Praise for
*The Interior*

"See's China is as vivid as Upton Sinclair's *Chicago*. . . . Hulan remains an intriguing heroine with a complex inner life that distills the contradictions of modern China. . . . One of the classier practitioners of the international thriller . . . See does more than strew mayhem—she draws her characters with convincing psychological depth, and she offers up documentary social detail that reeks of freshly made muck."
—*The New York Times*

"Sophisticated . . . See's writing is . . . graceful and she still has China passionately observed."
—*Los Angeles Times*

"Lisa See [does] for Beijing what Sir Arthur Conan Doyle did for turn-of-the-century London or Dashiell Hammett did for 1920s San Francisco: She discerns the hidden city lurking beneath the public façade."
—*The Washington Post Book World*

"Original and fresh, an absorbing look at an unfamiliar world."
—*Publishers Weekly*

"Immediate, haunting and exquisitely rendered, a fine line drawing of the sights and smells of the road overseas."
—*San Francisco Chronicle*

"A unique read . . . a thriller with a heart."
—*The Guardian*

"*The Interior* is packed with well-researched and nuanced reporting on today's China. . . . Hulan is an insightful guide to both Chinese corruption and those who resist it."
—*The Washington Post*

## ALSO BY LISA SEE

# THE INTERIOR

## A Novel

## LISA SEE

RANDOM HOUSE TRADE PAPERBACKS

NEW YORK

2008 Random House Trade Paperback Edition

Copyright © 1999 by Lisa See

Published in the United States by Random House Trade Paperbacks, an imprint of The Random House Publishing Group, a division of Random House, Inc., New York.

RANDOM HOUSE TRADE PAPERBACKS and colophon are trademarks of Random House, Inc.

Originally published in hardcover in the United States by HarperCollins Publishers, Inc. in 1999.

"Yesterday Once More" by John Bettis and Richard Carpenter © 1973 Almo Music Corp. and Hammer & Nails Music (ASCAP). All Rights Reserved. Used by permission. Warner Bros. Publications U.S. Inc., Miami, FL 33014.

LIBRARY OF CONGRESS CATALOGING-IN-PUBLICATION DATA

See, Lisa.
The interior: a novel/Lisa See.—Random House trade pbk. ed.
p.   cm.
ISBN 978-0-8129-7869-8
1. Women detectives—China—Beijing—Fiction.   2. Government attorneys—United States—Fiction.   3. Americans—China—Beijing—Fiction.   4. Murder—Investigation—Fiction.   5. China—Relations—United States—Fiction.   6. United States—Relations—China—Fiction.
I. Title
PS3569.E3334I58 2008
813'.54—dc22       2007014491

Printed in the United States of America

www.atrandom.com

2 4 6 8 9 7 5 3 1

*For my mother,*
*who's taught me a lot about*
*courage, persistence, and loyalty*

# Prologue

TODAY PROMISED TO BE ONE OF THE HOTTEST OF THE LONG summer in the interior of China. Here, the heat and humidity baked the earth and all upon it, so that by the time Ling Suchee reached the patch of ground where she grew her home vegetables, her clothes had already begun to stick to her skin. Suchee selected a turnip and two green onions, and pulled them gently from the red earth. Straightening up, she looked around. The fields stretched out before her, and the air shimmered in undulating waves. There were no trees to provide shade or a place to hide.

Where was her daughter?

Suchee glanced over to the rubble wall that served as the primary barrier between the fields and the pigsty. Last night she had seen Miaoshan lingering there as if it held some secret. But she wasn't there now, and Suchee went back inside. She sliced open the buns, tucked an onion and a piece of turnip in each, and squeezed the bread closed. No point in waiting for Miaoshan, Suchee decided, taking her first pungent bite of breakfast. Miaoshan must have gone to see her fiancé Tsai Bing. They had talked last night and probably met again this morning to make plans. Suchee took another bite of the bun and tried to push the embarrassment of her daughter's pregnancy from her mind, knowing she should focus instead on the joy that lay ahead of them. A wedding. A baby. All this to come so soon.

But it was not so easy to put away fear. During the night Suchee's dreams had been uneasy, disturbing, and now, sweating not just from the summer heat but from deep anxiety, she was reminded of the old saying: Fifteen buckets drawing water from the well—seven moving up, eight moving down. Last night she had lost more buckets of sleep than she had gained. Suchee shook away this unpleasant memory. She gathered the crumbs from the table, took them outside, and scattered them on the ground for the chickens. She walked around to the back of her one-room cottage, silently chastising herself for letting her night dreams become her daytime worries. Nevertheless she couldn't help but survey her surroundings, taking inventory of her property as she crossed the hard-packed earth. She counted her wealth—three chickens in the front, six ducks out back— all healthy, all here. She saw the pig—fine, alive. But where was that girl?

Suchee stared out again across her fields, this time looking at the white-hot sky. There were no clouds, so there would not be any rain to bring relief from the heat. This was as it should be. Most peasants knew when a big storm was coming, for when it did the rain would pour out of the sky in sheets for days and days, sometimes washing away an entire crop, an entire farm, an entire village. Did this day hold a dust storm in its minutes and hours? Is that what she sensed? Dust storms were common in spring, and Suchee and Miaoshan had watched many times as the soil was lifted up and carried out of sight to some other farmer's tract in a neighboring district. Could this be what she felt? Some tragedy that had stirred itself in the wrong season and would ruin her crops by day's end? Suchee held her hand to her forehead to shield her eyes from the sun and searched the sky, but it was perfectly blue and clear.

But as Suchee approached the shed, she was once again flooded with the sense that something was not right. She saw her tools propped against the mud siding. Someone had rearranged them. She was not stupid like the lowest barefoot peasant, and so she took care of her tools. They were the means by which she had kept herself and her daughter alive all these years. Had Miaoshan moved them? That couldn't be right, because mother had taught daughter the value of care and neatness. Just then Suchee realized that her ladder was missing. Hooligans must have come in the night and stolen it! If they had taken the ladder, could they have pirated away her ox too?

Suchee hurried to the shed, lifted the latch, and pushed open the door. Before her eyes could adjust to the dim interior, she stepped into the little room and gasped as she stumbled to the ground. She tried to sit up, but found herself tangled in the rungs of the ladder. Extricating herself, she sat there, rubbing first her shin, then an elbow, wondering what the ladder was doing here, right inside the door where anyone could fall.

As she peered into the darkness, she saw two feet swinging back and forth ever so slowly. With growing dread Suchee's eyes followed those feet up to the knees, then thighs, then hips, then torso, and finally to the neck and head of her daughter. A scream started to form in Suchee's throat as she saw Miaoshan's head tilted at an inhuman angle. Part of a rope necklace was buried in the swollen flesh of her neck; the other end was slip-tied to a rough-hewn support beam. Her tongue—purple and grossly swollen—protruded from her mouth. Her eyes bulged as though someone were pushing them from the inside. They were open, bloodshot, unseeing. "No-o-o-o," Suchee wailed as she saw one of the flies that already buzzed around her daughter's head break away from the swarm, dive down, and land at the corner of Miaoshan's unmoving right eye.

Suchee tried to scramble to her feet, once again tripping in the rungs of the ladder. Regaining her balance, she reached for her daughter. With a swoop Suchee wrapped her powerful arms around Miaoshan's thighs and lifted her body to take the weight off her neck. Standing there—her head against the small, hard mound of her daughter's stomach—Suchee knew it was too late. Miaoshan was dead, as was the grandchild that lay inside her.

The three generations stood this way together for a long time. Finally, Suchee gently released her daughter's legs and went back outside to get the scythe, feeling an emptiness that stretched beyond the distant horizon.

Those first moments after finding Miaoshan would be indelibly printed on Suchee's mind: cutting down the body, laying it out on the dirt floor of the shed, then running along the raised pathways between the fields to the land of her closest neighbors. The Tsai family—mother, father, and only son—were already working, bent over as they pulled weeds from around their crop plants. At the sound of Suchee's screams they looked up simultaneously, almost as a small herd of deer startled by a predator. Then they too were screaming and running back to the Ling farm.

Faced with this crisis, Tsai Bing, Miaoshan's betrothed, finally put his head to use. With promises that he would be back, he took off, jogging down the red dirt road that led first to the highway and then to the village of Da Shui. An hour later he returned with policemen from the local Public Security Bureau. By this time some other neighbors had gathered around to watch the unfolding catastrophe. The man in charge introduced himself formally as Captain Woo, although they had known him all of their lives. He firmly insisted that the neighbors return to their own farms. As they shuffled past, a few murmured their condolences. Tang Dan, the wealthiest of Suchee's neighbors, stopped before her and addressed her formally, "We are so sorry, Ling Taitai. If you need anything, remember to come to me. I will help you in any way I can." Then he too left, so that the only people remaining were the police, Suchee, and the Tsais.

"Auntie Tsai, Uncle Tsai," Woo said, using the polite honorific, "you have much work to do. We will take care of things here. And you, Tsai Bing, help your parents. We will come for you if we need you."

Madame Tsai looked questioningly from Suchee to Captain Woo and back again. But all of them knew one thing: The Tsais were insignificant people. They could not disobey a policeman. And so the Tsais padded away, with Tsai Bing occasionally glancing back over his shoulder.

Each time he looked back, Suchee was rocked by memories of the young couple together. She recalled how Miaoshan and Tsai Bing had liked to walk out across the raised pathways that divided the fields. Their laughter had drifted on the air, so sweet in the early spring months. Recently they had looked as happy as when they had been small children, not the usual wariness they had shown to each other during the early period of their betrothal.

Once Tsai Bing was out of sight, Suchee stood there dumbly as the policemen, sweating in their wrinkled khaki uniforms, walked around the shed and poked at Miaoshan's bruised neck with their rough fingers. When they said that suicide was a terrible thing, she insisted they were wrong, that Miaoshan would never take her own life; nor was she foolish enough to have caused her own death by accident. She told them again and again, but they would not hear her. "Girls," Captain Woo said, "they can be temperamental. They are too emotional. And Miaoshan . . . I have known her since she was a little girl. I am sorry, but she was a wild one. You never could control her."

Then the police put away their notepads and got into their cars. Just before driving down the rutted red dirt road, Captain Woo rolled down his window. He was not a man without sympathy, and he called out politely, "Ling Taitai, you don't need me to tell you this is hot weather. There is little time to waste. Miaoshan needs to be taken care of and soon. We are going back to the village. Would you like to ride with us?"

But Suchee shook her head, went back inside the shed, sat down again next to her daughter's body, and lifted the girl gently into her arms. She looked at Miaoshan's lifeless face and thought of her stubbornness. As a caring mother, Suchee should have made her daughter marry Tsai Bing long ago, but Miaoshan had resisted, saying, "An arranged marriage is old-fashioned. Besides, I do not love Tsai Bing. He is too much like a brother to me." Still, the mothers had persevered, and two years ago the parties had settled the terms of the bride price even though the two children were below marriage-certificate age.

Despite the engagement, Miaoshan had begged her mother again and again to be allowed to work at the new American toy factory that had opened in the area. "I can make more money as a worker, and I'll be less of a burden to you," Miaoshan had said. This had been only partly true. She could indeed make more money, but Suchee always needed Miaoshan's help watering and working the land. Still, Miaoshan had persisted with the same willfulness that she had shown since the age of three, when all Chinese children begin to show their true personalities. "The local ginger is not spicy enough for Miaoshan," neighbors often said, meaning that she always had her eyes on the horizon, thinking that things were better beyond its unseen edge. So when Miaoshan repeated her request to go to the factory, Suchee, despite her regret at losing her daughter as a helper and companion, had let her leave six months ago in the darkest month of winter. *Never, never, never* should she have let this happen.

When Miaoshan came home for her first visit, she had changed. Underneath her same old jacket she wore a store-bought sweater and American *nu zai ku*—what were called "cow boy pants." But what really shocked Suchee was her daughter's face. Miaoshan had always been considered plain. When other mothers had seen her as a baby, they had shaken their heads in sympathy, which was one reason that Suchee was so relieved when Tsai Bing's mother had sent the matchmaker. But upon her return from the factory, Miaoshan's cheekbones, which had always looked angular and pale next to the perfect round faces of the neighbor girls, were tinted pink. Her lips were painted a rich ruby color. Her eyes were outlined with black, and her lids were heavy with a deep gray. She looked like the famous movie star Gong Li. No, she looked like an American movie star. Suchee saw that even in death her daughter looked beautiful, Western, absolutely foreign.

Every time that Miaoshan came home, Suchee grew increasingly disturbed by the changes in her daughter. But during her last visit she had said something that made Suchee go cold inside. Miaoshan had been talking about a meeting she'd had at the factory with some of the other girls. "The right information is better than a bullet," she had said. "With it, you can't lose. Without it, you won't survive." Then she'd laughed lightly and changed the subject, but the memory of those words stayed with Suchee, because she could remember back many years to when people who recited slogans like that were punished. And now Miaoshan had been . . . destroyed.

She smoothed the hair away from Miaoshan's face, feeling how the warmth of the day was seeping into her skin instead of out. Captain Woo was right. Suchee could not let her daughter rot here in the summer heat. Suchee put aside her grief and temporarily covered the private hard purpose that was already growing inside her like a seed after a fresh spring rain, and began to plan her daughter's burial. She was a poor woman, this was true. But she was also a widow, and during the ten years since her husband's death she had conserved a little here, a little there, always thinking that the future was uncertain. One could never tell when there might be a drought, an illness, a political upheaval, a funeral.

She carefully set Miaoshan's body back on the ground, stood, stared

for a moment at the motionless form, then went outside for a shovel. She walked along the route that she alone had memorized. Suchee found her spot and dug until the shovel hit the metal chest where she kept her savings and her important papers. After taking the money and once again burying the box, Suchee was sweaty and dirty, but she did not stop to splash water on her face or clean her arms and legs. Instead she simply replaced the shovel and set off down the dirt road.

Her first stop in town was with the local *feng shui* man. The diviner promised he would weigh, as thousands of years of custom dictated, the attributes of *feng shui*—wind and water—to find the burial location that was most propitious for the new spirit. To that end he would also examine Miaoshan's horoscope and contemplate the political backgrounds of her parents. After that he would go to the cemetery and consult with the spirits who already resided there. All of this he explained to Suchee, but when she placed a larger number of bills in his hand than was usual he finalized his decision. Miaoshan would be buried on a slight rise in the cemetery where she might face the warmth of the south for all eternity.

Leaving the *feng shui* man, Suchee hurriedly did her other errands. But how difficult it was for her now to walk down the main street of this village. She saw the familiar faces—the woman who sold dishes decorated with gaily painted enamel flowers, the man who filled gallon cans with kerosene for lanterns, the old man who fixed broken bicycles. News traveled quickly in Da Shui Village. As she walked past these people, their faces darkened with sympathy and they bowed their heads in respect, but Suchee registered none of it.

Instead her mind filled again with images of Miaoshan in life. As a toddler in split pants. As a girl dressed in a faded blue padded jacket who was devoted to her studies, diligently practicing her Chinese ideograms and reciting her English. As the young woman she had recently become who sometimes seemed such a stranger. "One day I will earn enough money that we will leave this place," she had often said with such conviction that Suchee had believed her. "We will go to Shenzhen, maybe even America. . . ." Silently Suchee pulled at her hair, trying to drive away her dream-ghost daughter. Silently she screamed, *How could this have happened?*

From the dry-goods store, Suchee purchased paper in assorted colors

so that tonight she might cut them into offerings, which would be burned at the grave. In this way Miaoshan, who was so poor in life, would be accompanied to the afterworld with clothes, a car, a house, friends. To distract Hungry Ghosts from Miaoshan's funeral belongings, Suchee would cook up a pot of rice to sprinkle on the bonfire. When the flames died down, her daughter would truly be gone forever.

Suchee had one more purchase to make—a coffin. Undertaker Wang, knowing that Suchee was almost as poor as he, suggested that the girl be cremated. But Suchee shook her head. "I want a coffin, a good one," she insisted.

"I can make you something nice," Wang said. "See this wood over here? This will be perfect for you."

But when Suchee ran her fingertips over the rough grain, she shook her head again. She looked about her until her eyes rested on a crimson lacquer coffin with hand-wrought hardware. "That one there," she said, pointing. "That is the one for Miaoshan."

"Oh, too expensive! My nephew buys that one in Beijing and sends it here to me. At first I'm thinking, my nephew has put me out of business! That kind of coffin is for a Red Prince, not someone in our poor village. But these days . . ." The undertaker rubbed his chin. "We have some prosperity in our village now. I am keeping it for one of the village elders. They are all old men, and they can't live forever."

But Suchee didn't appear to be listening. She crossed the small, hot room and placed her hands on the crimson surface of the coffin. After a moment she turned and said, "I will take it." Before Wang could voice his objections, Suchee reached into a pocket, pulled out a wad of old bills, and began counting them. She was not prepared to bargain with him as she might have under other circumstances, and, to his honor, he did not cheat her but accepted a fair price with a solid profit. Undertaker Wang considered that if a peasant woman like Ling Suchee was willing to buy a coffin like this for a no-account daughter, then perhaps that nephew of his should send a few more lacquer coffins to the village.

Her business with Wang completed, Suchee stepped back outside into the harsh sunlight. With each of these stops her determination grew. She would make Captain Woo hear her. She crossed the street to the building that housed the Public Security Bureau, then waited while a

secretary went into one of the offices to speak with the captain. When she came out, her face was set in a disapproving grimace. "The captain is busy," the woman said. "He says you should go back home. Be a proper mother. You have a duty, you know. Take care of your daughter." The woman's voice softened just a little. "You have things you need to do for her. Go on."

"But I have to tell him—"

The secretary's firmness returned. "Your case has been heard. Captain Woo has already finished the paperwork."

"How can this be?" Suchee asked. "Captain Woo has not interviewed anyone. He has not asked me if Miaoshan had any enemies. We are a small village, but you and I both know there are many secrets here. Why isn't he asking about those?"

Instead of answering these questions, the secretary said, "The official file is complete." As an afterthought she added, "Do not cause trouble for yourself."

Suchee bent her head, looked at her callused feet, and tried to absorb what she had heard.

"Go on," the secretary insisted, a strident tone creeping into her voice. "We are sorry for your loss, but you must go away. If you don't, I will have to call . . ."

Suchee slowly stood, looked the woman directly in the eye, and uttered the worst curse she could think of. "Fuck your mother," she said and walked out.

She headed straight for the post office, knowing she would have to pass the Silk Thread Café. Approaching it, she saw the elders of the town—some old, some not so old, but all of them in clean and ironed white shirts that seemed an affront to all those who labored in the rocky fields that surrounded this village—sitting at their customary tables at the front of the establishment. When the men saw her approaching, their banter quieted so that all that could be heard was the sound of the café's television in the background.

She met their stares straight on. With the vision of her daughter hanging in the shed looming before her eyes, she said, "You will pay. I will make you pay if it takes my last breath and my last drop of blood."

Then she lifted her chin and continued on to the post office, where she bought paper, a pen, and an envelope. At the counter she slowly, painstakingly wrote out a few characters. It was important to her that their form be neat, that their content be as clear as her simple mastery of the written language would allow. Then—copying from a slip of paper that she had brought with her from that buried box in her fields—she wrote on the envelope the name and address of the only government official she knew, Liu Hulan, who had lived and worked in the village so many years before.

1

THIS MORNING, AS EVERY MORNING THIS SUMMER IN Beijing, Liu Hulan woke before dawn to the deafening sounds of drums, cymbals, gongs, and, worst of all, the horrible squeals of a *suo-na*, a many-piped wind instrument that resounded for blocks, maybe even miles. Competing to be heard over the instruments were the exuberant voices, cheers, and yelps of the Shisha Hutong Yang Ge Folk Dance and Music Troupe. This was the beginning of what would be a three-hour session, and this morning it appeared to be taking place directly outside Hulan's family compound.

Hulan hurriedly wrapped her silk robe around her, slipped on a pair of tennis shoes, and stepped outside onto the covered veranda outside her bedroom. Though it was only four, the air was already thick as custard with heat, humidity, and smog. Once the summer solstice passed, Beijingers prepared for the arrival of *Xiao Shu*, or Slight Heat Days. But this year *Da Shu*, Great Heat, had come early. This past week had seen five straight days with temperatures over forty-two degrees centigrade and humidity hovering at about ninety-eight percent.

Hulan quickly crossed the innermost courtyard, passing the other pavilions where in the old days the different branches of her extended family had lived. On the steps of one of these, her mother's nurse—already dressed in simple cotton trousers and a short-sleeve white blouse—waited for her. "Hurry, Hulan. Make them stop. Your mother is bad this morning." Hulan didn't respond, she didn't need to. She and the nurse had followed this routine now for the past three weeks.

Hulan reached the first courtyard, pushed open the gate, and stepped into the alleyway that ran before her family compound. There were perhaps seventy people here, all of them senior citizens. Most were dressed in pink silk tunics, while a few wore electric green. The latter, Hulan had learned a week ago, had come from the Heavenly Gate Dance Brigade after an argument about who would lead the dancing in their own neighborhood. The people looked colorful and—Hulan had to admit it— rather sweet in their costumes: Sequins decorated their fans, while glittering tinsel and tufts of white fluff fluttered in time to the music. The bodies of the old people happily gyrated to the drums and cymbals in a dance that was a cross between the bunny hop and the stroll.

"Friends, neighbors," Hulan called out, trying to be heard, "please, I must ask you to move." Of course no one paid her any attention. Hulan stepped into the dancers just as they began marching out of their circle and into rows.

"Oh, Inspector! Beautiful morning!" This greeting came from Ri Lihan, a woman in her eighties who lived five compounds away. Before Hulan could respond, Madame Ri twirled away.

Hulan tried to stop first one, then another dancer, but always they slipped past, laughing, their wrinkled faces flushed and sweaty. Hulan made her way through the dancers to the musicians. The cheeks of the man blowing on the *suo-na* were puffed out and red. The sound emanating from that instrument was high, loud, and discordant. Speech was impossible, but when the musicians saw Hulan pat at the pockets of her robe, they exchanged knowing glances. They had seen their neighbor, Liu Hulan, do this before. She was looking for her Ministry of Public Security identification, but, as was so often the case on these early morning excursions, she had left it behind. The musicians beamed and nodded agreeably to the inspector.

Still clanking, drumming, and blowing, the musicians slowly set off down the alley. Following this cue, the old folks—continuing their dancing rhythm—filed past Hulan. She waited for Madame Zhang to pirouette by, but when she didn't Hulan walked to the old woman's home, silently cursing this current wave of nostalgia to sweep through the city.

One month it was restaurants celebrating "the long-past good days" of the Cultural Revolution; the next month there was a run on collectible Mao buttons. One month there was a craze for Western-style white wine mixed with Coca-Cola and ice; the next month old people were bringing their rumpled *yang ge* costumes and instruments out of trunks and closets and taking to the streets like a bunch of teenagers.

*Yang ge* music had originated among the peasants of China's northeast and had been brought to Beijing by the People's Liberation Army in 1949. Now, after years of deprivations and political upheavals, the old people had resurrected twin passions—dancing and singing. The only problems—and they were big ones as far as Hulan was concerned—were the time of day and the noise. China, although a large country, operated on one time zone. While in the far west farmers might not go to their fields until the sun came up at nine, in Beijing the day started unconscionably early. Psychologically Hulan hated waking up before six, let alone four in the morning, to the ungodly racket of the *yang ge* troupe.

This constant clamoring had also been extremely upsetting to Hulan's mother. Rather than filling Liu Jinli with sentimental longings or carefree memories, these raucous sounds made the older woman quite querulous. Since the Cultural Revolution, Jinli had been confined to a wheelchair and still suffered from bouts of catatonia. During the first weeks that she'd come back to the quiet of the *hutong*, her health had improved considerably. But with the *yang ge* music stirring up the past, Jinli's condition had once again spiraled downward. Which was why Hulan had gone several times already this summer to Neighborhood Committee Director Zhang to register complaints. But the old woman, whose duty it was to keep tabs on the comings and goings of the residents of this Beijing neighborhood, had joined the troupe herself and for once seemed completely immune to Hulan's imprecations.

"*Huanying, huanying,*" Madame Zhang Junying said automatically, opening the door to Hulan. Then, seeing how her neighbor was dressed, the older woman quickly pulled Hulan inside. "Where are your day clothes? You are trying to scare the neighbors?"

"There's nothing to see that they haven't seen before," Hulan said, pulling her robe more tightly around her.

Madame Zhang considered these words, then said, "For most people this is true. After all, what surprises can any of us have? But with you . . ." The Committee director shook her head in a maternal show of disapproval. "Come sit down. Will you drink tea?"

Hulan, as custom dictated, politely refused.

But Madame Zhang would have none of it. "Sit down here. You pour. I'll put these papers away." As Hulan did as she was told, the old woman continued, "Today no fun for me. I have to file my report. So much paperwork, right, Hulan?"

"I have something for you to add to your report."

"Don't worry," the Committee director chortled. "I have already put in your complaints. Formal, as you requested."

"Then why isn't anything done?"

"You think you are the only one to complain? Remember that hot line the government set up for people to call? They got almost two thousand calls the first day. *Then* they turned off the phone!" Madame Zhang clapped her hands on her knees.

"The musicians are not supposed to be near residences . . ."

"Or hospitals. I know. You don't have to tell *me*. But you must look on the positive side. We are together maybe sixty thousand old people in different dance troupes. We are going outside the house and giving young people time at home alone. Daughters-in-law are happy. Sons are happy. Maybe next year we get a grandchild or great-grandchild—"

"Auntie," Hulan cut in sternly.

At her tone Madame Zhang finally turned serious. "I remember when your mother returned to our neighborhood from the countryside all those years ago," she said. "*She's* the one who taught us these songs. *She's* the one who taught us these dances. Now you tell me she doesn't want us to make noise? Ha!"

"But do they have to do it so early in the morning?"

At this Madame Zhang put her head back and laughed and laughed. "This is summer, Hulan. We are in Beijing. What is the temperature at this hour? Thirty-eight degrees centigrade? The people want to practice early before it gets too hot."

The old woman watched Hulan's face as she struggled to come up with another argument. Finally Madame Zhang leaned over and put a hand on Hulan's knee. "I know this must be hard for your mother. But she is just one person, and the people want to have fun." Her voice changed, becoming gruffer, deeper. "We all went through so much. We just want to enjoy the rest of our lives."

Later, as Hulan walked back to her compound, she thought over Madame Zhang's words. It was true, they'd all been through so much, too much really. In China the past would always be a part of the present. But unlike her neighbors, Hulan had the money and connections to make sure her family could escape it on occasion. And so Hulan made a plan. When she reached the Liu compound she went directly to her mother's quarters. The nurse had dressed Jinli, who now sat in her wheelchair. Her eyes were red and swollen from crying. Hulan tried to speak to her, but Jinli had retreated into silence. Hulan sat on the bed, dialed the phone, and made arrangements to send her mother and her nurse to the seaside resort of Beidaihe. They would be cooler there and away from the disturbing sounds of the *yang ge* troupes.

When Hulan was done, she carefully explained everything to Jinli, knowing that she might not understand anything that was said. Then Hulan kissed her mother, gave a few last instructions to the nurse, and made her way back to her own quarters.

At seven, Liu Hulan, dressed in a cream-colored silk dress, once again stepped through the gate of her *hutong* home to a waiting black Mercedes. A young man leaned against the back passenger door. "Good morning, Inspector," he said as he opened the door and motioned for her to get in. "Step inside quickly. I have kept the car running. The air conditioning is good."

Hulan sank into the soft leather cushions. Her driver, Investigator Lo, stepped on the gas and began heading toward Tiananmen Square and the Ministry of Public Security compound. Lo was a compact man— short, muscular, and prudent with his thoughts and emotions. From reading his secret personal file, Hulan knew that he was from Fujian Province, single, and an expert at several martial arts disciplines.

Several times during the last two months since Investigator Lo had been assigned to her, Hulan had tried to include him in the analytical aspects of her investigations, but he'd seemed circumspect, preferring to concern himself only with his chauffeuring duties. She'd invited him out for drinks, hoping that over a beer they might begin a friendship, but Lo had politely refused these offers as well. All of this was odd. Who would turn down an offer to "climb the ladder" at the ministry? It was through the successful conclusion of cases, recommendations from superiors, or political activities that investigators usually earned promotions. Investigator Lo appeared to have either no inkling of these rules or no aptitude for accomplishing any of these things, but Hulan was not surprised.

Her old driver, Peter, had been assigned to spy on her. Despite his lack of personal loyalty, Hulan had learned to depend on his judgment and instincts. She had hoped to build a similar relationship with Lo, but he seemed focused solely on his instructions from Vice Minister Zai, which apparently were limited to keeping tabs on her and working as some sort of bodyguard—a moving block of muscle with her protection as his goal. More than once she had needed to restrain Investigator Lo, who took it upon himself to physically bully witnesses who did not respond quickly enough to Hulan's questions.

When she had gone to Vice Minister Zai to request that Lo be transferred, he had shaken his head and said, "This is how it will be, Inspector." His manner—the way he dismissed her complaints and concerns—was new to her. But he, like all of them, was still trying to adjust and adapt to the changes that the last few months had brought. As the saying went, the blade of grass points where the wind blows. The only problem was that the wind was blowing in so many directions these days no one could completely protect himself.

These past months had been especially strange for Hulan. Her family had literally been ripped apart. Her father had died under bad circumstances when Hulan exposed him as a smuggler, conspirator, and killer. The press—regulated as it was by the government—had made the story headline news. There had been features about Hulan's parents, her grandparents, even her great-grandparents—all of them shown in a bad light. But for a time the government had seen in Hulan's own story a politically advantageous message, so her life had also been examined. Photographs had been dredged out of newspaper files as well as government records showing Hulan at various crime scenes, at political rallies from her youth, even as the baby daughter of one of Beijing's then-most promising couples. Hulan had been compared time and again to her namesake—Liu Hulan, martyr for the Revolution.

Hulan had thought that this interest would pass. But instead of dwindling, the coverage had swung in another direction thanks to Bi Peng, a reporter for the *People's Daily*. In a country that loved puns, Bi Peng was well known for his name. Bi was just a family name, but the tone sounded like *bi*, the word for pen. What he wrote about soon spread across the country. Now, to Hulan's growing embarrassment and anger, several newspapers and magazines had run photographs of her as one of Beijing's elite class—a Red Princess. Here was Hulan in a grainy photograph copied from a security tape dressed in a fuchsia silk *cheongsam* and dancing at the Rumours nightclub with an American. This showed her decadence as clearly as if she'd been caught buying silk lingerie at one of Beijing's new department stores.

But all this was just propaganda. Hulan remembered that night at Rumours perfectly well. She had not been there for fun, but rather to investigate a crime. The American in the photo was David Stark, an assistant U.S. attorney, who had come to China to help solve that case. The two of them had been successful and had been hailed as heroes. But it wasn't safe for anyone in China to climb too high. Bi and other reporters had turned her relationship with David into a national scandal. Could the same Liu Hulan who had been treated as a brave woman now have succumbed to the depravity of the West in the form of this American man? Couldn't she say *bai bai*—a mutant Mandarin-English phrase meaning to say "bye-bye" to lovers—to this foreign attorney? Hadn't Inspector Liu read *China Can Say No*, the book that stressed the importance of just saying no to American imperialism, materialism, and sexism?

None of this should have surprised Hulan. All the world over, the press liked to build people up, then bring them down, then build them up again. The only difference between the rest of the world and China was that here the government helped to color what was said.

At the iron gates to the Ministry of Public Security compound, Investigator Lo flashed his identification and the car was waved through. Lo dropped Hulan as close to the entrance as possible, then drove away to find a parking spot in the shade. Hulan hurried inside, walked across the lobby, and climbed the back stairs to her office.

Like most public buildings in Beijing, this one had neither heat nor air conditioning to protect the inhabitants from the vicissitudes of the weather. In winter she worked with her coat on. In summer she wore simple silk dresses or linen shifts and used old-fashioned methods of conserving cool air. She kept her windows open at night so that the room would cool down, then closed them first thing in the morning to keep the hot air out for as long as possible. In the late afternoons, when she couldn't stand it anymore, she cracked the windows again. On the very hottest days she draped wet cloths on the window openings and hoped for a breeze.

Hulan settled in at her desk, opened a file, and tried to concentrate, but she found her mind wandering. Her caseload was, to her mind at least, uninteresting. During these last months she'd been assigned to several murder cases. They'd been easy to solve, with nothing for her to do but fill out the paperwork, deposit the prisoners at the jail, and turn up in court when the prosecutor called. That she knew all this was Vice Minister Zai's plan to keep her safe didn't make her feel any better about it.

A few hours later, the mailboy came by with a stack of envelopes. She went through them quickly. One held an inter-office report from Pathologist Fong. She didn't need to read it, as the entry wound on the body at the temple pretty much told the story on that case. There were a couple of forms to be signed and sent back to the prosecutor's office. Again, nothing interesting on cases she could barely remember. But when she saw the return address on the last envelope, her breath caught. She set it down on her desk and swung around to look out the window. Memories flooded back. A destitute village on a scorched plain. Pigs crying at slaughter. The smell of the red soil. The searing brightness of a brutal sun. And then other images— girls in pigtails berating a man until he broke down and confessed. People being beaten. Blood running as freely as sweat. Her heart pounding, Hulan picked up the envelope and tore it open.

"Inspector Liu Hulan," Hulan read, "I am Ling Suchee. I hope you remember me from your days at the Red Soil Farm." Hulan remembered. How could she not remember? In 1970, at age twelve, Hulan had been sent to the countryside to "learn from the peasants." Now, sitting in her stifling office, Hulan was transported back across the years to when she was that young girl. Suchee had been her best friend. In those days of severity they had built a teasing relationship. With great affection Hulan had called Suchee her *maor ye*, or country bumpkin. Suchee had called Hulan *bei kuan*, literally meaning "north-wealth"—or a person of wealth from the north. Suchee had been funny, strong, and honest, while Hulan had been somber, had covered her city ways with false courage, and had already learned the political advantages of not always telling the truth. But for all of Hulan's so-called sophistication, Suchee had gotten them out of trouble more than once.

Hulan looked back at the characters on the page. "Today, on June 29 of the Western calendar, my daughter Ling Miaoshan died." Reading the circumstances of the girl's death, Hulan's hand instinctively went down to the early swell of her own pregnancy. "My daughter worked for an American company. It is called"—and here the crude characters gave way to even cruder print letters—"Knight International. I see and know things, but no one will listen to me. My daughter is dead. My daughter is gone from me. You once said you would help me if I ever needed it. I need your help now. Please come quickly."

Hulan ran a finger over the characters of Ling Suchee's name. Then she checked the date and realized that Miaoshan had died only five days ago. Taking a deep breath, she put away the letter, left her office, and went up a flight of stairs to Vice Minister Zai's office. He smiled when she came in and motioned for her to sit.

"I have sent Mama to Beidaihe," she said.

"This is good. I will go and see her on the weekend."

"I will also be leaving the city."

Vice Minister Zai cocked an eye.

"I am going to Da Shui Village."

Hulan saw a flicker of worry cross her mentor's face as he realized this would be a personal conversation. It was said that there was no such thing as a wind-proof wall in China and that no one could ever be sure who was listening or not. People also said that things had relaxed, that there was too much going on—meaning that everyone, including the generals in the army, were trying to get rich—for so much time and effort to be given over to observation. But only a fool would take the risk that this was so. Even assuming the unlikely possibility that there was no electronic surveillance in the building, any of Vice Minister Zai's assistants or tea girls could be made to repeat conversations they'd heard if push came to shove. Knowing this and knowing that their private lives had long been a matter of government record, Hulan and Zai attempted to continue their conversation. There was no mistaking the concern in Zai's voice as he asked, "Do you think that is wise?"

"Do you think I have a choice?" Her tone was sharp.

"You of all people have choice," he reminded her.

She chose to ignore this, saying, "The daughter of Ling Suchee has died. She is skeptical of the local police bureau's official version of the case. Her suspicions are probably just her grief speaking, but I can go to her as a friend."

"Hulan, the past is behind you. Forget about it."

She sighed. "You have read my personal file. You know what happened out there. If Ling Suchee asks for my help, then I must go."

"And if I forbid you?" he asked gently.

"Then I will use my vacation time," she said.

"Hulan—"

She held up a hand to stop him from continuing. "I will come back as soon as I can." She stood, crossed the room, then hesitated at the door. "Don't worry, uncle," she said, ironing the tension out of her voice. "Everything will be fine. It may even do me good to get out of the city for a while." She paused, thinking he might add something, but they both knew her words had many meanings and some of them might even be right. "And please, do visit Mama. Your companionship helps her."

A few minutes later she stepped out into the ministry's courtyard. Heat radiated up from the asphalt. Investigator Lo started the car, and as he pulled out of the compound she felt sweat trickle between her breasts down to her stomach, where her and David's child grew. She brushed her palm across her brow and thought of what Uncle Zai had said. "The past is behind you." But he was so wrong. The past was never far from her. It was with her every day in the crippled form of her mother. It was in the joyous voices and rhythmic drums of the *yang ge* troupe. It was in the blurry photographs that she saw in the newspapers. It was in the scratchy writing on a cheap paper envelope. She carried within her the future, but what kind of a future would any of them have if she didn't drive the past away forever?

D AVID STARK'S HAND REACHED FOR THE RINGING PHONE. At five in the morning, the call could mean one of two things. Either a case had broken and an agent wanted David to come down and look at the scene, or Hulan was calling.

"Hello," he said, his eyes still closed.

"David." Hulan's voice coming to him at eight in the evening from thousands of miles away across the international dateline jolted him awake.

"Is everything all right? Are you okay?"

"Of course."

Her next words were lost in a wave of static. Hulan insisted on using a cell phone to call him, despite the poor sound quality. She said she didn't trust the phone in her office for their personal calls. More recently she'd begun to suspect the phone in her home. The cell phone was in no way perfect. Just about anyone could listen in if they wanted. Hulan took solace in this. There might even be an element of protection in more than one party—even an innocent person—listening in on their private calls.

The transmission cleared and David asked, "Where are you?" It eased his mind to visualize her. Usually she called from her garden and she might describe for him what was in bloom or the feel of the sun on her skin. He could almost see her there—the wisps of black hair that framed her face, her black eyes that often revealed the real meaning of her words, her delicate frame that belied profound inner strength.

"I'm on the train."

David sat up, squinting as he turned on the light. "Where are you going? Is it for a case?"

"Not exactly. An old friend has asked for my help. I'm going to see what I can do."

David thought this over. He had to be careful how he questioned her. "I thought you were trying to wrap things up. I thought your next trip would be here."

"I'll come . . ."

"One day? Eventually?"

She chose to ignore this. "You know I miss you. Can't you come to me?"

David was just barely awake. He couldn't face that conversation again right now.

"So, where are you?"

"I'm on my way to Shanxi Province in the interior." She paused, then said, "I'm going to a village near Taiyuan."

He could hear the hesitancy in her voice even over all these miles, even with the static. "What village exactly?" He tried to keep his tone light.

"Da Shui. It's where the Red Soil Farm was during the Cultural Revolution."

"Oh God, Hulan. Why?"

"It's okay. Don't worry. You don't know everything about that place." (That's probably the understatement of the year, David thought.) "I had a friend out there. She . . . Well, it doesn't matter right now. Her daughter died, an apparent suicide. Suchee thinks it's something else."

"Sounds like she should go to the local authorities."

"She went to the Public Security Bureau. That's the local level of the ministry. But you know how things are here."

Corrupt, sure he knew it.

"Look, it's probably nothing," Hulan continued, "but the least I can do is ask a couple of questions and put Suchee's mind at rest. She's a mother." That word came over the line with tremendous weight. It was another thing that Hulan didn't like to discuss. "She lost her only child."

"When will you be back?"

"I was lucky enough to get a seat on a semi-express train to Datong. That means we'll only be making about ten stops over the next six or so hours. Tomorrow I'll take another train to Taiyuan. Then a few days in Da Shui, then the trip back. I'll be back in Beijing next week." When David didn't respond, she added, "This is nothing to worry about."

"How will I reach you?"

"I don't know what our days are going to be like, so I'll call you."

He didn't like it, but he said, "Fine."

Across the line came the sound of a train whistle. Hulan said, "Listen, we're about to make a stop. With all the people getting on and off, we won't be able to hear each other. So let me ask you something. Knight International. Ever hear of it?"

"That came out of nowhere."

"It's where Miaoshan worked. It's an American company. Have you heard of it?"

"Who hasn't?" David replied. "It's huge. It's based back East somewhere, but the company has a lot of Hollywood connections."

"So what is Knight?"

"They—a father and son—make toys. Do you know *Sam & His Friends*? Do you have that over there? It's a TV show for kids. *Sam & His Friends* is a cartoon. I've never seen the actual show, of course, but the advertising! I think Knight makes dolls. No! What's the word? Action figures! They've got an action figure for every one of those damn 'friends' and ads to go with them. Knight makes those over there? Jesus!"

"It's that big?"

"Remember the rage over Cabbage Patch dolls? Did you have those in China?"

"No. I don't think so."

"Tickle Me Elmo?"

"No."

"Beanie Babies?"

"No. Barbie, I know Barbie."

"Sam isn't like Barbie. These Sam toys are a fad. Kids are crazy for them."

"How do you know so much about it?"

"That's what I'm trying to say. It's on the local news every time a new shipment hits the stores. Parents line up around the block to buy these things. The supply can't meet the demand. It's in the business pages practically every day. Knight stock has gone through the roof. Here's a company that was percolating along for about seventy years, then this show comes on and kids go nuts. It's a phenomenon."

"And Knight is manufacturing the toys in Shanxi," Hulan mused thoughtfully.

"I guess it shouldn't be that strange, Hulan. Half of everything is made in China."

"Sure, in the Special Economic Zone in Shenzhen," Hulan said as the train whistle blew again. "In Guangdong Province. Around Shanghai. But Shanxi? There's *nothing* out there, David."

These last words were almost lost in the noise behind Hulan. "We're at the station," she said. "I'll call you later. I love you." And then she was gone.


After putting the receiver back in the cradle, David couldn't go back to sleep. By the time he pulled on shoes and shorts, there was enough light for him to head out for a run around Lake Hollywood. Tall and lean, he had dark hair, graying a bit at the temples. His blue eyes tended to pick up the hues of whatever environment he was in. This morning, with the fog still hiding nature's sky and water tones, his eyes were flecked with highlights from the greenery around him.

His pace was fast today and he knew why. Certain words Hulan had used this morning—the Red Soil Farm, the Cultural Revolution, an apparent suicide—had sent tremors of anxiety into his bloodstream. Could Hulan have more secrets from him? Would she be placing herself in danger out in the countryside? Was it even healthy—physically or mentally—for her to go out there? With each stride he tried to convince himself that there was nothing to worry about. Hulan worked for the Ministry of Public Security. No one would mess with her, especially in the countryside. Besides, a girl had committed suicide. That was about as open and shut as you could get in law enforcement.

Maybe after Hulan settled this thing, she would go back to Beijing, pack up, and come to him. Who was he kidding? They had gone around this way for three months now, talking on the phone and communicating by e-mail. Back in March Hulan had promised she would come to Los Angeles. "We'll be together," she'd said, and he'd believed her. He'd begun talking to government officials and filling out forms for a permanent-residency card. But days had turned into weeks, weeks into months as Hulan's doubts kicked in. She had lost so much in her life that, as much as she loved him—and he had no reservations about the depth of her passion—she was still afraid to commit for fear of what she could lose. But she would never say this, and he could never push her into that conversation without her skittering away from the subject. Instead Hulan would say that she didn't want to uproot her mother. "You should have seen Mama today. We talked for half an hour." Or, "Mama had a bad time today. How can I ever repair the damage?"

"Bring her here," David might say. "Bring the nurse. I'll make the arrangements." But Hulan always seemed to have another excuse.

And so their conversations had changed. Instead of Hulan coming to California, she now wanted him to move to China. "You said that if I didn't come, you'd come back for me. Well?"

But how could he? He had his job at the U.S. Attorney's Office. His family was here in America. His friends were here. All of which was true for Hulan as well. She too had her job, her family. Which was why they were at an impasse. "We're both strong-willed people," David had said once. "I guess it's not in either of our natures to give in."

Hulan's laugh had come floating over the line. "It has nothing to do with that. Relationships are always like this in China." Then she'd babbled on about other people she knew. So-and-so got married, spent one day with his wife, then was transferred down to Shanghai. That was two years ago. Since then the couple had spent a total of three nights together. Another couple she knew had met at Beijing University and gotten married. Chai Hong and Mu Hua had struggled hard to get a wedding permit. The problem was that she was from Hebei Province and he was from Zhejiang Province. Officials might give them the marriage permit, but they couldn't guarantee that the next bureau would give them residency permits for the same city. But Hong and Hua, persistent and idealistic, finally received their marriage permit and got married. But after their education was completed, twenty years ago now, they had each returned to their home provinces. They hadn't lived together again except for a week or two here and there during annual vacations. For people from different countries the problems were even greater.

And here was where David would typically interrupt and remind Hulan that she had promised to come to him. She would again launch into the excuses about her mother. Around and around they went. Who was going to concede first? On what issue would he or she cave in? Career? Family? Friends?

David stopped in the middle of the path that led around the lake. He was on the far side now, just a little past the halfway mark. He looked out across the city: Hollywood below him, downtown to his left. To his right, way in the distance, he should have been able to see the ocean, but the morning fog still shrouded the western side of the city. But David wasn't thinking about weather conditions. He was thinking about friends. Hulan didn't have "friends." Vice Minister Zai was Hulan's superior and her mentor. She seemed to have an amicable relationship with a neighbor woman, but Madame Zhang was decades older than Hulan. She had her colleagues, whom she treated with a polite coolness. *Friends.* Hulan had called Suchee a friend. He felt another wave of worry ripple through him.

Even as he stood there looking out across the city in the early morning coolness, he saw clearly that his emotions and concerns were primitive, base, elemental. Hulan was pregnant with his child. He remembered with absolute clarity when she'd told him. For weeks their conversations had revolved around anecdotes about cases they were working on, how the harshness of the Beijing winter was fading, how much she loved him, how much he loved her. But when she'd spoken the words "I'm pregnant," his life changed and the tenor of their conversation shifted. David wanted his child to be born in the U.S., where he or she would automatically become a citizen. "This is a Chinese baby too," Hulan said. "Why can't it have Chinese citizenship?"

That had been their only real argument. David had reminded her of the Great Leap Forward, when Mao had attempted to revolutionize agriculture and industry, but instead had created the largest famine in history, resulting in the deaths of thirty million people. He'd reminded her of the One Hundred Flowers Campaign, when people were encouraged to criticize the new society, then those who had made those criticisms were thrown in jail or worse. He'd reminded her of the Cultural Revolution, which had been so devastating to Hulan's own family. And then he reminded her that she had been the one who told him all of these horror stories. "And you want our child to remain in China?" He had pushed her too far, argued her into a corner, and they hadn't spoken about the baby since.

Ridiculous Chinese laws might be acceptable to couples like Chai Hong and Mu Hua. In fact, they might even work. David knew of many couples even in the U.S. who kept bicoastal relationships romantic and alive. But ten thousand miles was too great a distance with a woman like Hulan. He needed to see her eyes when she told him she was pregnant. He needed to be face to face with her to ask why she'd waited so long to tell him. Today he'd needed to see her eyes when she said the word *friend.*

David arrived at the U.S. Attorney's Office at nine. He was dressed in corduroys and a Polo shirt instead of his usual suit and tie. He grabbed a cup of coffee and headed down the hall to his office. Today he had no appointments or court appearances. In fact, for the first time in years he had nothing on his calendar. No cases on the docket. No depositions to set up. No special assignments. All he planned to do today was clean up his office after months of trial work. Later, workmen would come by with dollies to take away all the boxes and put them in the file room for temporary residence before moving them to a big government warehouse.

David sat for a few moments behind his desk, where files and correspondence were piled together haphazardly. Along the walls were stacked dozens of boxes already filled with trial transcripts, interviews with witnesses, and photocopies of evidence from the Rising Phoenix cases. Against many of the boxes were propped large poster boards. Some charted evidence, some served as time lines, others showed diagrams of crime scenes. Facedown on a set of boxes near David's desk

were post-mortem photographs, which graphically showed the handiwork of the Rising Phoenix. The triad had once been the most powerful
Asian organized-crime syndicate in the city. Now, after a series of trials
that David had headed—at one point he'd supervised four cases involving other gang members in addition to his own trials involving the triad
leader and his lieutenants—the Rising Phoenix's members were either
dead, behind bars, or had been absorbed by other gangs.

During the trials David had received several death threats. He hadn't
taken them seriously, but the FBI had. They put a trace on his phone and
arranged for round-the-clock surveillance. The routine was claustrophobic and enervating, but—as the agents had reminded him on their last
night of duty after the trial was over—he was still alive. Better to be safe
than sorry, they said.

David took a sip of coffee, grabbed a box, then began sifting through
the papers on his desk. There was a time when he would have kept
the congratulatory letters, but now he tossed them, even the one from
his ex-wife, in the trash. His secretary had grouped about a dozen invitations together with a rubber band. Without opening them, David
dumped these as well. Why should he look at them? He knew what they
were. Ever since the O.J. case, lawyers had become pseudo celebrities.
Hostesses and fund-raising groups liked to invite lawyers who'd been on
the news every night to give their parties a buzz. Other invitations were
issued by private law firms. With his rise in celebrity—and with every
Rising Phoenix conviction—several headhunters had phoned to inquire
if he wanted to go back into private practice. Old friends, who'd been
ensconced in firms for years, had called out of the blue to ask if David
would like to have lunch with the senior partners or stop by for drinks.
David had said no. He understood that this chapter of his life was over,
but not knowing what would happen with Hulan had put his career in
limbo.

By eleven, David had gone through the easy piles. Now he moved on
to the everyday materials that he'd needed during these last months of
back-to-back trials. As he began looking at the folders—knowing that
they held so many lives that had been lost or ruined—he couldn't help
but be aware of his own dejection.

Like most lawyers, David often experienced melancholy after the completion of a trial. But this time he was also hounded by a sense of futility. Sure, he'd been successful. The Rising Phoenix had been brought down, but as David had predicted, other triads had filled the vacuum. A couple of months ago, the Sun Yee On had become more active in Southern California. At that time David was deep into trial, so the case had been handled to someone else in this office. More recently the Wah Ching group had been caught with a shipment of heroin coming in from the Golden Triangle. That case had gone to the narcotics unit. The media loved a big drug case, and attention had finally shifted from David's work. The baton, so to speak, had been passed.

After the favorable conclusion of a big case, an assistant U.S. attorney was expected to parlay that triumph into a lucrative job in the private sector. The calls from the headhunters only verified for David that it was time to move on and that there were opportunities out there. At the same time, his name was being bandied about for U.S. attorney. If he believed the newspapers, his appointment and confirmation were assured. The current U.S. attorney, Madeleine Prentice, was behind him too. She'd been encouraging him to throw his name into the hat ever since her nomination to the federal bench. Madeleine's was a path that David had once aspired to, but he no longer desired it. True, he no longer trusted his own government, but it was more personal than that: he wanted to be with Hulan, to be with her when she gave birth to their child, to live together as a family.

So he had come back to thoughts of Hulan. Hours had passed since her call, and he was still worried about her. David hadn't been completely forthright with Hulan this morning, and it bothered him now. He knew how he could get information about Knight International, but he hadn't mentioned it. Recent press coverage had focused on speculation that the company was about to be bought by mega-toy company Tartan International. His old law firm, Phillips, MacKenzie & Stout, had long done Tartan's legal work. Tartan, a major client, paid millions of dollars in legal fees each year. As name partner and firm rainmaker, it was expected that Miles Stout would keep a close guard on his best client, and he had. He had managed the acquisition of several smaller companies by the conglomerate and had served as Tartan's spokesman for many years. Additionally, he represented Randall Craig, the chairman of

Tartan. But when it came to the actual grunt work for the company—licensing deals, handling esoteric copyright-infringement violations, or performing due diligence during contract negotiations—Miles passed most of it on to junior partners and a flock of associates.

When David had been at the firm, he'd been friendly with Keith Baxter, one of the young attorneys who'd been corraled by Miles into the Tartan work. David reached for his Rolodex, found the number for Keith's private line, and put through a call. After a couple of minutes, David and Keith had made arrangements to meet at the Water Grill on Grand Avenue for drinks and dinner. Keith was a good guy, pretty open. The next time Hulan called, David was sure he'd be ready with whatever information she might want on Knight.

At seven, the Water Grill was jammed with the pre-theater dinner crowd, as well as people who'd come down out of their office towers for business dinners or romantic evenings with their spouses. The Water Grill specialized in seafood, and here and there men and women wore big plastic bibs to protect their clothes from the splatter of bouillabaisse or flying pieces of cracked crab. At other tables customers attacked towering *fruits de mer* platters piled high with shrimp, oysters, mussels, and sea urchins.

David followed the hostess as she wended her way through the main room to one of the banquettes along the far wall. Keith was already seated and nursing a scotch on the rocks. A waitress came up and asked if David wanted a drink. "Shall we get a bottle of wine?" David asked Keith. When Keith nodded, David ordered a bottle of Chateau St. Jean. Moments later, wine had been poured for David, and Keith was working on another tumbler of brown liquor. During this time David sized up his old colleague.

Ten years ago, Keith had come to Phillips, MacKenzie fresh out of law school. He hadn't known much about law except how to take a test and argue with a teacher. And, with the exception of moot court, he'd never tried a case in front of a jury. But at the law firm, as it was in private law firms across the country, he hadn't been expected to try a case for many, many years. He'd been assigned to several of David's matters, had written briefs, done document reviews, and summarized witness testimony. When David left Phillips, MacKenzie, Keith was a senior associate. A couple of years ago he'd made partner and decided to focus more on mergers and acquisitions. But as a junior partner he was nothing more than a glorified associate—working hard but getting little of the credit or the fun.

Sitting across from Keith now, David saw that the past decade had been hard on the younger man. He'd once been a bit of an athlete, but he'd put on weight and begun to lose his hair. And the drinking? That was something David didn't remember.

Over dinner—Hawaiian mahi mahi on nori rice with blackened sesame seeds for David, grouper with an ancho chili sauce for Keith—the conversation concerned mutual friends, legal committees they were involved with, and news from the headlines. They bantered about David's captivity at the hands of the FBI security team—the fast-food meals, the lingo, the sense of importance the men and women agents brought to a job that David thought totally unnecessary. Once the dishes were cleared, Keith ordered brandy while David settled for coffee.

Finally David asked, "They still have you slaving away over there?"

"Yeah, you know how it is," Keith said.

"Have you tried any cases yet?"

"Shit no. I'm corporate all the way now."

"It's not too late to go back to litigation. If you want experience, come to the U.S. Attorney's Office. By the end of the first year, you'll have been in court so many times—"

"But my bank account would be empty."

David shrugged. "There are things other than money."

"Really, what?" The bitterness in Keith's tone made David look up.

"Doing right, working on the side of justice, putting away bad guys." David said the words, but he didn't know if he believed them anymore. So much had happened in his own life and to his sense of who he was and what he did.

As if reading these thoughts, Keith asked, "How can you still spout that stuff after all you've been through?" When David didn't respond, Keith continued, "After everything that happened to you in China . . ."

No one was supposed to know exactly *what* had happened to David in China. Was Keith speculating or did he actually know something? David decided to dismiss the comment with a laugh.

"All I'm saying is that you might have more fun if you changed jobs," David said. "It doesn't have to be the government. There are other things you can do."

"What about my clients?"

When David raised an eyebrow inquiringly, Keith continued: "Okay, so they aren't my clients exactly, but I still feel responsible for them. I may not be the name partner, but I'm the one the clients talk to day to day."

"Who are you working for?"

"In the firm? Miles, of course."

"Some things never change."

"Oh, they change, all right." There again was that bitter tone.

"How do you mean?"

"David, you don't want to know. I mean, you'd recognize the place. We've got the same carpet and draperies and oak desks and all that shit, but, man, we're at the end of the millennium. Practicing isn't the same."

"We all get burnt out," David offered, but Keith just shook his head and took another sip of brandy.

After a pause Keith said, "You didn't ask me out to dinner to catch up. What's up? You want to come back to the firm? You throwing a bone my way? If I get you to come back, I'd be guaranteed a bonus at the end of the year."

The two men stared at each other for a moment, then both cracked up. David realized that it was the first time this evening he'd seen anything of Keith's old sense of humor.

"It's not that, but when the time comes, you'll be the first to know."

"I doubt it. The name partners talk about you all the time. I'm surprised you haven't heard from them yet."

David thought about the unopened invitations he'd thrown away, but before he could follow up, Keith's smile faded and the moment passed.

"So what do you want?" Keith asked.

"It's about Knight International. Since Tartan's buying the company, I thought you could tell me about it."

"Anything I could tell you would fall under the auspices of privileged information."

David waited, hoping Keith would say more. Instead Keith took another swallow of brandy, then waved his empty glass in the air to signal the waitress he wanted another. As Keith brought his hand back down, David noticed it was shaking. Had he been nervous all night?

"Come on," David said at last. "What's Knight up to these days?"

"Why are you asking? Is this some Justice Department investigation? Because if it is, you're way out of line."

"That's a leap! I ask a simple question and you give me that?"

Keith shrugged. "I told you. Things are different at the firm. We have to be careful of outsiders."

"I'm not an outsider."

"But you're not bound by what I tell you either."

"The way you're talking makes me think you or the firm or Tartan has something to hide. Lighten up! I just wanted some background on Knight. I thought you'd be a knowledgeable source."

"Do me a favor and read about Knight in the papers."

The conversation had taken a bizarre turn. Sweat had formed on Keith's forehead, and he wiped it with a napkin. His face was flushed— from drink, from anger, from the heat of the room, David couldn't tell. But there was something more here. Since when wouldn't an old friend answer a simple question? Did Keith think it was some kind of ethics test? And that nonsense about an investigation? All this was probably just the alcohol talking. David could wait to ask his questions until tomorrow, when Keith would probably call and say his head hurt like hell and he was sorry for acting like such an ass. Instead David decided to lay his cards on the table.

"My girlfriend . . ." It was strange to call Hulan his girlfriend, but what was the proper word? He cleared his throat and tried again. "My girlfriend lives in China."

Keith grinned, his mood switching again. "Liu Hulan. I never met her, but I remember you talking about her. When we first met you were about as brokenhearted as they come. I heard you reconnected, shall we say?"

David ignored Keith's kidding. "One of her friends had a daughter who worked at a Knight factory in China," David continued. "I didn't know they had factories over there."

"They have one. Old man Knight thinks of himself as cutting-edge when it comes to manufacturing. What could be more cutting-edge than China?" When David didn't respond, Keith went on, "I've been over there, you know, doing the due diligence work and working with Knight's American accountants to get all the financials in order for review by the Securities and Exchange Commission. I've seen a lot of stuff."

"Like?"

Keith considered, then said, "Nothing exciting. It's a factory out in the boonies, and I can tell you that those accountants Knight flew in suffered from major culture shock from the food and the strangeness of the place. Those guys came and went as fast as they could." Almost as an afterthought he added, "Although I don't know why. Knight only employs women—some pretty ones too." He wiped his forehead again.

David stared at Keith, trying to make sense of the strange fluctuations in the other man's behavior. Finally David asked, "What's going on?"

"What do you mean?" There again was that testy tone, a response that was far removed from what David expected from his friend and colleague of many years.

"You seem to be under a lot more pressure than I've ever seen you. What's happening?"

Keith's eyes seemed to get watery, but he covered this by lifting the snifter and taking another sip of brandy.

"I can't help you if you don't confide in me," David persisted.

Keith put the snifter down. "I'm in a bind," he said, keeping his eyes focused on the inside lip of the glass. "I'm in trouble and I don't know what to do."

"What is it? Can I help?"

"It's personal."

"Keith, we've known each other a long time—"

"And it's professional," he said, raising his eyes to meet David's.

For the second time this evening, the honorable, yet sometimes horrible, code of ethics to which honest lawyers adhered had come into the conversation. They could skirt around the code: David could ask general questions about a client (Tartan) or about what that client was involved in (the acquisition of Knight), and Keith might even answer them, although he certainly hadn't tonight. But to exchange real information about a particular case, a particular client, a particular act involving jurisprudence? To actually divulge that a lawyer had been involved in something shady or sinister or straight-on illegal was another matter entirely. They both knew it was taboo.

David took a deep breath. "Is there something I can do?" He hesitated, then asked, "Do you need to talk to someone at the Justice Department or the FBI? You know I can arrange it."

But Keith just shook his head. "I don't know what I'm going to do. All I know is that I want to set things right."

The conversation had run aground. Keith was up against the wall, but still at a point that he couldn't or wouldn't talk about it. Keith smiled wanly, then looked away. "Man, I'm beat. Let's get the hell out of here." He flagged down the waitress, got the check, and paid it, saying, "Don't worry about it. I can expense it out." When he stood, his body swayed slightly. Then he made an unsteady line for the door.

They emerged into the cool night air. Tomorrow would be the Fourth of July. In Los Angeles that could just as easily mean dense fog or a heat wave. This year it looked to be foggy. Standing in the cool white dampness, David and Keith chatted a few more minutes. He wondered if Keith, who'd consumed far more alcohol than David, should drive.

"I left my car with the valet," David said. "You want a lift?"

Keith shook his head. "I'll just walk back to the office. I have a couple of faxes I need to send."

The offices of Phillips, MacKenzie were in one of the skyscrapers on Bunker Hill. All Keith had to do was cross Grand, walk past the library, cross Fifth, then climb the "Spanish Steps" up to Hope. The distance wasn't far, but downtown wasn't all that safe at night after the day workers had gone home to the suburbs.

"I can drive you up there if you want."

"No, I'll walk. It'll do me good. Clear my head."

They shook hands. "Lunch next week?" David asked.

"Sure, I'll give you a call."

Grand was a one-way street downtown. Keith looked right, saw nothing, then stepped off the curb. Up the street David saw headlights through the mist. Keith was halfway across the road, oblivious to the car. For a moment David thought the car was going to hit Keith, but then the driver decelerated.

To David it seemed then that everything slowed down so that he could see every detail as, maybe even before, it happened. A hand with a gun in it reached out the rear left window and swung toward David. He heard the gunfire and saw the flashes of light from the muzzle. Instinctively he fell to the ground. He heard screams behind him—probably other customers who'd left the restaurant just behind David and Keith and were on their way to the valet. David heard the bullets ricochet off the wall and felt pieces of stone and stucco rain down on him. From his position on the sidewalk, he saw Keith look back and left over his shoulder. If he'd looked right, he would have seen the car and hustled out of the way. Instead the car hit him. Keith's body flew up into the air, moving fast, arms and legs flailing, then slammed into the back wall of the library with a sickening thud. The car sped away, skidding as it turned the corner.

There was a period of silence, then David heard behind him the clatter of high heels on the sidewalk, the sound of men shouting, and someone begin to whimper in pain. All the while he didn't take his eyes off the motionless form of Keith across the street. Shakily David got to his feet, staggered across the asphalt, and knelt next to his friend. The bones in Keith's left arm were jagged sticks of white protruding from flesh. His legs were at unnatural angles, not moving. Blood gushed from a deep gash in one of his legs, probably where the chrome of the bumper had cut into flesh. David felt Keith's neck for a pulse. Somehow he was still alive.

"Help! Somebody help us!" David screamed.

David had never taken a CPR class, but he had an idea of how it worked. But should he tilt Keith's head back to give mouth-to-mouth? Maybe Keith had a broken neck—this seemed likely given that his limbs weren't moving. Should David massage Keith's chest? Maybe the internal injuries were too great; maybe David would cause more damage. At least he could do something about the blood. He put his hand over the gash and pressed hard to stanch the flow. Just then Keith opened his eyes. He moaned. When he tried to speak, blood bubbled out of his mouth and his eyes widened in terror.

"It's all right," David said. "I'm here. You're going to be okay."

Looking at the blood that oozed out over his hands and the blood that had now spread out like a halo around Keith's head, David knew that what he'd said was a lie. His friend was dying and he was terrified.

In the distance David heard a siren. "You hear that? It's an ambulance. Hang on. The paramedics will be here soon."

Keith tried to speak, but again all that came out was a ragged gurgle and a froth of foaming blood. Then Keith's body went into convulsions. Blood spattered the wall, the sidewalk, David. Then Keith took a last anguished gasp for air and went still.

Kneeling next to the body, blood on his hands and clothes, David did what he usually did in an emergency. He retreated into linear thought. When the police arrived, he'd help them with their report. He'd seen the Jeep: black, newer model, but he hadn't caught the license plate. He'd say that he'd been the target, that the locals would be smart to call the FBI right away, that an APB should be put out on those remaining Rising Phoenix members whom David had so grievously misjudged. Instead of scattering as he'd thought, they'd formed a deadly plan. Only they'd erred, killing Keith and injuring another passerby whose misfortune it had been to be in the wrong place at the wrong time.

He'd tell the police that the driver obviously hadn't seen Keith since he didn't attempt to swerve out of the way. Then David would get his car from valet parking and go home. By the time he got there, a team from the FBI would probably have already checked the rooms and once again set up residence. In the coming weeks David could look forward to the company of agents, no privacy and no freedom. But before all that he'd have to call the offices of Phillips, MacKenzie & Stout. He might even be the first one to tell Miles Stout about Keith's death. He'd fill in the particulars, offer to help with funeral arrangements, knowing perfectly well that Miles would want to control those details as he controlled so many things. Even the mundane thought that he'd have to make sure that his dark blue suit was back from the dry cleaner in time for the funeral flickered across David's brain.

But this time he identified something else, something different, amidst all these practical thoughts. Not anguish. Not despair. Not disgust at the rusty smell of the blood or the other bodily odors that now came drifting up from the corpse. Not worry over whether all that blood was clean. Not fear that he'd been the intended victim. It was an overwhelming sense of guilt. His complacency had led to Keith's death.

3

DA SHUI VILLAGE LAY ABOUT TEN MILES FROM TAIYUAN City in Shanxi Province. Although Taiyuan was only about three hundred miles from Beijing, it took Hulan almost two full days to reach. It had been too late to book a flight, and Hulan hadn't wanted to risk wasting time by offering a bribe if a seat couldn't be guaranteed. Driving was also out of the question, since the roads were painfully slow due to pedestrians, wheelbarrows, oxen-pulled carts, and bicycles, as well as cars, buses, and trucks. Besides, Vice Minister Zai would never have permitted Hulan to make the drive alone. He would have insisted that Investigator Lo accompany her, and that would have defeated part of her purpose for this trip. She wanted to get away, be alone for a while. As they said in the West, she needed to think things through.

The most convenient rail route to Taiyuan was on the Beijing-Guangzhou express, which required a train change at Shijiazhuang—a journey of about seven hours. Typically reservations were made ten days in advance, but since Hulan had made her arrangements on the spur of the moment, no seats had been available. Instead she'd traveled to Taiyuan via Datong, where she'd changed trains. And instead of booking a soft seat for the first leg, she'd only been able to buy a hard seat and even that required an extra "gift" paid to the reservations clerk.

On Friday morning Hulan had arrived at the massive North Beijing Railroad Station. Inside the air was dense with cigarette smoke. The steel-frame windows were open but didn't seem to have any effect on the overheated and stuffy atmosphere. Thousands upon thousands of people waited for trains for distant provinces. Some slept. Some ate. Some fanned themselves with torn sheets of newspaper. Several men sat with their T-shirts rolled up over their bellies to under their armpits and with their trouser legs rolled up over their knees.

At ten-thirty departure had been announced, and hundreds of men, women, and children had smashed up against each other as they tried to get their tickets punched. Then they pushed through the turnstiles that led to the train platform. Once on board, an attendant—a stern-faced woman in a starched pale green shirt with red emblems on the shoulders—took Hulan's paper ticket and exchanged it for a hard plastic ticket. Hulan took her assigned seat—the middle position on a hard bench that accommodated three people. There was no air conditioning, and all but two of the windows in the car had been sealed shut. Most of those on board were going on to Huhhot in Mongolia.

By eleven the train had left the station and had rolled through the crowded environs of Beijing. Gradually the high-rises and traffic jams of the city had been left behind. Within an hour the landscape had changed. Fields spread out to the horizon. Villages appeared, then disappeared as the express chugged through the rural western counties. Soon the train began a slow but steady climb. Occasionally she caught glimpses of the Great Wall as it snaked over the hills. Then the train leveled out again, and outside the window were fields of beans, corn, tomatoes, peppers, and eggplant. By the time the train reached Zhangjiakounan, with its massive nuclear power plant, the land had become harsher. Along the track were piles of coal, and the stations they passed through were dingy with coal dust. Hulan saw peasants—the poorest of the poor—working land that was filled with too many minerals to sustain proper life. Most people in this area had given up farming entirely and now worked in coal and salt mines.

Hulan had tried to keep her attention on what was passing outside the window, but it had been hard. Her compartment teemed with life. Babies wailed, spat up, peed (or worse) on the floor. Men chain-smoked rough-smelling cigarettes, occasionally hawking murky sputum toward the spittoons which had been strategically placed at either end of the compartment.

But usually the men hadn't bothered to move from their seats, and horrible globs of mucus ended up on the floor with the produce, the souvenirs, and gifts that people had bought in the capital, and the toddlers and those travelers who'd had it with their hard seats and had stretched out among the bags. Most of the passengers had brought their own provisions and throughout the day pulled out fragrant—sometimes too fragrant—containers of noodles. Others got by on slivers of garlic on cold buns. Most everyone had brought their own jar for tea, and the attendant passed through the aisle every hour or so with hot water refills. As the hours ticked by, these odors had blended with those from the bathroom at the end of the compartment. Many of the passengers were rural people who'd never seen indoor plumbing before, even if it was only a hole in the floor leading straight down to the track. The combination of smells could be nauseating under ordinary circumstances but were made worse by the train's constant movement. Indeed several people had lost their meals into plastic bags or straight onto the floor in desperate dashes to the bathroom.

Hulan, still in the early enough stages of pregnancy to be sorely affected by odors of any sort, had fought her feelings of queasiness by sucking on preserved plums and sipping from a thermos of ginger tea. Dr. Du, a traditional Chinese herbal medicine doctor in Beijing and Hulan's mother's longtime physician, had recently taken over Hulan's care. However, she had been extremely skeptical of his prescriptions for morning sickness—especially the Emperor of Heaven's Special Pill to Tonify the Heart, reputed to bring strength to the blood and calm the spirit—and had made the mistake of saying so to Madame Zhang.

The next day Madame Zhang had come calling with a bag of individually wrapped preserved plums and the mixture for the tea. "Doctors! Men! What do they know?" the Neighborhood Committee director asked. "I'm an old woman and you listen to me. You put one plum in your mouth and you wait. No chewing. Just suck. When the meat is gone, you keep sucking on the pit, too. You will feel much better." With this advice Madame Zhang had given her tacit but unspoken agreement to allow the pregnancy to continue without a permit. Sitting on the train, with her bag of plums half-empty, Hulan had been glad to have them. Old wives' tale or simple placebo, Hulan didn't care, so long as the plums continued to settle her stomach.

On the train went. So much dust, grit, and coal dust had blown in from the two open windows that they were closed until the heat became unbearable and were opened again. From loudspeakers music and a constant stream of announcements had competed with the human cacophony. Traditional Chinese songs were interspersed with newer romantic ballads. But the music was a relief compared to the broadcast declarations, during which a shrill voice announced train stops, cigarettes and liquor for sale, news of the day, and political reminders on birth control, politeness in society, and the importance of increased production. Not for the first time Hulan had marveled at her compatriots' ability—willingness—to have this noise, whether in music or propaganda, intrude into their daily lives.

Hulan had made reservations at the Yungang Hotel, a so-called five-star hotel and the only establishment in Datong that attempted to cater to foreigners. Driving there by taxi, Hulan saw a grimy city filled with coal trucks. Black drifts of coal dust tufted the edge of the road. Despite the taxi driver's high hopes that Datong would become a tourist center— "We are especially popular with the Japanese because they occupied Datong during the war and like to renew their memories"—the hotel and Hulan's room were desperately dreary. Cigarette burns marred the carpet, and grimy gray curtains hung in limp shreds. Hot water ran only from seven to nine in the morning, she was informed, and the television broadcast only local news and state channels. The cavernous hotel dining room had a staff of about fifty women dressed in powder blue *cheongsams* who looked listless and bored. Hulan had dinner alone, while a tour group of twenty Japanese silently picked through a meal of cold canned string beans, cold meat, sautéed pork with vegetables, french fries, watermelon, and lemon cake. A Karen Carpenter song played on a continuous loop with the waitresses joining in occasionally, "Every sha-la-la-la, every wo-oh-wo-oh, every shing-a-ling-a-ling . . ."

By eight the next morning Hulan was back on the train and heading south another seven hours to Taiyuan. She had been fortunate enough to book a soft seat for this second day. The compartment had two sets of bunks, and each person was required to sit on his or her own bed for the duration of the trip. The man who occupied the bunk across from Hulan put a newspaper over his face, fell asleep, and began to snore, prompting another man to shout out, "Roll over! You're making it impossible for any of us to sleep." The man did as he was told, and soon the other two occupants drifted off as well. On the table by the window, a brochure extolled this train's modern virtues in quaint, imaginative English:

Dear passengers, security, polite, and hospitality are the service aim of our crew. Please remember:

1. Never speak taboo words.
2. Keep the interior of the car clean and tidy. The environment must be graceful.
3. Our food dishes are meticulously prepared and have four features—color, fragrance, taste, and shape. Moslem food is also available.
4. When you are in car, please use the complement gloves.

Under the table Hulan found a basket with the gloves, a large thermos filled with hot water, and porcelain cups with lids. When a young woman attendant came by with packets of tea for purchase, Hulan inquired if there was some way to turn down the loudspeaker. The attendant not only said that she could but offered to turn the speaker off entirely. Soon the high-pitched announcements were replaced by the gentle sighs of the sleeping men and the soothing pulse of the train moving along the track. And although this train was also bereft of air conditioning, an oscillating fan circulated the warm air. This, combined with the hot towels that the attendant brought by periodically, made this day's journey almost pleasant.

How different all this was from the last time Hulan traveled to and from Da Shui Village! In 1970 she had joined other friends and neighbors from Beijing on a train that superficially looked like this. That train had been packed, overflowing really, with other young Beijingers. (She remembered one whole brigade of kids who'd climbed on the roof of the train and had stayed there for the whole trip.) Hulan and the others had worn old army uniforms handed down from parents. They had spouted slogans, although secretly they'd rejoiced that they were just being sent to the west instead of the Great Northern Wilderness along the desolate and inhospitable Russian border. They had harassed the compartment attendants, even booting some of them off the train. In one village, a group—not one of them over sixteen years old—had decided that the train's engineer and those who helped him were running dogs of capitalism tied to the old ways. These people were set on the station platform and harangued for two days. Villagers came out to watch the spectacle. Finally someone realized that none of them was ever going to get out of that godforsaken place unless the engineer and his helpers were put back on the train.

Coming back to Beijing two years later had been no different. That trip too was plagued by numerous stops for rallies and struggle meetings. Instead of reaching Beijing by sundown on the direct route, it had also taken two days. That time Hulan, fourteen years old and still filled with the wild passions that were so much a part of the Cultural Revolution, had traveled in the safe and comforting company of Uncle Zai. Meanwhile her father had been under house arrest in their *hutong* home and her mother, having fallen from a second-story balcony, had lain in the dirt outside an office building during Zai's four-day round trip to retrieve Hulan from the countryside. The people at the office had worked for Hulan's father for many years. They had all known Jinli, but they had been forbidden to come to her aid. By the time Zai and Hulan reached Beijing, Jinli was crippled and her mind destroyed.

The closer Hulan got to Taiyuan, the capital of Shanxi Province, the more she worried about coming back to this place of so much bloodshed and sorrow. *Shanxi* meant "west of the mountains," and the entire province was a mountainous plateau that looked out over the fertile North China Plain. That rich land had been attractive to foreign aggressors for millennia. In ancient times invaders had come from the north. Their first obstacle was the Great Wall; their second and more formidable barrier was Taiyuan. This city had seen more violence over the last two thousand years than any other in China. Those centuries of bloody turmoil lay buried in the soil and in the souls of the people of this province.

Hulan's train pulled into Taiyuan at three-thirty. She made her way out onto the street, flagged down a dented Chinese-made taxi, and asked to be taken to the bus stop for Da Shui Village. As a young girl she had been to Taiyuan only a few times—when she'd come and left on the train and on those occasions when her team at the Red Soil Farm had participated in demonstrations at the Twin Pagodas, the double temples located on a hill that served as the city's emblem. In those days few automobiles or trucks plied the streets. Instead the avenues and alleyways that made up the city had been filled with the reassuring hum of bicycles transporting people and merchandise. The air—even on a hot and humid day like this one—had been clear and filled with the perfume of flowering trees and the rich soil that even in the middle of the city exuded a warm scent.

Twenty-five years had passed, and Taiyuan was not at all what Hulan expected. Her taxi driver jolted the car in and out of bumper-to-bumper traffic. He kept his hand on the horn, despite Hulan's repeated requests that he stop. She rolled down her window—it was too hot not to—and her nostrils filled with exhaust and other fumes that spewed from factory chimneys.

These last ten years had seen an invasion of another sort to Taiyuan. American companies, the driver explained, had set up joint-venture coal mines in the outlying areas and export companies in town. Australians were raising special pigs, which were not as fat as local pigs and considered to be far more tasty. New Zealanders had arrived with sheep to grow wool for carpets. Germans and Italians, meanwhile, had gotten into heavy industry. These varied enterprises had brought prosperity to the city. All around Hulan saw construction sites for offices and foreign hotels. For now, though, foreigners stayed at the Shanxi Grand Hotel. "Year in, year out, they live there," the driver said. "Those VIP-ers have water every day, all day, while in the rest of the city we only get water on certain days of the week." Then he added, bragging, "I went inside the Shanxi once. It was amazing, but then you think of the new hotels . . ." He sucked air through his teeth. "The Shanxi Grand will seem like nothing once they open."

After the driver dropped her off, she discovered that the bus to outlying villages to the south wouldn't arrive for another hour. Carrying her bag, she walked down the block, passing an open-air café filled with customers. Another two doors down she found another café all but deserted. If she'd wanted a meal she would have gone back to the first place, but in such heat all she wanted was a bit of shade, a little solitude, a place to pass the time, and something cold to drink. The Coke came cool but not cold. At five, the owner of the establishment, a woman, returned to the table.

"You have been sitting here too long! You have to leave so I have room for other customers!"

Hulan looked around. There were no other customers. "I am a traveler."

"A Beijinger! Big-city woman! So what! I am a business owner, an entrepreneur. You are taking up space."

"As an entrepreneur you should be more welcoming to your customers," Hulan retorted.

"If you don't like it, go somewhere else."

Hulan gazed at the café owner in surprise. This woman was insulting her in the same way a salesclerk in a Beijing department store might. Customer service had gotten so bad in Beijing that the government had inaugurated a politeness campaign and issued a list of fifty phrases that were to be omitted from speech. Either this campaign hadn't filtered out to Shanxi Province, or the people here simply didn't care.

But maybe this campaign, like others before it, was doomed to fail no matter who ordered it. Hulan could remember back when the government had launched the Four Beautifications and Five Spruce-Ups Campaigns to combat incivility. In those days people had been accustomed to obeying every decree, and still no one had carried out the new orders. The masses argued that it was bourgeois to wait on customers, but Hulan had always seen the lack of manners in another way. It was hard to be polite to strangers when the government assigned the job and guaranteed the paltry salary no matter how rudely you acted. Now the pattern was hard to break. But clearly China's most successful entrepreneurs had learned the benefits of good customer service, which might have been why the first café had been filled with diners and this one was about to lose its only patron.

Hulan paid her bill and headed back to the bus stop. By now the sun had passed behind a tall building and shadowed the sidewalk. Hulan sat on the curb and waited.

The bus, when it arrived, was filled to capacity with commuters. Still, Hulan and five more people were able to squeeze onto the back-door steps. At first the bus moved slowly through the crowded city streets. After twenty minutes and only two miles, the bus reached the huge bridge that traversed the Fen River. Hulan couldn't believe what she saw.

Twenty-five years ago the Fen had been a huge, raging river a half mile wide. Today it was a meandering stream. The now-wide banks were lush with river grasses and shrubs. Children played. Families picnicked. A few people flew homemade kites.

But this wasn't the biggest surprise. In another few blocks the bus driver stopped at a toll booth, paid a fare, then entered a brand-new, four-lane expressway. What had once taken hours of start-and-stop driving accompanied by honking at the pedestrians and animals that crowded the roadway now zipped along. Within minutes the bus passed the turnoff for the Jinci Temple, renowned for its Song Dynasty Mother Temple and for its Three Everlasting Springs. Another few miles and the bus was flanked by undulating oceans of millet and vast areas planted with corn and sorghum.

The bus made quick stops in Xian Dian, Liu Jia Bu, and Qing Shu before arriving at the crossroads for Da Shui Village. Alone, Hulan stepped off the bus. After it pulled away, she took a moment to orient herself. Behind her, the expressway led back to Taiyuan. Before her, if she was recalling correctly, lay the village of Chao Jia and town of Ping Yao. About three miles down the road to her right—and this she would never forget—was where the Red Soil Farm had once had its compound of dormitories, storage buildings, work sheds, and kitchens. The land all around her for as far as she could see had been a part of that commune. Undoubtedly this land had been redistributed in 1984, when China's entire collective system was dismantled and individual plots were given to peasant families.

It was now about seven o'clock. Da Shui lay about two miles to her left, but she wouldn't have to walk that far. If Suchee's directions were correct, Hulan would have to go only about one *li*, or a third of a mile, to reach the farm. The evening couldn't be described as cool, but the air felt fresh and clean compared to that on the train, in Taiyuan, or on the bus. As Hulan began to walk, she took her time, enjoying the gentle bombardment of the country on her senses. The moisture-laden air hung heavily over the fields, creating a pale haze. The humidity gathered on her skin in a fine, damp, vaguely soothing film. One of the fields had just been irrigated, and the smell of the wet red soil and the fragrance coming off the plants was heady. She heard no sounds of technology, only the crunch of gravel under her shoes and the thrumming of cicadas in their evensong.

At last Hulan left the road to walk along a raised pathway that led left through the fields. Now that she was among the plants, she saw things a little more clearly. From afar the fields had looked green and lush, but these crops weren't thriving. They were barely hanging on. This was the height of the growing season, yet the green leaves were stunted. If this was happening aboveground, it was surely happening below, repressing and deforming the growth of the edible tubers. How odd, Hulan thought. The climate here was no worse for growing than in other parts of China. Irrigation had never been a problem, for this entire region was known for its springs and wells. Water had always been so abundant in this particular area that the village had honored the fact. Da Shui meant Big Water. But from what Hulan saw around her, these plants were starved for that very substance.

When the next two fields seemed far more healthy, Hulan allowed her optimism to rise, but this was deflated when Suchee's home came into view. These days one way to gauge a peasant family's prosperity was if the old mud-brick house had been torn down and replaced with one made from fired brick. On the train Hulan had seen many fired-brick houses. Then, on seeing the changes in Taiyuan, she'd supposed that some of that city's prosperity was a reflection of greater prosperity in the surrounding countryside, but her hopes and guesses had been wrong. Only three hundred miles from Beijing, this was the primitive interior.

Suchee's small compound had been built according to old customs, based on practical and political considerations. The building faced south toward the warmth of the sun and away from the north from which invaders had always come. There was a small walled-in courtyard of ten by ten feet, which protected a well. Other than this, the hard-packed land that nestled between these walls was devoid of buckets, potted plants, a bicycle, or any of those items that spelled a life lived above a subsistence level. This side of the house had a door with a window opening on each side. There was no glass, which was fine at this time of year, but cruel during the winter when Suchee would have to stuff the openings with dried grass. If she were feeling particularly prosperous, she might even seal the window further with newspaper held in place with glue made from flour and water.

"Ling Suchee!" Hulan called out. "I am here! It is Liu Hulan!"

From inside the house Hulan heard a squeal, then her own name called out. A moment later an old woman stood in the doorway. "I didn't think you would come," the old woman said. "But you have."

"Suchee?"

Seeing Hulan's uncertainty, the woman came forward and took her arm. "It is I, Suchee, your friend. Come in. I will make tea. Have you eaten?"

Hulan stepped over the high threshold, which was designed to keep flood waters out. Except for the single bare lightbulb that hung from a rafter in the center of the room, she could have been stepping back in time a hundred, even a thousand years. The room held two *kangs*, beds made from wooden platforms. Once again memories rushed back. Hulan remembered her shock as a twelve-year-old on learning that people slept on these platforms instead of in soft beds. How the bones of Hulan and her young comrades had ached until the peasants had shown them how to make mattresses out of straw. Later that year, when freezing winds had come down from the north, the peasants had taught them to make quilts from raw cotton and to set braziers filled with hot coal under the platforms for warmth.

"Sit, Hulan. You must be tired."

Hulan did as she was told, perching on a stool made from a crate turned on end. She glanced around. There was so little here. The table, the upturned crates, the two beds. A shelf held two cups, four bowls—two large for noodles, two small for rice—three serving dishes, and an old soy sauce container filled with cooking utensils and chopsticks. To the right of the door was a small cabinet where Hulan supposed Suchee kept clothes and linens. On top Suchee had put together a simple altar with some sticks of incense, three oranges, a crudely carved Buddha, and two photographs. These would be of Suchee's husband and daughter.

Once the water was on, Suchee joined Hulan at the table. Too many things had happened in the last twenty-five years for these women to go straight to the reason Hulan had come. They needed to reconnect, to reestablish a rapport, to build again the trust that had once bound them almost as blood relatives. Yes, there would be time to talk about Miaoshan, but for now the two women spoke of Hulan's trip, of the changes she'd seen in Taiyuan, of life in Beijing, of Hulan's coming baby; of

Suchee's crops of millet, corn, and beans, of the water shortage, of the oppressive heat.

Years ago they had been girls together, but since then they'd traveled very different roads. Except for those two years on the Red Soil Farm, Hulan had lived the sheltered and privileged life of a Red Princess. She had never wanted for clothes or food. Her position had allowed her considerable freedom to travel not only across China but also to the United States. She was not afraid of the government or of nature. All this showed in Hulan's clothes, in her smooth, pale skin, in the way she held herself as she sat on the upended crate, whereas, if she had seen Suchee on the street in Beijing, she would have taken her for someone sixty or seventy years old.

As twilight faded into darkness, Hulan began to see her girlhood friend hiding behind the old woman's face. Under the flickering light of a kerosene lantern—electricity was too expensive to use on a daily basis— Hulan saw how a lifetime of backbreaking work under an unforgiving sun had taken its toll. As a twelve-year-old Suchee had been stronger and far more robust than Hulan. But Hulan had spent the rest of her teenage years in America, eating meat at almost every meal, so now she was perhaps four inches taller than Suchee. Beyond this, Suchee's back was already curving into a dowager's hump due to years of carrying water and produce on a pole slung across her shoulders. Suchee's face pained Hulan most of all. As a girl Suchee had been beautiful. Her face had been round and full of life. Her cheeks had glowed pink. Now her skin was wrinkled and stained dark brown from the sun.

Of course, she had lived a much fuller life than Hulan. She had married and borne a child. She had also lost both her husband and her child. When Hulan looked straight into Suchee's eyes, she had to turn away. Behind the polite words Suchee was suffering from a loss that Hulan could not begin to imagine. Hardening her heart against the details that she knew would come, Hulan reached across the table and took Suchee's hand. "I think it's time you tell me about your daughter."

Suchee talked late into the night, recalling in painful detail Miao-shan's last day. Suchee had just finished locking the ox into its shed when she met her daughter, who was coming home for the weekend, having been away for several weeks at the Knight factory. Seeing Miao-shan on the dusty pathway that led to the house, Suchee instantly knew that her only child was pregnant. Miaoshan denied this accusation. "I told her, 'I am a peasant. I have grown up on the land. Do you think I don't know when an animal comes into season? Do you think I don't know when a creature is with child?'" Faced with these basic truths, Miaoshan had broken down completely. With tears streaming down her face—the Western display of emotion doing little to settle Suchee's fears—Miaoshan had confessed everything.

There were so many sayings that covered chastity and what happened when one didn't protect it: Guard your body like a piece of jade, or, One blunder can lead to remorse. But Suchee didn't believe in these kinds of reproaches. She had been young once herself. She knew what could happen in a moment of passion. "I told her that there was nothing wrong that couldn't be fixed." Then Suchee went on as if her daughter were in the room with her at this moment. "You can be married to Tsai Bing next month," she said. "You know he has waited a long time. Tomorrow I will go to the Neighborhood Committee director. That old grandma will understand. You will have your marriage permission certificate by the end of the week. The child permission certificate may be a little more difficult. You and Tsai Bing are still young, and this will be your only child. But I am not concerned. I have known that busybody director for so long. If she wants to make trouble for you, I will tell stories of when she was young, eh? So don't worry. I will take care of everything."

But her comforting words had done little to calm Suchee's own emotions, and during the night she'd been jarred awake many times, feeling a sense of foreboding that went beyond the news of the pregnancy. "The next morning Miaoshan was dead, and the police wouldn't listen when I said that the men in our village were getting rich by sending girls and women to that factory," Suchee continued. "They don't care what happens so long as they make their profit." Before Hulan could question her about this, Suchee said in a voice filled with remorse, "But I let her go there! And when I saw she was happy, I let her stay! She liked the work and brought home most of her salary." With that money Suchee had been able to buy extra seed and some new tools. But her worries blossomed again with each visit home, which became increasingly rare as Miaoshan began spending her weekends at the factory too. One minute Miaoshan talked sweetly, the next her words were filled with turpentine.

One day she combed her hair into pigtails, and the next week she came home from the factory in new clothes and with makeup all over her face. She talked about marriage, then almost in the next sentence switched to the subject of her desire to leave Da Shui and go to a big city—somewhere much larger than either Taiyuan or Datong.

As Suchee talked, Hulan wondered if these were just the naïve dreams of a simple country girl. In her job at the MPS, Hulan had first-hand experience with members of this class who were illegally leaving their villages and flooding cities like Beijing and Shanghai, looking in vain for a better life, only to find bitterness. In their innocence they were often the victims of criminals and crime syndicates. Without residency permits or work units in the cities, they were also subject to harassment and arrest by the police. Was Miaoshan just another one of these dreamers?

And parts of Suchee's story didn't make sense. Where was Miaoshan getting the money for new clothes, especially if she was giving the bulk of her salary to her mother? Where did Tsai Bing fit in? And what about Suchee's comment about the men in the village? If Hulan had been in Beijing and if Suchee had been a stranger, she would have felt no compunctions about asking whatever she wanted, but she was in the countryside now and Suchee was a friend. She would need to tread softly.

"I'm wondering about Tsai Bing and Ling Miaoshan," Hulan ventured. "Was theirs a true love or an arrangement?"

Instead of answering the question, Suchee asked one of her own: "Are you asking if we were following a feudal custom? Arranged marriages are against the law."

"There are many laws in China. That doesn't mean we follow all of them."

"True." Suchee allowed herself a small smile. "It is also true that in the countryside many people still prefer arranged marriages. This way we are able to consolidate our land or resolve disputes. These days we have even more concerns. The one-child policy—"

"I know," Hulan interrupted. "Too many abortions or girl babies given up for adoption. Now not enough girls to go around. Of course families want to make sure their sons will have wives."

Suchee nodded. In the golden light of the lantern, Hulan saw Suchee's eyes mist up again. "As a neighbor, Tsai Bing was always a good match for my daughter, but you know me, Hulan. I myself married for love."

"Ling Shaoyi." As Hulan spoke Suchee's husband's name, she was cast back again over the years. Hulan had met Shaoyi on the train from Beijing. He was older, perhaps sixteen, and not so afraid to be leaving home. He was a city boy clean through. Like all of them who'd come from Beijing, he knew nothing about farm life. Suchee had been the peasant placed on their team to teach them. At that time Western ideas like "love at first sight" were considered bourgeois at best and capitalist roader at worst. For a long while the kids in the brigade decided to look the other way when they saw Shaoyi's blushing face each time he spoke with Suchee, or when they observed her bringing him home-cooked treats while the rest of them were subsisting on bowls of millet porridge. After those years of turmoil were over, Shaoyi could have gone home to Beijing. He could have resumed his studies, maybe even become a party official. Everyone was surprised when he married Suchee, stayed in Da Shui, and became a peasant.

Suchee's voice cut into Hulan's thoughts. "Do you think I could let my daughter marry for anything less than true love?"

"No, not you," Hulan answered, knowing that this still might not be the full truth. The aphorism "Only speak thirty percent of the truth" was valid even in the countryside, even between old friends.

"Is there anything else I should know about Miaoshan?" Hulan asked. "Did she keep any papers here? A diary perhaps or letters?"

Suchee stood and went to one of the beds. From underneath she pulled out an oversize manila envelope, then laid it on the table.

"Miaoshan had a special place where she kept her private things," Suchee explained, "but I am a mother and this is a small farm. I knew that she hid her treasures in the shed behind the grain bin. After she died, I went there to look for objects to put on the altar." She took a deep breath, then continued, "I know some ABC letters and words that I learned in the Peasant Woman's School, but I can't understand these papers. And there are drawings . . ."

Hulan opened the clasp and pulled out three sets of papers. One set was folded into quarters, which Hulan opened and smoothed out on the table. Quickly Hulan leafed through them, while Suchee held up the lantern so they might see better.

"It says Knight International," Suchee said, "but what are they?"

"They look like specifications for an assembly line, and these look like they could be the floor plan for the factory itself. Have you been there? Can you tell?"

"I have seen the outside, but I've never gone inside. Even so, I don't understand the pictures."

Hulan drew with her finger along the lines. "This must be the exterior wall. And see, this says workroom, bathroom, office. . . . Let's see what else you have." She refolded the plans and picked up a stack of papers held together by a paper clip. It was a list of some sort with several columns. On the left were names—Sam, Uta, Nick, and the like. In the adjacent columns were account numbers and what looked like deposit amounts.

Silently Hulan put the papers back in the envelope, then took her friend's hand. "I'll tell you the truth. When I came here, it was because you were my friend and I thought I could offer help in your time of mourning, but now I don't know. So many things you've told me don't make sense. What you said about the men in the town and the fact that Miaoshan was pregnant, well, these are common occurrences in our country. But these papers make me look at things differently. What are they? Why did Miaoshan have them? Even more important, why did she hide them?"

"Are these ABC papers why she was killed?"

"I don't know, but I want you to put them back in Miaoshan's hiding place. Don't mention them to anyone. Can you promise me that?"

Suchee nodded, then asked, "What will you do now?"

"If Miaoshan was murdered, then the best way for me to find her killer is to understand who Miaoshan was. As I begin to know her, I will begin to know her killer. Once I know her, I will know her killer." Hulan paused, then added, "But, Suchee, remember this. There may not even be a murderer. Your daughter may have simply killed herself. Either way, are you prepared for whatever I find?"

"I have lost my only child," Suchee answered. "I'm an end-of-the-liner now. With no family to take care of me, I will end up in the government old people's courtyard in the village. So am I prepared? No. Ready? No. But if I'm going to spend the rest of my life alone, then I need to know."

# 4

H ULAN WOKE BEFORE DAWN THINKING ABOUT MIAOSHAN. Last night she'd been distracted by her friendship with Suchee and hadn't used the investigative tools she usually employed when conducting an inquiry into a crime or interviewing a witness. Ordinarily she would have thought about motive. She would have tried to categorize the murder. Was it a contract killing? Was it murder motivated by an argument, personal or financial profit, sex, revenge, politics, or religion? Or was this simply a suicide? She would have focused her attentions much more clearly on Miaoshan herself. As Hulan had said last night, to catch a murderer, an investigator needed to understand the victim.

Hulan quietly dressed and went outside. Coming from Beijing, with its cars and trucks and millions of people, Hulan was accustomed to noise. Here there was noise of another sort. She heard birds enthralled in their morning song and the whirring of cicadas. Although it was Sunday, she heard the low reverberations from a piece of farm equipment somewhere in the distance. Beyond these sounds and hiding just below the surface quiet was the hum of the earth itself. As a girl she had thought of it as the roar of plants pushing up through the soil.

She slowly walked to the shed where Miaoshan had been found. If she'd been here on the day of the discovery of Miaoshan's body, Hulan would have kept everyone away from this area so that she could examine the fine dust that covered the hard-packed earth. But if there had been footprints, they were long gone now, so Hulan pushed opened the door and entered. Immediately her senses were assaulted with the sights and smells of long ago. In this small, enclosed, dark room, the aromas of burlap, dirt, insecticide, kerosene, and seed mingled into a muskiness at once intoxicating and repugnant, heady and earthy. She closed the door behind her. As she waited for her eyes to adjust, she forced herself to put away her girlhood memories and preconceptions.

She tried to visualize Miaoshan hanging from the beam, the ladder below her. She called to her mind the suicides she'd seen before: the young mother in Beijing who'd killed herself by drinking carbolic acid; the old woman from Hulan's own neighborhood who—for reasons that never became clear—had slipped some rocks into her pockets and walked into Shisha Lake; the man who'd taken his village's savings, invested it in the stock market, lost it all, then had leaped from his hotel window rather than go home and face the people of his village. Then she remembered her own father, seeing him put the muzzle of a gun to his head and pull the trigger.

Hulan let her body slip down into a sitting position with her back against the wall of the shed, and thought. Typically vanity—even at this most desperate moment—kept women from using guns to kill themselves. They preferred to take pills, swim out to sea, or even slit their wrists—options that would not alter the face and also allowed the possibility of a rescue. Death by hanging was also primarily a male act, involving as it did a certain level of mechanical expertise: securing a rope to a beam, tying a knot that would have the ability to slip, then hold, positioning an object on which to stand but could easily be knocked out of the way when the time came. Of course, a farm girl would have these abilities, but death by hanging did not result in a beautiful corpse. From everything Suchee had said about her daughter—that she was in the midst of transforming herself into a Western ideal of beauty—a broken neck, swollen tongue, and purple face didn't fit the pattern for this particular victim.

Something else bothered Hulan. While suicide stemmed from deep melancholy, very often victims used the act as a way of getting the last word, of inflicting permanent guilt on those left behind. As a result, suicides were often planned so that the people who discovered the body were the actual targets of the victim's rage or despair. The young woman in Beijing, for example, had taken her baby to a neighbor's house, come home, dressed in her wedding clothes, drunk the carbolic acid, and, despite her agonizing abdominal spasms, positioned herself so that her husband—who turned out to have had a series of affairs—would find her on their marriage bed.

Out here on the farm only one person could find Miaoshan. But so far Suchee had said nothing that would indicate that there had been any hard feelings between herself and Miaoshan. Twenty-five years was a long time, but could Suchee have changed so much that she could hide her emotions and motives so cleverly that Hulan wouldn't be able to see through them? If Suchee had felt guilt or remorse, would she have asked Hulan to come out here at all? No, Hulan decided, the mother was convinced that something had happened to her daughter, and the longer Hulan spent out here in this shed, the more convinced she became as well.

Without obvious physical evidence Hulan knew that the only way to understand what had happened was to take steps back from the scene of the crime. With each step a clearer picture would emerge. Her first step would be to interview Tsai Bing, since so often murders were committed by husbands or boyfriends. Nothing in what Suchee had said about Tsai Bing suggested any animosity between him and his fiancée, but mothers could be blind when it came to such personal matters.

Hulan stood, pushed open the door, and went back outside. She scanned the fields and spotted Suchee. Hulan walked along a raised berm running between a field of corn and a field of budding sunflowers until she reached her friend, who was working the soil with a hoe.

"I've been thinking, Suchee," Hulan said. "It would be a mistake for me to talk to people as an investigator for the Ministry of Public Security. They would be too scared."

Suchee frowned. "My daughter's murderer deserves to be scared."

"Yes, of course, but if you want him caught, then we can't frighten him into hiding. Let him think he's gotten away with it. Let him think I'm merely a relative or friend who's come to visit. He'll let down his defenses. When he does, I'll be there."

"But who?"

"I don't know yet, but for me to flush him out, I must understand him. To understand him, I must understand Miaoshan. To understand her, I believe I must blend in."

"Not like that," Suchee said, nodding at Hulan's clothes. "You can wear Miaoshan's things, at least until that baby you're carrying gets bigger."

Back in the house, Suchee opened a low cabinet. On two shelves were neatly folded cotton clothes. "These were Miaoshan's. She was thin like you."

Many times in Hulan's life she'd been required to change personas. On some occasions these had been at the whim of politics, as when she'd been thrust out of her routine as a model child of privilege and sent to the countryside. Other times had been the result of geographical circumstance—from Chinese countryside girl to Connecticut boarding school student. Jobs and money had also affected her attire—as a law student, then as an associate at Phillips, MacKenzie & Stout. In recent years she'd changed her dress to meet the needs of a particular case. Hulan thought of this less as working undercover than simply blending into a landscape so she could hear people's real voices.

Hulan stripped off her dress, then pulled on a simple short-sleeve white blouse worn soft by years of wear and washings, and pants that came to just above her ankles. Suchee then handed her a pair of homemade shoes. Slipping these on, Hulan thought about the kind of life that a person wearing them would have out here in the countryside. She felt her body losing its attitude of self-possession and assuredness, to be replaced by a woman who had survived only at the caprice of nature. Within minutes, and aided by these few garments and a change in demeanor, Liu Hulan devolved from Red Princess to peasant.

"Can you tell me the way to the Bing farm?"

"They won't know anything," Suchee said.

"I'm going to see Tsai Bing," Hulan clarified, then added, "but if you want me to do this, then you'll have to let me do it my way. Please don't question me."

After a brief discussion, Suchee reluctantly agreed.

"One more thing," Hulan said as they left the house and headed out across the fields. "Please don't tell anyone who I am."

"What if someone remembers you?"

Hulan shook her head. "I was here long ago. You were one of the few local people who came to the Red Soil Farm to teach us. The others who were older are probably dead."

Suchee acknowledged that this was so.

"And the people who were our age, well, most of them went back to the city. Am I right? Besides, twenty-five years is a long time. Few of us look as we once did."

"Yes, but there may be people who will remember you for your name—Liu Hulan, martyr for the Revolution."

"Maybe, maybe not. It was a popular name once, so I am only one of many my age. What's important is that even if people do recognize my face for some reason . . ." She thought about the photographs from the newspapers, then strengthened herself and her voice. "No one can know I work for the ministry. No one. Do you understand?"

The two women stopped walking. Suchee contemplated Hulan. Would she have thought to write Hulan if she hadn't seen that photograph of her dancing in that tight dress in the nightclub pasted to the news wall in the village? At that time Suchee had heard no gossip and didn't mention that the decadent woman in the picture had once lived in the area. As Hulan said, that was a long time ago, and she had been only one soft city face among thousands of other soft city faces. Today, if someone saw Hulan in Miaoshan's clothes they would not think Beijing woman, let alone Ministry of Public Security inspector. She would be just another peasant. To Hulan's question, Suchee nodded solemnly. Hulan put a hand on her friend's arm. "And you're sure this is what you want? Because if you have any doubts, now is the time to stop me."

"I'm sure."

"Okay, then, how much farther is it?"

Suchee raised an arm and pointed out across a bean field. "Go one more *li*. You will see the house."

Hulan took a couple of steps, then looked back at her friend. "I may be gone for some time. Go back to work and don't worry about me." Then she turned and walked along the pathway.

It was still early, maybe only eight, but the sun beat down unrelieved by any breeze. Hot air undulated up off the earth, heavy with humidity.

Soon enough Hulan's body would become acclimated, but for now she endured the heat as best she could. She felt sweat running down the backs of her legs, but she kept her pace steady. To go more slowly would prolong her time under the direct sun; to hurry would only hasten dehydration.

Eventually the rows of beans changed back again into corn. The air was moderately cooler here with banks of corn coming up above Hulan's head on both sides of her, but in many ways she would have preferred the low-lying bean fields to the slashing leaves of the corn stalks that sometimes breached their orderly rows. Suddenly Hulan heard voices. She held still for a moment and decided that they were ahead of her. It was late enough now that the Tsais would already be out in the fields, but these were not the sounds of mother, father, and son working side by side. These were low murmurs punctuated by a young woman's giggle. With her homemade shoes, Hulan's footsteps were virtually silent as she passed along the earth, so she brushed her hands against the corn, causing the leaves to rustle so that whoever was out here would hear her approach. Abruptly the corn opened up to reveal a small area of about six by six feet where the corners of four different plots met. Where the pathways created a cross sat a young couple, face to face, with their legs draped over each side of the berm.

"*Ni hao.*" The young man's greeting came out more as a question: Who are you and what are you doing here?

"*Zenmeyyang,*" Hulan replied. This translated to something casual along the lines of "What's happening?" Without waiting for a response, she continued, "I am looking for the farm of the Tsai family. Am I close?"

The girl giggled. The boy said, "I am Tsai Bing. This is our family's land. Can I help you? Are you looking for my parents? They are in the field on the other side of the house."

Instead of answering his questions, Hulan asked, "May I sit down?"

The two young people looked at each other, then back at Hulan. Finally the boy motioned for her to sit.

"I am Liu Hulan, a friend of Ling Suchee."

"This is Tang Siang," the boy said, motioning to the young woman seated across from him. "She is the one-child daughter of our neighbor. The Tang lands are over there." He raised a dirty finger and pointed to his left. "They go for many *li*. For so many *li* that Tang Dan and his daughter are able to live in Da Shui Village."

In another culture Hulan might have taken this thorough introduction for nervous jabbering, but here in China it was not only common but expected that an introduction would include identification of place, status, and, most important, family position.

Hulan did not respond with similar information on herself. Instead she said, "I have come to visit Suchee. She is sad to lose her daughter." As she spoke, Hulan observed Tsai Bing. The boy's face had not yet developed into manhood, and he had an open look to his features. His eyes were bright. His smile was friendly. He was countryside thin, meaning that he was just bones and skin. His shorts—several sizes too large for him—were held up by a tightly cinched belt. His black hair was long and stuck out in unruly chunks. Whether this was from home cutting or from his time alone with the girl at his side Hulan couldn't say. "It must be hard for you too."

"Oh, yes," he said. He sounded sincere, but Hulan caught the quick look that passed between him and Siang.

Addressing the girl directly, she said, "You and Miaoshan must have been friends. Everyone knows everyone in the countryside."

"I have known Miaoshan since we were both in first school." The words sounded pleasant enough, but Siang wasn't sophisticated enough to hide the scorn in her voice, which practically shouted, *She was poor. My father is a landowner. She lived here in these fields. I live in the town.*

"I'm sure that Miaoshan's mother will be comforted to hear of your grief and that you have come to offer solace to her daughter's fiancé."

Siang's cheeks reddened, but she said nothing.

Hulan let the silence stretch out. She was in no hurry, and the longer she kept quiet, the sooner these two would wish to fill the void. Siang noiselessly etched a groove into the dirt with the edge of her tennis shoe, while Tsai Bing looked around nervously. Finally he said, "I didn't see Miaoshan so much anymore. She was always at work or in the dormitory. I am always here working in the fields. Different lives, different choices."

"But it was to be same lives, same choices, no?" Hulan commented. "Marriage brings two people together. You must have talked about that on her last night, making plans for your wedding—"

"I didn't see Miaoshan," he interrupted, genuinely surprised. "I hadn't seen her for a couple of weeks before she killed herself."

"But the baby and your wedding?"

Now it was Tsai Bing's turn to blush. Again he glanced over at Siang, looking first embarrassed, then defiant. When he turned back to Hulan, he jutted his chin indifferently.

"Who's to say that Tsai Bing was the father?" Siang said suddenly. "Miaoshan was living away from home. Who knows what she did or where she did it?"

"That's right," Tsai Bing chimed in.

Tsai Bing and Siang had to be lovers. How else to explain Tsai Bing's odd indifference to losing his fiancée or Siang's callous remarks? But the young woman with the pretty face wasn't finished.

"Miaoshan was always showing off. With her new clothes and her painted face, she thought she was telling the whole village she was better than the rest of us. But everyone looked at her and thought she was acting like a sister of the cave, like a prostitute."

"I see," Hulan said, and she did see Siang's jealousy very clearly.

"Everyone felt sorry for Tsai Bing," Siang continued. "He is a good man and a good peasant. He obeys family and public rules. The law says it's too early for him to marry without parental permission and a special exemption permit. Maybe one day he will marry. When he does, he will go through the proper channels and not through the back door."

Hulan had heard enough. She slowly stood and asked, "Tsai Bing, you're sure you didn't see Miaoshan that last night or in the morning? Her mother thought she was with you."

Instead of answering with words, the boy reached out and took Siang's hand. Hulan said good-bye and that she hoped they might meet again, but what she was thinking was that Tsai Bing, a sweet enough kid, was in over his head with Siang. If this obstinate woman had her way, he would become a husband sooner than later. When he did, he would quickly catch *qi guan yan*. The words meant "inflammation of the wind-pipe," but the pronunciation was similar to the words for "wife's tight control," creating the meaning of a henpecked husband. But Hulan's mind jumped beyond this superficial assessment. If she believed these two and they had been together on that last night, then where was

Miaoshan? Perhaps, like Hulan today, she had gone to find her fiancé and overheard him and Siang in the cornfield. There were many women—and men, for that matter—who killed themselves over broken hearts.

Hulan kept coming back to Tang Siang. She was obviously envious of Miaoshan. More than that, her comments had been unnecessarily cruel. They seemed less the observations of someone who was sure of her relationship with Tsai Bing than someone who was still trying to solidify her position or—if she was as clever as she thought herself—trying to distract Hulan from the truth, whatever that was. This, coupled with the blatant intimacy between Tsai Bing and Siang, caused Hulan to wonder: Could either Tang Siang or Tsai Bing have killed Miaoshan? Murders of passion were as old as the human heart.

It was still early in the morning, but late by countryside standards when Hulan left the fields and stepped onto the road for Da Shui. Peasants who had gone to the village to sell their produce or to do business were already heading back to their farms, so that Hulan had to thread her way through the oncoming traffic of people, pushcarts, bicycle carts, and bicycles. At first she kept to the far side of the road, nervous of the cars, trucks, and buses that drove past, but soon she fell into the rhythm of the road—the even strides, the occasional greeting, the beeping of the vehicles, the smells of exhaust, sweat, earth, and the greens that grew upon it.

An hour later, with the sun directly above her head, Hulan entered Da Shui. In many ways it still looked the same. The streets leading into the village were too narrow for cars to pass through. (She'd seen three cars parked on a vacant stretch of land just outside the village.) The unpainted gray-brick houses were small, mostly one or two rooms with a small courtyard holding a family pig. Tiled roofs inclined steeply. A few had upturned eaves, which showed their older age. In the center of the town was a square of sorts—a large, barren area of earth where a few chickens pecked. As in most of China, there was trash of every variety lying about—twisted pieces of iron, scraggly baskets, some old barrels.

But to Hulan's eyes Da Shui had changed dramatically. A few feet of cement sidewalk edged the north side of the square. Where once there had been one or two little shops with government-controlled prices,

Hulan now saw store after store—all small establishments, all competing against each other to sell toiletries, rice, produce, crackers, and other dry goods. Painted on empty walls were advertisements for chewing gum, appliances, and face cream. She even saw a couple of billboards.

Twenty-five years ago the only decoration in the village had been larger-than-life posters and paintings of the Great Helmsman. Of course, there had been other embellishments in the form of revolutionary slogans promoting Mao's Cultural Revolution ("Universal Redness With No Exceptions" or "Fight With Words, Not With Weapons") and in *dazibao*, the big character posters that proclaimed the real and imagined crimes of this or that villager. In those days loudspeakers had blared Chairman Mao's quotations all day and long into the night.

Even today cone-shaped speakers wired to the eaves of buildings played a set routine of programs, beginning at six in the morning with news and commentary. At noon, those fortunate enough to have fields near the village would have lunch accompanied by news and maybe a little music. At dusk, when peasants from the surrounding area converged on the town for a cup of tea, a little conversation, and a game of cards, the programming would start up again with what had traditionally been political indoctrination. Right now an old-fashioned military march accompanied Hulan as she walked down the dusty street.

She went straight to the local Public Security Bureau. The linoleum floor was worn and dirty. An electric fan hung from the ceiling, flanked by two sets of fluorescent lights, but none of them was turned on. Hulan went to the counter. Two women sat at desks against the wall. One was eating from a bowl of food she'd brought from home; the other was doing nothing as far as Hulan could tell. Neither woman looked up. The police bureau was not part of what might be considered the service industry. Manners had no place here. There were no forbidden phrases or outlawed attitudes. To the contrary, people in law enforcement—even if they were simply office staff—were allowed to be rude. Hulan understood the routine, but that didn't make her like it any more.

Finally Hulan cleared her throat.

"What do you want?" the woman eating noodles asked.

"I was hoping to see whoever is in charge."

"Captain Woo is busy. He can't see you now."

"I can wait."

The two women exchanged glances. The woman eating noodles smirked as she said, "You can sit or you can go, we don't care."

What came to Hulan's mind as she stood there in the hot room was a centuries-old saying: To be an official for one lifetime means seven rebirths as a beggar. Wisely, she didn't say this and sat down instead. She picked up a newspaper, but there was little news in the province this week. A while later, she got up and walked to the bulletin board. Here were the usual posters promoting the one-child policy, a flyer for employment at the Knight factory, a chart showing farming quotas, and a government-sponsored list of slogans encouraging better work habits, personal hygiene, and good attitudes such as "Time Is Money, Efficiency Is Life" and "Persist in Reform and Open Policy."

At last a door behind the counter opened and a man came out. Seeing Hulan, he leaned down and spoke quietly to one of the secretaries, then straightened and addressed Hulan directly. "You may come in, but only for five minutes."

The sign on the door said Captain Woo. He motioned for Hulan to sit and asked, "What's your name?"

"Liu Hulan."

"An old-fashioned name. People don't use that name much anymore."

"This is so."

Captain Woo poured himself a cup of tea from a thermos but didn't offer any to the woman who sat before him. "You are not from Da Shui."

"I have come to visit a friend."

"And you find that you argue, that things aren't as they were? This happens sometimes. Friends grow apart."

"No, that isn't it—"

But the captain wasn't listening. "The bureau doesn't get involved in domestic disputes. That is something for the Neighborhood Committee or the manager of the work unit to handle, but"—he sighed deeply—"I have people like you coming to me more and more. Soon, I think, the government will need to come up with a directive on how to handle these problems, for neither I nor my colleagues are equipped to deal with petty arguments when we have so much more important work."

"Excuse me, Captain, but I am not here over a dispute with a friend."

"If you have a problem with a husband running away to our village, then you must go to the village leader. Make a petition. He will listen."

Hulan's patience was wearing thin, but she couldn't interrupt him or stop him in her usual manner without giving herself away as an educated woman, a Beijinger, a Red Princess, or an inspector for the Ministry of Public Security. This last was most crucial. Local Public Security Bureaus had little respect for the more important Ministry of Public Security in Beijing. This attitude wasn't unique to China. Every country had its jurisdictional arguments between local police and national law enforcement, whether it be the FBI, KGB, or Scotland Yard. So, instead of putting Woo in his place, Hulan acted as a peasant, more than a little afraid of his power.

"Please, Captain," she said as meekly as was possible for her.

He frowned at her impertinence, then nodded for her to go ahead.

"I am here because my friend's daughter died. The mother is very sad. I am hoping you can tell me what happened so that I can help the mother with her grief."

Woo's eyes narrowed. "You must be speaking of Ling Miaoshan. She killed herself."

"How can this be?" Hulan asked. "She was young, beautiful, and she was to be married. Suicide isn't the act of a bride."

Hulan had hoped that Captain Woo would recognize the inconsistencies just as she had. Instead, he dropped his pseudo-polite demeanor and spoke in a tone designed to halt any more questions from this know-nothing woman.

"Ling Miaoshan had a bad character. The whole district knew she was a loose girl who opened her legs for any man with a beating heart. As for marriage? Well, no one ever saw an invitation to the wedding."

"Are you saying that Tsai Bing never intended to marry Miaoshan?"

"No, I'm saying I'm done with you. Go on your way before you get into trouble here." This time there was no mistaking the threat. Hulan stood, bowed her head in feigned gratitude, and left the office.

Later, as she walked along the road leading out of the village, she thought over Captain Woo's words. How could Miaoshan have had such a bad reputation? The answer was as old as womankind—she'd probably earned it. But again, this seemed at odds with Suchee's description of her daughter. Was this just a mother's blindness to her daughter's weakness? Or were the villagers intimidated enough in some way by Miaoshan to create a portrait that explained a disparity that they couldn't understand? Hulan knew how that worked. It had happened to Hulan her entire life. Even at work her colleagues recognized her differences and translated them into misjudgments such as that she held herself too high or dressed peculiarly, yes, even that she was a loose woman who had had unmarried sex—with a foreigner, no less.

# 5

SUNDAY MORNING DAWNED DAMP AND FOGGY. DAVID, dressed in boxers and an old T-shirt, padded down to the kitchen and started a large pot of coffee for himself and special agents George Baldwin and Eddie Wiley. Within hours of Keith's death, the agents had arrived back at the house. George and Eddie were pretty good guys, and during their last few months together on the Rising Phoenix case, they'd learned how to accommodate one another. Eddie, who'd spent years doing undercover work, was more of an athlete and accompanied David on his morning runs around Lake Hollywood. George, on the other hand, had come out of the bank robbery squad. He was accustomed to sitting all day in courtrooms and waiting in offices, so he had a great deal of patience with David's typical workday. During the previous months a kind of frat house atmosphere had prevailed. But circumstances had changed.

David had thought his life had been circumscribed the last time around, but after two full days with George and Eddie he felt as if he were in jail. After the shooting outside the Water Grill, the agents were taking everything much more seriously. David was never alone in his own home. Never alone when he ate. Never allowed to go outside and pick up the paper. Never alone when he walked or ran or went to work. Even now David could hear George on the phone setting up shifts, which meant there'd be new agents to get to know, more traffic all around the periphery of his life, and even less freedom.

Eddie entered the room, then in a swift series of motions slipped his hand to where he kept his weapon holstered behind his back, opened the door, looked around, went outside, picked up the paper, brought it in, and dropped it on the kitchen counter. Then, without a word, he opened a cupboard and poured himself a bowl of Cheerios. He'd already showered, shaved, and dressed for the funeral in an outfit that wasn't much different from what he wore on every other day of the week—gray slacks perfectly pressed, a starched light blue shirt, sports jacket, and a tie with a blue and red pattern. He was in his thirties, and because of his undercover work kept his hair longer than most agents. Eddie had a girlfriend he talked to every night on his cellular phone. David had overheard more than one conversation between the two agents about how and when Eddie should propose.

David waited silently for the coffee to finish, poured himself a cup, grabbed the paper, and went back to his bedroom. He stood for a minute or two looking out at the view. Usually it gave him a sense of expansiveness, but today he only felt the pressure of the four walls around him. His mood might have lifted if he could have spoken to Hulan, but she hadn't called since that day on the train and he couldn't reach her—not because she was out of satellite range but because she hadn't turned on her phone. Hulan had a 139 phone that allowed her to place and receive calls from anywhere in the world. Since phones were such a rarity in homes both in the countryside and in large cities like Beijing and Shanghai, most people who could afford cell phones—and they and their ancillary rates were outrageously high in China but minuscule compared to U.S. standards—had them. The government had facilitated this by making sure that satellites covered all but the most remote or difficult to reach areas such as the Three Gorges. With Hulan separated from him— by choice? The idea made him even more depressed—she didn't even know that Keith had died, or that David was responsible.

David still had two hours before the funeral, so he propped himself up in bed and opened the paper. There were the usual stories—trouble in the Middle East in the front section, a profile of one of the Dodgers in Sports, the second of a two-parter on infidelity in Life & Style, and, because it was an industry town, there was a piece about a film that had run over budget in Calendar. He was about halfway through the business section when he saw Knight International in bold type.

Despite troubles in the Asian markets, he read, Knight's stock had climbed another seventeen points in the last week. The reporter, a Pearl Jenner, had interviewed a couple of brokers who observed that the recent action was due to the fact that Knight's board and its minority shareholders had accepted a bid for purchase by media and manufacturing giant Tartan Incorporated. She also interviewed Henry Knight, the colorful chairman of the company, who said, "I've spent my life building this company. We've always done well. But in this last year our sales have skyrocketed thanks to Sam & His Friends. If there's a time to sell, this is it."

The reporter didn't see it that way. Why sell the company when the financial forecast looked so rosy, with Knight's new technologies guaranteed to expand profits geometrically in the next century? She went on to answer her question. Henry Knight wasn't as young as he once was. He'd been in and out of the hospital for heart problems during the last two years. Most important, several sources, who refused to be named, suggested that Henry didn't want to leave the company to his son, Douglas Knight. "The old man is a visionary, but he's a hard man," offered one observer. "He should have stepped down and turned the company over to Doug years ago, but he won't let go." When asked why, the unnamed source answered, "Henry's the kind of man who brought himself up by his bootstraps. If it was good enough for him, then it's good enough for his son." Pearl Jenner noted several examples of other family-owned businesses where the founders preferred to sell or hand the running of a company over to outsiders rather than give it to their less talented offspring. Ironically, however, Henry hadn't founded Knight, his father had. Perhaps a more logical explanation was that by selling now—when profits were at an all-time high—the company would get the best price. This had the added benefit of giving Henry the chance to help his son with estate taxes while he was still alive.

In the last paragraph David saw something that made him sit upright. "Family considerations aside, Mr. Knight's concerns may have lessened lately," Pearl Jenner wrote. "Just two days ago, Keith Baxter, an attorney at Phillips, MacKenzie & Stout, the law firm which represents Tartan Incorporated, was killed in a traffic accident. Baxter had been the target of a recent federal inquiry into alleged violations of the U.S.

Foreign Corrupt Practices Act, which occurred during the Knight sale negotiations. Until now Henry Knight has refused to comment on the inquiry, but speaking by phone yesterday, he said, 'I always believed that these allegations were unfounded. Now the government will have no choice but to drop their charges. I want to add that Keith Baxter was a fine young man and his death comes as a shock to my family and me. Our sympathies go out to the Baxters. To honor his memory we will continue to move ahead with the sale. I know Keith would have wanted that.'" The article ended with a summary of Knight International's annual gross revenues and net profits.

David put the newspaper down and closed his eyes. Bribery was practically a way of life in China, with roots that could be traced back thousands of years. Keith must have slipped a bribe or two to some official, hoping to work out a conflict or smooth over some mistake in the paperwork. The practice might be customary in China, but it was beyond stupid here. No wonder Keith had reacted so strangely to David's questions about what he was doing at the firm, suggesting that David had come as part of some federal investigation. If Keith had confided in him, David would have insisted that he go straight to the U.S. Attorney's Office. Considering Keith's background—a lawyer with no priors—he might have gotten away with probation and a fine.

The service was held at Westwood Village Mortuary. David signed the guest book and looked for a seat. Hoping to be as inconspicuous as possible, he and the two FBI agents who accompanied him slipped into pews toward the rear of the chapel. But really, how inconspicuous could they be? Even if the shooting hadn't been in the news, even if David hadn't been the real target of the murderer with Keith's death as the consequence, David's companions would have marked him for at least a few stares. It wasn't their fault: FBI agents looked like FBI agents.

Keith's coffin lay on a raised platform at the front of the chapel. A few bouquets—some daisies, some roses, even one of those carnation things on an easel—surrounded it. A man walked to the podium and introduced himself as Reverend Roland Graft from Westwood Presbyterian. He opened with a few perfunctory remarks on the nature of death and the

tragedy of a life taken so young and violently. However, the Reverend
Graft had obviously never met Keith and quickly turned the microphone
over to Miles Stout.

The last time David had seen Miles was at the annual dinner for current and former assistant U.S. attorneys. He hadn't changed, he never
did. His Scandinavian background was prominent in his features. He was
tall, blond, blue-eyed, tan, athletic-looking despite his almost sixty years.
It was said that he still played tennis every day before going in to the
office. He spent his vacations skiing in Vail or white-water rafting down
some river no one had ever heard of in some remote area of the globe.

At the podium Miles appeared to take a moment to gather his
thoughts. Probably half the people in the chapel knew this was mere the-
atrics. Miles was brilliant on his feet whether in court or as an after-
dinner speaker.

"What can I say about Keith?" Miles asked in the buttery-smooth
tones that so captivated juries. "How do I sum up a life?" He let the questions hang in the air unanswered, then dropped his voice. "Keith came to
the firm still wet behind the ears, but he was a quick study. I learned to
trust his judgment and admire his insights."

It was classic Miles Stout: sincerity combined with hackneyed
images, false regret, and just a slight bending of the facts. Miles, knowing
his audience and recognizing that they would be seeing right through
him, continued.

"But again, how do we remember a man? With platitudes? No. With
empty sentiments? Never. Today I want to remember the good times.
Sure, they all involve the firm, but that's the kind of man Keith was.
Perhaps through my stories, you will remember some of your own."

He paused, let a gentle smile come to the corners of his mouth, then
said, "Just last week Keith and I were working on the acquisition of
Knight International by Tartan Incorporated. Our team had been up for
two nights straight. We'd been eating pizza and Chinese takeout till we
were all longing for a home-cooked meal. I called down to the office . . ."

David allowed his mind to drift. He hadn't been at the firm for the
Tartan-Knight negotiations, but he didn't need to be to know that Miles
hadn't been working twenty-four hours a day and eating food brought in
from the nearest fast-food restaurant. Miles said it himself. "I called

down to the office." He was the billing partner. It didn't matter if he went out to dinner with Mary Elizabeth, his high school sweetheart and wife of thirty-five years, to dine on linguini with black truffles so long as he brought in the work. And he did, big-time.

Miles was a legend of sorts in the Los Angeles legal community. Like Keith, he'd been raised on a farm somewhere in the Midwest. He'd gotten a scholarship to Michigan, then had been accepted to Harvard Law School. Upon graduation he clerked for a judge, then went directly to the U.S. Attorney's Office. When he was ready to leave, Phillips & MacKenzie offered Miles a position as partner. Ten years later, after he threatened to leave and take his substantial client list with him, the partnership voted to add his name to the firm's, turning it into Phillips, MacKenzie & Stout. Despite his good fortune, Miles never forgot his roots, which was why he often had parties on days that the Wolverines played and probably why he mentored Keith, who'd come from such a similar background.

David tuned back in to the eulogy as he heard Miles's voice suddenly go mournful. "I want to end now with how I saw Keith on that last day. We were in the conference room. There were half-eaten sandwiches, Cokes, cold cups of coffee. Keith was taking me through the contract point by point. He was thorough. He didn't stumble over a number or a clause. At one point he opened a file cabinet and pulled out some papers. He saw the mistakes. He saw the problems. He didn't miss a thing. Because that's the kind of lawyer . . . No! That's the kind of man he was."

Miles looked over at the coffin. "Keith, we're gonna miss you, buddy." He turned back to the audience, murmured a barely audible thank-you, and walked back toward the condolence room, crossing paths with Keith's sister, Anne Baxter Hooper, who said a few words. Then Reverend Graft thanked everyone for coming and invited the mourners to the Stouts' home for refreshments.

Twenty minutes later, David and the two agents turned north off Sunset and began climbing into the Brentwood hills, where grand mansions were hidden behind stone walls, wrought iron gates, or carefully trimmed hedges. A valet stand was set up at the entrance to the Stout property, but George flashed his credentials and the car was waved through.

The Stout estate had been built at the turn of the century by an East Coast robber baron who'd come out to California for the winter season and decided to stay. He brought with him traditional ideas of living, but for his new home he had also asked the architect to include the very best ideals of Southern California living. The house—built in the Spanish style with cream-colored walls, extensive terraces, and a tiled roof—was gracious, large, and perfect for entertaining. Over the years the property had passed through many hands. When the Stouts purchased it in 1980, they decided to bring the property back to its former glory, first restoring, then embellishing its fine bones. Nowhere was this more evident than in the gardens.

The landscaping had been designed on a semi-European scheme with "rooms" representing different countries and themes: a Japanese garden, a rose garden for viewing, a citrus orchard for Southern California, a tropical garden with bougainvillea, birds of paradise, and flowering silk floss and jacaranda trees. Colorful annuals bordered the driveway. Manicured lawns spread out lush and green. Hundred-year-old sycamores and California oaks provided shade. David remembered that somewhere on the property there was a greenhouse filled with orchids and another hidden garden for cut flowers. In this way Mary Elizabeth Stout was able to have fresh flowers in every room virtually all year.

Someone from the catering staff showed David and the agents through the living room and out onto the terrace. Heading down to the pool, David and the FBI agents were flanked by a series of terraces, each draped with flowers and vines. George and Eddie took up discreet positions at either end of the cabana, while David went straight for the bar. He ordered a beer and watched as the other guests came down the stairs. They were the predictable assortment of lawyers from different law firms and government entities, as well as a smattering of judges. David waved to Rob Butler from the U.S. Attorney's Office and said hello to Kate Seigel from Taylor & Steinberg.

No one seemed particularly upset. In fact, as they picked up drinks and mingled at the bar, they looked more like guests at a garden party than at a funeral. But what did David expect? If Keith had died a week ago, would he have reacted differently? Certainly he would have felt bad about a friend and colleague's death, but he would have compartmentalized it and, like most of these people, come more out of duty than friendship. How strange, David thought, the way people avoided grief, avoided any unpleasant emotions, as if that would protect them from tragedy or make them invisible to evil.

Phil Collingsworth, who'd been at the firm even longer than Miles Stout, clapped David on the back and said that the three of them should grab some time later to talk. David spoke with another partner, who, after Hulan left him years ago, had encouraged him to date, then marry Jean. The marriage had been a mistake, but when they'd divorced, Marjorie, like so many people and things, had gone into Jean's half of the communal property. But now here was Marjorie, giving David a hug, saying how nice it was to see him after such a long time, and asking if he wouldn't like to come over for dinner and see how big the kids had grown.

It felt good to be back among friends, but there was a shadow over most of his conversations. No one mentioned the accusations surrounding Keith or David's presence at Keith's death, but he felt these subjects intruding into all of his encounters. Soon enough small talk evaporated into awkward silence. The little grouping would disperse and another one would form.

At one point David found himself standing alone. He glanced around, caught a sympathetic nod from Agent Baldwin, and quickly looked away. His eyes came to rest on Keith's sister, sitting with an older couple. The three of them looked exhausted and definitely out of place in the party atmosphere. David passed through the little eddies of people, reached Keith's family, extended his hand, and introduced himself.

At the older woman's quick intake of breath, the man at her side put a protective arm around her shoulder. With his other hand he reached out and firmly gripped David's. "Matt Baxter. I'm—I was—Keith's dad. This is Keith's mother, Marie. And this is Anne." But these introductions seemed about all he could manage. David watched as Matt squeezed his wife's shoulder, this time to strengthen himself.

A moment passed before anyone spoke, then Anne, her eyes welling with tears, looked up at David. "You're the person who was with Keith when . . ."

"That's right," David finished for her. "May I sit down?"

"Of course," she said.

David dragged a lawn chair over to Anne and her folks. As soon as he sat down he smelled an overpowering and sickeningly sweet scent that reminded him of death.

"Can you tell us about Keith on that last night?" Anne asked.

David had been so wrapped up in his guilt that he hadn't considered that Keith's family would ask him this question if given the opportunity. What should he say? That Keith had drunk too much? That he'd been worried about work? These weren't words that would bring solace. Instead David answered in half-truths.

"We had a bottle of wine. We ate fish. He was in a good humor. He teased me about coming back to the firm," David said.

Keith's folks nodded and smiled sadly.

"But did he *say* anything?" Anne pressed.

Was she asking about Pearl Jenner's allegations in the *Times*? She couldn't be.

"At the time nothing seemed that important," he said, trying to keep the conversation light. "We were just friends catching up on what we'd been doing. He asked about some trials that I'd had. It was just lawyer talk . . ."

"I don't know how you could say that," Anne said, not bothering to disguise her sarcasm.

"Anne," Matt implored his daughter, but she ignored him.

"I talked to him that day too, you know." Her voice had shifted into something hard and edgy. Her eyes stayed steady on David as she waited for him to respond. How much did Anne know? Was she, like David, worried about her brother's reputation? All he knew was that he didn't want to talk about these things in front of Keith's parents.

"My brother was in anguish. His girlfriend had just died . . ." Anne began to cry.

His girlfriend? Keith hadn't mentioned anything about that. Could David have misread the evening? No, not if what the *Times* said was true.

"We haven't thanked you for calling that night," Keith's mother said. "It meant a lot to us that it was a friend and not the police. I don't think I could have taken that."

"If the situation had been reversed, I'm sure Keith would have done the same for me."

"Do you think so?" Anne asked.

"Of course I do."

"What I mean is, do you think the situation *could* have been reversed?"

"Anne," Matt Baxter gently pleaded with his daughter.

Anne took an angry swipe at her tears, then turned impatiently to her father. "What is it, Dad? Do you want me to forget that my brother died because of this man? Well, I'm not going to forget that. I don't think anyone here—except for maybe you and Mom—is going to forget that."

Hearing those words, David felt his gut tighten. Was this how people would think of him from now on?

"Excuse me."

They all looked up to see Special Agent Eddie Wiley, sounding extremely official. "Mr. Stark, I need for you to step this way."

David rose. He kept eye contact with Anne but spoke to her parents. "Again, I can't begin to tell you how sorry I am." He tipped his head, broke away from Anne's hard gaze, and followed Eddie into the cabana.

"Thanks," he said.

"No thanks required. You looked like you needed rescuing."

"Yeah, I guess I did."

"You're going to have to learn how to deal with shit like that." When David regarded him in puzzlement, Eddie explained, "With people asking questions that they really don't want the answers to."

"And?"

"Shine them on."

David frowned. "Could I do that? Could you?"

"It's part of the job."

"Maybe yours . . ."

Eddie didn't respond. He didn't have to. They both knew how many deaths the Rising Phoenix had brought to David's job. "Eddie, can you do something for me?"

"You know I can."

"I want to meet alone with Keith's sister."

"What? In the fucking greenhouse or something? I don't think so."

"I have to explain to her about that night."

"No, you don't."

"I want . . ." David took a step toward the cabana's French doors, but Eddie moved to block his way.

"Haven't you heard what I've been saying? You can't let guilt run you, man." Eddie lowered his voice. "Believe me, I know."

For the second time in about as many minutes David was in a stand-off. And, for the second time, he was rescued by a familiar voice.

"Ah, David, there you are," Miles called out from the French doors. "I've been looking for you. Phil and I want you to take a walk with us." He cocked his head to Eddie. "Is that all right with you? We'll stay on the property. I'll tell you what. We'll even stay down here on the lower ter-race. Just give me a few minutes of privacy with my former colleague."

Eddie stood his ground a moment longer, then stepped aside. David and Miles threaded their way through the crowd and walked out along the terrace.

"It's been a rough few days," Miles said. "How are you holding up?"

David stared down into the canyon below him, where sumac and other scrub brush served as a counterpoint to the luxury and refinement of the Stout grounds.

Since David didn't seem willing to answer, Miles said, "It was a bad break. You need to know that none of us blames you."

David snorted. "I think Keith's sister does."

"What does she know? She wasn't there." Miles closed his eyes and tilted his face up to the sun. "Why did you and Keith get together any-way?"

"It was nothing really, just dinner." Here again was another half-truth, but he just didn't want to cover this material again.

"Did he talk about work, the firm?"

"I suppose." David shrugged. "We talked a little about Tartan and Knight."

"He was working with me on the acquisition. We've been working on the deal for a year. The firm's been consumed with it."

Miles loved to discuss business. David, relieved by the change in focus, accommodated him. "From what I've read, I'm surprised Knight would sell."

"It came as a surprise to me too when I got the call from Henry say-ing he wanted to sell and did I think Tartan would be interested. Of course, Randall Craig was interested and made an offer right away. That was a year ago."

"You must be slipping," David needled good-naturedly.

"It wasn't me. It was that damn Henry Knight. He's one strange bird. He doesn't like to use attorneys, and he only hires accountants on an as-needed basis."

"Is he covering up something?"

"No, he's just eccentric. But look, eccentric or not, he built his company himself. He was already rich. Soon he'll be filthy rich."

David had a father who sounded a lot like Henry Knight, so he knew that eccentricity could be charming and irritating at the same time. David also knew from his experiences at the U.S. Attorney's Office that such men were not immune to the temptations of crime. Instead of committing a crime himself, had Keith found some problem in the Knight records? Was there a mistake in the deal? Is that what had so worried him? Or had he discovered some irregularities, something that might involve a federal investigation? If so, why not tell Miles? Or, if it was really bad, why not go straight to the U.S. Attorney's Office, the FBI, or the SEC himself?

"What was Keith working on exactly?" David inquired.

"You know, doing the due diligence, gathering together the various representations and warranties for the SEC and FTC. It was just the usual antitrust and securities formalities."

David lowered his voice even though they were alone. "What about those accusations in the *Times* this morning?"

"All lies." Miles's eyes flashed angrily. "That reporter made that stuff up and has been able to get away with it for months by throwing in the word *alleged* here and there."

"For months? I didn't know it was going on at all."

"It wasn't something the firm or Keith advertised. Fortunately Jenner's stories were always buried deep in the business section."

"And Keith never came to you with any concerns?"

"Oh, he was concerned, all right. Wouldn't you be? What that woman wrote was totally unfounded." Miles shook his head sadly. "When I think of how tortured Keith was . . . Certainly you must have noticed how upset he was."

"I did, as a matter of fact. I wish he'd explained—"

"He didn't like to talk about it. As unfounded as those articles were, they were deeply embarrassing to him."

"The death of his girlfriend couldn't have helped matters. Did you know her?"

"No, she didn't live here. Her death was a tough break for Keith. Well, there's no point dwelling on it now." He paused, then said, "Ah, here's Phil."

"Have you asked him yet?" Phil inquired.

"No," Miles answered. "I was waiting for you."

"Good," Phil said, smiling warmly at David, "because I want you to know that this proposal comes from all of us at the firm. Go ahead, Miles."

David waited, listening.

"We've all watched your progress at the U.S. Attorney's Office," Miles began. "You've done some amazing work in China and certainly with the triads. We're all proud of you for that."

"Thanks."

"I'm going to lay our cards on the table," Miles continued. "We'd like you to come back to the firm and open an office in China." He held up a hand to keep David from speaking. "We've got a lot of work over there even without the Tartan business. We're subbing it out to lawyers in Beijing. Remember Nixon Chen, who came over from China to train with us all those years ago?"

"Not only do I remember him, but I had lunch with him about three months ago."

"He does a lot of our China work, and he bills at rates almost as high as ours," Phil said. "We're giving him hundreds of thousands in legal fees each year. The firm's thinking is, why should we give Nixon all that work? We've been wanting to open a branch office in Beijing for quite some time, but we needed the right person to get it up and running."

"And you think I'm that person?"

Phil stared earnestly at David. "Look, you're a litigator, but a lot of your cases have involved big companies with complex financials, so you've become quite a good corporate lawyer too."

David hadn't thought of his career this way before, but it made perfect sense.

"But you bring something more to the equation," Miles picked up. "The Chinese care about *guanxi*—connections. Nixon's a Red Prince, so his connections are impeccable. But you also have some pretty interesting connections—with the Ministry of Public Security . . ."

"If you're thinking about Hulan, forget it. She's happy where she is."

"I didn't mention her name. You did. We haven't asked Hulan to open the office. We're asking you."

David shook his head. "Thanks, but I like what I do too."

"We're prepared to make a substantial offer," Miles said. "Just name your price."

"Money's never mattered to me."

"I know that, and if you want our offer to take that into consideration, I'm sure we can oblige." Seeing the look on David's face, Miles grinned triumphantly, as if he'd caught a witness in a lie. "I knew it," he said. "We never would have gotten this far in the conversation if you weren't just a little bit intrigued. So do us a favor. Think about it and come see us tomorrow."

"All right, but don't count on anything."

Miles smiled, gloated, convinced he'd achieved victory, then looked back toward his waiting guests. "I bet Mary Elizabeth's wondering where I am. You mind if we head back?"

As the three men slowly walked along the path leading to the pool, David said, "I'm not saying I'll do it, but what kind of time frame are we talking about?"

"The visa won't be a problem," Miles said. "The Chinese know you and you've been there before. We'd love to get you on a plane to Beijing by the end of the week."

"Jesus! What's the rush?"

Miles stopped. "Frankly I thought you'd be in a hurry. You'll be safe in China. And"—Miles allowed himself a small smile—"you could be reunited with Hulan."

"Actually," Phil interjected, "we've been thinking about this for a long time. We have a window of opportunity in China. We've thought about talking to other attorneys, but you know how long it takes to integrate a lateral hire into a firm like ours. You already know us, and we know you. Really the only way we can go ahead in a timely fashion is with someone we know. That's why you've always been our first choice, but you weren't going to leave the U.S. Attorney's Office in the middle of the Rising Phoenix cases. Those trials are done now, and let's face it, David, it's time for you to move on. So I say, if we're going to act, let's do it fast. All the work's been done on the Knight deal. All we need now are the signatures. So, let's get you in there in time to deal with the last-minute logistics and to meet all of Tartan's top players. That will smooth the transition and put you in prime position to continue handling Tartan's China business. But again, for that to work, we need to move quickly."

"Do you think the others will want me back after what happened with Keith?"

Phil momentarily dropped his friendly senior-statesman demeanor. "I mean no disrespect to the dead. What happened was bad luck. But let's face facts. Keith was a mediocre lawyer who barely got enough votes to make partner. You've got real talent. We've known that for a long time."

"Still—"

"Let me put it to you another way," Miles interrupted. "There's lots of money to be made in China. The lawyers of Phillips, MacKenzie & Stout might as well be the ones to make it." Registering David's shocked expression, Miles held his hands palms up. "For once in your life try to divorce yourself from your so-called good intentions. You've done your time, you've given back to the community and all that. Now you should think about what's best for you. And Hulan."

An hour later, the agents whisked David away from the gathering. Once he got home, he opened a beer and sat down ostensibly to watch the news, but his mind was on his conversation with Miles and Phil. Could David work with Miles again? They'd never gotten along all that well. David was born with all the things that Miles had worked hard to attain. David had lived in the city his entire life, had grown up surrounded by culture, had gone to the best schools, had fast-tracked into a partnership at the firm where—at least according to Miles—David had never quite been able to "get with the program." Of course, David saw it differently. Coming from a position of professional security, David had had little patience for either Miles's mannerisms or his compulsive desire to be respected and obeyed. Miles was as smart and savvy as anyone David had ever met, but in many ways he was still an insecure farm boy. He could truly be a friend and benefactor to someone like Keith who kowtowed to him, but David had never been able to do that. Then David had done something almost unfathomable to Miles. David had given it all up—meaning the six-, almost seven-figure salary—to go to the U.S. Attorney's Office, where he felt he could make a difference. But the door, so to speak, had obviously been left open. Miles might not have liked David, but he recognized that he was always among the top billers at the firm.

Phil especially had nailed the situation: it was time to move on. Coming back to Phillips, MacKenzie could benefit both David and the firm, and timing was everything in business. David had been further reassured when Phil had said, "The fees to our clients in China are cover-ing the financial risk for us, so that in the unlikely event that this doesn't work out, the firm won't hold it against you and you can come back to the L.A. office. We want this to be a win-win for both parties right on down the line. We're partners."

All of this brought back to David that last dinner with Keith, who'd mentioned in passing that the partners had been talking about him. Somehow that knowledge—that link to Keith—made the offer all the more appealing. And then there was the deeper consideration: Hulan. The only way he could deal with her fears was if they were together. If he could hold her in his arms, he knew he could banish the inner demons that haunted her so.

Just then Eddie came in, sprawled out on the couch, and said, "You should do it, you know."

"What?"

"Do what they say. Get the hell out of here. Take them up on their offer."

"How did you know . . . ?"

Eddie cocked an eyebrow. "Man, we're the FBI. You didn't think you could have a private conversation without us knowing about it, did you?"

He paused, then added, "Anyway, for what it's worth, you should go."

"How can I?"

"How can you not? Look at it this way, Stark, you've got a guy like me on your couch here and a woman waiting for you in China. That's a no-brainer from where I sit."

# 6

I F HULAN HAD BEEN IN BEIJING, SHE WOULD HAVE COM-
pleted all of her interviews in one day. But she was in the countryside
now, where the pace was slow. Activity happened early or late in the day
to avoid the brutal heat. Part of blending in meant that she would have
to melt into those rhythms. So on Monday morning Hulan once again set
out for the village, where she planned to stop at a café and strike up a
casual—and hopefully informative—conversation with the owner.

With its sign in English posted on the door, the Silk Thread Café
seemed particularly receptive to people from afar:

WELCOME DISTINGUISH
ED GUESTS
GOOD FOOD
COFFEE

It was too hot to sit on the sidewalk, so Hulan stepped inside the single room of the establishment, where several men sat clustered together
at two tables. When she entered, she saw one of the men pick up a
remote control and change the television channel. From Hulan's seat in
the corner she could see the television, which was hung from the ceiling
in one of the corners. On the screen she recognized *The Three Amigos*, an
American movie that was very popular in China.

The proprietress took Hulan's order and soon came back with a pot of tea, a large bowl of *congee*, and condiments. The eating bowl and spoon were filthy and still covered with leavings from last night's dinner. Hulan poured some of the hot tea into her bowl, swirled it around, then poured the dirty tea on the floor, where others had tossed their leftover bones and gristle and had cleaned their eating utensils in the same manner.

The men seemed to forget about Hulan—either that or they decided she was unimportant—and turned the television back to CNN. Hulan was halfway through her meal when one of the men called out, "You!"

It was rude, but Hulan responded nevertheless with a curt nod.

"Are you looking for work?" the man asked.

"No."

"Don't be shy," he said. "There is no need for that."

"But I don't need work."

The man scowled. "Then why are you here?"

"For lunch."

"Women don't come in here *for lunch*," the man said, his voice filled with innuendo. The other men laughed.

Hulan chose to disregard the insinuation. "I'm not from here," she said. "I don't know your village customs."

Ignoring everything Hulan had said, the man asked, "Do you have proper work papers?"

Faced with his persistence and the curious stares of his table companions, Hulan decided to see where this would lead. "Of course," she answered. She did indeed have work and residency permits for Beijing, but not for any other village or city in China, so she added, "But not for Da Shui."

The man waved his hand dismissively. "No matter. It is a small problem easily fixed." The man pushed his chair away from the table, the legs scraping against the floor. With the other men watching, he stood, crossed to Hulan, and handed her some papers. "You can read, I hope."

Hulan nodded.

"That is good but not essential," the man continued. "We"—he gestured to his companions—"we see women like you every day. Some come from close by, some come from as far away as Qinghai Province.

These days so many country people go to Beijing or Shanghai for work, but we say there's no need for that. Come here. We'll make sure you get work."

"For a fee? I have no money," Hulan said, playing along for now.

The man smiled broadly, pleased at how cleverly he'd gotten his fish to take the hook. "No cost to you. The company pays us a small token."

"What company? What's the work? I don't want to work in the fields anymore. That's why I left my village."

"It's a factory. American. They give you food. They give you a room. And the salary is very good."

"How good?"

"Five hundred *yuan* each month."

Hulan calculated that would be about $60 each month or about $720 U.S. a year. By American standards the pay was indecently low. By Beijing standards, where there were now all kinds of jobs with American companies, it was still quite low. In the countryside, where a peasant might hope to earn only about 300 *yuan* a month or just over a dollar a day—the official poverty level—it was fantastic, especially if this income was considered a second or third or even a fourth to be added to the family pot.

"When can you start?" the man asked.

Hulan studied the contract. It appeared straightforward.

As if reading her thoughts, the man said, "Take it. Read it. Come back tomorrow or the next day or the day after that. We'll be here." Then the man went back to his table.

Hulan finished her meal, paid her bill, and left the café. As she walked out of town, she felt the oppression not only of the heat but also of Da Shui itself. Yesterday's visit with Tsai Bing and Siang had been disconcerting. The people at the Public Security Bureau had been rude. The villagers and the Silk Thread's proprietress had been closed-mouthed. But none of them had been as disturbing as the men in the café. On this day, as Hulan followed her investigative custom of stepping back and back again from the scene of a crime, she found no answers, only more questions. The main question that now played in her mind was the role of the Knight factory. Miaoshan had worked there. The men of the town made no pretense of hiding the fact that they were earning some sort of kickback from Knight by placing women—with or without proper papers—at that factory.

Just as Hulan had a method for looking at a crime scene, she also had routines for getting questions answered. One was direct, the other circuitous. To ease her mind, she would have to follow both. This afternoon she would make an "official" visit to the Knight factory. Tomorrow she would go back to the café, sign her contract, and see what happened. The idea that either of these plans might be dangerous to her or her baby did not enter her mind.

An hour later, wearing a simple linen dress and a light jacket, Hulan took the bus back to Taiyuan. From the bus stop she hailed a taxi and rode to the Shanxi Grand Hotel, where she arranged for a car and driver for the day. An hour after that she was back on the expressway.

Eventually the driver turned off the main road and followed signs decorated with cartoon figures of what Hulan assumed were Sam & His Friends. The car made one last turn, and the Knight factory rose up stark and white against the sky. In the traditional Chinese manner, a high wall protected the entire compound. The driver stopped at the guardhouse. Hulan introduced herself and opened her MPS credentials. The guard paled, stepped back inside his shelter, and made a call. A moment later the gate lifted, and the car pulled into the compound.

The driver steered down the center road of the complex. On either side were buildings—some immense, others little more than single rooms—each with their own sign designating what they were: DORMITORY, ASSEMBLY, CAFETERIA, ADMINISTRATION, SHIPPING, WAREHOUSE, COMPANY STORE. Next to each of these words was a different cartoon character. Since this was still a new complex, the trees were not yet tall enough or broad enough to provide shade. A few shrubs withered against the white walls of the buildings.

The car stopped before the building marked ADMINISTRATION. A man with light blond hair and pale skin opened Hulan's door and said, "Good morning and welcome to Knight International. I'm Sandy Newheart. I'm the project director here."

Hulan introduced herself and showed her Ministry of Public Security identification. That Sandy Newheart didn't demonstrate the fear that the guard had shown didn't surprise her. It was conceivable that Sandy had never heard of the MPS, or if he had, he didn't realize its power.

"I wish you'd told us you were coming," Sandy said. "I would have prepared a proper welcome, perhaps even a banquet."

"That wouldn't have been necessary," Hulan said.

Sandy's forehead crinkled as if he hadn't understood what she'd said. Then his features smoothed. "Well then, what can I do for you?"

"I have come about one of your employees, a Ling Miaoshan."

"I don't know anything about that, so I doubt there's much I can help you with."

"Still . . . Perhaps there's a place we can talk."

"Of course. What was I thinking? Please come inside." As he mounted the steps, he glanced back at the car. "Can I get your driver anything?"

"No, he's fine."

With the air conditioning, the lobby was at least five degrees centigrade cooler than outside. Under her lightweight jacket goose bumps popped up along Hulan's arms. Air conditioning was an extravagance in China, used almost exclusively in Western hotels and businesses. As they walked down a long corridor, Sandy kept up a one-sided dialogue.

"Henry Knight, our founder, came to China for the first time during World War II. He didn't return until the winter of 1990, just after the troubles at Tiananmen Square. That was a time when most American businesses were leaving."

"I remember," Hulan remarked, thinking it odd that Sandy felt compelled to bring up a subject that was still touchy, especially with government officials.

"But China has long held a fascination for Mr. Knight," Sandy continued as they passed a large room broken into individual work stations, where a flock of nicely dressed Chinese women sat before computer screens. Between the aisles that separated the cubicles walked a handful of supervisors—also women, all Chinese. From this central room Hulan could see four hallways leading outward at the four points of the compass. Sandy turned down the corridor that led to the left. "So at a time when others were unsure, when even our own government was suggesting that America should beware of China, Mr. Knight took a chance."

Hulan bet he'd also hoped for an extraordinary deal.

"But as you know, things move slowly here, and we didn't get this place up and running until two years ago." Sandy stopped before a display of animation cels, products, and a company history. "This is our brag wall," he explained, then began pointing out the various highlights in Knight's corporate history.

After years in the lucrative preschool market, Knight had struck gold in the post-war years with the Sally Doll—one of the first baby dolls on the market to drink from a bottle and pee in its diaper. The company had experienced another growth surge during the mid-eighties, when deregulation under Reagan led to relaxed limitations on advertising during children's programming. But none of the products introduced at that time had experienced the phenomenal success of the Sam line. The action figures had been designed as a team of ten. Sam was the leader, but he was never seen without Cactus at his side. After Cactus there were—in order of military rank—Magnificent, Glory, Gaseous, Uta, Annabel, Notorious, Nick, and Rachel. Ironically, although children were supposed to want all the figures equally or at least in order of rank, the ones with the most common names lagged behind in popularity and sales.

Sandy's patter came to a close, and he continued down the hall. Following behind him, Hulan realized that the names of the Sam figures were the same as those on the financial papers at Suchee's. Again Hulan wondered how those documents had gotten into Miaoshan's hands.

Sandy stopped, pushed open a door, and gestured inside. "Here, this is my office."

A huge black lacquer desk dominated the sleekly modern room. In front of the desk the room was divided into two sections: to the left, a mini conference area made up of a round table and four chairs; to the right, two couches with a coffee table between them. Sandy took a seat on one of the couches and motioned for Hulan to sit across from him.

This entire experience puzzled Hulan, and she tried to reconcile what she knew about Americans and American business with what she understood as a Chinese woman. In China great value was placed on titles. Sandy Newheart had said he was the project director, and certainly the size and opulence of this office suggested that he was the top person here. But in China it was practically unheard of for someone of importance to meet directly with an unknown quantity, let alone go outdoors to meet that guest. Was he being polite or trying to control the situation?

"Are you the person I should talk to about Miss Ling?" Hulan asked.

"I can take you over to meet Aaron Rodgers. He's the manager of what we call assembly. I believe that's where Miss Ling worked."

"I thought you said you didn't know her."

"I didn't. I just know she didn't work in the heart."

"The heart?"

"That's the area we just passed through," Sandy explained. "That's the heart of what we do. Those girls handle all orders from the U.S. They track shipments and money transactions. I doubt that poor girl was ever in this building. But tell me—and please forgive my ignorance—why are you here? Her death has nothing to do with us."

Only tell one-third of the truth, Hulan thought for the second time since coming to the countryside. "I'm an investigator for Public Security. It's my duty to investigate suspicious deaths in this province. Ling Miaoshan committed suicide."

"You're with the police?" Sandy asked, finally grasping what this was all about.

Hulan tipped her head in acknowledgment.

"But a suicide—" he tried again.

Hulan held up a hand to keep the project director from repeating himself. "You're absolutely right, but as you've noted, we have our own ways in China. I'm here to understand this girl. It will help me if I can see where she worked and how she spent her last days."

Sandy's eyes narrowed. His fingers drummed on the armrest. Finally he asked, "Have you met with Governor Sun?"

"No, I haven't," she responded, startled by the question.

"Governor Sun Gan represents the province," he explained. "He also serves as the provincial liaison between American companies and the Chinese bureaucracy, I mean, government. I'm surprised you don't know him."

Hulan smiled thinly. "Everyone has heard of Governor Sun, but China is a big country and I haven't met him." She stood. "Now, I'd like to see where Miss Ling lived and worked. If you're too busy, then you can have one of your other workers take me around."

"No." The word came out sharply. "I mean, I'd be happy to show you our facility."

As they walked down the road between the buildings, Sandy once again took up his tour guide role. They stopped to look at the cafeteria, where Sandy showed her the private dining room used by himself, the department managers, and the Knights when they came to visit. Hulan was not allowed to see the area where the factory workers ate because, as Sandy explained, the room was being cleaned and readied for dinner.

Back outside, Sandy led her past the warehouse and several of the other buildings, all of which he said were places that an employee such as the girl who killed herself would never have entered. When Sandy passed the entrance to the dormitory, Hulan reminded him that she wanted to see where Miaoshan had lived. He said that regretfully this area was off limits today. "You can imagine that with nearly one thousand women living together that things can get quite messy. So once a month we send in a crew to do a thorough cleaning using high-strength disinfectants and such. I don't think you'd find that a particularly pleasant place to be today."

"But I'd still like to see it," she said, her eyes roaming over the harsh white exterior.

"Perhaps another time."

Noticing that the dormitory building had no windows, Hulan slowed and turned her head back the way she'd come. None of the buildings in the Knight complex had windows, at least not on the facades facing the center road.

Hulan followed Sandy up the couple of steps leading to the building marked ASSEMBLY. As he pulled open the door, Hulan felt again the rush of cool air. But once inside the lobby, she realized that this building was not nearly as cold as the Administration Building. A guard—a foreigner—sat at a desk.

"Jimmy, could you call Aaron out here? We have a visitor I'd like him to meet."

"Sure thing, Mr. Newheart," the guard said in an Australian accent. Hulan watched as his beefy fingers hit the number pads on the phone. Jimmy hung up the receiver and stood. He was at least six feet tall and well over two hundred and fifty pounds. Most of this weight bulked in the muscles of his arms and shoulders. Unlike Sandy Newheart, who seemed to have no inkling of what Hulan was, Jimmy's deep brown eyes sized her up and seemed to come to the automatic conclusion that she was in law enforcement. At the same time Hulan was coming to conclusions of her own: Jimmy was accustomed to physically settling scores and carrying out other people's orders. His recognition of her could only point to one thing: He had more than a passing acquaintance with cops. He might have been a policeman at some time in his life, he may have simply passed his working life as a guard of some sort, or he may have been a low-grade criminal himself, doing breaking and entering, maybe even "enforcement" for hire. Although how an Australian of such questionable background would end up working in an American-owned factory in Shanxi Province was a mystery, to say the least.

Behind Jimmy's desk a door opened, and Aaron Rodgers came through. He wore jeans, a cotton shirt with the sleeves rolled up, and tennis shoes. His smile showed perfectly straight white teeth.

"You're here for a tour, huh?" His voice was young and enthusiastic. "We don't get a lot of visitors, so I'd be happy to show you around."

Jimmy pressed a button under the desk, the door buzzed, and Aaron held it open for Hulan and Sandy. They followed Aaron through an inside foyer, then down several circuitous hallways lined with unmarked doors. Left, right, left again. Hulan felt lost and claustrophobic in here. This was compounded by the lack of air conditioning or windows. Finally Aaron opened one of the doors, and they stepped into a large room, which was obviously well soundproofed because Hulan had heard none of the hundred or so voices of the women who were working here until now. They sat at tables in long rows that ran the length of the room. They wore pink smocks and pink hair nets. Fans overhead kept the air circulating, but otherwise there was no mechanical noise. Everything in this room was done by hand.

Looking around, Hulan thought back to the plans she'd seen at Suchee's house. Why hadn't she studied them more closely? Shouldn't this room be much larger?

"As you may have guessed, this is our assembly area," Aaron said. "This is where the workers add the final details to Sam & His Friends, where we do inspections for quality, and, finally, where we package the finished products."

Hulan walked down the center aisle and got her first look at the Sam & His Friends figures. They were dolls, but the bodies were soft like stuffed animals. She stopped to watch a woman bend back the arms to keep the fabric limbs from interfering with her work, then begin to clip human-looking eyes into the plastic face.

"Have you seen Sam before?" Aaron asked.

Hulan shook her head. "We don't have this in China."

"You will soon enough. The cartoons will come here one day, and every child in China will want one."

How many times had Hulan encountered foreigners such as Sandy Newheart and Aaron Rodgers who thought that the China market was wide open to them if only they could break into it somehow? Just because something was manufactured here didn't mean that the Chinese wanted it. But then, who was she to underestimate the power of television? She had seen what the recent rash of news stories had done to her own life. If Knight—or the studio that made the *Sam & His Friends Show*—could actually get it broadcast in China, then these dolls probably would become a sought-after commodity.

Aaron leaned down and spoke softly into the woman's ear. She smiled prettily and put the doll in his hands. Aaron then held the doll out to Hulan. When she didn't immediately take it, he began twisting its limbs. "These products are unique in the world market. Sam, the cartoon, is an action figure in the traditional sense, but you would expect to see an action figure to be made of molded plastic and be no taller than four inches. Mr. Knight had a different idea and one that took some persuading when it came to the studio and advertising guys. G.I. Joe, Batman, Ghostbusters—all of them followed the same four-inch model. Hell, more than a few of them were made in the same molds. Mr. Knight took a big risk going soft."

Aaron squeezed the Sam doll to show Hulan what he meant, then grinned boyishly. "But Sam's insides are as tough as any hero's." Seeing Hulan's look of bewilderment, he added, "We provide Sam & His Friends with a steel wire skeleton. You can bend him into any shape you want."

"Don't all stuffed animals have that?"

"Most just have stuffing and don't move at all. Some have articulated limbs but, again, no flexibility."

"I know I've seen stuffed animals that can bend like that."

"Oh sure, cheap things made in Hong Kong. Manufacturers have been running hanger wire through kapok for years. But this is different. Sam can *hold* his position, he can grasp a weapon, he can sit in a jeep. And that skeleton is guaranteed not to poke through. That means no hurt fingers or injured eyes."

"I see."

But Aaron wasn't done. "Traditionally the toy market has been extraordinarily biased by sex. Girls like Barbie; boys want G.I. Joe. But we have something unique here," he repeated as he continued to twist the figure. "We're able to appeal to girls because Sam & His Friends are soft like dolls and we make female characters who conform to modern attitudes of girl power while still maintaining their femininity. At the same time, boys want them and all the accoutrements—the weapons and vehicles—for their practical uses in war and other action scenarios. And it's all because of the steel skeleton. We—I mean Knight International—have patented this technology. It'll have practical applications for toys well into the next century."

"That will translate into lots of money, I suppose."

"Absolutely, Inspector."

"And you still haven't shown her the best part," Sandy interrupted.

Aaron blushed, grinned again, and said, "Sam talks too."

He pressed something on the yellow figure, and it said in a surprisingly tough voice, "Give me a hand here, Cactus." This was followed by: "All's quiet now." Then: "This is Sam. Until next time."

"Sam & His Friends come factory-equipped with standard phrases such as these," Aaron explained. "But this is just the beginning. Our deluxe model comes with a microchip that allows kids to program different conversations. We're talking about a fully interactive toy. The technology is still in the early stages and rather expensive—about ninety dollars U.S. for the full package. But in a year or so we'll be able to bring the deluxe models way down in price."

At last Aaron handed the figure back to the Chinese worker. Again he leaned down and softly spoke into her ear.

"Your Mandarin is very good," Hulan observed.

"Thank you. I studied it in college. It was my major, actually. That's how I got the job."

The trio continued down the aisle. On either side of them women applied different features to the faces of the colorful figures. When they came to the end of the row, they turned the corner and came up another aisle, where women packed the figures in boxes. This involved taking clear plastic straps and winding them around the neck, arms, and legs of the figures and tightening them into place on a cardboard backing. On the next aisle women attached various gizmos to the cardboard. Some got combs, brushes, mirrors, and knives. Others got pistols, machine guns, grenades, and miniature backpacks.

At last Hulan and her guides came to the door leading back to the hallway. "May I see where the other women work?"

"I beg your pardon?" Sandy asked.

"You said you have a thousand women working here. I'm guessing they're on the other side of the corridor."

"That's an empty room," Sandy answered, irritation spilling from his mouth like oil running from a bottle.

"Then you won't mind if I see it."

"Actually, our time is up."

"What about the other women who work here?"

"I'm sorry. I can't help you anymore. Aaron and I have a meeting, right, Aaron?"

"Yes, that's so." But the young man couldn't help blushing again.

"Our office will be sorry to hear that you haven't cooperated," Hulan said.

With any Chinese citizen this comment would have been understood for the threat that it was, but Sandy Newheart seemed unimpressed.

"Perhaps on another day you can come again and we'll be properly prepared to receive you." Sandy opened the door and led the way back through the labyrinth of corridors and doors. As they entered the foyer, Jimmy stood, moved his bulky frame around the desk, planted his feet apart, and crossed his arms.

"I'll come back," Hulan said. "But I doubt I'll be calling first. You are guests in my country and you must abide by our rules."

Sandy grimaced as he opened the outside door. "Until our next meeting, then."

Hulan held his gaze, nodded, then passed through the door to the courtyard. Aware that three sets of eyes were on her, she looked toward the Administration building and held up her arm to get her driver's attention. Waiting for him to pick her up, she once again took in the vast emptiness of the courtyard complex. Where were the signs of life? She expected to see people walking from building to building either on break or moving merchandise, people sitting together for a late lunch, even people sprawled out asleep for *xiuxi*. How did this company, administered as it was by what appeared to be just three foreign men and a handful of Chinese women, manage to control such a large population of workers? How had Knight ended up out here at all? Most important, what was going on in those other buildings and on the other side of the Assembly wall?

Once the car had turned back onto the expressway, Hulan pulled out her cell phone, punched in David's number, and waited several seconds for the line to connect. If it was 3:00 P.M. here, then it was midnight in Los Angeles. David would be up. She was sure of it.

## 7

W HEN THE PHONE RANG, DAVID KNEW IT HAD TO BE HULAN. It had been four days since they'd spoken, longer than any time since he'd left Beijing. "Where are you?" he asked. "I've been worried."

"I'm fine."

"I have so much to tell you," he said. She did too, but what he said next made her stories seem unimportant. "I'm coming, Hulan. I'll be in Beijing . . ." He paused to calculate the time and the dateline, and said, "Day after tomorrow."

"How? What for?"

"I have a job. I'm moving to Beijing."

She heard static on the line; then she asked with deliberation, "Is this the truth?"

He laughed. "Yes! Yes!"

"Oh, David. I can't believe it." Then she asked again, "How?"

He started four days back with Keith's horrible death and what that meant about the triads and the FBI surveillance. He confided in her his concerns about Keith and what he'd read in the paper. Then he told her about going back to his office the day after the funeral. . . .

He'd picked up his voice-mail messages, including one from Keith's sister. "I'm sorry about yesterday," she said. "We're going home today, but

I'd like to talk to you about Keith when you have a chance." She left her home number in Russell, Kansas, then closed with, "I hope you'll call."

At the time he'd had no desire to hear more of her recriminations, so he'd written the number down and put it in his briefcase.

A few minutes later he'd walked down the hall to U.S. Attorney Madeleine Prentice's office. She was blonde, beautiful, smart, and politically astute. Rob Butler, the chief of the Criminal Division, was also there. David had known Rob since law school. They'd played tennis together for years. Like Madeleine, he was a brilliant lawyer. David needed to clear up one aspect of Keith's death before he made any other decisions and hoped now to confirm what Miles had told him after the funeral.

"What can you tell me about the Keith Baxter investigation?" he asked.

"There isn't one," Madeleine responded.

"It was in the paper yesterday," he said.

"Don't believe everything you read in the papers," Rob said. "Haven't you learned that yet?"

David ignored the barb. "He was accused of doing something in violation of the Foreign Corrupt Practices Act."

"Bribery?" Madeleine asked.

"I assumed so, but I don't know."

"Well, it's not in our office," Madeleine said. "We haven't had a single Foreign Corrupt Practices case since the statute was written."

"Maybe his name has come up in another matter," Rob suggested.

"But we don't have *any* bribery cases right now," Madeleine said.

"What about in the Washington office?" David asked.

"Your friend lived in L.A., right? If he was up to something, don't you think Washington would tell us?"

David still didn't know what was bothering Keith, but if Miles said there was nothing to worry about, and Madeleine and Rob verified that, then he could move on—emotionally and perhaps professionally. Except . . .

"Can I ask something else? Do you think Keith could have been the target the other night and not me? I mean, the Rising Phoenix has had lots of other opportunities. So why now? Could there be some connection between Keith and the triads? He was doing work in China . . ."

Madeleine sighed. "David, you *know* what happened that night. Accept it, then put it behind you."

David looked at Rob, who said, "She's right."

David considered, then announced, "Miles Stout has asked me to set up an office in Beijing."

Without hesitation Madeleine asked, "How soon?"

"I'd leave in a couple of days."

"A week or two's notice would have been nice, but it wouldn't be the first time an assistant left on the spur of the moment," Madeleine said. Then eerily echoing Phil Collingsworth, she added, "When it's time, it's time."

David laughed and shook his head. "What's this? Here's your hat, what's your hurry?"

"Not at all, David," Madeleine said. "It's a practical move for you. More than that, I'd call it wise. You've finished the Rising Phoenix trials, so if you have to leave suddenly, this is a good time to do it. For the office, I mean," she amended. "Obviously we'll hate to see you go, but there are other things to consider. You've got people after you. We can surmise it's some last vestige of the Rising Phoenix. Can we prove it? Not yet. Is there any evidence that points directly to them so that we could get a wiretap and go roust some folks? No. So what you're looking at is uncertainty and having those Feebies following you around. You can't tell me you like that."

"I don't, but should I run away to China?"

"You're not running away," Madeleine said. "You're getting out of harm's way so the FBI can do its job and find those assholes."

"But China? The Rising Phoenix is a Chinese gang," David pointed out.

"Based in Los Angeles," Madeleine added as if David didn't know. "There may be a few hotheads still hanging around the city, but there can't be any left in Beijing."

David knew this was true. The gang members in China had been caught. Those who'd confessed had been treated leniently with hard labor in China's hinterlands. Those who hadn't had been tried, sentenced, and executed.

"Even if they aren't all dead," Rob added, "the Chinese will be able to protect you in a way that we simply can't."

David hesitated. There was one more question he had to ask, but it wasn't an easy one to ask of friends. "This isn't some setup, is it? You aren't trying to get me into something I don't yet know about? We've been down that road before and—"

"David," Madeleine interrupted wearily, "just get out of here. Be safe . . ."

The taxi's windows were open, and hot hair blew across Hulan's face. She gazed out over the fields, thinking of the time she'd spent in the U.S. Attorney's Office with Madeleine Prentice and Rob Butler earlier this year, and of the life that David would be giving up to come here.

"You love being a prosecutor," she said into the phone receiver.

"Yes, but I don't look at that work the same way anymore." He was referring to the case that had brought them back together. Both of their governments had played them for fools. She'd expected it; he hadn't. She'd accepted it; he felt betrayed.

"Have you spoken to Miles again?" In her mind's eye she conjured up Miles's handsome face. He'd always been nice to her—he was polite to everyone—but she'd always felt uncomfortable around him, probably because she'd never been able to read behind his smooth Nordic exterior.

Picking up on her tone, David said, "I'm not particularly fond of Miles either, and frankly I sense a certain ambivalence in him about this arrangement too. But the firm is made up of many people. Phil and the others have been great, but you guessed right. My negotiations were with Miles. After my meeting with Madeleine and Rob, I met Miles for lunch to go over the particulars. He said he'd give me free rein. 'Sink your teeth into it. Run with it. The Knights are good people. . . .'"

"The Knights?"

"Remember the factory you asked me about? The firm wants me to handle the sale of Knight to Tartan, then stay on—"

"David, you don't know anything about those people or their business. I've seen things—"

"Look, they don't need to be my friends. They sell, we buy. Hell, in twelve days Knight won't exist anymore except as a division of Tartan. Don't you see, Hulan? I'll be going to China *with* business. I won't just be representing Tartan, but other business the firm has lined up. Marcia, Miles's secretary, has already set up appointments for next Monday. Don't ask me where they're going to be. I don't have an office yet."

Hulan had many questions, but David just kept talking. . . .


It was amazing how easily he walked away from one life and into another. After lunch he'd gone back to the firm with Miles. Just as Keith had said on the night of his death, the offices of Phillips, MacKenzie & Stout hadn't changed. The public areas were dark, plush, and conservative. Each partner was given an allowance to decorate his or her own office, which meant that there was a little of everything—from Louis XV to Early American, from mahogany to bird's-eye maple, from cheap posters to original Hockneys on the walls. As a partner in the top echelon, David was entitled to a corner office on any of the firm's five floors, the top of which was the acknowledged power center. But since David was going to China, he was assigned a large office between Miles's on one corner and Phil Collingsworth's on the other.

Under ordinary circumstances the partners would have needed to meet to vote on accepting a new partner, but, as Phil had pointed out the day of the funeral, everyone here knew David. A few phone calls to the executive committee resulted in a unanimous decision. Five minutes later Miles asked David for his passport, which he pulled out of his breast pocket. Miles laughed when he saw it and said, "I guess I should have negotiated your points a little harder." Both men had laughed then, for there was no denying that David had wanted to go back to China from the first moment that Miles mentioned it. The senior partner gave the passport to his secretary and told her to hustle down to the Chinese consulate for a visa. After that Miles and David joined Phil and some of the other partners for an impromptu champagne toast. It had felt like old times . . .


"Did you ask about Keith?" Hulan interrupted.

"What do you mean?"

"About the bribery?"

David's voice was lost in static, and she asked him to repeat his answer.

"I asked Miles, and I talked to Madeleine and Rob about it too. They all said something along the lines of you can't believe everything you read in the papers. After what you and I have been through, I have to agree. I can't remember the last time I was quoted correctly."

"I don't like it," she said.

Even over this great distance she heard him sigh.

"What part?" he asked, the pain in his voice palpable. "Is it that you don't want me in China?"

"That's not it at all," she said quickly. "I love you. I want you to come, but I don't like what I've seen at the Knight factory and—I don't know—this is happening so fast. Miles never does anything without deliberation."

"But that's what I've been trying to tell you. Miles isn't the only voice here. Everyone at Phillips, MacKenzie has been thinking about this for a long time." His voice faltered, and she understood how deeply she'd hurt him. "It's sudden," he said, "but it's an opportunity. It's *our* opportunity." His words got lost in another wave of static, then: "No more bad connections, just the two of us together."

"When does your flight get in?"

"Seven-fifteen on the tenth," he said, then clarified, "your Thursday."

"You may beat me back to Beijing," she said. Hulan had yet to tell David about the peculiar circumstances of Miaoshan's death, the strangeness of the Knight compound, or her now postponed plan to go into the factory, but she would when they met in Beijing. "I don't know how easy it will be for me to get back to the city, but I'll try to return in time to meet your plane. If I'm not there, I'll send my new driver. Don't worry, he'll find you."

They spoke for a few more minutes, then David said, "Soon we'll have all the time in the world to talk, but I should go. I have to be at Phillips, MacKenzie in the morning. I have a lot to do tomorrow to close up this life. We're going to be together, Hulan. We're going to be happy."

Suddenly that old caution crept back into Hulan's voice. "I hope so, David, I really hope so."

They hung up, both knowing that a lot had gone unasked and unanswered.

The next day David spent his first hour back in the luxurious fold of the firm with Miles's secretary. Marcia explained that she would handle David's time sheets and billings from here. She'd manage his workload when he was in town and take care of personal things like forwarding his mail to China. She'd also make sure that he received all interoffice memos in Beijing—or wherever in the world he happened to be—and that any phone calls that did come in for him were routed to his as-yet unknown number in China. She told him that the firm had just hired a Miss Quo Xuesheng as a secretary and interpreter in China. Miss Quo was already scouting out office space and setting up appointments for him upon his arrival.

Then Marcia left him alone with several files, which would bring him up-to-date on the firm's overall business and strategic plan. At noon, David swung back down to the U.S. Attorney's Office, where Rob and Madeleine held a farewell gathering. Then he went back to Miles's office for a final briefing on the Knight matter.

"I've handled business for Tartan and Randall Craig for twenty years," Miles said. "The Knight deal is a great opportunity. There's a lot of money involved—seven hundred million—but not much can happen now to sour the deal. We're at that point where the sale has its own momentum and we're just along for the ride."

"Are there any problems I should know about?"

Miles shook his head. "Smooth sailing. Henry Knight is a widower and has one grown son. Henry's an ethical guy, a lot like you actually. He's run his business cleanly even when he could have made shortcuts here and there. Top profit has never been his main motivator."

But the factory was in China, David pointed out. That had to cut costs.

"Sure," Miles said, "but that's just a side benefit. He sees himself as a philanthropist. He's given money to hospitals, children's organizations, various shelters. For Henry, China's just another cause. He's always loved the place. I don't know. It goes back to the war, I think. Anyway, he thinks he's helping the people he hires. Having come from a farm myself, I know what a shit life that can be." Miles shrugged as if to shake away the memories. "When you get over there, you'll meet Governor Sun and his assistant, Amy Gao. They're with the local government."

"You've met them?"

"I met Sun on my first trip to China, but otherwise I've just dealt with his assistant. She has a Chinese name, but like so many of them she goes with an American version of her first name and puts her family name second. Amy Gao is a smart woman, ambitious. She's come over here, been up at the firm. You'll like her. If you have any problems, talk to her. I'll come over for the final signing." He paused, then said, "Now, don't get worried that I'll be butting in. This is your matter now. I mean it when I say go with it. Although I can't say there'll be much to *go* with. The work is done. All we need now are the John Hancocks. And as far as *that* goes, I couldn't miss the final signing. Randall Craig and Tartan have been a big part of my career."

That night, after David finished packing, he tried calling his parents, but they were both out of the country. His father, an international businessman, had separated from David's mother shortly after David was born and played little part in his life. David's mother, a concert pianist, was on tour. David left messages on each machine, then went to bed.

The next morning, Eddie—having promised to house-sit for as long as David wanted—drove him down to LAX. At eleven-fifteen David boarded a 747 and sank into his first-class seat—one of the many perks of being back in private practice. He remembered back to just four and a half months ago when he'd been on this same flight. He'd been nervous and unsure of what to expect. He'd plotted every move, using his legal background to logically plan his life. He'd hoped that somehow he would see Hulan, not knowing at the time that others had long planned their meeting. Looking back, he saw someone lacking in spontaneity, afraid of living on the edge, often in the position of reacting instead of setting things in motion himself.

Four months later he was a very different man. Sure, he still sought his friends' counsel and advice before making a decision. (He was cautious. He always would be.) Most definitely he'd haggled over his compensation, firm points, title, and expenses. He'd also thought a lot about

Keith's death. Was David running away now to escape his guilt? But Madeleine and Rob were right. With him out of the picture, the last of the Rising Phoenix renegades might make a mistake. When they did, the FBI would be there.

As for what had troubled Keith on that last night, David might never know the full story. Clearly an ethical issue had troubled Keith, but maybe it wasn't as bad as he thought; maybe he'd been more upset about his girlfriend's death but didn't know how to talk about it. And maybe, David thought ruefully, Keith had just been tired and stressed, worn down by these brutal transpacific flights and the strain of the deal. What mattered now was that David had found an honorable way to get back to Hulan.

Although David had tried these last two days not to read too much into their last phone call, he wondered what Hulan hadn't told him. When he'd said he was coming and she'd asked, "What for?" it had momentarily taken his breath away. Then he'd decided to take her query at face value. He hadn't told her his plan from the beginning, thinking that if it didn't work out she'd be disappointed. But as their conversation went on, he couldn't help but hear her wariness. Maybe that was just Hulan. She was always so guarded, always afraid of the ways that good things could be ruined by bad. Despite this, he convinced himself she was glad he was coming. He knew he could make her happy. In a few more hours they would be together with no ocean or secrets between them.


When he'd last flown out of Beijing it was March 1. The sun had just begun to warm the city, but the vacant land between the runways had still been frozen hard and the airport had been cold and damp. On July 10, at a little before midnight, as the plane taxied to the terminal, David looked out the window and saw men working under the lights wearing only loose shorts, sandals, and earphones to block the noise. When the door of the plane swung open, a wall of heat and humidity flowed into the first-class cabin.

David took a place in line for passport control behind another business traveler and watched as the back of the man's shirt quickly darkened with sweat. An officer dressed in a drab green short-sleeve shirt took David's passport and leafed through the pages. He briefly looked up, compared the photo to David's face, stamped the book, then handed it back without a word. David grabbed a luggage cart, loaded his bags, passed through Customs, then pushed his way through the exit and to the curb, where a man dressed in a black suit stepped forward and extended his hand.

"I am Investigator Lo," he said in heavily accented English. "I am here to drive you to Inspector Liu's home. She arrived a short while ago and is waiting for you there. She has instructed me to take you to your appointments tomorrow."

A few minutes later Lo threw the car into gear, honked his way through the airport, and roared onto the toll road. This route didn't offer all the sights of the old road, which ran parallel to this one, but within twenty minutes Lo had reached the city. Even at this late hour the streets were awash in neon, filled with people walking and on bicycles, and aromatic with the rich smells coming from street vendor carts. Soon the car began snaking its way through the narrow alleyways of Hulan's *hutong* neighborhood. The car pulled to a stop before a simple wood door set in an austere gray wall.

Lo unlocked the gate, handed David his bags, and said good night. David stepped over the threshold into the first courtyard, and his nostrils filled with the fragrance of night-blooming jasmine. He wandered farther into the compound, past the first, plain courtyards, then into the more elaborate courtyards, past colonnaded buildings that had once housed the many generations of Hulan's mother's family, and finally to the door of Hulan's quarters. It was unlocked and he walked in.

He very much felt her presence in these rooms. Her scent hung lightly on the air. There was a bowl of oranges on the table and a silk blouse draped over the back of a chair. David's longing for Hulan was greater now than during all the months of separation. He stepped into the bedroom and saw her in bed, waiting for him. He stripped, sank onto the bed, and wrapped his arms around the woman he loved. She nuzzled into him. Her body was warm and her words were tender. Soon their murmured words were replaced by soft groans of pleasure.

David marveled at the changes in Hulan's body. Her breasts felt larger under his fingertips. Her stomach—always hard and flat—had a gentle swell. He let his tongue and lips move lower, constantly aware of her breathing, listening to the changes that would signal she was ready for him. Finally her hands gripped his shoulders, pulling him back into her arms. She wrapped her legs around him, guiding him into her. Her eyes met his, and he knew he was truly home.

David was wide awake at three the next morning. He nudged Hulan. Without opening her eyes, she kissed him and snuggled closer. He listened until her breathing deepened again, then slipped out of bed, made himself a pot of tea, pulled out his laptop, and checked his e-mail. Just before dawn, he put on trunks and a singlet, and set off for a run. By six, he was back at Hulan's. At about the time he stepped out of the shower, the *yang ge* troupe began banging its cymbals and drums somewhere in the far distance. Despite Hulan's grumblings by phone, her descriptions of the troupe had sounded colorful and quaint, but David didn't go out to investigate, knowing his appearance would attract too much attention. So he made another pot of tea, rummaged through cupboards for crackers, and peeled himself an orange.

At eight, when Investigator Lo arrived to take him to his appointments, Hulan still hadn't wakened. David kissed her gently, then quietly left the compound. Lo drove him to the Kempinski Hotel in the Chaoyang District. In the lobby he was met by a pert young woman, Miss Quo Xuesheng, a Chinese national and until now the only employee of Phillips, MacKenzie on Chinese soil. She wore a bright red suit hemmed well above her knees. Four-inch high heels brought Miss Quo to a still petite height of five feet two inches. To David's eyes she looked very young. In a few questions he determined that she wasn't a lawyer by training, but she did have a lot of experience with foreign companies, for which she'd worked for several years, perfecting her English and working her way up from tea girl to secretary to personal assistant.

"Our first appointment is to look at an apartment and office space in the Kempinski's business complex next door," she said as she led the way back outside and across the hot asphalt to an adjacent high-rise.

"I don't need an apartment," David said, but he was about to have his first lessons in doing business in China. First, Miss Quo had very strong ideas about what foreigners wanted and needed. Second, she was not easily swayed by his opinions or, as he would later find out, direct orders. Third, foreigners who wanted to set up businesses in Beijing were easy marks for every manner of scheme and bribe.

The next three hours were spent going in and out of buildings, up and down elevators, listening to the attributes of particular complexes and neighborhoods. The buildings followed one of two models: either separate structures within the same compound for housing and offices, or both together in the same building. After the Kempinski they got back in the car and drove a few blocks and into a motor court that looked uncomfortably familiar. "This is the Capital Mansion," she said. "Again, you can have housing *and* office space. I believe this is best for you."

"I don't want to be here," David said, vividly remembering the body that he and Hulan had found here not so long ago—the intestines splayed out, the blood, the smell.

"Because of what happened before," she said amiably. "This I understand, but I have already begun our arrangements."

"Undo them."

"See the rooms, then we'll decide."

David followed Miss Quo, but he barely paid attention to her or the building's director of real estate. When David stepped back outside, Miss Quo stayed behind to talk to the realtor, who was obviously agitated. David wondered just how far the negotiations had gone and if they had gone as far as he suspected, why? As Hulan often said, there were no secrets in Beijing. Certainly Miss Quo seemed to know a lot about him. Clearly she knew about the murder of Cao Hua in this very building. Wouldn't she know this place would upset him?

At last Miss Quo came through the revolving door, got in the car, and snapped out some orders to Investigator Lo in Mandarin. Their next stop was the Manhattan Garden residential complex next to the Chaoyang Golf Course. David explained once again that he didn't need an apartment, but Miss Quo smiled, pretended she didn't understand him, and went on to show him the Manhattan Garden, followed by the Parkview Towers in downtown Beijing, the North Star Commercial and Residential Community, where a thousand foreign families lived and many more worked, and the Bright China Chang An Building, which housed numerous foreign enterprises including Citibank, Samsung, and Abdul Latif Jameel Co., Ltd.

At this point Miss Quo took him to the coffee shop in the Palace Hotel. Miss Quo waved away the menus and ordered in Chinese. Hoping for dumplings or noodles, David was disappointed to have a club sandwich with some limp french fries placed before him. Miss Quo seemed to know almost everyone here, and she waved friends over to meet David and explain that he was opening an office. Each time before they left, she said, "Attorney Stark is a good friend to China, as I'm sure you already know. If you ever need help with business transactions, he will be happy to assist you." She placed a business card with David's name and that of Phillips, MacKenzie & Stout in English and Mandarin into each palm. "We will have our office soon," she said. "Until then you know how to reach me." Then there were more handshakes, words of congratulation, and promises of receptions and banquets.

After lunch, he was taken out as far as the Woodlands. Billed as "villas in a resort-like setting," they seemed to David more like tract housing in the San Fernando Valley. Then it was on to something called Beijing Riviera, which boasted luxuriously furnished resort homes complete with central air conditioning, steam showers, Jacuzzis, and heated towel racks. From here they swung back to central Beijing and the Evergreen Gardens.

"This is a wonderful place for families," Miss Quo explained.

"I don't have a family," David said.

Miss Quo's face crinkled. Between her giggles he ascertained that rentals were $18 U.S. per square meter for lease or $1,188 U.S. per meter if he wanted to buy. He would have needed a calculator to figure this out, but it seemed expensive. But all the prices seemed either confusing or staggering. At the Beijing International Friendship Garden, David was told that he could make "a fifty percent investment and realize a hundred and twenty percent realization of aspiration"—whatever that meant. During the day, as he'd tried to pin down actual prices, he'd heard everything from a low of $6,000 U.S. to a high of $12,000 U.S. a month for a suite with one office and a reception area for Miss Quo.

"You're telling me that in a city where the annual income is— what?—about a thousand dollars, that I have to pay this much for a couple of rooms?"

Miss Quo smiled prettily. "These are your choices. Which one do you want?"

But this was nothing compared to the exorbitant sums that were thrown around for what he considered basic office necessities. Installing a phone line ranged from a paltry $20 to an outlandish $1,400. A fax line cost even more. If he wanted a telex machine, one could be brought in, he was assured, but this too could range anywhere from $100 to $2,800. Even basic essentials like electricity weren't fixed and depended on the building, on the development company's representative, and on Miss Quo's rapport with that person. And they hadn't even gotten to the question of a car and driver.

At four, Lo dropped Miss Quo back at the Kempinski, then edged into the thickening late afternoon traffic. David closed his eyes and dozed off into a jet-lag nap. The next thing he knew, the car had pulled to a stop and someone had opened his door. He felt cool breath on his cheek, then heard Hulan say, "Wake up, David."

As soon as they were inside the compound with the door closed behind them, David took her in his arms, burying his face in her neck. He pulled away and looked down into her face. She was beautiful. She took one of his hands, and together they wordlessly walked to her quarters at the back of the compound. In her living room they kissed. There was no need for words: they were desperate for each other's touch. Hulan pulled at his shoulders, edging him quickly into the bedroom.

Several hours later they lay entwined in one another's arms. They were parched, exhausted, and happy. Finally Hulan got up, slipped on her silk robe, wandered out to the kitchen, and came back with glasses of cool mineral water and a tray laden with grapes, slices of watermelon, and slivers of orange. She placed the tray on the sheet, puffed up the pillows, and propped herself up next to David.

"So," she asked, "how was your day?"

He told her how he'd been pushed in and out of buildings by a highly organized little demon named Miss Quo.

"You're very fortunate to have Quo Xuesheng," Hulan said, breaking off a piece of watermelon.

"You know her?" David asked rather dubiously.

"Since she was a baby. She's the daughter of the minister of the Foreign Enterprise Service Corporation. You were assigned someone very high up. You must have very good *guanxi*," she said in mock serious tones, then popped a grape into her mouth.

"You arranged this?"

"You have to hire someone. You might as well have a friend. After I got off the phone with you, I called Miss Quo's father. The minister was very happy to place his daughter with you."

"Do the people at Phillips, MacKenzie know?"

Hulan shrugged.

"And she's a Red Princess?" David asked.

"In two ways. Her grandfather was on the Long March, while her father has made millions in his government position."

"So she knows who I am."

Hulan smiled and nodded.

"And she knew perfectly well that I didn't need an apartment."

"Um, I don't know about that. That may have been a test for both of us." She leaned over and reached for another grape. As she did this, her robe fell open, exposing the curve of her breasts. "It wouldn't be a bad idea for you to take a small apartment just to keep gossip down."

"Will it be better for you?"

She closed her eyes and played out different scenarios in her head. When she opened them, she said, "Take an apartment, but you'll live here."

"She showed me space in the Capital Mansion."

Hulan shook her head and laughed. "That's because she lives there, just like Guang Henglai and Cao Hua did. It's very popular with the young crowd."

"Well, I'm not going there."

"No, of course not. I know a good space for you. It's not fancy, but it is close by. We'll look at it tomorrow."

"Okay, but I don't want to pay through the nose."

Hulan smiled. "It's not you. It's the firm."

"Still, I don't like to be treated like a sucker."

"You'll be treated like a foreigner no matter what."

"Which means getting fleeced?"

David told her about the prices that he was expected to pay for a fax line.

"That's not so bad," she said. "Consider this: Until a couple of years ago, foreigners could only send faxes during the day because the government surveillance people who monitored the lines all went home at five."

"But that's no longer in effect?" he asked, relieved.

"No, it's still in effect. We just have people working all night now."

"They can't possibly monitor *every* fax!"

Hulan shrugged again, and a little more flesh was exposed. "Believe what you want to believe." She pulled another grape from the stem. This time she slipped it and the tip of her index finger into David's mouth. "If you think that's unfair, think about what you—or rather the firm—must be paying your Miss Quo."

But David didn't respond with words, overcome as he was by the reflexive stirring he felt in his loins. Hulan let her finger languidly trace a path from his lips, down across his chest, to where the cotton sheet edged against his skin. Her voice was husky as she said, "The typical translator makes about seven hundred dollars U.S. a month of which the state-run agency receives about six hundred and thirty dollars. Then you look at someone like your Miss Quo, a Red Princess, very well connected. Phillips, MacKenzie is probably paying her a hundred thousand dollars a year." But David had heard enough. He covered her mouth with his, and they continued a far more intimate conversation.

8

ON DAVID AND HULAN'S FIRST FULL DAY TOGETHER, SAT-
urday, Investigator Lo picked them up and took them to a building
not far from her home. The corner office suite was simple. The walls were
painted white; the furniture was restrained; there was a phone, a copy
machine, a fax, and a television set. The view presented a panorama of
Beijing. Looking behind him, David could see into the courtyards of
Hulan's—and his—*hutong* neighborhood. Stretching out in front of him
were the red burnished walls of the Forbidden City. After looking at the
office, they rode the elevator up four flights to see an apartment, which
came fully furnished and with the same spectacular view. Miss Quo
arrived and she and Hulan carried on a lively conversation in Mandarin.
At the end of it, Hulan switched back to English. "Good, then everything
is taken care of. Attorney Stark will be here Tuesday at nine."

On Sunday and Monday, they stayed home. While Hulan puttered
around the house, David continued familiarizing himself with the
Tartan-Knight paperwork and the list of prospective clients given to him
by Miles Stout. On Tuesday, July 15, they both rose to the sounds of the
*yang ge* troupe. David showered, shaved, and dressed in a lightweight
suit. When he came out to the kitchen, Hulan was standing over the
stove, stirring a pot of *congee*. David ate, then it was time for him to leave.
Arrangements still hadn't been made for a driver, so Investigator Lo took
David down to his new office.

At this point Hulan should have showered, dressed, and gotten on her Flying Pigeon bicycle to go to the Ministry of Public Security. She did none of these things. Instead she went back to bed, took a nap, got up just before noon, then rode her bike down to David's new office and took him out for lunch. That afternoon she went to the open-air market, bought some greens, ginger, garlic, salted black beans, and a little fresh pork, carried them home, and prepared dinner. When David returned, she asked him about his day.

In the morning he'd met with the representative of a hotel that was in a dispute with a California winery over a shipment of chardonnay. His next appointment was with an American man who came with his Chinese partner. They had a factory that manufactured women's clothing made from pigskin. For five years this venture had operated smoothly, with the products having a steady growth in the United States. Unfortunately, the tanner had become involved with some unsavory types, and now the whole enterprise faced investigation by the government. The American in particular was worried about his rights. Was there anything that David could do to help?

At a quarter to five, David and Miss Quo left the office, and Investigator Lo drove them to the Zhongnanhai compound next to the Forbidden City to meet with Governor Sun Gan, who served on the Central Committee representing Shanxi Province. As the car pushed through traffic, Miss Quo ran through David's itinerary for his trip to Knight International. On Thursday, he would have private meetings with the American managers of the factory and the Knights—father and son. On Friday, they would meet with Governor Sun and the other VIP-ers, as Miss Quo called Randall Craig and the Tartan team. On Saturday, after a ceremony at the Knight compound, they would all fly back to Beijing on the two companies' private jets for a series of banquets and meetings with top officials from Knight, Tartan, and the Chinese government. Miles Stout would also fly in to attend. The Sunday evening banquet would culminate in the signing of the closing documents.

Once at the Zhongnanhai compound, Miss Quo led the way to the small private office the governor used while in Beijing. She made the introductions, carefully translating the conversation. By the quality of the fabric and cut, David surmised that Sun's navy blue pinstripe suit had been tailored either in Hong Kong or London. Despite this surface sophistication and his age—Sun looked to be in his late sixties—his ruddy complexion and the strength of his handshake attested to a life spent largely outdoors in physical labor.

The two men sat down in overstuffed burgundy velvet chairs, while Miss Quo took a straight-back chair a little to David's left. For the next couple of minutes Miss Quo spoke in Mandarin. David recognized certain words—*baba* and *cha*—and knew that they were exchanging pleasantries about Miss Quo's father and negotiating the ever important issue of whether or not the guests would drink tea. Their chatter came to a close. Sun himself poured three cups of tea, and then he began to speak in a smooth, confident voice, pausing occasionally to let Miss Quo translate. During the next twenty minutes, as Sun spoke in glowing terms of the attributes of his home province, he never took his eyes off David. Under other circumstances David might have chafed under this scrutiny, but Sun had a warmth about him. He was down-to-earth and, if Miss Quo's translation was accurate, very direct.

"Governor Sun wishes you to know that he has encouraged many foreign businesses to come to his province," Miss Quo said as Sun came to the conclusion of his remarks. "Every year it becomes easier to reach. Shanxi has built a new expressway, making Taiyuan only five hours away from Beijing by car or bus, while a plane takes only minutes. He thinks it's important for you to know that he believes that within ten years his province will be a leader for economic investment in the interior."

"How does Governor Sun plan to accomplish his goals?"

Miss Quo dutifully translated David's question, listened as Sun replied in Mandarin, then said, "As you know, China is in a period of great change. Supreme Leader Deng Xiaoping encouraged us to move forward with economic reform."

"To get rich is glorious," David quoted.

"Precisely." Miss Quo nodded. "But there are some things that he did not want to see change. Since his death our country can now move forward on some of those programs. This is what Governor Sun is promoting here in Beijing as well as in Shanxi. Historically, he says, change can only come from the countryside. He has proposed one-person, one-vote balloting in local elections that would be open to party and non-party candidates alike. He has worked hard to abolish rice-eating finance."

At David's puzzled look, she explained, "This is a phrase used by Premier Zhu Rongji. It means he wants to cut our country's bureaucracy, which so often promotes corruption. Governor Sun greatly supports these new ideas and believes that they will eventually lead to greater freedoms for the Chinese people, increased prosperity, and a better relationship with our brothers in the West."

"That all sounds wonderful," David said. "But why has Governor Sun invited me here?"

Miss Quo didn't attempt to hide her displeasure. "You ask too forward a question."

"It doesn't matter, Miss Quo," Sun said, speaking in near-perfect English.

David had fallen for one of the oldest tricks in the Chinese book. Of course this man would speak English.

"I thought it would be wise to meet you before we see each other at Knight International," Sun said. "I have nothing but the greatest respect for Mr. Knight and Mr. Craig. Henry Knight is an old friend while Mr. Craig is new. Still, I think it is good for us to become friends ourselves. In this manner the road of business is smooth."

"I agree fully," David said.

Sun offered David a saucer filled with dried watermelon seeds. "But I must admit that I have what you would probably call ulterior reasons for meeting with you today," Sun continued. "Like many of us in China who read the newspaper or watch television, I'm familiar with the good work you did for our country earlier this year. But we both know that what was in the news was not the full truth of those days. I do hope you'll forgive my immodesty when I say that I've been permitted the great privilege of sitting in on conversations with people very high in our government who are aware of the true nature of your deeds. Our nation has been honored by your work in uncovering corruption in our government as well as in your own."

David was in a country with the world's largest population, and yet he felt as though he had moved to a small town where everyone knew everyone else's business. Before he could say anything, however, Sun went on.

"I too am very concerned about corruption. As Premier Zhu has observed, the collecting of illegal fees sows seething discontent among the people. So, as you might say, you and I are on the same wavelength. I think that two people of such like minds should work together. I would be honored if you would accept me as a client."

"Are you in trouble?" David asked, the litigator in him showing through.

An awkward silence followed, and David felt Miss Quo's disapproving eyes on him. Then Sun laughed heartily and said, "Some people say that bluntness is the worst trait of Americans. In China we would never use words so freely. Well, maybe after you and I had known each other for ten thousand years and had been meeting here every day for ten thousand weeks, perhaps then you would have shown this weakness. But actually this characteristic is what I love about Americans as a people. You speak your mind. It makes you so very transparent, but I must admit it is refreshing."

The remarks were condescending, but Sun's affability took the sting out of them.

"To answer your question," Sun continued, "no, I'm not in trouble. But people have many reasons to need lawyers."

"I'm not an expert on Chinese law," David said. "You'd be better served by a Chinese law firm."

"You see, Miss Quo, there he is showing his open heart to us again," Sun said.

Miss Quo cast her eyes down modestly, pleased that her new boss had fallen into favor with such a powerful man.

"I don't need someone who is familiar with Chinese law," Sun said after a moment. "As your Miss Quo has already explained, I act on behalf of my province and my country when foreign companies come calling. I have actively sought foreign investment in Shanxi. You must understand, until very recently we didn't do much business using contracts. You don't need things like that when the government owns every business, factory, and farm. So in China we've had many problems with outsiders as we negotiate our deals. I think foreigners would be pleased to deal with someone like you who understands their ways. What I'm proposing is that you represent me both as an individual, for I have many investments of my own, and as the representative of Shanxi Province."

"It would be a conflict for me to represent you in any dealings with Tartan," David said.

"Again, that's just one deal. It's my job to bring many foreign companies to Shanxi."

"If I represent you, I'll be privy to many aspects of your business. There may be things you won't want Tartan to know and vice versa."

"Lawyers are supposed to be discreet."

"Discretion isn't the problem," David said. "Many clients simply prefer to know that there'll never be a chance that their affairs will be anything other than completely private, that work product won't somehow get misplaced or misfiled, that no one will be in the office and glance at something they shouldn't see."

"What you're saying, Attorney Stark, is making me nervous about you *and* Phillips, MacKenzie . . ."

"We are scrupulous with all work product, but accidents can happen. Not to mention . . ."

When David hesitated, Sun finished for him. "You're in China and you can't guarantee complete confidentiality anyway."

David turned his palms up and surrendered to that truth, then added, "In addition, what if five years from now there's a disagreement between you and Tartan?"

"There won't be," Sun said.

"But what if there were?" David persisted. "Wouldn't you want to know that your affairs had always been totally secure?"

"We're both working toward the same ends," Sun said. "There are no conflicts and there never will be."

"Still, if there were, I'd have to choose which client I'd represent. I'm afraid it would have to be Tartan."

"Because it's a bigger client than I am."

"And because my firm has represented Tartan longer."

"This is all right with me."

"Then let me call my office and Tartan to see how they feel about it. I'll get back to you as soon as I can with their answers as well as a waiver that you'll need to sign."

Governor Sun stood, signaling the end of the meeting. He shook David's hand, looked deeply into his eyes, and said, "As soon as you get your waiver, I'll send you a report of my various activities." He walked David and Miss Quo to the door. He bowed his head. "If you need anything before I see you later this week, please call my assistant Amy Gao." Then Sun turned his attention to a delegation of businessmen waiting in the foyer.

"There's something quite wonderful about listening to people's troubles, then trying to help them," David said to Hulan that night. "I made a couple of phone calls this afternoon and was able to resolve the problems with the winery. The pig thing will be a little more difficult, but Miss Quo has already drafted a couple of letters to whom she says are the right people. Hopefully we'll be able to have some meetings at the beginning of next week after the signing of the Knight deal and those pig guys can go back to their manufacturing with no more problems."

Hulan thought David still had a lot to learn about the way things worked in China.

He'd saved the news of his meeting with Governor Sun for last. Hulan absorbed the details, listening carefully for the usual Chinese nuances that David might have missed. They both laughed when he told her about the new Beijing-Taiyuan expressway. "How was I supposed to know it existed?" Hulan asked, groaning in mock horror at the needless misery she'd put herself through on those two trains, while at the same time thinking just how far removed Suchee and the others she'd met in Da Shui were from this life-changing news.

They laughed even harder when David got to the part about Sun speaking perfect English. "I should have known better," David said. "I *do* know better!"

"But?"

"Jet lag?" he tried. And again they laughed. Then he said, "Thank you."

"For what?"

"For Sun. Landing him as a client is a coup. I know I owe that to you."

"But I didn't do anything."

"He isn't a friend or some part of the Red Prince network?"

"I've never met him. I've seen him, of course. He was at Deng's funeral. He's a powerful man, David. Very important."

"So how did he . . ."

"As Sun said himself, your reputation precedes you. Besides, Miss Quo has impeccable connections."

David thought for a moment, then asked, "All that pro-democracy, pro-capitalism talk, isn't that dangerous?"

"A year ago, even three months ago I would have said yes. But Deng is dead. Look at who runs the country now. President Jiang Zemin is trying to recast the U.S. as China's friend, not its enemy. As mayor of Shanghai, Zhu Rongzi brought that city back to world prominence. Now that he's premier, he hopes to do the same for the whole country. I don't know much about Sun, except that he's trying to do for his entire province what Zhu did for Shanghai. It doesn't take a mathematician to add this up. Today Sun is one of one hundred and seventy-five people on the Central Committee. People say he's vying to become one of the seventeen members of the Politburo. From there maybe he'll go onto the five-man Standing Committee. Then again, maybe he can bypass those steps entirely and go straight to the top. In ten, twenty years, he could have it all."

"You like him."

Hulan shrugged. "Again, I don't know him personally, but I like what he says. He'll be a great client for you."

"I don't know," David said. When Hulan looked at him quizzically, he continued, "I don't know much about the way things work here. I don't understand the politics. I go out on the streets and see capitalism. I come home and you tell me about communist party rule. I have trouble meshing those two ideas."

"But you don't have to. Listen to what he said: He wants your help in working with foreigners, because the rituals are different. He said it; you just didn't hear it. In a Chinese deal the negotiations are intricate: will tea be offered, will you accept it, who will sit at what part of the table, who enters the room first. Effusive compliments are exchanged but never accepted. You can never say what you want or what you'll concede. The 'final' contract is never the last version. On the eve of signing or just before a big banquet, there are always 'a few last matters to attend to.' Negotiations can go on for months, sometimes years. This is true in business and personal relationships, but it's absolutely contrary to the American way. When you tell me Sun wants you to help him cut through all that, I like him even more."

"But he's a politician, Hulan."

"He's not just any politician. He's a forward thinker. If he needs help, I think you should give it to him. That's what you do best—help people who are on the side of right."

David didn't like the idea of getting involved in politics, but if Hulan thought Sun was a good guy, then what could David do but help him, because as Hulan said, this was what he did best. He tried to explain the heart of it to Hulan.

"I guess it doesn't matter to me if a client is big or not. Like today with those people who were manufacturing clothes out of pigskin. I enjoyed talking to them. It pleased me that with a couple of phone calls I could fix their problem or at least make some headway. But a politician is different. I'm not convinced about how complex his deals are. I worry about integrity. I worry about what I won't understand. I worry about what Sun's real problems are and why he wasn't forthright about them. Because he must have them or else he wouldn't come to me. Still, as a lawyer I can look at his problems and steer him in the right direction, but . . ." He drew the word out as he thought back. "I remember once seeing a painting of a shipwreck. There was a lighthouse and the beam reflected over the water, but that still hadn't prevented the ship from hitting the rocks. That's how I see what I do, Hulan. There's the sense that you can orient to the light in the darkness and even know the waters, but if a surprise current comes up or a fog descends, then suddenly logic and experience might not be enough to stop disaster from occurring."

On Wednesday they were awakened as usual by the *yang ge* troupe. This time David said he wanted to go out and see it. They dressed and a few minutes later stepped out into the alleyway. Standing at David's side, Hulan saw the dancers in a new way. How sweet they were in their colorful costumes. How dear to see these old people like Madame Zhang and Madame Ri with their smiling faces and delicate movements. Even the music that had sounded so loud and inharmonic to her ears now sounded festive and gay. And at her side was David. He was dressed casually in khakis, a button-down shirt open at the neck, and loafers. His body was loose and relaxed as he leaned lackadaisically with one shoulder against the wall of the Liu family compound. Hulan edged closer to him, and he draped his arm easily over her shoulder. She felt cautiously happy.

Still, David was a foreigner and Hulan's neighbors had been aware of his presence since the night he had arrived in the *hutong*. So, when Neighborhood Committee Director Zhang came knocking at the door an hour after the troupe dispersed, Hulan was ready for her. She escorted Madame Zhang out to the garden, where David was on the phone speaking to Miles Stout about Governor Sun and explaining all the conflict issues. David looked up, said into the phone, "Miles, I have to go, but if you get a waiver from Tartan, fax it to me as soon as possible. I'd like to represent Sun if we can." Then he hung up, stood, and took Madame Zhang's knobby hand in his for a light handshake.

Madame Zhang took an appreciatively noisy sip of chrysanthemum tea, then said in Chinese, "The foreigner has come again. I see he has been here for five days already."

"Yes, auntie," Hulan agreed.

"I suspect that he has plans to stay longer."

"I hope so," Hulan said.

"You have not come to me for a marriage permit."

Hulan glanced over to David, who was trying to look interested, but was totally unaware of the meaning of the conversation. "There is no plan for marriage."

"This man is the father of your baby," Madame Zhang stated.

"You know that to be true."

Madame Zhang grunted. She shifted her frame in her chair to stare at David directly. She leaned forward and said to him as if in confidence, "One drop of piss can ruin the well for everyone. The people of our neighborhood would not like to see this happen. Our citizens are good people. We don't want trouble with the higher-ups."

David smiled and asked Hulan what the Neighborhood Committee director had said.

"On behalf of all our neighbors, she welcomes you to the *hutong*. She says that America is an inspiring country, and she looks forward to many interesting conversations with you in the future."

"*Xie-xie*," David said to the older woman. Then he addressed Hulan, "Please tell Madame Zhang that I'm very happy to call this place my home."

Hulan translated this as "Attorney Stark says that he is happy to visit China again, and he will do his best to obey all rules of the neighborhood and the country."

Madame Zhang snorted, then roughly cleared her throat. "Well then," she said again to David. "I expect to have a request for a marriage certificate very soon, as it is not a custom in our country for this certificate to come *after* the one for a baby."

Again Hulan translated: "Our Committee director says that when good things come, they come in a pair. She is gladdened that you have come and that we are together."

David reached over and took the startled older woman's hand. "I will do everything I can to make Hulan happy."

Madame Zhang pulled her scrabbly hand out of the foreigner's grasp and hastily stood. "We make allowances for you, Liu Hulan, but please remember to be careful." Then she bowed to David and hurriedly left the compound muttering to herself about the curious ways of *wai guo ren*.

Hulan might have been able to camouflage Madame Zhang's disapproval, but she had a far more difficult time when she and David met Vice Minister Zai later at a restaurant for dim sum. Vice Minister Zai spoke English. He was a shrewd man and a survivor of many political upheavals. Once the assortment of little dishes and miniature steamers were set on the table, he said to Hulan, "Your mother was well enough to speak with me on the phone yesterday."

These words hit Hulan deeply. She hadn't forgotten Jinli—she'd spoken to her mother's nurse every day since they'd gone to Beidaihe—but she'd selfishly guarded her happiness and her privacy with David.

"I think the sea air agrees with Mama," Hulan said. "I'm happy she's where she can enjoy the cool ocean breezes."

"She was away from you for many years . . ."

"I know this, uncle."

Hulan always used the honorific when she wanted to imply a closer relationship. In truth, theirs was much closer than even uncle and niece. With her own father there had always been layer upon layer of hidden meaning, but with Zai, Hulan knew that his hidden meanings—even when they preyed upon her filial duties and underlying guilt—were always in her best interests.

"Then she will be returning to Beijing soon?"

"After David and I return from the countryside."

David put down his chopsticks and smiled. "I didn't know you were coming with me."

"I asked Miss Quo to buy tickets for both of us."

"She didn't tell me," David said.

"You didn't ask."

In the excitement of the last few days, David and Hulan hadn't talked about her visit to the countryside, nor had she seen Vice Minister Zai to tell him about it. Now Hulan quickly recounted her trip and what she'd seen—the mysterious floor plans and other records Suchee had shown her, the incongruity of the death scene, the bizarre encounter she'd had in the village café, the official visit to the factory during which she'd seen little, and finally her decision that the only way to know what was going on there was to get inside.

"There's something strange about that place," she said. "Otherwise they would have let me see the whole facility."

"But whatever is happening there surely has nothing to do with the suicide of your daughter's friend," Zai said.

"Not to mention that Knight is important to me right now," David added. "The sale's my main reason for being in Beijing."

"I thought I was your reason for being here," Hulan said.

"You know what I mean, Hulan."

Vice Minister Zai held up his hands to silence the two of them. "There's no need to disagree, because Hulan has no reason to go out to the countryside at all." He turned to Hulan. "You have a job here in the city. I gave you a few personal days off to visit your friend, which you did. Now, although you have returned to the capital, you have not come back to work."

"David needs my help getting settled in."

"He has Miss Quo for that." Zai paused, then said, "When I was a boy, we had a saying about women. Never come out the front gate, or walk across the second gate. Do you know what that means? In a compound like your family's, women not only didn't go out into the street, but most were not expected to go into the far courtyards. But you were not born in feudal times, Hulan. You don't need to stay at home to be considered a good woman."

Hulan blushed and looked down at her plate.

"I will put this another way," Zai continued. "If you were anyone else, you would have already been reprimanded."

David looked at Hulan, confused. "What's he talking about?"

"Hulan dismissed," Zai explained, "and you expelled from the country."

"I've done nothing wrong," David said.

"Foreigners are not allowed to have affairs with Chinese citizens," Hulan said softly.

"We're not having an affair," David corrected.

Hulan shrugged. "You call it one thing. The government calls it another."

Zai spoke to Hulan in Mandarin: "I protected your father for many years, Hulan. I don't regret that. But you make a mistake if you think my actions aren't being monitored. As for you, I want to remind you of the newspapers. You have money, but that can't always protect you. Again, I refer to what happened to your father."

"Excuse me," David interrupted. "Please speak in English."

But no one translated the last exchange for him.

"I need to get into that factory," Hulan repeated, switching back to English for David's benefit.

"And what of the baby, Hulan?" Zai asked. "If you can't be concerned for yourself, shouldn't you be concerned for its safety?"

With these words the past few weeks rippled through Hulan's mind—the boring cases, the light workload, the protectiveness of Investigator Lo. Zai must have known about the pregnancy all along.

Hulan tried a different tack. "A minute ago you were chiding me for being old-fashioned. Now you're telling me I can't do something because I'm pregnant."

"These are two different things," he said. "Am I not right, David?"

As an American, David was having trouble with this conversation. It was too personal to be having with his girlfriend's boss. Besides, what Zai said went to deep questions about the roles of men and women, of fathers and mothers, to which David wasn't sure he knew the answers. But David was a lawyer and knew how to move a conversation in another direction if he had to.

"If you're so worried about corruption," David said to Hulan, "you don't need to go out to the countryside to find it. In a few days here in Beijing I've seen several instances of corruption involving foreigners: those office buildings, the fees for hooking up phones, what you told me about the salaries for translators—"

"Everything you've seen is perfectly legal," Hulan interrupted impatiently. "Foreigners have more money than the Chinese people. They should pay more."

"A hundred grand for a secretary?"

"Could your secretary in Los Angeles set you up with new clients? Could she introduce you to the most important people in the city? How do you think you got your new legal matters so quickly?"

Again Zai attempted to act as peacemaker. "What David says is true. You don't need to go to the countryside to find corruption. You can find it right here in Beijing."

"I don't like to hear you say those words," she said.

"And I don't like the idea of you, my true heart daughter, going into that place."

"Uncle, you trained me. You taught me how to look. There is something going on in that factory. I feel it."

"If there is, then leave it to the local police," Zai said.

"And what if they're involved?"

When Zai jutted his chin, dismissing the accusation, Hulan felt David's hand cover hers.

"I don't like it," David said to Zai. "You don't like it. But can we stop her? Let her come down with me. She might not even be able to get into the factory. Then this whole thing will be over."

"And if I don't agree?" Zai asked.

"She'll probably do it anyway." David turned to Hulan. "I'm telling you, nothing's going on at Knight. I've seen the records. But if you want to spend a day in the factory, if that will put your mind at ease, then fine. Do it. But then let's not hear about it ever again."

"One day in the factory. No more," Zai conceded. "And I have one other condition. Investigator Lo accompanies you to the countryside. He can act as David's driver if you choose, but I want someone nearby who can look out for you if things go bad."

"They won't," David said. "She'll be perfectly safe, because the factory is perfectly safe. At the end of the day she'll come out of there tired, and that will be the end of it."

"She needs to be back in the office on Monday," Zai insisted, continuing the negotiation. "No more days off until the baby comes."

"Agreed," David said.

The men, having reached an understanding, looked at Hulan for her approval. But in listening to them debate what she could and could not do, Hulan had the strangest sensation of her life options drifting out of her control. She weighed what David had said. She trusted his judgment, but what if he was wrong and something criminal *was* going on at Knight? What if he was reading this with the same eyes that told him that his own reputation had brought in his first round of clients and not Miss Quo's connections?

There were deeper issues too. She didn't like to show her emotions either in public or private. Yet when David said he'd come here for work and not for her, she'd immediately revealed her hurt. When David made the comment about corruption in Beijing, she'd reacted by criticizing the U.S. Two hours ago she'd seen happiness before her; now she felt trapped. But had these feelings come from the realities of the conversation, from her own fluctuating hormones, or from a deeper belief that she didn't deserve happiness?

Finally, if something illegal was going on at Knight and it was somehow connected to Miaoshan's suicide, then going into the factory *could* put her and her child in danger. Why hadn't she thought of that? Why hadn't she thought of that all the way down the line—when she'd gone out on those easy cases in Beijing, when she'd hopped the train to go out to Da Shui, when she'd traipsed through the fields to see Tsai Bing, when she'd entered that strange café, when she'd visited the local police, or when she'd questioned Sandy Newheart and Aaron Rodgers?

Hulan raised her eyes to meet Zai's. "One week," she said, "and I will go back to my place." Those words could have many meanings, and she wasn't sure she understood any of them.

# 9

HULAN HAD FORGOTTEN HOW EASY IT WAS TO TRAVEL with a foreigner. By paying almost double what a typical Chinese national would pay, Miss Quo picked up two round-trip airline tickets from a travel agency. David gave instructions for Investigator Lo to fly down tomorrow, rent a car, and meet him at the Shanxi Grand Hotel. Hulan packed clothes that would be appropriate for any official meetings that might come up, as well as some old work clothes she found in the back of her closet.

An hour and twenty minutes after takeoff, they arrived in Taiyuan. A half hour after that they registered in the hotel. Upon check-in David was handed several envelopes. In their room, while Hulan unpacked, David read the faxes. Most were inconsequential, but two were important. One was from Miles, saying that Tartan saw no problems with David representing Governor Sun. In fact, it might prove useful. The second was the promised waiver from Tartan. The last was from Rob Butler; no new leads had turned up in the Rising Phoenix investigation. David wrote a couple of letters himself, and on their way through the lobby he handed them to the concierge to be faxed ASAP.

They ate in the hotel dining room, where they ordered the specialties of the region—thick *tounao* soup, steamed pork with pickled greens, and a plate of flavorful noodles. Hulan drank tea, while David sipped *fen jiu*, a strong wine from vineyards located to the north of the city. After dinner

Hulan packed a separate bag with simple clothes, kissed David good-bye, promised that she would be back the next night, and left. She took the local bus back out to the crossroads near Da Shui Village and walked the final few *li* to Suchee's home.

The following morning, as David was taking a hot shower, Hulan washed her face with cold water. While David shaved, Hulan took a pair of Suchee's blunt scissors and cut her hair until the edges were uneven. While he put on a lightweight suit, Hulan slipped on some loose gray pants that came mid-calf and a short-sleeve white blouse, both of which were soft and thin from years of wear and many washings. (As the saying went: New for three years, old for three years, mending and fixing for another three years. These clothes fit the last category.) Then, while David perused the many dishes adorning the hotel's elaborate breakfast buffet, Hulan joined Suchee for a simple breakfast of a green onion pulled fresh from the earth tucked into a bun. At about the time that David opened his laptop to check his e-mail, Hulan took one last look at herself in Suchee's hand mirror and then set out across the fields.

By seven, when Hulan arrived at the Silk Thread Café, the old-timers had already taken their places for the day and were sucking at cups of tea, picking their teeth with toothpicks, and smoking cigarettes. The man who'd so brazenly spoken to Hulan during her last visit called out, "Good morning! You have come to see us again. Perhaps you have reconsidered our offer!"

Hulan kept her eyes lowered. She spoke softly, humbly. "I have."

The man pulled himself out of his chair and crossed to Hulan. "Where have you been all this time?"

"I went to Beijing. People in my village say it's easy to go there and find work, but no one would hire me." Hulan's voice filled with anxiety. "They are not nice to country bumpkins like me."

"Like you? Like me, too!" The man signaled the waitress to bring tea, then said, "Sit down. I can help you."

The waitress brought the tea, poured it, and left without a word. Hulan's fingers shyly edged across the tabletop to her cup. The man said, "Take the tea. It will relax you and we can talk." As Hulan sipped, she kept her eyes focused on the greasy tabletop. The whole time she could feel the man appraising her. "Do you still have the papers I gave you?" he asked at last.

Hulan nodded and gave them back already filled out. She'd tried to answer each question as simply as possible, knowing that the closer to the truth her lies were, the easier they would be to remember.

"Liu Hulan," the man read aloud, glancing up at her. "A good, common name for women your age. There are probably some other Liu Hulans at the factory. You might enjoy meeting them. Your birthplace? Umm . . ." He crossed out what Hulan had written, then wrote in new characters. "We'll say Da Shui Village. It's less complicated that way. Now, what are your special skills?"

"Until my husband died, I worked in our fields. I can also cook, sew, clean, wash . . ."

The man shook his head impatiently. "They will teach you everything you need to know. Any illnesses?"

"No."

"Good," the man said. "Now sign here." When Hulan faltered, he said, "What is it?"

"How much will I earn?"

"Ah," he said, drawing out the syllable and assessing her again. "You are a thinking woman. Impudent but thinking."

Hulan stared at the man noncommittally.

"The contract is for three years," he said. "As I told you before, the factory will pay you five hundred *yuan* a month, plus room and board. You will have Saturday afternoons and Sundays off. You may leave the compound during those times, but since you don't live in a neighboring village, you will be allowed to stay in the dormitory for a small fee. You won't be lonesome, because most of the women who work there are from far away."

Hulan picked up the pen and signed.

The man's solicitous attitude instantly evaporated. "The bus comes at eight o'clock. It will stop right outside the village. Please wait there." With that he scooped up her contract and walked away.

Hulan raised her eyes and saw the man hunker back down into his group. She picked up her satchel, left the village, and went to stand on the dusty patch of land that passed for Da Shui's parking lot. At quarter to eight two other women arrived. Hulan ascertained that one of them, Jingren, about eighteen, had—like Hulan's cover story—retraced her steps to this town after failing to find work in Beijing. The other, Mayli, was about fifteen. She'd come here from Sichuan Province after some labor scouts had come to her village promising work in either Guang- dong Province or Shanxi Province, even though she was below legal hirable age. The salaries were the same, Mayli explained, but if she came here, she was only a six-day bus ride from her village.

"And no other women came with you?"

"Oh, there were many girls from my village who got on the buses. Have you been on a bus before?" When Hulan said she hadn't, Mayli said, "Everyone has her own meals packed. This is okay on the first day, but on the second day, with the smells and the winding road, many people were getting sick. For me it was very bad. The other girls are com- plaining, because I am so sick. Finally the bus driver can't stand it any- more. He leaves me in another village. I am there for five days. Can you believe it? But I had signed my contract, and the bus had to come back for me. I got here last night." She gestured back toward the village. "They found me a place to sleep. They said they usually send new girls to the factory on Sunday nights, so they can get processed first thing in the morning and work a full week. But they also have a bus that comes every day to nearby villages to pick up stragglers." Mayli looked at Hulan and Jingren. "What does that mean, to be processed?"

Before either woman could answer, the bus rounded the corner. It was neither a city nor a provincial bus, for it was far older than even those that usually plied country roads. The bus stopped and the door wheezed open. The three women picked up their parcels and climbed aboard. About a dozen women were already on the bus. Most of them had spread out their possessions so that no one would sit next to them. The driver ground the gears and began to pull away even before the three newcomers had found seats. Then someone at the back of the bus shouted, "Wait! Someone's coming!" The driver stopped, threw open the door, and Tang Siang, her hair a windblown mess, hopped up the steps. "I don't wait for people," the driver said. "Next time I will keep driving."

"It won't happen again," Siang called out over her shoulder as she came down the aisle, trailing her belongings behind her. She plopped down in a seat across from Hulan. After she'd arranged her gear, she looked across the aisle at Hulan, trying to place her. "I know you."

"I am the friend of Ling Suchee."

"Yes, I remember now, but you look different."

Hulan ignored the remark, introduced her to Mayli and Jingren, then said, "I'm surprised to see you here."

Tang Siang ran her fingers through her hair. "It will surprise everyone, I think."

"Did you run away from home?" Mayli asked.

"Something like that, yes." Looking at the expectant faces, Siang said, "My father is a strong man. I can even say he is a wealthy man in our village, but he is old-fashioned. He thinks he can tell me what to do, but I don't have to do it."

"What about Tsai Bing?" Hulan asked.

When Siang didn't answer, Mayli, her voice filled with girlish excitement, asked a series of questions. "Do you have a boyfriend? Are you betrothed? Is it for love or is it arranged?"

Listening to the three young women, Hulan thought back to her own girlhood—first on the Red Soil Farm, then later as a foreign student at the boarding school in Connecticut. She remembered her own naïve dreams of how her life would be and realized that those dreams weren't much different on either continent, nor had they been truly changed by time or culture.

"I am not engaged," Siang said. "Not yet anyway."

"Your father doesn't approve," Mayli said sympathetically.

"Men want a lot of things," Siang said, trying to sound worldly. "But that doesn't mean I have to give it to them."

Hulan wondered if Siang was talking about her father or Tsai Bing.

"So, did you run away?" Mayli repeated.

Siang tossed her long black hair over her shoulder. "Last night I went to the café. I said I wanted a job. But those men are cowards. They said they couldn't hire me. They said they would tell my father. You want to know what I said?"

Mayli and Jingren nodded.

"I said they would have far more trouble if they didn't hire me. So they let me sign the paper. Then this morning when my father went out to walk his land, I packed my things and came running."

"Won't your father come after you?" Mayli asked.

"My father will not interfere with the foreigners' business. That is one reason I know my plan will work."

Siang had left out some crucial details, but the two other girls didn't seem to mind.

Hulan, who'd listened quietly to their prattling, trying to parse truth from fiction, now went back to a conversation that had started on the dusty street outside the village. "Mayli, when the scouts said you could go to Guangdong or come here, did they say what the difference was in the kinds of work you'd be doing?"

Mayli frowned. "Work is work. What does it matter?"

The other girls agreed. "At least it isn't the fields," Jingren said. "I saw my mother and father die in those fields. Now I'm alone. Maybe now I can earn enough money to go back to my home village and start a business."

Mayli smiled. "My dream is to open a little shop, maybe for clothes."

"I was thinking maybe I'd open a place for hair cutting," Jingren said. "What about you, Siang?"

"My future is beautiful, that I can tell you."

The bus stopped at the big gates to the Knight compound. The driver handed down a clipboard, which the guard checked before stepping back into his kiosk. The gate lifted and the bus drove inside. Now everyone on the bus was silent as they took in the new sights. For Hulan, however, nothing seemed different from when she'd visited before.

As soon as the bus stopped, everyone stood up and started to gather together their belongings until the driver called out, "Stay seated." He left the bus, disappeared into a building marked PROCESSING, and came back five minutes later with a woman dressed in a powder blue gabardine suit, white blouse, nude knee-highs, and black pumps. Her hair was cut in a bob, making her look as familiar as an auntie.

Taking a place at the front of the bus, she said, "Welcome to your new home. I am Party Secretary Leung. I am here to serve the needs of the workers. If you have problems, you come to me." The party secretary motioned to the building to her right. "Your first stop today is the

Processing Center. You may now stand and follow me. Talking is not necessary."

The women on the bus did as they were told. Once inside, other uniformed women guided the new arrivals into two lines. From here Hulan and her companions went through a dizzying round of paperwork. Then they were gathered into another large room and ordered to strip down to their underwear. A nurse did a cursory inspection of all the women, inquiring about rashes, checking eyes and throats, asking about infectious diseases. But all this was perfunctory. There were no reproductive questions, and Hulan didn't volunteer any information about her pregnancy. Even naked she looked almost as thin as the others.

Next they were herded into an auditorium of sorts—a great hangar of a building where the air temperature hovered at about forty degrees centigrade. There were enough benches to seat perhaps a thousand people, but today the handful of new arrivals dotted only the first couple of rows. As soon as the last woman had taken a seat, the lights dimmed and a video about the facility began to play. Narrated by Party Secretary Leung, the video tour was far more complete than what Sandy Newheart had shown Hulan on her previous visit. The dormitories looked clean if utilitarian. This was followed by quick shots of the clinic (with the voice-over explaining that the one-child policy was strictly enforced at this facility), the cafeteria (where smiling women lined up to receive trays of steaming food), the company store (where workers could buy snacks, feminine hygiene products, and Sam & His Friends dolls for friends and family at deep discounts), and the assembly room (which looked no different from what Hulan had seen on her tour).

When the lights came back on, Madame Leung went to stand at a podium. Speaking rapidly, she described the routine—lights on at 6:00, breakfast at 6:30, at your station not one minute later than 7:00, fifteen-minute break at 10:00, a half-hour lunch at 1:00 P.M. At 7:00 the workers were dismissed from their stations. At 7:30 dinner was served. Lights-out occurred promptly at 10:00. "If all the workers meet their quotas," she said, "you can expect to be rewarded with the occasional *xiuxi*." Looking around her, Hulan saw the shock on the other women's faces. *Xiuxi*, late-afternoon naptime, was considered customary throughout the country. "Yes, I know it sounds harsh," Madame Leung acknowledged. "But this is an American company. These foreigners have different ideas about work-days and workers' rights. They expect you to be on time. They do not want to see you eating, spitting, or sleeping at your workplace. Again, I must emphasize, no sleeping on the factory floor, on the cafeteria benches, or anywhere on the grounds outside."

Hulan had spent her teenage and young adult years in the United States, and when she returned to China as an adult she'd been amazed at her countrymen's ability to sleep anywhere, at any time: at cosmetics counters in department stores, slumped on stools in the vegetable mar-ket, or even on the floor in the post office. Workers—usually man-agers—who'd been assigned individual offices were often given a cot as a perk. Even at the MPS many of Hulan's coworkers had cots in their offices.

"Most important," Madame Leung continued, "no men are allowed in the dormitory—ever. This means that all repairs and clean-up are done by us. The Party worked hard to achieve this so that the women who work here will be safe not only from the foreigners but from our own countrymen who would question our virtue."

Hulan felt the relief in the room. How many of these women had fled abusive fathers or unwanted marriages? And with the one-child pol-icy, which had resulted in millions of abortions of female fetuses, women, for the first time in the history of the country, were a valued commodity. If what the party secretary said was true, then these women—some still teenagers—would no longer be at the mercy of ban-dits or other rogue groups who swept through remote villages kidnap-ping women to sell into marriages in distant provinces.

"Punishment for infractions is automatic and severe," Madame Leung went on. "For every missed minute of evening curfew, an extra hour of work will be added to your day. This means if you are not in your dormitory room precisely at ten, the next day you will work until eight. *This* means you will miss dinner."

Madame Leung held up a hand to silence the murmurs of dissatisfac-tion. "This is how things are done in America, so this is how things will be done at your new home," she said sternly. Her hands clasped the podium as she waited for full silence. "Let me continue. If you miss one day of work, you will lose three *yuan* from your salary of two hundred *yuan.* If you miss three days of work in a row, you will be fired."

Again the women muttered among themselves. "I thought the salary was five hundred *yuan* a month," a voice called out.

Madame Leung's disapproving eyes scanned the room. "Who asks this question?" When no one answered, she said, "One day, after you complete your full training, you will be promoted. Until then all of you will be paid two hundred *yuan* a month." She surveyed the room, daring the women to complain. None did. "In a moment you will begin your education, but before you go I want to remind you that I am your government liaison. Please, if you have any problems, come to me. You will always find a receptive ear."

Twenty minutes later, Hulan found herself in yet another vast room, which had the capacity to seat a hundred or more at long tables. But since this was the middle of the week, the instructor explained, there would be only these few women for training. During the rest of the afternoon Hulan moved from one station to the next, getting timed on how quickly she could run fabric through a sewing machine, clip on button eyes, attach the extra gizmos to the cardboard packaging. She thought she was getting quite adept at installing the box that contained the software, until she saw that the others in her group were faster. She kept sneezing when filling the body with its polyester-fiber stuffing and saw the supervisor put a red mark next to her name for that activity. Her next chore was to punch hair into the heads of the dolls. This involved using a tool to run clumps of plastic hair through tiny pre-made holes, then tying off the strands along the interior of the skulls. At each stop the supervisor made a note of Hulan's progress on her clipboard.

Hulan then moved on to a stamping machine. Unused to working with her hands, she was slow at this job, which required quickly moving the doll's plastic face into position so that special attaching holes could be punched through. Within a minute the cutters came down and slashed through the flesh between Hulan's thumb and forefinger on her left hand. Madame Leung shut down the machine and hustled Hulan to the clinic. The nurse pulled out a needle and thread, then, without the aid of either anesthetic or disinfectant, stitched the wound closed. The nurse wrapped gauze around Hulan's hand, tied two torn strips together, told her that the injury was neither significant nor permanent, then said,

"You may go back to work." Madame Leung nodded and escorted Hulan back to the training room. The bandage and the pain exacerbated Hulan's clumsiness, but she found that although she was still not as swift as the others, she could still do the work. More red marks, however, were made next to her name.

At 6:30 they were shown into the deserted cafeteria and given bowls of rice with stir-fried vegetables on top. At seven they heard a siren. Madame Leung reappeared, ushered them into an adjoining room, and told them they could rest for fifteen minutes. Just as Hulan heard the cafeteria filling with the regular workers, Madame Leung returned, opened a door to the outside, and led them through the late afternoon sunshine to the Assembly Building. Jimmy, the Australian, was not at his post in the lobby, so Madame Leung reached under the desk and pressed the button to release the lock on the door.

On the other side was the small foyer that Hulan had passed through on her tour. Madame Leung opened one of the doors that led from it, and the women followed her down a hallway, turned right, left, right again, then two lefts. In each corridor they passed more closed doors. Hulan had no idea where she was in relation to the final assembly room she'd been in before, let alone the main courtyard from which she'd come. At last they stepped into a huge room that logic said must be on the other side of the wall from the final assembly area.

The room was divided into two open areas. The first and largest held the cutting tables and sewing machines. The second area was dominated by gigantic machines, some of which measured eight feet high and twenty feet long. Madame Leung explained their various purposes: "molders" for making the plastic body parts, "flockers" to create the hair, and another machine with knife-like claws that grabbed compacted bricks of polyester fiber, drew it along a conveyor belt and shredded it into fluffy stuffing, which emerged out the other end of the machine to be packed loosely into burlap sacks. As she followed behind Madame Leung, Hulan could still feel waves of heat coming off the machines. The temperature, even this late in the day, was as hot as anything Hulan had ever felt. Fine beads of sweat broke out on Mayli's forehead, and Siang whispered, "We are standing in an oven. In an hour we will be as cooked as a piece of pottery."

"This is where you will begin work tomorrow," Madame Leung said. "You will be assigned a station and a guide. She will teach you how to work your machine. Once you have mastered the work in this room, you will be promoted to other jobs. Some of you might even make it into what the foreigners call the heart. This is a place with air conditioning. This is a special American invention that makes the air feel as cool as ice even in the hottest month. Many of you have come here with big dreams. I am here to tell you that they can come true. I can promise you this, because once I too was like you. I came from a village far away. I started in this room. I earned only two hundred *yuan*, but I kept working because I had my dreams."

Madame Leung paused, looked around at the newcomers, and smiled. Everyone in the room could see that the party secretary's dreams had come true by her nice suit, her nice haircut, and her nice figure that was neither too thin nor too fat. "In a moment you will go to your dormitory. If you think you will be unhappy here, this is the time to say so. You have all signed a three-year contract. Tonight—and only tonight—we are willing to let you walk away from your obligation. Tomorrow you will be fully committed, and there will be no crying, no changing your mind, no saying this isn't the way to your dreams."

For the second time that day Madame Leung inspected the group, looking for any signs of weakness. Again there were none.

"Our countrymen know hard work," Madame Leung said. "We are proud of what we can do. Through our American friends we can reap the rewards." She straightened her shoulders, then said, "Good night. Sleep well, for tomorrow you start your new life."

The dormitory rooms were hot, stuffy, and humid. Three smells hung in the air—women, overflowing (or unflushed) toilets, and scented toiletries. The women who'd accompanied Hulan thus far now separated and went looking for beds. Each room had four bunks, each with three beds apiece. Underneath the bottom beds were stashed the belongings of all the women in the room. A single bare lightbulb hung from the center of the ceiling. Most of the rooms were fully occupied, and since the other women had set out before Hulan, the few bunks that were available were quickly taken. Hulan was about to enter one room when she saw Jingren coming out.

"You don't want to go in there," Jingren said. "The only free bed belonged to a dead girl."

If the dead girl was who Hulan thought it was, then this was exactly where she wanted to be. She entered the room and asked which bed was open. One of the women pointed at a middle bunk. "But if you sleep there, a ghost spirit will visit you."

"I don't believe in ghosts," Hulan said.

A couple of the women laughed. "You say that now," a girl of about fourteen said. "Tomorrow morning you will move out like the other women who have tried to sleep here." She feigned a frightened voice and twisted her face into a humorous crinkled mask. "She was sitting on my chest all night! She was howling! She was nibbling at my ears!" Her voice shifted again. "Sleep here if you want, but tomorrow you will be gone."

Hulan threw her satchel on the bed and slid into the space. She couldn't fully extend her arm when lying down, and there certainly wasn't room to sit up. Poorly written Chinese characters had been scribbled on the wall with pen and pencil: "Protect me," "Home," "Work is reward." Had Miaoshan written these words and phrases, or were they the work of the women who had come before and after her death?

Hulan stretched out. The sheets were unwashed and they smelled.

"Excuse me," she said. "Where do I get fresh linens?"

The other women looked at her as if she were crazy.

The girl who'd spoken before said, "Same bed. Same sheets. Don't worry about it. You'll get used to it, if you can last the night." Her forehead wrinkled again and she giggled.

"I am Hulan."

"People call me Peanut," the girl said. "They call me that because I am small like a peanut." She was small, but Hulan thought it was the girl's peanut shape combined with her goofy facial expression that had earned her the nickname. "You'd better hurry. Lights go off in twenty minutes. If you want to use the bathroom, you should go now. It's down the hall on the left. You won't miss it."

Hulan followed the directions, passing room upon room of women and girls—some barely teenagers. By and large there was little conversation. Chinese people had always lived in crowded conditions. With so many generations living in a few rooms, Hulan's compatriots had learned how to be alone in a crowded space. Most of the women were already in their beds, their backs turned to the doors, trying to sleep or already asleep. Others lay on their backs, staring at the ceiling or the bunk above them. A few sat on the concrete floor talking, while others changed from their pink uniforms into extra-large T-shirts for sleeping. She passed one room where a girl no more than twelve sat cross-legged in the middle of the floor crying. She was obviously too young to be away from home, and yet Hulan had also been on her own in this very county at that age.

Peanut had been right about finding the bathroom. The smell led Hulan straight to it and she was shocked by what she saw. This was an American company, so she'd expected to find American-style facilities. Instead this was almost as bad as a public latrine. There were stalls but no doors. There were toilets but no seats, and the floor was slippery and wet. The big vats of water that lined the opposite wall told Hulan that this place had no running water. Hulan dipped a pail into the water and went to a toilet. Looking around, Hulan asked a woman where the toilet paper was stored. "In the company store," the woman responded gruffly, turning her head away. "You can buy it tomorrow before breakfast or during lunch." Without looking Hulan's way, she tore some paper off her roll and said, "Here, you can have this."

When Hulan was done, she poured the water into the back of the tank, flushed, and took the empty pail back to the water vats. She then went to the sink—a long trough with several spigots but again no running water.

"We have water for one hour in the morning and from eight to nine in the evening," the woman said.

"Is the water safe for drinking?"

"Even in my home village we boiled our drinking water, but the Americans won't let us have braziers or any other cooking utensils." Then she added dryly, "You can buy bottled water in the store tomorrow."

When Hulan got back to her room, she slipped off her shoes, lay down on the bed, and waited. At five minutes to ten she got up again. Just as she was about to leave, Peanut whispered, "You have to stay here.

Lights out in a few minutes. You can't get caught outside the room."

Hulan put a hand on her stomach. "I think the bus made me sick. I have to use the toilet again."

"Just come back as soon as you can."

Hulan threaded her way not toward the bathroom but toward the exit. A few feet before she reached it, the lights went out and the hall was pitched into utter blackness. Hulan groped her way forward, found the door handle, and pushed her way outside. The moon glowed through the thick, humid air. She edged around the side of the building, pulled out her phone, dialed the number for the Shanxi Grand Hotel, and asked for David's room.

"Hello?" His greeting sounded worried.

"I'm okay," she reassured him.

"Where are you? You said you'd be back here for dinner."

"I couldn't get away. This place . . . It's worse than I thought." She flexed her wounded hand and winced at the pain.

"I'll have Investigator Lo come and get you."

"No!" Hulan glanced around but still didn't see anyone. She lowered her voice. "I can't leave now. They have us locked in the compound."

"I don't like this. I know I sound like some dumb male, and I'll admit it, maybe that's part of it. But Jesus, I wish you weren't in there."

She cut him off. "Have you met the Knights yet? What are they like?"

He sighed. "They didn't show. They had bad weather in Tokyo. A typhoon, I think. Anyway, we'll have to try and cram everything in tomorrow."

"Then how did you spend your day?"

"I came back to the hotel and went for a run down along that creek they call a river. The rest of the day I was either on the phone or on the Internet. What else? Governor Sun just sent over a carton of papers, along with his signed waiver."

"So what are they?"

"I'm not sure," he said. "Financials of some sort. I'll look more closely before I meet with him." He hesitated. "But you know we shouldn't talk about them anyway. He's a client."

He was right, but Hulan wasn't so sure she liked it. Still, he had his professional ethics and she had hers, which made answering his next question much easier.

"Hulan, how do you think it will look if you're caught in there?"

"It's going to be bad if I find something."

"But you're not going to find anything."

"We've already covered this," Hulan sighed. "This place isn't what you think."

"You promised Zai and me—"

"I know."

"I'll be at the factory tomorrow at ten. I don't want to see you there."

"You won't," she said.

They exchanged good nights. Hulan punched the OFF button, put the phone back in her pocket, and went around to the entrance to the dormitory. She opened the door and waited for her eyes to adjust to the inky blackness. Suddenly a light flicked on.

"What are you doing out here?" Madame Leung asked.

Hulan looked down at the floor and didn't answer.

"You know the rules."

"I'm new, Party Secretary," Hulan said tremulously. "I got lost."

"Your name?"

"Liu Hulan, and I promise it won't happen again."

Hulan felt Madame Leung's eyes appraising her.

"Are you the one who was asking those questions today?"

"No, Party Secretary."

Looking at the ground, Hulan could see Madame Leung's foot slowly tap on the concrete floor.

"I will look the other way this one time," the party secretary said at last. "There will be no penalty."

"Thank you."

"You may go back to your room. I'll turn on all the lights so everyone will see you. If they ever see someone up and out again, they will know whom to report. Do you understand?"

"Yes, Party Secretary."

Madame Leung reached up and threw a series of switches. Without looking up, Hulan scurried past the party secretary. Hurrying back to her room, she felt the eyes of hundreds of women upon her. Moments after she settled onto her bunk, the lights were turned off. Hulan held her hand in front of her face and couldn't see it. She lay there for a few minutes, listening to the breathing and occasional shifting of the other women in the room. Her thoughts were on Miaoshan. The mattress was only a few inches deep, but from within it Hulan could smell a distinctive scent that she remembered from America. It was White Shoulders perfume. No wonder the women who slept here talked of ghost spirits. The oppressively sweet odor had always reminded Hulan of death. As Hulan drifted off, she wondered how White Shoulders had found its way into a dormitory room deep in the interior of China.

By quarter to seven the next morning Hulan had already had a cold shower, had dressed in her pink smock, had stopped in the company store to buy toilet paper and bottled water at three times Beijing prices, had slurped down a breakfast of *congee* with pickled turnip, and had finagled a spot in line with Siang to enter the Assembly Building. At 6:50 a bell rang and the line began to move. Madame Leung and the guard Jimmy stood in the middle of the lobby. If Jimmy recognized Hulan, this would all be over. When she reached him, he stared directly at her, but she was just another woman in a pink smock with a pink bandana covering her black hair. Madame Leung put an arm out to stop the line. She handed Hulan and Siang passes, looked around, spotted Peanut, and said, "Take them to your post and teach them what to do." Peanut nodded, and Hulan thought how strange it was that this place seemed to have so much security and the workers were so much under the control of the managers, and yet actual assignments could be as haphazard as who happened to be standing nearby at the time.

"We'll be watching you today," Madame Leung said. "Remember, if you do well, you'll be promoted. We reward good work. If you cannot do the work, do not despair. There are many jobs here at Knight. We will find something for you."

The line moved forward again. Peanut showed Hulan and Siang how to wave their passes over the bar code reader. Then they entered the door. The women ahead of them automatically divided into two groups, each going down different corridors. Hulan's line snaked left and right through the halls until she felt completely disoriented. Siang must have felt the same way, because she reached out and grabbed a pinch of Hulan's smock. Peanut bounced along rapidly, once turning her head back over her shoulder to say, "Everyone feels lost in here when they start, but you'll get used to it in a few days." They entered the main workroom, the women moving briskly to their positions before the various machines. At 7:00 the machines clamored to life. Within minutes the clatter and clanking of the machines had created a deafening roar.

Fortunately, Hulan and Tang Siang had been assigned to work with Peanut, who, although young, had a cheerful disposition and a great deal of patience. Peanut explained that they had been given the easy job of punching strands of plastic hair into minuscule holes in the heads of the dolls. Hulan remembered this task from the day before and thought that she'd gotten a lucky break. She was mistaken. Yesterday she'd been seated and she hadn't yet hurt her hand. Today she stood before a conveyor that sped up as the morning progressed. What had seemed relatively easy the day before as the trainees had moved from station to station soon became impossibly difficult. As the machines continued to churn, the room's temperature rose until the only respite came in the form of the slight oven-hot breeze that came off the moving parts of the equipment. After three hours Hulan's hands burned with fatigue, her wound throbbed, her fingers were scratched, and her smock was damp with sweat.

Siang's hands, however, moved deftly, competently. After the morning break Aaron Rodgers, who circulated between this room and the final assembly area, stopped to compliment Siang on her abilities. "Thank you very much," she said in heavily accented English.

Aaron's face broke into a smile. He leaned his head toward Siang's and spoke into her ear. With the sound of the machines, Hulan couldn't hear what he said, but she could see Siang blush, return his smile, and reply, "No, I am not a city girl. I am educated here in our local school. My father says English is very important."

Aaron Rodgers agreed, massaged Siang's shoulders for a moment, then turned his attention to Hulan. Again there was absolutely no sign of recognition. Aaron looked right into her face and, keeping a proper distance, spoke Mandarin in a tone loud enough to be just barely heard over the din of the machines. "Your fingers are bleeding. We can't have that on the figures."

"I'm sorry," she responded in Mandarin.

Aaron reached into his pocket and pulled out a couple of Band-Aids. "Use these. During the break, come to me. I will try to find you another job."

"I'll do better," Hulan vowed.

"We'll see," he said. "For now, just get back to—"

A woman's high-pitched screams cut him off. Instantly a quiet fell just under the continuing drone of the machines as all of the talking among the women came to an abrupt halt. Once the machines were shut down, the woman's screams seemed even louder as they reverberated through the echoing vastness of the room. Aaron took off at a trot; then the others left their posts and began crowding around the injured woman. Hulan edged into the throng, using her elbows to push her way to the front.

A woman sat on the floor before the fiber-shredding machine. Her right hand gripped her left elbow, holding that arm up and away from her body as she tried vainly to stanch the flow of blood. The flesh along her forearm was sliced open, and two of her fingers were gone. Aaron knelt beside her, pulled his shirt off, and wrapped it around the arm. Without any hesitancy he picked her up. The crowd parted to create an aisle. As he walked toward the door, the woman began to struggle. "No! No! No!" Her screams now seemed louder, more terrified than before. Instinctively the other girls stepped back even farther. A few turned their eyes away. A minute later Aaron stepped out of the room, the door shut, and the woman's screams faded. Someone near Hulan muttered, "We won't see Xiao Yang again." Then Madame Leung's voice came over a loudspeaker. "Please return to your places." The girls obeyed. Levers were pulled and buttons pushed. The machines revved back to speed, and the girls went back to their labors. Hulan held her spot just long enough to see the still bloody claws reach out, grab another fiber brick, and draw it into the machine's thrashing maw.

# 10

TWO HOURS AFTER HULAN TOOK HER PLACE ON THE assembly line for her first full day of work, Investigator Lo dropped David off in front of the Administration Building. As with Hulan's initial visit, Sandy Newheart stood on the steps to greet him. The two men shook hands, then went into the building, making their way down a corridor to a conference room where Henry and Douglas Knight awaited their arrival. There were no other attorneys present.

Henry Knight's handshake was straightforward and firm. He was of average height and lean. His silvery hair curled just over his collar. "It's great to have you here," he said. "Randall Craig and Miles Stout said they'd send us someone who was familiar with China, our company, and was quick on his feet. They say you fit the bill." He looked over to where his son sat. "That's my boy, Doug."

Doug raised a hand and waved. He looked to be about forty-five. Like his father, he was thin. But while Henry seemed spry and full of vigor, Doug came across as gaunt and lethargic.

"Can I get anyone coffee?" Sandy asked. "I can have it brought in."

"No, thanks," Henry said. "I don't want some damn tea girl hovering around. We can break later." Then, "That okay with you, Stark?"

"Just fine."

The four men sat at one end of the table, leaving the other dozen seats empty.

"We're on a tight schedule with Tartan and I want to keep things moving along, so I'll start with a quick review for your benefit." Henry opened the file in front of him, waited for the others to follow suit, and said with a grin, "I've always liked the Tartan offer. They're acquiring us outright. Doug retains his position as chief financial officer for five years. I gracefully exit and enjoy my retirement. Tartan asked for and received a non-compete clause, so that if I come up with any new ideas they'll come straight here as they always have."

Henry checked the others, then went on. "But I don't plan to do much in the way of development. I want to enjoy myself—travel a bit, visit my old haunts. Doug, on the other hand, is still young. I built this company and grew it to where it is today. We have these new technologies, and who knows where they'll end up?" He turned his steel gray eyes on David. "I want my boy to be a part of that excitement."

"As I see it, everything you've asked for is right here," David assured him. "But I wouldn't be completely honest if I didn't tell you that once a conglomerate like Tartan buys a company like this, it gets to do what it wants. Sometimes the people who are left behind are squeezed out. Sometimes they're uncomfortable with all the changes. Sometimes it's a perfect fit. There are no guarantees."

"Is that what Miles told you to say?" Henry asked, grinning at David.

"No," David answered, "no, he probably wouldn't have liked that I said that."

"An honest lawyer," Henry said. "I guess that's why they pay you the big bucks."

The others in the room laughed, as they were supposed to. David did too, realizing that despite Henry's hard eyes and years of business, he fancied himself as a bit of a cutup.

"All right, then," David said, trying for a more lawyerly tone. "As I understand it, Miles Stout and Keith Baxter have gone through this about twenty times, so I know they're satisfied. And I'm assuming that none of you or your lawyers are worried about the substance of the agreement—"

"Yes, we've had lawyers look at things, but the buck stops with me," Henry said. "I'm the one who makes the decisions."

"Are you sure you don't want your attorneys here?" David asked.

"Only a fool would go into a transaction like this without having representation."

"I've come a long way in business without using too many lawyers," Henry said. "Mine have vetted everything. It looks good to them. My feeling is, why fly them out here first-class, put them up in a hotel, and hire them companions for the night, when I know my company better than anyone else? Put another way, it's my money that's at stake, and I'm satisfied."

David looked at Sandy and Doug to gauge their reaction to this outburst. Sandy drummed on the papers in front of him with his pen; Doug seemed to be daydreaming. Both were reactions that David had experienced with his own father on occasion. No, Henry Knight wasn't the first entrepreneur to be a little eccentric. If that's the way they wanted to play it, it was fine with David.

"The final deal is slated to be signed in Beijing on July 21, with monies and power transferring on that date," David continued. "I know Miles and Keith have covered all this. Still, my main area of expertise is litigation, so I always like to double-check potential trouble spots. I don't mean those places where anyone is trying to slip something clever past the other side. By my reading and from what Miles has told me, all that's been taken care of to the satisfaction of both parties. I'm talking about places where Tartan might be exposed to future litigation."

"Are you asking me if I have anything to hide?" Henry asked in a friendly tone.

"You can put it that way if you like," David replied, also keeping his voice light.

"Well, we don't. Keith made sure about that."

"That's good, because you've got a good deal here. Seven hundred million is a lot of money. You don't want something to come up three years from now and bite Tartan on the ass. Because I can guarantee you that we'll come back to you full force."

Henry threw his head back and hooted with laughter. "Miles said you were full of vinegar. I like that."

David continued evenly, "So, I hope you can answer some questions, if only for my benefit."

"Fire away."

"Do you have any outstanding lawsuits or any threats of lawsuits that you know are lurking out there somewhere?"

Henry glanced at his son and Sandy, then said, "None. I've always run a clean shop. We've paid our bills. We've never gotten in trouble with the unions."

"How about product liability?"

"None," Henry answered.

"You manufacture toys," David pressed. "It seems to me I've read about cases where some kid swallows a part or gets bitten by a doll or some crazy thing."

"Hasn't happened with my products," the older man answered swiftly.

"You're sure—"

"I already told you, twice."

David leaned back in his chair, quietly evaluating the meeting. In the U.S. Attorney's Office he asked questions and, for the most part, people had to answer them. Now he was back in the private sector, where he had clients. He was here because Tartan had hired him for his expertise and advice. But as everyone kept reminding him, the due diligence was done and so was the deal. His role in these final days was reduced to that of cruise director: keep everyone happy, keep the deal moving along, and watch out for possible diplomatic snafus. The problem was that David didn't know the Knights and they didn't know him. They were all working against a deadline, but they still needed to trust each other.

"How long have you been in business?" David asked, changing strategies, hoping to get to know the man behind this enterprise.

Henry thought for a moment, regarding David the whole while. Then he nodded as if to say he understood what the younger man was doing. "My grandparents emigrated from Poland in 1910, when my father was ten," he began. "He was supposed to go to school. Instead he went to work shining shoes. When he was fifteen, he got a job selling penny banks. By the time he was twenty, he'd started a little company for school supplies. Ironic, isn't it? Here was a man who didn't finish school, but he made his living selling pencils, slate boards, notebooks, chalk."

Henry peered over at David. "Knight International. Such a grandiose name for a one-person operation, but my dad liked it. Obviously our last name wasn't Knight back then. You'd have thought he would have taken a name that was somehow more American, but he loved the idea of knights—the pageantry, the jousts on horseback, the gallantry. The name and all it implied were about as far from Poland and his childhood as he could get."

"Did he manufacture chess sets?"

Henry shook his head. "No, only school supplies. We didn't get into chess sets until much later. We were the first to make the pieces out of plastic, but that's getting ahead of the story. My dad married the daughter of one of his customers. I came along soon enough. I was five when the Depression hit. Schools stayed open, thank God, but really most people couldn't afford much in the way of extras. Times were hard, sure. But my dad also let people take advantage of him, because, he said, if someone was that desperate he probably needed that something more than we did. Then there was a lawyer who told my father all of the wrong things. He was nearly ruined."

"Which is why you don't like lawyers."

"I just like to make my own decisions. My father almost lost Knight, this company that was his whole life. I was just a little kid, but I'll never forget it."

"Something like that can make you pretty tough," David observed. "Both of my parents were kids during the Depression. They were both raised in families that struggled. I look at my parents now and think that that period—those 'formative' years—defined them for life." David thought for a moment, then added, "That and the war."

Henry nodded. "Where was your dad?"

"He was in the army, stationed in London."

"Not bad duty, if you can get it."

"In some ways it was the most fun my father ever had," David said.

"And in others?"

"War is hell. That's what he always said."

"Well, sport, he was right on both counts."

David shrugged. He rarely spoke about his family with strangers, but Henry made it seem easy.

"I was stationed in China," Henry said. "First in Kunming, then . . . I got around, especially in those months after the Japanese surrender."

"What were you doing?"

Henry didn't answer the question; instead he said, "Like your father, I had the time of my life. You just can't imagine what Shanghai was like back then. Every night we went out dancing and drinking and womanizing. It was fast. Exotic. That's a word that gets shit on these days, but I'm telling you, back then Shanghai was exotic."

"And what were you doing?" David repeated.

But before Henry could answer, his son asked, "Dad, shouldn't we get to work here?"

It was the first time Doug had spoken, and it took everyone by surprise. Henry checked his watch and said, "Give me another minute, then we'll take a quick break, grab some of that coffee Sandy's got brewing somewhere, then come back and get down to it. All right?"

Doug looked away. David wondered if Henry always dismissed his son's suggestions so casually.

But Henry's stride had been broken, and he hurriedly finished. "I thought I'd stay out here after the war. I got to know some people and had some pretty good ideas now that I look back on it. But then China closed and that was that. I went back home to New Jersey and started working for my dad. The baby boom came on strong, but the company wasn't going to feel it until those kids hit kindergarten. I began to think of ways to reach them earlier."

"Mr. Knight practically invented the preschool market," Sandy interjected. "That's why he's in the Toy Industry Hall of Fame in New York."

"I can't take any real credit for that," Henry said modestly. "Ruth and I wanted children. We wanted them to have something fun and educational to play with. That's all."

The phone rang. Sandy picked it up, spoke a few words into the receiver, hung up, and said to the others, "Something's come up in the Assembly Building that I need to take care of, so let's go ahead and take that break."

They left the room and together walked back to what Henry Knight explained to David was the heart of the company. Then the three company men left David to peruse Knight's brag wall. After about ten minutes, David had seen enough and decided to see if he could find the others. He stepped outside into the heat, looked around, and saw Henry and some other men clustered together next to a pile of something in front of a building to his left. David strolled their way, taking off his jacket and loosening his tie.

"I don't see how this could happen," Henry was saying in a quavering voice as David neared. When he reached them, the men stepped aside and David saw the figure of a woman dressed in a pink smock lying crumpled on the hard-packed earth. The smock was stained dark red with blood. The woman's arm was mangled, but this was nothing compared to the terrible thing that had happened to her head, which had flattened and split against the ground. Her dark eyes stared at the sky. Her injuries and the rag-doll quality of her limbs reminded David of Keith, but the familiarity of that nightmare didn't make this one any easier to take.

"Come on, Dad," Doug pleaded. "Step away. Let the others take care of it."

"No!" Henry jerked his son's hand off his shoulder. "Sandy, I'm asking again. How could this happen?"

But Sandy didn't answer. Instead he bolted away, leaned over, and threw up.

"Sir." This wavering syllable came from one of the men in the group. He was young and his face was as white as alabaster. "Sir," he tried again. He swallowed a couple of times and turned his eyes away from the bloody mess at his feet. "It's my fault. I shouldn't have left her alone."

"Who are you?"

"Aaron Rodgers, sir. I'm the manager for the assembly area. There was an accident. She . . . Does anyone know her name?" When no one answered, the young man gulped again and continued. "Her arm got caught in the shredder. It was bad, but not this bad." Aaron started to sway. David stepped forward, grabbed him, and led him over to the Assembly Building steps.

"Put your head down for a minute," David said. He looked around. "Can someone get some water, maybe a cold cloth?"

A heavyset Caucasian man whom David had yet to meet nodded with military precision, went into the building, and returned with a couple of paper cups filled with water which he gave to David. Then the man went over to the dead woman, flipped open some fabric, and let it settle on her. From here he walked to Sandy and escorted him to the steps to sit with Aaron Rodgers. "Drink this," he said in an Australian accent. Then, as Sandy stared over at the body, the other man said, "I'll get this cleaned up before the women have their lunch break."

"Go ahead, Jimmy," Sandy said.

"Don't you think you should wait for the police?" David asked.

Jimmy turned his squinty eyes on David. "We're way the hell out here in the middle of nowhere. You want to wait for the police and have a thousand women go hysterical when they come outside on their lunch break and see their friend or whatever squashed like a melon?" he asked sarcastically. "Or how about this? You want to sit around and wait five hours for the locals to arrive and have that thing over there start stinking up the place?"

"All I'm saying is, we don't know what happened," David said.

This was Aaron's cue, and he resumed his narration. "I carried her upstairs to my office," he said. "You know how we have those cots in there?" David didn't, but he nodded anyway. "I laid her down. She was upset, screaming about not wanting to die. Why did I leave her alone? Why did I go to another office to make my calls? Why didn't I just carry her straight to the clinic?" His whole body shook as if trying to shake away his guilt. "I don't know what I was thinking. I wasn't, I guess. I called Sandy. I knew Mr. Knight would be here today, and I wanted to tell him about the accident in person. After I called Sandy, I tried Madame Leung. When she wasn't in her office, I called the nurse straightaway."

David thought, Straightaway? It must have been five minutes at least.

"Then I went to find Madame Leung. I wanted her to stay with . . . with . . . the injured girl. I thought she would want a woman with her. Madame Leung was in the control area, speaking over the loudspeaker to the workers down on the floor. It was important to keep them calm, don't you think?" The young man looked earnestly at David. "But when we got back to the office, the girl was gone." Aaron's face went a few shades whiter. David put a hand on the back of Aaron's neck and pushed his head back down between his knees.

Doug Knight said, "She must have jumped out of your window."

"No," Aaron mumbled. "My office isn't on this side. My office faces the back and looks out over the wall."

David looked up at the building. There were no windows on this side.

"Well," Doug said conversationally, "she must have climbed up to the roof, then."

"Christ almighty, you're a cold-hearted bastard!" Henry stared at his son, his fists in tight balls at his side. "A woman has died here. Our family has been in business for more than seventy years. We've never lost an employee."

"All I'm saying, Dad, is that she killed herself," Doug went on calmly. "It's not your fault."

The older man, reacting to his son's soothing tones, gradually regained his composure. Then he turned away, walked back to the body, and knelt beside it.

"He's old," Doug said to no one in particular. "I hope he'll be strong enough to deal with this." Then Doug went over to his father, put an arm on his shoulder, and spoke softly to him.

Hurriedly the body was removed and the blood washed away. Several times Doug pleaded with his father to go back to the conference room, but the old man couldn't seem to tear himself away. Since he wouldn't leave, the rest of them couldn't either. At one, the bell rang and hundreds of women began filing out of the Assembly Building. Soon the courtyard was a sea of women in pink smocks with pink bandanas. Many of them walked arm in arm, chatting and laughing together. A couple of the younger women—perhaps on dares from their compatriots—waved and smiled at the foreigners, then began calling out greetings. David couldn't understand the words, but he could tell they were friendly from the women's smiles and infectious giggles. As the women eddied by, David searched for Hulan, but how could he find one face amidst this basically faceless crowd? Once they were past, David glanced over at Aaron Rodgers and was relieved to see that color had come back to his cheeks.

At last Henry turned and headed in the direction of the Administration Building, the others following close behind. Once back in the conference room, Henry still appeared unsteady, but his son moved to sit next to him, which seemed to bring the older man a measure of comfort. David suggested that they break for the day, but Henry dismissed the idea, saying, "There's nothing more we can do about that poor woman now. Let's keep this moving." Then he turned to Sandy and added, "But I want you to find out who she was. Make sure her family has the means for a proper burial. The Chinese set great store in that, you know. Make a payment to the family. Cash is always good. And if she had children—"

"I'll take care of it," Sandy said.

"Okay, then." Henry turned his gray eyes on David. "I guess I spoke too soon about liabilities."

"A suicide could hardly be Knight International's fault," David said.

"What about the injury that happened on the factory floor?"

"We'll have to look into it," David replied. "Have there been other accidents?"

"None," Henry said.

David looked questioningly over at Sandy.

"This is a first," Sandy said. "Sure, we have some problems, but nothing that a little peroxide and a Band-Aid won't cure."

Again, a week ago David could have demanded answers, but he was back in private practice. The finalization of the deal was the most important thing for his client as well as the Knights, so he didn't have the luxury of grilling these people. Besides, Keith must have covered this material a hundred times over. So David moved on, re-addressing the due diligence issues that he'd brought up earlier in the day. Did Knight have any outstanding lawsuits? Henry answered no.

"Looking ahead, do you foresee any lawsuits?"

"Maybe from that woman's family," Henry replied glumly.

David shook his head. "I think you can take care of that. As you've said, you'll provide for the woman's family even though it's a suicide. Your generosity will go a long way in a peasant family. But I'm not talking about what happened today. Right now Tartan is concerned with any possible liabilities it will be facing when it acquires your company. So I want you to think broadly about such things as copyright infringement, manufacturing defects, patents, licensing agreements."

They spent the next couple of hours going over each issue. Henry let Doug and Sandy do most of the talking, but this made sense. Not long after Henry had decided to move operations to China, he'd had the first of his heart attacks, so the responsibility for building this compound had fallen on Doug and to a lesser extent Sandy. All of which had ultimately worked to the company's advantage. If Henry hadn't been home recovering, he never would have stayed put long enough to come up with not only the idea for Sam & His Friends but also the technology. During the months he'd been homebound, he'd brought in all manner of toy and software designers to help him turn his concepts into reality. All of it— even the things that had been invented by others—was owned entirely by Knight International.

Even in a worst-case scenario Knight looked good. They had patents pending on some of the new technologies and materials used in the Sam & His Friends line. The Knights insisted that there were no manufacturing defects, and they reiterated what David already knew: Knight International had a fair record with labor. Still, part of the reason Knight had come to China was to avoid dealing with the American unions.

"Our workers here do have a union of sorts," Sandy explained. "The elected union leader also serves as on-site party secretary. We've found Madame Leung very easy to deal with. Actually, we couldn't get along without her. She's like a den mother, troubleshooter, and conflict resolver rolled into one. Our workers go to her when they have problems at work, but also when they have problems at home. Since most of our workers live right here in dormitories, you can imagine how conflicts might come up. But," he added, "a lot of the women get lonely for their husbands or children. We've had a few cases of women having affairs with the men here."

"I haven't seen many men," David noted. "In fact, I haven't seen many people at all except during the lunch break."

"We try to keep the men and women separated from each other as much as possible," Sandy said. "All of the men are locals. They crate the packaged products for shipping, load the trucks, deal with refuse. We've trained them how to use forklifts and . . ." Sandy smiled sheepishly. "Well, you get the idea. The point is, they're almost always in the warehouse or the shipping building. Their lunch break is at a different time than the women's. The only time they see each other is at the end of the day when the men go home and the women go to their dorms."

"All that to discourage fraternizing?"

"Madame Leung thinks it's best," Sandy said. "I'm sure you've heard a lot about how inhibited the Chinese are about sex. They're especially puritanical about extracurricular sex. I'm talking about serious penalties for screwing around. Did you know there was a time you could get sent to a labor camp for having an affair with a married woman? Things have always been a bit looser in the countryside, where the government isn't watching as closely and the attitudes are, shall we say, cruder. Nevertheless, we employ married women and single girls. Most of them are far from home and lonely. While there are still plenty of ways for the men and women to get together—this is a big place and all it takes is a few minutes—we're trying to do what we can to prevent broken hearts and unwanted pregnancies."

David moved on to licensing agreements. Like Sam & His Friends, several of the older products had also originated from television or movie characters, but those licenses had been locked into place years ago. In fact, Knight's relationship with the various studios had only improved with the wild success of Sam & His Friends. David finally had to ask Henry the question that had been gnawing at him since he'd read about the sale on the day of Keith's funeral. "With so much opportunity out there, plus the way you love your company, why are you selling?"

"Haven't you heard? I'm a dying man," Henry said.

David regarded the older man. He still looked shaken from seeing the dead woman, but death seemed very far from him personally. Henry looked strong and fit for a man his age. "Ill or not, how can you give up something you so obviously love?"

"It's a new world. I've lived my life in the toy business. Sure, I've made my forays into Hollywood, and they've been very profitable. But I don't want to spend the rest of my years in New York and L.A., going to lunches in fancy restaurants or commissaries, chatting up studio marketing and licensing people."

"You could let someone else do those things," David said.

"But it's my company. I like to be in control. Oh, not everything. I've never cared much for everyday operations."

"He means," Sandy clarified, "that he likes to sit on the floor and invent toys. He likes to work with the test groups—kids and moms. He likes to go to the toy fairs and put our products into the hands of the people who'll sell them. There isn't another company where the inventor is so closely linked with the end user. It's what's made Knight so successful."

"Then why sell?" David pressed.

"Because we've come to a crossroads," Henry said. "I just don't like the outside demands on my time." He got an almost dreamy look on his face. "I'll travel, maybe find an island or someplace around here, set up a little workshop out back . . ."

As he spoke, David understood why this was such a great deal for Tartan. Knight International had done extremely well over the years and Henry was a genius, but his iron-fisted control over the company and its practically nonexistent board of directors had undoubtedly kept Knight from expanding. With a host of managers, lawyers, accountants, and designers set to come in, and with Henry's commitment to bringing his products "home," the Knight brands under the Tartan umbrella could skyrocket.

And the conglomerate wasn't just buying a company with great potential, but would also continue to avail itself of the services and connections of Phillips, MacKenzie & Stout, in particular Miles Stout. Henry Knight had made his connections in Hollywood, but for years he'd been isolated in New Jersey and more recently isolated because of ill health. Tartan was in L.A., as was Phillips, MacKenzie. Miles, David recalled, had spent a lot of the firm's money on entertaining Hollywood bigwigs over the years. By getting his children into the right private schools, he'd developed personal relationships with studio heads. He'd coached Michael Ovitz's kid for a soccer season. His wife had set up play dates with the Roth kids. He'd helped Lew Wasserman get his grandchild into Brentwood Elementary. In turn, these media giants had invited Miles to be a fourth for tennis, to play a round of golf at the Riviera Country Club, to give money to their favorite charities, to go to screenings and premieres, and to join their Oscar-night parties. David could remember those evenings in years past when Miles and Mary Elizabeth had been whooshed away in a limousine to go party-hopping from the MCA Universal tent to the Paramount soirée to the Sony bash. Those studio relationships, while not part of the building blocks of the contracts, did act as the mortar. Add to this a final bonus: an independent contractor—in this case an eccentric toy inventor—coming up with new products on his island hideaway.

So, if the information Sandy Newheart and the Knights were giving him was correct—and David would have to check that it was—then he felt confident that this aspect of the deal would be all right. That still left what Tartan and Knight, as public companies, needed to disclose to the government: the financial details on past performance as well as what the consolidated company would look like, what the shareholders would get and if it was fair, documents dealing with antitrust issues since the original companies were both in the toy business, and affidavits stating that their officers and directors were in compliance with their respective companies' codes of conduct—meaning no instances of bribery, undisclosed transactions with vendors, or violations of the laws of the countries in which they operated.

"I see that Keith and your people have already provided the SEC with what it needs to know," David said, flipping through the papers.

"As you say, we're square on all of that," Henry said. "You've got the evidence right in front of you."

And on it went.

At four a young woman escorted Governor Sun Gan and Assistant Secretary Amy Gao into the room. Unlike the last time that David had met Sun in Beijing, for this occasion he was dressed quite casually in slacks and a short-sleeve white shirt which emphasized his physical strength. From his vantage point David could see the incredible charisma that Sun exuded as he circumnavigated the table, exchanging individual greetings with everyone in the room. David supposed that Sun's ability to make people feel special was what had made him such a successful politician.

All the while Amy Gao stood patiently with her back against the wall, her impenetrable brown eyes coolly surveying the room. David was aware that in China an underling was hardly ever addressed or acknowledged and would never be presumptuous enough to step forward and introduce him- or herself. So David decided to approach Amy, for the very simple reason that if he was to represent Sun, then he would need to have a good relationship with his right-hand woman. Most likely Amy Gao would be able to provide more details on a particular matter or be able to look up information more quickly than the governor himself. But where Sun projected ease, his assistant appeared beautiful but undeniably stiff and formal. Her response to David's self-introduction was a brief handshake and a clipped "How do you do?"

Once they all resumed their seats, with Amy taking a chair against the wall behind her superior, Sun addressed Henry. "I know you're all very busy with your sale, but I wanted to come and see if there's anything I can do to help facilitate matters."

"I'm always grateful for any help that the governor can provide," Henry said. "But in this instance things are moving along fine. We see nothing but clear weather ahead."

"This is good news," Sun responded, keeping his official demeanor. He cocked his head in David's direction. "You may not know this, but Henry Knight was the first to recognize the possibilities of Shanxi Province."

"Oh, now, Sun," Henry interrupted. "We're all friends here. You don't need to give David the full treatment, you know."

The two men laughed, and the others from Knight quickly joined in.

Then Henry, still beaming, explained to David, "We've known each other since the war. Hell, we were a couple of kids, but we did some serious carousing, didn't we, Sun? When I came back to China, I knew whom I had to find. Only I didn't know *what* I'd find—some broken peasant, maybe he was dead, I didn't know. But I get over here and look who's practically running the show. I can't tell you how easy he made it for us. He found this property. When we were building the compound and I was home in the hospital, he got the tradesmen here on time, he kept the work moving steadily forward, and he dealt with all the red tape. We never would have gotten up and running if not for him."

Sun acknowledged this with a slight bow of his head, then said, "It is I who owe much to you. I had a vision for my province. You were the first to turn it into reality. Now we have other companies from France, England, Australia, Germany, and, of course, the United States. We may not have Mattel, Nike, or Boeing yet, but once they see what we've done here, they'll come. Why? Because our land and labor prices are cheaper than on the coast. But the real gift is not what we can give you. It is what you have given us. You remember, Henry, what it was like here fifty years ago? Terrible poverty. Always we were having famine or drought or flood, then you add to that war . . . It was bad. Even when you first came back to visit in 1990, life for common people had not changed so much. But today you can see what prosperity has done not only to our big provincial cities of Taiyuan and Datong but also to our villages."

David glanced around the room, noting that the others looked bored with this ongoing mutual admiration fest. Perhaps they'd listened to it too many times and no longer heard the real content of the words, but David heard them. Sun had obviously done a lot to make things run smoothly for his old friend. In the West this might have meant a few phone calls, but in China it could mean anything from a few phone calls to coercion, graft, or bribery. Despite these red flags, David couldn't imagine that the governor—with his straightforward manner, his ease with people, his obvious love of his home province, and his rapid rise in power—could be personally involved with such underhanded business practices. For that matter, neither could Henry Knight. Watching the two of them together, David saw two mannerly gents bound together by some good times in the past. On different continents and in vastly different cultures, they had both risen to prominence. They had made money. They had achieved success.

# 11

WHEN THE BELL RANG FOR LUNCH, HULAN AND THE other women filed out into the courtyard. Except for one fifteen-minute break, Hulan had stood in exactly the same spot for six hours, so she was grateful to have the opportunity to stretch her legs. And, hot as it was under the sun, it was far cooler outside than on the factory floor. She was thankful as well for Peanut's take-charge attitude. Smiling, Peanut had linked arms with Hulan and Siang, pulling them along. Through the crowd Hulan caught a glimpse of Mayli and Jingren, but they were in the company of their own teams. In fact, all of the groups seemed to be made up of people who worked together. After standing or sitting in such close proximity to the same people day after day, week after week, how could they not be friends, how could they not know each other's most intimate secrets?

For a moment Peanut broke into an old harvest song. Her voice sounded sweet, and a few of the women around them joined in for a verse or two. Then someone spotted the foreigners, and word quickly passed that Old Man Knight himself was in the courtyard. Hulan rose up on tiptoes to see the foreigners. Dressed in suits and ties, they looked wilted and suprisingly indistinguishable as individuals. Then she spotted David. She looked right at him, but he didn't see her. Around her, the women dared each other to go up and talk to the Americans.

"Suchan, tell that young one over there you are burning hot for him."

"Um, no, I like the old one. Who wants a hard *jiji* when you can have hard currency?"

The women laughed appreciatively at this tart rejoinder. Then another voice called out.

"In this hot place I am parched. I long for clouds and rain." The time-honored euphemism for the sexual act made the women laugh louder.

Looking at the men's faces, Hulan knew they had no understanding of the words being hurled their way. None, that is, except Aaron Rodgers. Even from a distance Hulan could see that his ears had gone bright red. She wasn't the only one to notice his discomfort.

"Hey! Look at Manager Red Face! I think we're making him hot!"

"Choose me! I will let you feel my love button!"

"No! Pick me! I will be so carried away I will forget to count the thrusts!"

"Forget your dreams, sister. He has found his new conquest. Where is that new girl? Who is she anyway?"

Hulan peered sideways and saw Siang in much the same condition as Aaron. Her eyes were cast down and she was blushing from embarrassment, but the smile on her face showed her pleasure.

Peanut, keeping her voice low, said, "Don't listen to them, Siang. They're just having fun."

"Do you think so?" Siang asked.

Peanut grinned conspiratorially. "Tell us. What did the manager say to you?"

"That I was doing good work. He said I was learning faster than anyone he had ever seen."

They entered the cafeteria building, picked up trays, and joined the line to receive a bowl of rice with some stewed meat on top. Peanut and Siang went to find a table, while Hulan got herself a mug of weak tea. By the time she reached her co-workers, they were deep in conversation, their heads together.

"Are you going to meet him?" Peanut asked Siang as Hulan sat down.

"Do you think I should?"

"Of course. I would if he asked me," Peanut answered.

Obviously a lot had happened in the few minutes Hulan had gotten her tea.

"But where?" Hulan asked. "I thought there were no places to be alone."

Peanut and Siang exchanged glances.

"The people who run this place think we have no needs, but we do," Peanut said delicately. "So we have found places to meet here inside the compound and ways to get out when we can."

"How?" Hulan asked. She picked up a piece of the meat, noticed that the hair was still attached to the skin, set it against the side of her bowl, and looked for another, more appetizing morsel.

"When you're here longer, you'll find out," Peanut answered.

"But Siang already knows, and we've been here the same amount of time."

"But she's different. The manager told her himself."

Hulan put down her chopsticks. "I don't think this is fair." The words seemed tame enough, but in China they were the first step toward public criticism.

Peanut sighed. "Okay, but if you get caught, don't tell them I told you. There are actually several ways to meet," she went on, trying to sound more worldly than her fourteen years. "Staying in the compound is the least dangerous, but it's hard to avoid their eyes."

"Last night Madame Leung caught me when I went outside," Hulan said.

"That's because you left after lights out," Peanut explained. "You have to be gone much earlier than that." Peanut looked around to make sure that none of the officials were nearby, then leaned forward and continued in a low voice, "Did you notice that when we came in here that we didn't have to check in? Well, the same goes for breakfast and dinner."

"So?"

"So they only check us when we go in and out of the factory. Otherwise they don't pay much attention."

"People sneak out during lunch?" Hulan asked dubiously.

"Lunch. Dinner." Peanut's eyes scanned the room. "I can tell you not everyone is having lunch right now."

"But where do they go?"

"Oh, the warehouse, the shipping area, the Administration Building, even here." Seeing Hulan's shocked look, Peanut laughed. "They aren't doing it in here right now! That's only at night after lights out and the men have supposedly gone home. Outside, you put a man and a woman together, how long does it take? Not so long and then the man goes to sleep. But"—Peanut's eyes gleamed—"if you stay in the compound—if you're in here perhaps—you do your thing and then you have all night to talk, because these floors are too hard for much sleeping. Believe me, I know!"

"Still, won't you get caught?"

"Depends where you go," Peanut said, "depends who with."

"What if I wanted to leave the compound?" Hulan asked.

"Do you have a special man too?" Peanut wanted to know.

"Maybe," Hulan said. "Maybe I just don't believe you. What about the gate? What about the guard?"

"Oh, leaving is easy!" Peanut bragged. "We're dismissed at seven and so are the men. You take off your smock, give it to a friend, join the men—walking in the middle of the group—and go right out through the gate. In the morning, you just reverse the process. And if you really want out, you can always pay the guard. He's very greedy."

Hulan remembered back to the first time she entered the compound and how the guard had paled when he'd seen her identification. He must have thought he was on his way to a labor camp.

"You've done this yourself?" Hulan asked. "Paid the guard?"

"Me? No. I'm here to make money, not spend it." Peanut turned her attention back to Siang. "So, where did the manager want to meet you?"

Siang studied her empty bowl. "He said to come to his office. He said we would have dinner there and we could talk about my promotion."

"Um." Peanut nodded sagely. "He wants to talk." Then she burst out in raucous laughter, stood, and called out across the room in a shrill voice, "Manager Red Face wants to talk!" The laughter that followed was accompanied by a few more comments on Aaron Rodgers's prowess.

Feeling sorry for Siang, Hulan reached across the table and patted her hand. "You don't have to do what he says."

Siang looked up not in embarrassment but in defiance. "Why wouldn't I go?"

"Isn't it obvious that he does this with other girls?"

"So what?"

"So you could get hurt. You could get a disease. You could—"

"You only say those things because you're old." Siang filled the last word with as much contempt as she could marshal. As Hulan recoiled at the insult, Siang went on. "Don't look so surprised. It's true you look young, almost like one of us. But you are a friend of Ling Suchee. Tsai Bing's mother says you are girlhood friends. Well, if you are friends for that many years, then you are as old as that old woman."

Peanut consumed all this with considerable interest, and Hulan had no doubts that their conversation would be common knowledge by lights out tonight.

"And what about Tsai Bing?" Hulan asked.

"He's the reason I'll do it." Siang pushed her tray away and stood. "We want to be together, but how can we without money?"

Hulan and Peanut watched Siang wend her way through the tables. "True-heart love, eh?" Peanut asked. Hulan nodded. "Parental objection too?" When Hulan nodded again, Peanut sighed at the hopelessness of it all.

During the long, hot afternoon, as Hulan continued to jab hair through tiny holes in the Sam dolls, Peanut peppered them both with questions: What villages were they from? How had they been hired? What were they saving money for? Fortunately, Hulan didn't have to worry too much about her answers due to Siang's repeated interruptions. Eventually Peanut directed her questions solely to Siang, who responded with an insolent brashness, as though she were taunting them with her family's superiority.

"A hundred years ago my family was important in this area," Siang said. "They were landowners, the worst of the worst, but even so, they didn't have so much. They weren't Mandarins or educated, but they'd been in this district for many centuries. They were slave owners. They bought girls to work in the house and eventually become the concubines of my great-great-uncles."

All of these words were spoken with perfunctory contrition, for there was no masking Siang's pride in her family's past. Still, to be on the safe side, she covered her haughtiness by adding, "I had a great-uncle—a younger brother naturally—who joined the People's Army. It's a good thing too. Otherwise my entire family would have been killed during Liberation or during Land Reform."

"What about the Cultural Revolution?" Peanut asked. "Your family must have paid then."

"I wasn't born yet, so I only know the stories," Siang said. "In those days there was a big commune not far from here where thousands of youths from the city came to learn the ways of the people. Can you imagine?"

"In my home village," Peanut said, "we also had a work camp for people from the black classes."

"Maybe that's where my father was sent. Who knows?" Siang said. "But always I have thought this was kind of funny, because it isn't so easy to live here even now. The whole time that my father was gone from Da Shui, the villagers held criticism meetings against our family. Eventually they sent away my aunties. They never returned. Then the team leaders of the commune assigned my grandparents the worst jobs—filling buckets of shit from the public latrine and carrying them to the fields. My grandparents, already weak, died very quickly. By the time my father returned, he no longer had a family. His home, tools, and land had long been confiscated and incorporated into the commune."

"This was life for people everywhere," Peanut observed. "Your family is not so unique."

"A little less talking and maybe the new girls would get more work done," a voice cut in. Hulan looked over her shoulder to see Madame Leung.

"Sorry, Party Secretary."

"Peanut, I gave these two to you because you are fast. But"—she pointed at Hulan—"look at the job this one here is doing." Then she turned her attention from the work to the person doing it and instantly recognized Hulan. "You're the one from last night."

Hulan bowed her head. It was an admission of guilt and an act of repentance.

"This work will never pass inspection," Madame Leung said. Then she grabbed Hulan's hands. "And look at this! You're bleeding through your bandages. No one wants your blood on our products. Here," she said as she reached into her pocket and pulled out some gloves. "These ought to help your hands, but if I don't see an improvement in the work, we'll have to move you to a less demanding job." Madame Leung surveyed the room for her next targets. Once she spotted them, she said, "Get back to work, and, Peanut, you're responsible for this one."

When she walked away, Peanut said, "You'll have to try harder, Hulan. This is a bottom-rung job. I'm still here, but I'm team leader of Appendage Assembly. If you don't succeed, you'll be given an even lower job, like hauling water to the bathrooms or cleaning the floors. They'll drop your salary even more and you'll work longer hours. I know you didn't come here for that. Now, watch exactly what I do . . ."

Peanut devoted the next hour to helping Hulan. The work itself wasn't all that difficult, but Hulan's left hand was bandaged and awkward. Peanut taught Hulan to modify her grip on the doll's head. Soon enough muscles she didn't know she had in her hand started to ache, but at least she wasn't worried about driving the punching tool into her wound. The minutes ticked past and Hulan became aware of Siang's growing impatience, as she bumped into Peanut and cleared her throat, inexpertly trying to get the team leader's attention. Finally Peanut said to Hulan, "Your hands are clumsy and your arms don't have much strength, but you are doing better. Try it on your own for a while. The next time Madame Leung comes around, you'll be ready for her."

As soon as Peanut picked up her own tool, Siang began to speak as though no time had passed since her earlier speech. "When the responsibility system came in 1984, everything changed for us," Siang said.

"Things changed for everyone." For the first time Peanut's voice was edged with irritation. Then she leaned over and asked Hulan, "What about you? You haven't told us where you're from."

"You've been talking to her for an hour!" Siang blurted. "Are you going to listen to me, or are you going to keep talking to her?"

Peanut sighed, picked up another Sam head, and expertly jabbed the hair into the small holes.

"The brigade leaders got together to redistribute the land, seed, animals, and tools," Siang continued. "They took into consideration past hard work, familial ties to the land, the qualities of livestock and soil. Although the black marks against my mother and father had been removed through self-criticism, many villagers still held a grudge. So, while several people were reassigned to their ancestral land, my father wasn't given any of his. The leaders gave him a poor tract on the other side of the village. All the time he is working hard. One year he's so successful that he has enough money to buy extra seed. He went to one of the neighbors—an old couple—and said if they would let him plant it, he would provide for them the following winter. The next year that couple died and my father got their land. Since then, every year he gets a little here, a little there. And every day my father thanks Deng Xiaoping for instilling in us the desire to get rich."

"Is he a millionaire?" Peanut inquired.

"My father? No! He's a peasant like everyone else in our county. That's why his family attitudes are so backward."

The three of them kept working, their shoulders almost touching. Once Peanut leaned over and rewrapped Hulan's fingers around her tool. "Don't forget to do it this way," she said. "The work will go faster." Then again they drifted back into silence while all around them the machines roared and the other women chattered.

"After everything that happened to my family, what could my father do but obey every new law our country put forth?" Siang said at last. "The government said one child and that's what my parents had, but my father has never forgiven me for being a girl."

"Look around," Peanut said. "Do you think anyone in this building has been forgiven for being a girl? Sometimes I think that's why we're all here."

"I came here to break away from my father," Siang confessed.

Peanut raised an eyebrow. "Like a lot of us."

"But this is different," Siang insisted. "My father has plans for me. He has a boy picked out for me to marry. He's from Taiyuan City, not from the village."

"But you love someone else," Peanut said.

"My father says Tsai Bing is not good enough. He says Tsai Bing will never be more than a peasant. But more than anything he says I should be no man's second choice. You see, Tsai Bing was engaged before. His fiancée used to work here, but she died. Ling Miaoshan was her name. Did you know her?"

"She shared our room," Peanut said without much enthusiasm. "She was a troublemaker."

Hulan would have loved to have questioned Peanut about this, but Siang continued. "Her death made us free to be together. If I work here and earn enough money, then Tsai Bing and I can go away. Have you ever been to Beijing, Peanut? I've gone there with my father several times. You can't imagine what it's like. So much opportunity . . ."

Despite her companions' incessant gossiping and all of the information she learned about Siang's character, Hulan could no longer ignore her physical discomfort. By three her hands ached. By four her arms felt as heavy as they had the first time she'd worked a full day shoveling manure back when she was twelve. By five her legs and feet throbbed from standing in one position for so many hours. By six her neck burned from constantly staring down. By seven, when the bell finally signaled the end of the workday, she was sore, tired, famished, and ready to be as far away from this place as possible.

Siang, who'd scrupulously ignored Hulan all afternoon, whispered a few words to Peanut, shot a last impertinent look in Hulan's direction, and quickly headed for the exit. Peanut stretched her fingers out and closed them again.

"I like her," Peanut said, nodding toward Siang's retreating back. "But you see the landowner class all over her."

"Oh, I don't think it's that," Hulan said. "She's just young."

"She's older than me," Peanut corrected.

"In years, yes," Hulan said. "But unlike you, she's insecure. We should try to make allowances for that. She'll grow up in time."

"You say that after the way she treated you today?" Peanut asked as they walked toward the exit. "You're a good person."

"Not so good," Hulan responded, "just old like Tang Siang said earlier today."

Peanut giggled, then turned serious. "What I told you before about sneaking out of here . . ."

"Yes?"

"It's not as easy as I said."

"I didn't think it could be."

"Actually, I've never done any of those things that I said before," Peanut admitted.

"I won't tell."

"And only a handful of women have ever left the compound," Peanut said.

"Maybe some have kept it a secret."

"You think anyone could keep a secret around here?" Peanut quipped. "I'll tell you this: All of us have plotted ways to leave, but only a few have had the courage. They're so strict here. You would lose your job for sure if they caught you. That's why it's safer to be in the compound. It's easy to hide in here. Even if they spot you during lights out, you're only docked pay. On the other hand, if someone sees Tang Siang with the manager, no one will report them."

They stepped outside. The sun hung low in the sky, but the heat had not begun to abate.

"Funny, though," Peanut mused. "She's in love with the same village boy that Ling Miaoshan was supposed to marry. Now she's going off to do the house thing with Manager Red Face."

"When you're held under water, you only think of air," Hulan recited. "She thinks she's trapped, and like the lowest rat she'll do anything to get free."

"It's not for me."

"Or me either," Hulan agreed.

"Yet you're going to try and leave the compound tonight." With Peanut's eyes boring into her, Hulan couldn't lie. Peanut accepted the news with an abrupt nod of her head, then added, "I'm the designated room watcher. It's my responsibility to report you."

"But you won't."

"I never reported Miaoshan, because she always said she would report me as retribution even though I'd done nothing."

"I'd never report you even if I caught you."

"Be careful," Peanut warned. "You've already been given one chance. It's just like what happens if you're injured. You hurt your hand but not badly, so you can stay—for now. If you have a more severe injury or if you get hurt more than once, you disappear. The same goes for sneaking around. If they find out, maybe they'll give you another chance; maybe you'll disappear like the others."

"I'd just go home to my family."

"Maybe."

Hulan frowned, then asked, "The other women *do* go home to their families, don't they?"

"Sure. I've seen people go back to the villages around here, but how do I know what happens to the girls from far away? The factory hired them from a distant place and paid their way here, but how do I know what happens if they want to go home? For all I know, those girls go on to Beijing or south to Guangzhou or out in the fields here and die. I'm not there. I don't see it. All I'm saying is that if you get in trouble, you're gone. If you get hurt like Xiao Yang today, you're gone forever."

"If what you say is true, maybe you should report this to the Public Security Bureau," Hulan suggested in a mock serious tone, believing Peanut's words to be as much of an exaggeration as her various sexual escapades.

"Me? Never!" Peanut laughed. "Don't take everything so seriously."

Most of the women had already crossed the compound's yard and had disappeared into the cafeteria building. "Well, if I'm going to leave, I'd better do it now," Hulan said. She quickly took off her pink smock and handed it to Peanut. "See you tomorrow," she said, then walked down the steps and casually drifted into the cluster of a hundred or so men. A few of them looked at her curiously, but none said a word.

Hulan's breathing became shallow and her heart began to pound as she waited for the gate to open. She told herself that it didn't matter if she was caught, that she had nothing to lose. Still, the fear she felt made her realize why the women here rarely did this; the danger of losing their jobs, of being stranded miles from home, was too big a risk to take. When the gate drew up, Hulan kept to the thickest part of the crowd. With dozens of male bodies shielding her, she strolled as nonchalantly as possible out of the compound.

When she reached the hotel, she walked around to the back, slipped in through the employee entrance, rode up the freight elevator to the eleventh floor, and knocked on David's door. David drew her in and hugged her, but not before she glimpsed the momentary lack of recognition that flickered across his face. Hulan retired to the bathroom. Looking in the mirror, she saw that her newly cropped hair had come loose from its pins, and her face was streaked with dirt. She stepped into the shower, enjoying washing the grime of the factory from her skin and feeling the warmth of the water on her aching muscles. When Hulan reemerged, her hair was pulled back, she wore a sleeveless ecru dress of raw silk, and she'd applied a fresh bandage to her wound.

"Do you want dinner in the room?" David asked, admiring her transformation.

Hulan shook her head. "I'd like to go out, especially if we can walk somewhere."

They went back downstairs. Hulan checked with the concierge for a restaurant recommendation, but he insisted that all the restaurants in Taiyuan were for the masses. "You are only two people and he is a foreigner," the concierge said in Mandarin. "You will be an inconvenience to the other patrons. It is better that you stay here. If you really must go someplace else and you want authentic food, I can recommend the restaurant in the Hubin Hotel, which caters to our overseas compatriots."

When the concierge wouldn't budge on his suggestions—he probably received kickbacks from the two hotels' chefs—David and Hulan pushed through the revolving doors and into the sultry night air, crossed the street, and decided to take a chance on a small restaurant decorated with Christmas lights. Hulan conversed with the waiter about specialties and ingredients, then ordered. David asked for a Tsingtao beer, while Hulan accepted some chrysanthemum tea. A few minutes later, the waiter returned with fresh corn soup.

David and Hulan had both experienced a lot since the previous morning, but at first they shared only trivialities. David said he'd looked for her at lunch but hadn't seen her; she said she'd seen him. He said he was impressed by how cheerful the women seemed as they walked to the cafeteria. "They waved and called out to us," he said. Hulan smiled but didn't tell him what the women were really saying about Aaron Rodgers.

The waiter arrived and with a flurry set down three dishes: diced chicken sautéed with hot peppers, baby bok choy warmed with giant mushrooms, and prawns that had first been stir-fried with ginger, garlic, onions, and black beans, then dipped in molten lard to create morsels that were flavorful on the inside and crispy on the outside. It all tasted wonderful, especially to Hulan, who hadn't had a decent meal in twenty-four hours.

At last David asked, "So tell me about the factory."

"Last night when I called you, I'd only seen those places that were nice enough to keep me from walking out on the contract," she said, putting down her chopsticks. "But here's what it's actually like: There's running water only for an hour in the morning and an hour at night. To flush the toilets, you scoop water out of a barrel and dump it in the tank. There's no hot water at all. The shower stalls—if you can call them that— probably haven't been cleaned since the factory opened two years ago. The food in the cafeteria has hair on it. From what animal, I don't know. And then there's the factory floor itself—"

But before she could go on, David interrupted. "You're a Beijinger who's happened to have gone to a Connecticut boarding school. You're always telling me about dirty or backward conditions like on your train trip or in that hotel in Datong. Didn't that place only have hot water two hours a day?"

"There's a big difference between no running water and rationed hot water."

"To a peasant? The women I saw today looked perfectly content. It has to be better working in the factory, no matter how primitive, than being out on a farm."

His ignorance surprised her. "Is it that you don't believe me when I tell you that we're tricked into signing contracts that promise one thing but deliver another, or is it that you think that just because the women are peasants they should be grateful for what they get?"

"I'm saying neither of those things, Hulan," he replied patiently. "I'm saying they were singing. They seemed happy to me."

"I'm sure that's what your slave owners used to say," she bristled.

"Hulan . . ."

"I just spent a day working shoulder to shoulder with two women. Siang and Peanut may not have been educated in the way that you or I have been, but they have a deeper understanding of how things work than either of us."

"Aren't you romanticizing them?"

Hulan thought back. "No," she said, "just the opposite. They've lived at the whim of so many things. They are truly close to the soil. You know what that means to me? A kind of earthiness."

"In my meeting Sandy said something like that as well. He was referring to crudeness, I think."

"Perhaps it's crude to live from hand to mouth, but it makes things very clear. The women I worked with today understand that they're being taken advantage of. The hours are long. The living facilities are substandard. The noise level on the factory floor has to be bad for our ears. A lot of what we're doing is dangerous. Look at my hands, David."

Of course, he'd already seen the gauze wrapped around her left hand and that wound remained covered. But the exposed flesh on both of her hands was scratched and scabbed, while her fingernails were broken and jagged.

"But this is nothing," she continued. "A woman was badly injured in the factory today. Her whole arm was torn up."

David waited for Hulan to tell him about the death. When she didn't, he said, incredulous, "Their security man was right. He cleaned it up and no one even knew what happened."

"What are you talking about?"

"The woman who was hurt jumped off the roof of the building. She's dead."

"Why didn't you tell me before?" she asked.

"I assumed you knew. I figured that's why you were so upset."

Hulan ignored his last comment and said, "Tell me everything."

"We were in a meeting. Sandy Newheart got a call. He said we should break for coffee. He and the Knights left. When they didn't come back, I went outside and found them with the body."

"And?"

"And nothing. A security guard wrapped her up and took her away. We went back to the conference room. The old man was pretty shaken up, but he's tough, focused. We continued our meeting."

"David," Hulan said, leaning forward intently, "tell me about the body. Where was it in relation to the building? How did it look exactly?"

"Oh, Hulan—"

"David, please."

"Okay." He sighed, then began to conjure up the picture in his mind. "She was on the ground, obviously."

"Right next to the building?" she inquired. "On the steps? Up against the wall?"

"No, she was on the dirt. I'd say seven to ten feet from the building."

"And how did she look?"

"How do you think?" he asked impatiently. "Her head was flat. There was lots of blood."

Hulan closed her eyes and slouched back in the chair. "On her side? Face up?"

"Face up."

Her eyes still closed, Hulan nodded grimly as if she'd seen the body herself. "Do you know what Peanut said?" she asked. "She said that Xiao Yang—Little Yang, that's the dead woman—wouldn't be coming back. I thought she was joking. At the time I thought she meant that Xiao Yang's injuries were so bad she'd have to go home. But now I see Peanut meant something quite different."

"Don't read anything into this, Hulan."

Hulan slowly opened her eyes and stared at David. "I'm only responding to what you saw."

"I saw a woman who jumped from a building and died."

"Look at it with me: A woman gets her arm half torn off. She loses a lot of blood. She's probably in shock. She can't walk off the factory floor—"

"Aaron Rodgers said he carried her to his office, but that doesn't mean she couldn't walk."

"*I'm* telling you she couldn't walk." Hulan waited for David to challenge her again. When he didn't, she continued, "He takes her somewhere—"

"His office . . ."

"And goes for help." David nodded, and Hulan went on. "Now, you're suggesting that Xiao Yang gets up, climbs a set of stairs, somehow finds her way onto the roof, goes to the edge of the building, and jumps?"

"That's what happened."

"David, think about that building. If you were on the second-floor roof and you jumped, do you think you would die?"

"Probably not, might break an ankle, though." He smiled, but Hulan would have none of it.

"So you'd go feet first?"

"Yeah, I suppose."

"Then how do you explain the fact that Xiao Yang landed ten feet from the building, with her head crushed?"

"What are you suggesting?"

"Someone threw her off the building," Hulan said gravely.

David disagreed. "If you jump, your body's going to have a forward trajectory. Even if she landed on her feet, she'd have to fall forward or backward. If the circumstances are right, the momentum could be enough to cause that damage."

"Three weeks ago Miaoshan supposedly kills herself. Today Xiao Yang also kills herself. Doesn't that seem strange to you?"

"Look, it's terrible what happened to Miaoshan, and it's sad what happened to that poor woman today, but you're seeing murder where there's only suicide. These things are tragic, but that's all they are."

On another day, maybe in other circumstances, Hulan might have heard these words differently. Instead she filtered out everything except for what she took to be his condescension.

She stood and put her purse on her shoulder.

"Where are you going?" he asked.

"I'm not sure yet."

"You're not going back to the factory."

Hulan's eyes flashed. "Are you telling me what I can and cannot do?"

"You said a day, Hulan. You were in there two days."

She looked at him in anger and disappointment. "You're a lawyer. You're supposed to look at things logically. Where is your *brain*, David?"

"You say that just because my interpretation deviates from yours?"

Hulan shrugged indifferently.

David didn't know where his next words came from and regretted them the moment they left his lips, but he said, "I forbid you to go."

Her eyes were cold as she said, "You're not my father." Then she left the restaurant.

# 12

WITHOUT THINKING, HULAN GRABBED A TAXI AND ASKED to be dropped at the bus stop for Da Shui Village. When the driver said that the last bus had already left for the day, she asked if he'd take her. Speaking into the rearview mirror, the driver said, "You're a Beijinger. Why do you want to go there?"

"You look at me and see only my face and my clothes," Hulan said. "Since that is the case, you know I also have money."

That seemed a good enough answer for the driver. He made a U-turn, stepped on the gas, and headed out of town. Soon the city lights were left behind them, and only the taxi's headlights illuminated the deserted road. Hulan stared out into the darkness. Again and again she went over the words of her argument with David. How could he tell her what to do? How could he see Siang and Peanut and Mayli and Jingren all as faceless, uneducated peasants? How could she be with someone like him? She felt as trapped as she had the day David and Zai had discussed her activities as though she weren't at the table with them.

At the crossroads, Hulan pointed left. Soon after, she asked the driver to stop. She got out of the car and paid her fare, supplementing it with a tip. But he waved away the extra money. "I have seen this on American television shows," he said. "And they say tips are now given in Beijing, but I cannot accept."

"Please take it," she said. "I was rude before, and tired. I hope you'll forgive me."

"Ha!" he said. "I thought you were just showing your city ways. So we are both mistaken." He looked out into the black fields. "You're sure this is where you want to be?" When Hulan nodded, he said good night, then sped away. In the far distance she could see the glow of Taiyuan's lights. In another direction Da Shui's electricity provided another smaller proof of civilization. But other than these two gentle luminescences, the night seemed an opaque blanket. Hulan walked along the road for a short way, then dipped down onto a raised pathway. Eventually she came to Ling Suchee's small compound.

She entered the tiny courtyard and was surprised to see Suchee sitting on a low-slung bamboo chair talking to a man. He looked very much at home as he sat on the metal cover of Suchee's well. Suchee introduced him as her neighbor, Tang Dan, and Hulan as an old friend.

"I've met your daughter," Hulan said, trying to camouflage her distress with the usual pleasantries.

Tang Dan gave a customary response. "She is disobedient and ugly." He regarded Hulan frankly, and she returned his stare. His eyebrows were bushy over dark eyes. A few white whiskers jutted from his chin. His stomach pressed against his shirt. His sandaled feet were callused and rough. The only family resemblance between Tang Dan and his daughter was in the strength of their jaws.

"She's at the Knight factory," Hulan said. "Siang is safe."

"I wasn't worried," Tang Dan replied. "When she comes home this weekend, I will make her see sense. By Monday morning all obstacles will be removed and she will once again obey."

The words "When a daughter, obey your father" ran through Hulan's mind. Then she thought of Siang's headstrong ways, her stubbornness, her sense of entitlement, and wondered which of the two—father or daughter—would win in this contest of wills.

With a grunt Tang Dan heaved himself to his feet. His legs bowed out under him. "Good night, Ling Suchee, Liu Hulan."

"See you tomorrow," Suchee responded.

As soon as Tang Dan left the courtyard, Suchee beckoned Hulan inside.

A few minutes later, Hulan sat at the small table in Suchee's single room, sipping tea. Etiquette prevented Suchee from asking her guest what she was doing here this late at night, so she went back to an earlier chore of making shoes. Silently she took some paste made from flour and water and applied it to sheaf after sheaf of cut newspaper, taking pains to press the sheets together so that there were no bubbles or uneven areas. Wordlessly Hulan watched her friend, remembering back to the days of the Red Soil Farm and how she herself had spent long evenings making the papier mâché soles, then dying them red in a vat tinted with soil, and sewing on scraps of cloth to create the tops.

"I've told you about David," Hulan said. Suchee nodded and continued her work. "Many years ago in America I left him with no explanation. It was cruel and unforgivable. All those years since that time I've been lonely. Of course, there were other men, but they meant nothing. Then, when David came back into my life, I wanted nothing more than for us to be together again. I thought we could be happy together, but I don't think we can."

"Because . . ."

"Because since he's come here, I don't know who I am," she said. "I act one way, he acts another. He's said terrible things."

"What terrible things were those?"

"That the women in the factory are uneducated, that our country is corrupt, that the people who run the factory are honest . . ."

"Ah, so it is a political disagreement."

"That, and he thinks he can treat me like a woman, like a *taitai*."

"Don't you want to be his wife?"

"It is a word that, like so many in our language, is a prison to me."

"I don't understand."

"*Mama, baba*. Separate words for older brother and younger brother—*gege* and *didi*. Separate words for older sister and younger sister—*jiejie* and *meimei*. *Yeye, nainai, bofu, shushu*," she rattled off the words for paternal grandfather, paternal grandmother, oldest paternal uncle and younger paternal uncle. "All these are different than the words for their maternal counterparts, and *those* words connote a lesser meaning because the female side is seen as unimportant."

Suchee picked up another piece of newsprint, coated it with the

paste, and pressed it to the growing sole. "You aren't telling me anything I don't know."

"My whole life I've known exactly where I fit in the family tree. Even when I lived in America, I felt the pressure of that. No, not pressure, the weight, the sense that I could never truly be myself."

"But our words are a comfort," Suchee said, glancing up from her work. "They tell us who we are. They are what make us Chinese."

"No, they are what keep us locked to the past," Hulan countered. "When a daughter, obey your father; when a wife, obey your husband; when a widow, obey your son," she said, completing the proverb she had thought of when talking to Tang Dan.

At this Suchee put down her work. Once again Hulan was struck by how much her friend had aged in this harsh environment. But Hulan was doing just what she had accused David and the taxi driver of doing, judging Suchee by her face. Behind the rough skin and tragic eyes, Suchee was as she'd always been—gentle, kind, and astute.

"It is sad, Hulan. You have not changed since you were a girl. You were always running away, even when you first came running to the countryside all those years ago."

Hulan disagreed. "I was sent to the Red Soil Farm."

"Yes, but even then you ran away from the truth of you."

"I don't understand."

Suchee's eyes narrowed as she appraised her girlhood friend; then she asked, "Do you want me to say this?"

Suddenly Hulan wasn't sure, but Suchee went on. "Here is what I remember about you: Unlike most of the girls sent here, you were happy to be away from your family. Oh, you said you were lonely, but no one ever saw you cry, no one ever saw you write a letter. When they had struggle meetings, you spoke out the loudest and said the worst words. No one wanted you on their team, because at any time you could turn against an individual person or the entire group."

"I know all this," Hulan said. "I'm sorry for the things I did."

"Are you sure? Because what I remember is that your words kept you safely alone."

"You think I spouted those slogans and reported on people's infractions because I didn't want friends? You're absolutely wrong."

"Am I?" When Hulan didn't answer, Suchee said, "If you couldn't run away from people physically, then you could distance yourself by being politically superior."

"I never treated you that way."

Suchee raised her eyebrows. A dark silence settled on them.

Finally Hulan said, "It was against the rules to have sex. That was the worst infraction."

"I was your friend," Suchee said. "You didn't have to report us."

"But everything worked out. Ling Shaoyi was able to stay here with you. The two of you had a life together."

Suchee shook her head. "Do you think a day goes by when I don't wish that you had never seen us on that day, that I had never married, that I had never given birth to a daughter? Shaoyi was sixteen and I was twelve when your train arrived. You remember how I loved him from afar? That was the love of a farm girl for a city boy. Two years later, he finally saw me, but we were not looking to spend our lives together. We both understood our differences. Like you, he was from a good family. They had always planned for him to go to university and become an engineer. But you said your words and then you ran away."

"I didn't run away. A family friend came to get me. Do you think I was happy about what happened next? I was made to say more terrible words and then was sent into exile in America—"

"Even after you left, Shaoyi was punished," Suchee pressed on. "There were more struggle meetings. He was called a counterrevolutionary, a revisionist, a cow demon. They made him write self-criticisms. The brigade leaders instructed us to get married. But what kind of a ceremony was it? We both wore dunce caps. We were paraded through the compound. We didn't have a wedding banquet, but people did throw rotten fruit at us. We didn't enjoy a wedding night. Instead I was sent back to my family and Shaoyi was put in the cow shed. I heard later that they kept him there for three months and only brought him out after he contracted pneumonia. I thought I would never see him again, but I was wrong. When the others went home, Shaoyi had to stay behind. When he came to my parents' house, I didn't recognize him. He had lost much weight and his color was that of a dead man. He looked sixty, not twenty."

"Everyone suffered in those days," Hulan said, echoing the words that Peanut had said earlier today. "Is there anyone in our country who wasn't affected by the Chaos?"

"Your words are true," Suchee said. "But many people were able to retrieve their old lives. Shaoyi was not one of them, and neither was I. Like most girls, I had been betrothed almost since birth. I know this is a feudal idea, but even in those dark times customs didn't change that much in the countryside. Naturally, the family heard of the cause of my mock marriage and called off the engagement. My parents tried to find another match for me, but who would take into their family a broken piece of jade? When Shaoyi came to our door, my father decided to accept him."

Hulan understood the devastating implications of what Suchee was telling her. In China a daughter was never considered to be a member of her birth family. She was raised as an outsider—someone who consumed valuable rice until she went to the family of her husband. Upon marriage the bride's family had to provide a dowry, while the groom's family had to pay a bride price. A poor family such as Suchee's might have anticipated a few bride cakes, a few slivers of pork, and maybe a *jin* or two of rice. But as a broken piece of jade—a girl who had lost her virginity— Suchee was effectively worthless. No family would pay for her, and her parents couldn't afford a larger dowry. However, Shaoyi too had been worthless. He no longer had access to his family. He certainly had no ties to anyone in Da Shui or any of the other neighboring villages. By being taken into his wife's home, Shaoyi lost his identity. He traded in his last name and took on Ling as his new surname.

"At first I was happy," Suchee continued. "Then I saw the way he suffered. You city people do not understand hard work. Do you think a man who's supposed to be an engineer is capable of chopping down trees for firewood, of plowing the fields with an ox, of using a long-handled hoe to work the land all day, every day, year after year? Even my father felt sorry for Shaoyi. Sometimes my father would say to him, 'Go help Mama and Suchee with their work.' And Shaoyi would have to obey, because he was no longer a true man. What could we give him to do? He couldn't cook. He didn't know how to patch clothes or"—and here she gestured to the work before her—"make shoes. My mother taught him how to shuck corn. Day after day he would sit outside stripping the cobs of their kernels, or separating seed, or cleaning the rice. Neighbor men saw him doing this work and ridiculed him.

"Every year Shaoyi wrote to his family in Beijing, hoping that they would be able to get him assigned to a work unit in the capital and get him a residency permit. But when the government saw he had a wife and child in the countryside, they ignored the applications and even the bribes. To our government he had become a country bumpkin like me. Each year he became thinner and quieter. He developed ulcers and arthritis. Every winter I wondered if his lungs, which had been so damaged during his confinement, would finally fail. I made him tea with ginger and onions. I held his head over steamed vinegar to clear the congestion. But every night he coughed. When his sputum turned from green to red, I knew there wasn't much time left. The barefoot doctor prescribed a tonic, but he died anyway. For too many years he had eaten bitterness."

"I'm sorry."

"Sorry is not the word I want to hear," Suchee said.

"Then what do you want? For me to make it up to you? I'm trying . . ."

"I'm glad you came for Miaoshan. And yes, that will help me. But I'm thinking of something else tonight. Despite all that happened, I know we were good friends. As I look back over the years, I can remember others. Madame Tsai on the next farm has always been free-spoken with me. Tang Dan's wife was also good and funny when we worked in the fields. She is dead many years now, but I will always remember her. But you were my closest friend."

"I feel the same way," Hulan admitted. "I have not had other friends since you."

"Then why did you report us?" Suchee implored. "It would have been so easy to look the other way."

"In those days I didn't believe in a one-eye-open, one-eye-closed policy—"

"No! You said those things and then you ran away. It's the same with your foreigner now."

"It's not," Hulan said. "David's trying to make me into something I'm not. He's trying to control me." But even to Hulan's ears these words rang hollow.

Suchee pressed her advantage, confronting her old friend on her weaknesses. "You accuse us and then you are gone. You meet your foreigner in America and then you run away from him. You come back here and work in the Ministry of Public Security, knowing, I think, that no one will be your friend if you do that job. And then you meet your foreigner again. You are together long enough to get pregnant. He wants you to come to him. Even if we don't admit it, every single person in China would like to leave. You have that opportunity handed to you—"

"You're twisting what happened—"

"And you decide to stay here," Suchee forged on. "So he comes to you. Here is what I think happens: You are seeing a future before you. You are thinking you will be happy. One minute later—not even long enough for the sun to go around the earth—you have turned things into bitterness, so that now you run away again. It is easier for you to be alone by your own actions than to be left by others—"

Suddenly a flashlight beam crossed the window opening. "Hulan! Hulan! Are you here?" David's voice called out.

Never had Hulan been so happy to hear his voice. Across the table, Suchee kept her eyes steady on Hulan, taking in her friend's reaction.

"You can run away from what I've said here," Suchee said in a low voice, "but it won't change the truth of it."

"If all you say is true, then why have you stayed my friend?"

"I don't know that I have," Suchee answered truthfully.

"Then why did you write to me?"

"Because I needed to know what happened to my child. I thought that if you had any decency, you would come—"

"Hulan!" David cried out again. "Are you here? Is anyone here?"

Suchee stood. "He's come for you," she said. "This must mean he loves you very much. And I can tell you love him or else you wouldn't be so tormented." She crossed to the threshold, looked back at Hulan almost in sympathy, then stepped outside. A moment later Hulan heard Suchee greet David in almost incomprehensible English. "Hello. I am Ling Suchee. Hulan is inside house."

Hulan covered her face with her hands, willed her heart to slow down, and tried to compose a look that would not betray her feelings. Suchee had distorted the facts, but that didn't make them any less painful to hear. Hulan heard David say her name. She took a breath, uncovered her eyes, and looked up to see him standing in the doorway.

"Where's Suchee?" she asked.

"Outside with Investigator Lo."

Hulan let the implications of that sink in. Vice Minister Zai must have told Lo about this place. She said, "I'm sorry."

"Me too."

Ignoring everything that Suchee had implied, Hulan said, "I'm not used to anyone telling me what to do. I reacted badly."

David sat down opposite her. "What about me? The words I spoke came from someone else. I'm not like that, Hulan."

"I know."

"This is a big change for both of us. Can we just leave it at that? Put this behind us and start again?"

"I'd like to." The relief Hulan heard in her voice embarrassed her. She eyed David to see if he'd noticed. He had. She watched him struggle with what to do next. Would they fight? Would they need to have an American-style discussion of feelings? Or would he stay true to his suggestion of "putting this behind them"? As for herself, she wondered if she'd be able to have a discussion of any sort. She *had* run away. Admitting that allowed the rest of Suchee's words to skitter around in Hulan's brain like free radicals. She needed time to give them form, to shove them out or accept them. She saw David studying her and realized that, as usual, he was calculating how much she could take before she shut down or ran away. Just as she felt another rise in panic, David seemed to come to a conclusion of his own.

He cleared his throat and said, "Driving out here, I thought about what you said about the factory. If it's true—"

"It is." These words sounded weak, as though she'd lost a great battle.

Again Hulan saw the wariness in David's eyes. "I have to trust what you saw," he cautiously went on. "Still, what you've told me doesn't jibe with how I experienced Henry Knight. He thinks he's doing good for these people, paying them well, providing housing. Beyond that, he said several times that his employees haven't had serious injuries. Have you seen anyone else get hurt?"

Apart from her own little scrapes, Hulan had to admit that she hadn't.

"So Xiao Yang's injury and suicide could have been a totally random thing."

"Except that Peanut said that when women *get hurt*, they disappear."

"For now let's just say they're fired, okay?" David said. Hulan could sense the emotions of the last hour falling away as he became caught up in Knight International's problems. "That still leaves the alleged injuries. To me this suggests a flaw in the design or that some part of the manufacturing process is inherently dangerous."

"Those machines *are* dangerous."

"But you could say that about every piece of machinery on the planet," he said. "The issue then changes from one about injuries to what happens if an employee gets hurt. And again, I have a hard time believing the Knights are irresponsible employers because I saw the way Henry reacted over that woman's death. I don't think he could have made that up. If he is, then he's putting on an incredible act."

"Maybe Henry doesn't know," Hulan offered.

"That's not plausible. It's his company. He built it. He takes pride in connecting to people, in knowing his products."

"But, David, how often does he come out here?"

"Not as much as he'd like. He's had heart problems . . ."

"So maybe he hasn't seen every part of the compound. Where are the worst conditions? On the main factory floor and in the dormitory. If he's an honorable man, like you say, then he can't enter the dormitory because it's against company policy."

"Are you defending him?"

"I don't even know him," she replied, "but I have to respect your judgment, especially when it comes to an American."

"But what about the factory floor?"

She thought about this, then asked, "Have you taken a tour of the compound yet?"

"I've seen parts—the Administration Building, a lunch room, the courtyard."

"One of the things I've noticed is that there are several places to meet with large groups of employees. There's an auditorium, but the cafeteria could also be a place to talk to people, not to mention the courtyard. You could easily gather all of the employees out there. Maybe Henry hasn't been on the factory floor because he's never had to. Oh, maybe back on opening day, or maybe he goes to the final assembly room, but otherwise why would he go in there? And even if he did, it would be easy to keep him focused on the product, not the environment."

"Today he said that since the factory moved to China, he's let Sandy and the others handle the manufacturing aspects of the business."

Hulan mulled this over, then nodded to herself.

"What?" David asked.

"What's that American saying? Something about out of sight, out of consciousness?"

"Out of sight, out of mind."

"That's it. The first time I went to the factory, Sandy Newheart took me into the final assembly area. When you're in there, it's huge, with a hundred women working. You don't think about what you're *not* seeing. When I asked about what was on the other side of the wall, he got upset. What I'm trying to say is that the architecture of that place hides things. No windows. Excellent soundproofing. Doors that seem to go nowhere. Circuitous hallways that hide direction and dimension."

"I'm not sure I follow what you mean. You can't 'hide' a room with seven hundred women in it."

"But you can," Hulan said as she stood up. David followed her outside. They found Suchee and Investigator Lo sitting on their haunches next to the Mercedes, smoking Marlboros.

"Suchee, can you get those plans you showed me before?"

Hulan's friend stood, went out to the shed where Miaoshan had been found, and came back with the manila envelope. Together they went back into the house. Suchee flipped on the single bare lightbulb. Hulan cleared Suchee's shoe project off the table and wiped the dampness away with her forearm. After Suchee pulled out the papers, Hulan riffled through until she found the factory plans. The four of them leaned in, hovering over the main site plan. Hulan spoke in English, pointing out each building to orient the others. Quickly she flipped this plan aside to show the second-story designs and, tapping her finger across the paper, showed those few places where there were windows—all on the second story, all facing out over the wall as opposed to into the courtyard. Then she went to the Assembly Building specs.

"Here's the front door and the lobby. Right here they have a desk. There's a button underneath the desk that unlocks the door into the main part of the building." With her finger she traced the route to that door, and crossed to the foyer on the other side where the women separated into two groups. "If you go right, you eventually end up in the final assembly room. If you go left, you end up in the main manufacturing area." From here she traveled along the serpentine hallways, hesitating before other doors which either led nowhere or to small closets or rooms. She tilted her eyes up to David's. "By the time you've gotten to this main room, you don't know whether you're facing north or south, or where you are in relation to the rest of the compound."

Suchee muttered something. Hulan asked her to repeat it, which Suchee attempted in English. "You talk fast. I do not understand. But this is like the fields. No straight . . ." Suchee frowned, looking for the word, then reverted to Mandarin, rattling off several sentences and gesturing this way and that.

Investigator Lo and Hulan nodded in understanding. Then Hulan explained to David that in the countryside paths between the fields were never built in a straight line; nor was there ever a direct route to a farm or a village. On the superstitious level, this was done to confuse ghosts. On the practical level, it had been done to baffle bandits, kidnappers, and invading armies. "The women who work in the factory—myself included—don't see it, because they're so accustomed to it."

"And Henry Knight designed his factory this way to confuse the people who work there?" David asked.

"What if it was designed this way to keep out prying eyes, including his own?"

"Hulan, if things are as bad as you say, is it conceivable that Henry Knight *wouldn't* know? Put another way, who's the only person who will benefit from a cover-up? It's Henry Knight's company. He's selling it for a huge profit. Obviously if there's something wrong, it needs to remain hidden until after the sale."

"What about his son?"

"Doug? He's going to make money with the sale, of course, but not as much as his father. And he'll stay on after the takeover. Henry's been fighting for that."

"So his son can take the blame when everything comes to light?" Hulan asked. "What kind of a father is he?"

An uncomfortable silence clamped down over the group. Every person in the room knew what had happened between Hulan and her father. Hulan looked into each of their faces, seeing their sympathy. Keeping her voice steady, Hulan said, "But this isn't a vendetta as far as we know. This isn't one man against . . ." She faltered. When she next spoke, her tone was hard. "This is a big factory. If Henry knows, wouldn't they all know? Madame Leung, Sandy Newheart, Aaron Rodgers, that security guard, even Doug Knight?"

"And Miaoshan," Suchee ventured.

David's and Hulan's eyes met across the table as they considered. "What else did Miaoshan bring home?" David asked.

Hulan opened up more building plans, but no one could see their significance. There were also plot plans of the surrounding area, indicating that perhaps the company had once considered expanding the compound. But when Hulan showed David the spreadsheet, she noticed his involuntary intake of breath, then the way he swiftly recovered. On the left of the page were the names of the various action figures. Next to these names were numbers, whether in dollars or *yuan* Hulan couldn't tell. She picked up one of the papers and stared at the names: Sam, Uta, Nick, Gaseous, Annabel, Notorious.

"Why is it these six Friends?" Hulan asked. "The ten characters were designed as a team. Where's Cactus?" She quoted the print ads and the history she'd seen on the brag wall at the Knight compound. "'Sam and Cactus are best buddies, doing right together.' It was a master stroke of marketing, don't you think? A child can't have Sam without at least having Cactus." Suddenly she yelped in triumph. "It's the stupidest code I've ever seen, but so stupid I would have missed it if I didn't know something about the toys."

As soon as she said this, David immediately discerned the pattern. *S*am, *U*ta, *N*ick, *G*aseous, *A*nnabel, *N*otorious. SUN GAN.

"This is so obvious it has to be a set up," Hulan said. Then, seeing David's hooded look, she asked, "Have you seen something like this before?"

David's jaw tightened. Hulan was sure he wasn't even aware of it. When he answered "No," she knew he was lying.

"What about the papers Sun sent you?" she pressed.

David stared at her resolutely. The documents in his room bore a striking resemblance to these. They had the same typeface, layout, and the Knight letterhead. But he couldn't tell Hulan any of that.

"Investigator Lo," Hulan said without taking her eyes off David, "perhaps you'd like to wait outside. This could mean political trouble for all of us, and I don't know if I'll be able to protect you."

Before Lo could respond, David sighed. "He doesn't have to go anywhere."

"David, this could be dangerous," she insisted. "I look at the Knight factory and think that they're making money by putting people's health and safety in jeopardy, but is it against the law? In China the answer is not really. I look at these papers and figure that Sun is connected somehow. Obviously the Knights wouldn't be able to operate out here without his help. But what do these papers even mean? As I said, Sun is a powerful man. More than that, he's popular, very, very popular. Even I," she said, "have admired him."

"You don't understand *my* concern," David said with a rueful smile. "Governor Sun is my client. You trained as a lawyer, Hulan. You know what that means. The papers he sent me are now privileged information. Ethically I can't turn them over to you or use them to damage him in any way, because he's my client, as is the Tartan corporation."

"You're a prosecutor," Hulan said after a long pause.

"I *was* a prosecutor. But even as a prosecutor I always respected the rights of the accused. Confidentiality is a cornerstone of our legal system."

"But you're in China . . ."

"I'm not saying that Governor Sun's papers are anything like these, but if they were, would I be free to pursue him as though he was a criminal rather than a client?"

"Article 3 of the Provisional Regulations Regarding Lawyers says that in carrying out their activities, lawyers 'shall take facts as the basis and the law as the criterion,'" she recited. "This means that lawyers should never fail to distinguish between right and wrong. They should expose contradictory facts and clarify erroneous errors. A lawyer also has the right to refuse to represent a client if he feels that the defendant has failed to reveal the entire truth."

"What are you leaving out?"

"As a lawyer operating in China, you must safeguard state sovereignty . . ."

"No problem."

"And the state's economic interests," Hulan continued. "At the same time, the rights and interests of foreign businessmen must be protected."

"Just tell me, do I have to maintain confidentiality here or not?"

"I'm afraid so. The code says that confidentiality of private matters must be maintained. It goes along with protecting state secrets."

"It seems to me there are a lot of contradictions in those rules."

"This is China."

"So what can and can I not do?"

"I didn't train in our system, and I've never practiced law here," Hulan said. "I don't know all of the subtleties or how to play them."

"You do have one thing in your favor," Lo interrupted, although he didn't fully understand David's dilemma. "Lawyers have the right to make investigations and visits pertaining to the cases they're handling."

"In that case," David said, "I'd like to go back to the hotel."

A few minutes later, Suchee walked the trio to the car. With great solemnity she extended the papers to Hulan, who refused them. "Keep them here for now," she said. "Your daughter knew how to keep them safe." Then, "I promise you I'll find out who killed her."

As soon as the car disappeared down the dirt road, Suchee turned toward the shed to restore to their hiding place the papers that might have cost her daughter's life.

# 13

A N HOUR LATER, AFTER MAKING A PLAN FOR THE NEXT
day, Investigator Lo dropped David and Hulan off at the entrance to
the Shanxi Grand Hotel, then drove away to park the car. As they passed
through the lobby on the way to the elevator, a woman's voice called
out, "David Stark!" He looked around and saw a woman he didn't recognize approaching him. She was Chinese, but dressed unlike most women
he'd seen here. She wore khaki trousers and a silk blouse. Her hair was
pulled back in a ponytail, and large gold earrings hung from her earlobes.
She extended her hand. "Mr. Stark, I'm Pearl Jenner. Would you join me
for a drink?"

He knew he'd heard the name before but couldn't place it. "I'm
sorry," he said. All he wanted to do was get to his room and look at Sun's
papers. "We're just on our way up. It's been a long day."

Pearl Jenner studied Hulan, then turned back to David. "I've come a
long way," she said. "This isn't the easiest place to get to."

"Yes, well . . ."

"I would think you'd want to talk to me. I'm from the *Times*. I've
been covering the Tartan acquisition."

Now David realized who this woman was. She'd written the article
he'd read on the day of Keith's funeral, saying that the federal investigation into bribery allegations would now be dismissed because of his

death. She had gotten her facts wrong and no doubt caused unnecessary pain for the Baxter family.

"I'm not interested in giving an interview at this time," he said, taking Hulan's elbow and leading her away.

"I know about Ling Miaoshan," Pearl called out after them.

David and Hulan stopped and turned around.

A triumphant smile played around Pearl's lips. "Why don't you join me in the bar? There's someone there I think you'll want to meet." She spun on her heel, utterly confident that David and his companion would follow.

The bar was in the basement next to the gift shops. She sat down at a table where a young man nursed a half-empty bottle of orange soda. "I want you to meet Guy Lin. Guy, this is David Stark and . . . Miss Liu, isn't it?" Hulan didn't acknowledge her. Instead she shook the young man's hand and sat down. Guy was young, twenty-two at most. His complexion was sallow and his eyes miserably sad. His shoulders sagged and his frayed cotton shirt hung loosely on his thin frame. To Hulan, he looked like an Overseas Chinese; to David, he looked like a mainlander. In a way they were both right.

"Guy is from Taiyuan, but like you, Miss Liu, he was educated in America. In fact, he's a graduate of your alma mater."

"You went to USC?" Hulan asked the boy. He nodded.

David kept his eyes on Pearl, reflecting on the fact that she had not been introduced to Hulan and yet knew not only who she was but also where she'd gone to school.

"Yes, he went to USC to study chemistry on a scholarship," Pearl went on. "But things didn't go according to plan. See, he gets there, takes a sociology class to fill an out-of-field science requirement, gets interested, and goes out to do a little community service for extra credit. Guess where he ends up? OSHA."

"I don't see what any of this has to do with us," David said.

"Hear me out." Pearl Jenner was attractive, but her smile was not in the least bit friendly. "First Guy volunteers in the office, assisting people with their claims, answering questions, filing papers. He begins to like it, and the folks there like him too. Pretty soon he's forgotten all about chemistry. All he wants to do is go out and help his new friends in their work. He especially likes going into factories and helping people who're being treated badly. Only one problem. He's in America on a student visa. He gets pulled over for a speeding ticket. No big deal, right? Only his name gets run through the computer and by now he's illegal. His friends at OSHA try to help him. They're government people, but even they can't do anything. Two weeks later he's back in China."

"Ms. Jenner, it's late. If you have something to tell me—"

Pearl raised her voice and spoke right over David. "He's seen the outside world. He's seen the good part of the U.S., but he's also seen the shit. You know what I mean? Put a greedy American and a hundred illegals together and you've got a nice sweatshop operation going. But he knows how it *should* be. So he's back in China and he starts poking around. He hears about these American companies that have been opening in his home province. He gets hired by one, works a couple of days, and if he were a different kind of person he probably would have stayed there because the pay's good, the dormitories are better than government-assigned housing, and the work's not too hard. But he quits and tries another factory—Knight International. The problem here is he's only a day worker in the warehouse, so he can't see what the place is really like. Then one Saturday he gets an idea. On Saturdays at one the local men and women leave the compound together. He sidles up to the most beautiful girl he can find and strikes up a conversation."

David interrupted, "How long ago was this?"

The young man looked up. "Three months," he said. "But she"—he motioned to Pearl with his elbow—"is making it into something it wasn't. I wanted to know about the factory, but when I first saw Miaoshan, all I wanted to know was her. On that day I walked her home. She didn't want me to come inside, but she said she would meet me the next day." He hesitated, then asked, "Did you know her?"

When David shook his head, Guy said, "She was *beautiful*, but she had inside of her so much . . ." He struggled to find the word, then said, "She wanted to know all about America, and I told her. When she found out why I was at the factory, she said she'd help me. She was alive with ideas. She told me what it was like in there: the girls who were too young to work, the way the managers lied about the pay, the way people got injured and how often."

"Did she have proof?" David asked, thinking that if the factory employed child labor, Hulan surely would have told him.

"She told me what she saw."

"But those could have been made-up stories," David suggested. "Just how young are the women? Did she get ID's from them? Was she able to introduce you to anyone who'd been hurt? Did she have medical records?"

"Mr. Stark, hear him out," Pearl said. "He'll get to all that." Then to Guy she said, "Tell him what you thought you'd do with the information you collected and why it was important."

Not knowing Hulan's background, Guy explained that in America things were very different. If someone got hurt from a product, then the manufacturer could be sued. If a product was made in an unsafe manner, then the workers could sue. Most amazing, if the manufacturing process caused damage to the environment, then neighbors or the government could go after the company to clean it up and even make retribution to the people and the state.

"When I left China, we didn't have any recourse if we were burned or dismembered by products," he continued. "But while I was away, a consumer-rights law went into effect. Now even state-owned enterprises can be sued! There have been about half a million individual suits each of the last three years. I am sure you have read of the different campaigns in regards to this movement."

Although Hulan always tried to avoid campaigns, she—like any other citizen of China—couldn't avoid them, especially since the cornerstone of any campaign involved the press. So of course she'd seen articles like "Is a Chinese Life Worth Less Than a Foreign Life?" and "A Needle in My Father's New Kidney!" In fact, the media was very much at the heart of the new consumer law. Since press reports could be introduced in court as evidence, smear campaigns went a long way in swaying judges. This resulted in costly counterattacks mounted in the media by the defendants. And while awards to plaintiffs weren't as lucrative as in the States—the record still stood at about $30,000 U.S., given to the family of a woman who'd been asphyxiated by a faulty water heater—judges regularly granted monies to dubious claimants based on a "fairness principle" that implied that the rich should help the poor.

"But what does this have to do with Knight?" David asked. "They've never had a product-liability case."

"It's not the products I care about," Guy said. "It's how they're made. For me that includes not using child labor and providing a safe environment. Three years ago we didn't have consumer rights or product liability, but we have them now. Why can't we take the next step and push for workers' rights?" Guy searched David's face. "Every country, including yours, had to start somewhere. Miaoshan and I thought that somewhere could be Knight. But the women in the factory never helped us. They never said a word because they were afraid they would lose their jobs. Still, she kept asking."

"Even after the women wouldn't respond?" Hulan asked.

Guy nodded. Hulan put two fingers to her lips and tapped gently, deep in thought.

"When the women wouldn't help," Guy continued, "I said, 'Let's forget it.' But Miaoshan had another idea. There was a man in the factory, an American, who liked her. Sometimes during the week she would go and talk to him at night. She said he was worried about the factory. He thought it was unfair how the women were treated. He began to tell her things—money things—that went on inside. That's when I knew we couldn't do everything on our own. I have a friend who's in business in Taiyuan. He has computers in his office, and he let me use one. I got on the Internet and looked for help."

"That's how he found me," Pearl interjected. "At the paper we get information out of China in the usual ways—press conferences and speeches by politicians. The things the government wants you to know are easy to find out. But what about something like Tiananmen? We had reporters in Beijing at the time, but we also relied heavily on the students who communicated with us through fax machines. The same goes for a lot of other stories. We hear about things, but it's difficult to work officially, if you know what I mean. Nowadays, with the Internet, getting information is easier than it used to be. China blocks the *Times'* website, but enterprising people like Guy are able to get around the firewalls."

"So for you it's not personal," Hulan said. "It's professional."

"What isn't?" Pearl asked. "There isn't a business reporter in the

States who hasn't tried to get at a story like this, but it's been completely closed to us by both the Chinese and the Americans."

"Why does it matter to you what happens in a factory in China?" Hulan asked.

"Because it's a human-rights issue and that's a hot-button issue that sells."

Hulan said, "The people who work in the Knight factory aren't prisoners . . ."

"Human-rights violations come in many forms: political prisoners in solitary confinement, prison laborers, but I would also include what happens to the women and girls in factories like Knight."

"I agree it's bad in there," Hulan said, "but is it worse than working in the fields?"

David hid his surprise. Hadn't Hulan just gotten on his case for using this same argument? Was she using this as a tactic to provoke Pearl?

"That's not the point."

"Really?" Hulan retorted. "Do you have any idea what a factory like Knight has done for the surrounding area? I'm not defending the company. I've been inside, but I also see a new prosperity in the countryside that was unimaginable twenty years ago."

Pearl seemed ready for Hulan's challenge. "You want the big picture? All right, here it is." For the next few minutes Pearl talked about her and her colleagues' efforts to cover American manufacturing practices in China and their deeper cultural and political implications. Manufacturers went overseas for cheap labor and great tax breaks, but they could also skirt around American laws by hiring children, by using chemicals that would never pass U.S. safety standards, by having working conditions that were dangerous, and by employing people for inhumane numbers of hours.

"Occasionally some company or person gets targeted by a watchdog group," Pearl said. "You've read about them. Some conglomerate hires a celebrity who endorses a line of children's clothing that turns out to be manufactured using child labor. What do the celebrity and conglomerate do when the truth comes out? They plead ignorance." Pearl sighed. "The truth is, they probably *are* ignorant, but that doesn't make it right. Then you get reporters who want to go and see what it's like in a factory like

Knight, but we can't get in. You have to wonder about that."

"But *does* anyone wonder about it?" Hulan asked.

Pearl's eyes narrowed. "Meaning?"

"Meaning I lived in the States for a while. I never noticed anyone caring much about China one way or the other."

Every once in a while Hulan said something that showed animosity toward the U.S. David knew she sometimes did it just to elicit a reaction. Other times he thought she was giving her real opinion. Right now, watching these two women—one Chinese, the other Chinese American— he wondered what exactly Hulan was doing.

"That's the beauty of the story," Pearl exclaimed. "Most Americans never think at all about China, and to me that's very strange, because China plays a part of our everyday lives."

"What are you talking about?" Hulan asked, agitated now.

"China's invisible," Pearl responded, "producing invisible work and invisible products. From the moment we wake up in the morning until we go to sleep at night, we are coming in contact with China. Our alarm clocks, our T-shirts, our designer clothes. The tires on our cars. The electronics we use all day. Take any holiday—Easter, Halloween, Christmas— all the decorations are made in China. The toys our kids play with, even those that we consider to be the most 'American'—Teenage Mutant Ninja Turtles, G.I. Joe, Sam & His Friends, and of course Barbie. Tens of millions of Barbies are made in China every year. Without naming names, I can say that there are some American factories in China that pay only about twenty-four dollars a month. That's six dollars a month *less* than what the Chinese laborers working on the transcontinental railroad were paid in the last century."

"But these things aren't unique to China," Hulan said, again defending her home country.

"You're right. They also happen in Indonesia, Sri Lanka, Pakistan, Haiti, but I'm Chinese American, and what happens here matters to me."

Seeing Hulan's dubious look, Pearl said, "When Guy first contacted me, I didn't know what to believe. Then he started e-mailing information about the factory's conditions. They sounded really awful." She turned to David. "Like lawyers, reporters also need proof. I tried to set up several appointments with Henry Knight, but he always canceled. Then, when I heard that Tartan was going to buy Knight, I tried Randall Craig, then Miles Stout. They were pleasant enough, but of course they told me nothing. About three months ago, I called Keith Baxter. He denied any wrongdoing by Knight or his client, Tartan. But I kept calling and giving him pieces of information that only someone on the inside, someone like Guy, could know. The more I pressed Keith with those tidbits, for lack of a better word, the more I could sense his softening. Did you know that Keith used to come out here a lot?"

David nodded. Miles had told him that Keith had been over here at least once a month for the last year, sometimes staying for a week or two at a time.

"He knew that what I was saying was true," she continued, "because he'd seen it himself. I think at the end he was ready to give me proof, tangible evidence of Knight's activities here."

"Of what?" David asked. "Here's what I'm hearing: Knight has a factory in China that has bad working conditions. But Tartan is about to buy Knight. Once that happens, any irregularities that exist—and I'm not saying they do—will be immediately remedied."

"Unless Henry Knight's hiding the truth from Tartan to keep his stock prices high. That should be of great concern to you and your client."

David had had enough of Pearl's insinuations. The papers he'd seen at Suchee's house already troubled him. He needed to get up to his room and see how they related to Sun's. Gnawing at him was the thought that he was representing a client who might be up to his eyeballs in illegal acts. If this was so, he was trapped by an ethical code that said he would have to continue to represent Sun. At the same time, he had a responsibility to Tartan to make sure the sale went through smoothly and without illicit shenanigans attached. What Pearl had just suggested about Knight International was fraud, pure and simple. He couldn't let Tartan get pulled into that muck. He had to know if she had any real information.

"Are you saying that the Securities and Exchange Commission is investigating the sale?"

"No," Pearl answered.

"Did Keith give you proof that there was a violation of the Foreign Corrupt Practices Act?"

"Of course not."

"Did Keith give you *any* reason at all to believe that there was a federal investigation of any sort?"

"No," she responded.

"And yet you wrote—"

"I had to pressure him somehow."

"You made that stuff up!" David jabbed out the words.

"I always said it was alleged," she answered defensively.

"*Alleged*? Alleged by whom? You made it sound like he was the target of a criminal investigation. Do you have any idea what that did to him?"

"Well, I had to keep the pressure on," she repeated lamely. "I had to make him believe that an investigation already existed so that he'd bring me the papers. You know, take his case to the press—"

"Do you have any concept of how your lies made his family feel after his death?"

"That's why I wrote that the case was no longer an issue. That's why I manufactured the quote from Henry Knight. It was unethical, but I'm not the first reporter to do it."

"But there never was a case!" David's hands bunched into fists. He'd never felt so strongly the desire to hit someone—a woman—before.

Pearl regarded him coolly, then asked, "Have you considered that Keith might have appreciated what I wrote? That maybe it provided a safe cover for him, especially if he was going to be a whistle blower?"

"We'll never know that, will we?" David said through clenched teeth.

David's fury grew as he realized Pearl's indifference to the pain she'd caused. Guy continued to sit there, pathetic in his misery. Around them business travelers swilled down a last beer or scotch before retiring.

"What are you doing in my country?" Hulan asked, her voice frigid in anger.

David looked over and saw on Hulan's face what he felt—utter loathing for this woman. But Pearl seemed indifferent.

"As you already know," Pearl said, "I knew about Miaoshan. A week before her death, Guy said that she'd smuggled papers out of the factory and that he'd send them to me once he got a copy. The day after she gave them to him, she killed herself." Pearl looked around. "But none of us believes that, do we? That's why I thought it would be good to get them in person."

Hearing of the papers, David stifled the desire to catch Hulan's eye.

"You say you have papers," Hulan said to Guy in a tone that revealed nothing but a kind of general interest. "What are they?"

"She never explained to me what they were," Guy said, "but she said they were the proof of many things."

"What did she mean by that?"

"Miaoshan always talked on many levels," he said. "She was very smart. I went to university, but she was much smarter than me." Guy reached down and pulled a sheaf of papers out of his satchel. "These plans show how the factory was designed. There aren't many doors and very few windows. If there were a fire, many people would die." David had thought the same thing when he'd seen them at Suchee's, but he didn't say so now. "But also, if they use chemicals, then there isn't proper ventilation."

David's thoughts turned instantly to the baby. His hand covered Hulan's as she said, "I haven't smelled anything when I've been there."

"I don't know if they use them," Guy admitted. "I'm just saying that if they did, it would be very dangerous."

"Was there anything else?" David asked, momentarily relieved.

Guy rummaged through his satchel again and pulled out a Xeroxed set of spreadsheets, but before David or Hulan could get a real look at them to verify that these were the same ones they'd seen at Suchee's, Pearl Jenner reached out and scooped them up.

"I don't think you need to see these," Pearl said with a grin. "But when you're ready to cooperate with me, I'll be happy to show them to you."

"At least tell us what they are," David said.

"I don't think so," Pearl responded.

Hulan interrupted this exchange by switching to Mandarin and addressing Guy directly. "How did Miaoshan get the papers?"

"I told you. There was a man at the factory, an American," Guy answered, also in Mandarin. "He helped her."

"Hey! Speak in English!" Pearl ordered.

"Aaron Rodgers? Sandy Newheart?"

"A man, that's all I know." Guy's sorrow was palpable. "She would go to him at night. He liked to talk and she listened. I told her to stop, because I was afraid. What if this man decided to stop talking? What if he wanted sex? She was alone with him. I worried about her and the baby."

Hulan squeezed David's hand. She switched back to Mandarin again. "Miaoshan was pregnant with your child."

Guy's eyes brimmed with tears, and he nodded. "I loved her," he said in Mandarin. "I saw a future for us. But I pushed her and pushed her. I wanted success for myself. And I have lost my family and my future in one moment."

"What are you saying?" Pearl demanded. When neither Hulan nor Guy translated, she looked at David. When she saw he wasn't going to help her, that characteristic hard smile came back to her lips. She stood and motioned for Guy to join her. They took a few steps, then Pearl stopped and came back to the table.

"You can't hide the truth from me," she said to David. "As you say, what Knight's doing may not be against the law, but it is against human law." When he didn't respond, she added, "Tartan can get its side out or not. Frankly, I don't care, because I'll do the story with or without you."

"Tartan Incorporated has no comment at this time," David said with all the lawyerly command he could muster.

Pearl Jenner flipped her ponytail behind her. She looked inordinately amused. "You have a reputation in Los Angeles. You're respected. People speak of you as one of the good guys. I'm going to have a lot of fun proving they're wrong."

# 14

SILENTLY DAVID AND HULAN WATCHED AS PEARL AND GUY stepped into the elevator and the doors closed. David didn't know what to say. What he'd thought of as a bad situation out at Suchee's house had just gotten much worse.

"If Pearl really has a copy of Miaoshan's papers," Hulan said at last, "then she knows no more than we do."

"But she's not going to stop until—"

"We have a lot to talk about. Let's not do it here."

In their room, David asked what Guy had said in Mandarin. Hulan told him, then added, "I knew I couldn't ask him in English. It was too private, and I didn't think he'd tell me in front of you or that woman."

David sat down on the edge of the bed. "I'm in trouble."

"Maybe, maybe not. In the last few hours we've been deluged with facts and innuendoes. We have to sort through them."

"Why? It's clear that Pearl Jenner has an agenda and I'm part of it. As she said, it doesn't matter whether I participate in her story or not. She's still going to write it."

"And destroy your reputation?"

"It's not just my reputation," he said. "It's who I am."

Hulan knelt before him, put her hands on his knees, and looked up into his face. "You know that what I have always loved most about you is your integrity, but ethics and honor are easy to live by as long as they aren't tested. This is your test."

"But I did nothing wrong. I'm just a lawyer who's bound by client confidentiality. That's not my fault."

"David, you know I love you, but maybe it's your fault in the sense that you chose not to know." Before he could say anything, she put a finger on his lips to keep him from speaking. "You took the job at Phillips, MacKenzie without asking enough questions. You took on the Tartan matter without knowing all the details. You agreed to represent Governor Sun without finding out what his problems were. Now that you represent him, you still don't know what it is exactly that he wants from you. I understand *why* you didn't ask. You wanted to be here with me. And I know this isn't the right time to say this, but you came here without even asking me if this was what I wanted."

Everything she said was true. He had put his wanting to be with Hulan before anything else. His love for her had always blinded him, but knowing this didn't change the way he operated. If anything, he'd always had to act for both of them. That's why he hadn't asked her if she wanted him to come. (What if she'd said no?) That's why when Hulan had run away from him during dinner, he'd gone straight back to the hotel, rousted Lo out of bed, and made the investigator drive him out into the pitch black of the countryside to Suchee's hovel. He could have said something about the poverty of that place, about the filth, about Hulan's sanity in risking her health and that of their child's by being there. He could have also demanded an explanation from Hulan about why she'd run away from him. But he did none of those things, because he really didn't want to know the answers. His desire not to know had gotten him into deep trouble both professionally and personally.

He looked down at Hulan and felt a deep despair. What if his actions and inactions had cost him everything?

"We're going to sort this out," Hulan soothed. "Too many things are happening here. What's going on in the factory. What Henry Knight may or may not know about all that. What Miaoshan's papers are and what they have to do with the ones that Governor Sun gave you. You're the smartest man I know . . ." He felt the warmth of her hand as she put it on his chest over his heart. "But you're dumb here. So now all we can do is try to work our way out of it."

"Where do we start?"

"There's only one place to start. With Miaoshan." Hulan rose and sat next to him.

"She got around," he noted dryly. "Tsai Bing, Guy Lin, the American in the factory."

"It's weird, isn't it?" Hulan said. "Our culture is repressed in many ways. Sex out of marriage . . . well, it's against the law in a lot of instances. But Miaoshan didn't seem to care. She was almost predatory about it. I want to believe it's because she was young or that she had a hard life, but that could apply to millions of women here."

"Maybe her promiscuity goes back to that earthiness you were talking about earlier," David offered. "If you grow up in the countryside everyone—even children—knows about animals mating. They see it with their own eyes; they participate in the breeding."

"Yes, and they joke about sex and go to the herbalist to increase their sexual prowess or fertility, but chastity is considered the highest female virtue. It's a weird double standard, but that's how it is. So at first when Captain Woo and Siang said Miaoshan had a bad reputation, I didn't believe it, because there are always village gossips willing to spread lies. But now how can I not? She was having sex with Tsai Bing recently enough that he thinks he was the father. Poor Guy Lin believes he was the father and maybe he was, but it could also have been Aaron Rodgers."

"That kid? Why him?"

"You should see 'that kid' with the young women in the factory."

"That doesn't mean he was fucking her."

"Believe me, David, he was. I see that now. Today Peanut said something about Tang Siang going off to rendezvous with Aaron in the context of talking about Miaoshan. When she said it was strange, she must have meant that Miaoshan and Tang Siang not only shared Tsai Bing but Aaron Rodgers as well."

"Three men, one woman. There are plenty of motives for murder in that setup."

"Yes, but there's more to Miaoshan than her promiscuity," Hulan said. "I think that in each case she used sex as a means to an end. With

Tsai Bing she had to keep up appearances. More than that, she knew that Siang loved him and probably used sex in the most petty way to get back at her rival. I think she saw Guy Lin as a ticket out, but to keep that relationship she had to give him information. That meant seducing Aaron Rodgers, although having watched him in action, I don't think she had to work too hard to do it. But she didn't stop with Aaron. The way that she went about getting other information from the women in the factory fascinates me. Guy said she repeatedly asked the women questions. Even Peanut complained about it, but I didn't know what she was talking about at the time."

"Why does it matter?"

"Because it shows such bad manners in our culture," Hulan responded. "If you ask a question and don't get an answer or you get an evasive one, you're supposed to drop the subject. When Miaoshan didn't, she was going beyond rude. I myself haven't asked many questions about Miaoshan in the factory, but you might expect stories about her to circulate. Apart from ridiculous ghost stories, I don't think there was any grief when she died. Neither Tang Siang nor Peanut liked her. So I've wondered, was it just jealousy or was it something else? I'm beginning to think that she was too foreign to them."

"Because of the way she looked."

"Yes, she was beautiful but in a foreign way. I think she played that up, buying Western-style clothes—"

"Or they were given to her by whomever it was in the factory who was helping her."

"Oh, absolutely. Even now, more than three weeks after her death, I can smell White Shoulders perfume on her bunk." When David frowned, she said, "Oh, you've smelled it before. It's strong and very sweet. I remember it from the States. I always hated that smell."

As David looked at her incredulously, Hulan went on. "And it's not something you can just pick up in the company store, in a dry-goods shop in Da Shui Village, or even here in Taiyuan. Which brings us to the papers Sun gave you."

"I can't show them to you."

"I understand."

David got up, sorted through some piles on the desk, then spread out

Sun's papers while shielding them from Hulan's view. Although they looked superficially the same as Miaoshan's, these weren't copies. Where the names of the action figures had been, now were the names of various companies—Toy World, Plush Supply, Mega Soft, and the like. To their right were account numbers and deposit dates. How did this material fit into the big picture? Had Sun sent these over knowing this moment was imminent, that as David's client he'd be protected, because instead of evidence these documents would fall under the rubric of privileged information?

What was very clear was that David and Hulan were now on different sides. She loved him and knew how to read him, so as much as he tried to cover his emotions, the look on his face as he read through the papers said much about Sun's guilt. So now her job was to garner information from David; his was to protect his client. Her job was to pin down the crime; his was to point suspicion elsewhere. He was fully aware that cooperation was a cornerstone of the legal system in any country. (Smart criminals hired attorneys with good relationships with investigators and prosecutors. Was this part of Sun's plan for David with Hulan?) David could speak to Hulan, of course, but only in hypotheticals, while she would try to pry as much information out of him as possible without him shutting her out completely.

"What are Miaoshan's papers actually proof of?" David asked. "What's the crime? I see so many levels, but which is the right one?" He paused, then said, "You didn't tell me before about the child labor."

"I didn't think it mattered. It's not really a prosecutable offense." She shook her head, then clarified, "What I mean is, child labor is against the law. The official labor age is eighteen for government factory work, but private companies can hire younger people."

"How young are we talking, Hulan?"

"At Knight I'd say the youngest I've seen is about twelve, but, David, you have to understand that if this was reported, Knight might be fined and those girls let go. I think the only way an owner might go to jail was if there was an international scandal, a story in the press . . ." Her breath came out in a disgusted rush. "Pearl Jenner."

"But Guy Lin said Miaoshan's papers were 'proof.' They may be proof of something, but it isn't child-labor violations. And despite the

SUN GAN code, I see nothing that would tie my client to child labor. Neither are the papers proof of the factory's conditions. You and I and Guy Lin may think they're deplorable, but they're still within Knight's rights, which means, I hate to say it, they're also within Tartan's rights. Then there's the dangerous machinery and the possibility of improper chemical use. But again, I didn't see anything in Miaoshan's papers that pointed to that or to my client."

Very aware that Sun's papers were just a few feet away from her, Hulan ventured, "Maybe the products themselves are somehow dangerous and the papers have to do with shipments or something."

"I don't think so. If there was a defect in Sam & His Friends, it would have been all over the American press. That's something they really can't cover up."

"The next level of crime would have to be the bribery," Hulan said. "Except we know that Pearl made that up."

David didn't respond.

"I'm going to lay out a scenario for you," she said. "Let's suppose Pearl was right but didn't know it. Could Sun have taken a bribe?" She held up a hand. "You needn't answer, but consider this: Would your client not take one? This is China and Sun's a smooth operator. If that's the case, then how did Knight hide it in their financials?"

David thought he knew the answer: Knight disguised the bribes as payments to dummy corporations. Hulan was close to the truth. Where would she go next?

"I'm guessing they did it with the skim," Hulan said suddenly. "We were told we'd be paid five hundred *yuan*. We actually get two hundred, which leaves three hundred *yuan* a month extra." She reached over and grabbed a notepad off the nightstand. "Let's figure some people do get paid more, because Knight has to promote sometimes, don't you think?" She didn't wait for an answer. "So let's take an average of two hundred *yuan* off the salaries. With a thousand workers . . ." She scribbled furiously, then announced, "That would be a little over twenty-four thousand U.S. dollars a month, or almost three hundred thousand dollars a year."

She put the notepad down. "Would your client have killed Miaoshan if he thought she had papers that implicated him in a scheme that netted him hundreds of thousands of dollars a year?" Hulan asked, then answered the question herself. "Yes."

"You're jumping to huge conclusions," David countered. "Let's remember that we still don't know what Miaoshan's papers actually mean. They don't give a complete picture."

"Well, I'm guessing you're holding a list of dummy corporations—"

"You've got deposits and dates and toys that spell out a code name, but where is the money actually going?" David interrupted, trying to keep Hulan focused on Miaoshan's documents. "All this"—his motion included the papers before him—"proves nothing unless you know where the money is. It could be down at the corner bank, in Beijing, or in Switzerland for all you know. And it could be going into *anyone's* account. What if Sun's been set up? You have to admit that was a pretty stupid code."

What he said next took Hulan completely by surprise. "We have to find a way to link the deaths of Miaoshan, Xiao Yang, and Keith." He amazed her again by focusing first on Xiao Yang. Then, as he spoke, she realized that he was laying out a defense—one in which he pointed blame everywhere but at his client—as clearly as if he'd been in a courtroom before a jury.

"Let's assume that the woman in the factory was killed as you suggested earlier tonight." David thought back to just three hours ago when that idea had seemed inconceivable. Now her death had become one more piece of the puzzle. "Was it to cover up the fact that Knight doesn't use safety precautions with its machinery? Was it because she saw something? Was it because she made financial demands on Aaron Rodgers or someone else in the company? Was she one of Aaron Rodgers's girls and now that he'd seen . . . what's the new girl's name?"

"Tang Siang."

"Now that he'd seen Tang Siang, he wanted to get rid of Xiao Yang. Maybe he's a serial killer who makes love to girls, then murders them when he's ready to move on." His questioning tone belied the implausibility of this scenario.

Hulan asked gently, "And where does Keith fit into all this?"

They hadn't talked much about his death. Just after the accident David hadn't been in contact with Hulan. Then when she'd finally called, they'd mostly talked about his coming to Beijing. Once he got there, he had been too happy to bring up Keith's gory death.

"I saw him die," David said. He stood and began to pace. "I accepted responsibility for that. The FBI, Madeleine, Rob, we all believed I was the target. But what if we were wrong? What if someone believed that Keith truly was the subject of a federal investigation as Pearl had written?"

"But what she wrote wasn't true."

David stopped in his pacing. "It doesn't matter. People believe what they read in the papers." He resumed walking, crossing the room in four long strides before pivoting and crossing the way he'd come. "And even if our murderer *didn't* believe the story, what if he saw right through to the fact that Keith was about to become a whistle-blower either about the conditions in the factory or about the bribery you're alleging?"

"But you don't know that he was."

"On that night he was worried about something. Maybe it was that he was going to be a whistle blower; maybe it was that he was going to violate attorney-client privilege. Either way, an ethical issue had torn him up. What if the killer or killers knew that?"

"But the deaths were on two continents. Are you suggesting a network of some sort—a gang, the triads, some form of organized-crime syndicate—operating in China and Los Angeles that goes beyond Sun and Knight?"

"It could just as easily be a couple of greedy people. Remember, the Knights, Aaron Rodgers, Sandy Newheart—all of them travel back and forth. They all had opportunity."

"Sun also travels," she pointed out. "He also had opportunity."

But listening to the facts the way David had laid them out had shifted Hulan's view. It was too easy, too obvious, to accept Sun as the guilty party, although she already had enough evidence for a conviction under Chinese law. Is that what the killers had planned all along?

Even if Sun was innocent, David was still in an ethical bind. He'd presented different possibilities. If Keith had been bothered by an ethical issue, as David suggested, then that pointed to Tartan's involvement. Tartan was David's client, as was Sun. If, on the other hand, Henry Knight or the Knight company was the guilty party, then David had no obligation to keep quiet. In fact, he would need to expose whatever had happened to his client, Tartan. Although if Sun had accepted payments from Knight, then David was back in his ethical quandary because he couldn't expose one client to another.

"It seems to me I have four choices." David held up his forefinger. "One, I can finish the deal and walk away. No one but you, Sun, Henry Knight, and I will be the wiser. That would be the easy way, maybe even the sensible way, but that's not going to happen." He held up a second finger. "I could tell Tartan an edited version of events. Obviously I wouldn't be able to tell them anything about Sun." He stopped. "I'm not saying he's involved . . ."

"I understand."

"So that would limit me to the child-labor issue and the unsavory working conditions, both of which may or may not be illegal in China. Three, I can go forward, continue representing Tartan and Sun, but ask the governor and the Knights straight out what this stuff is. Because here's the thing: What if you're wrong about the bribery? These papers could be nothing. Maybe Miaoshan committed suicide because she was pregnant and didn't know who the father was. Maybe Xiao Yang, in shock from loss of blood, wandered out on the roof and fell. Maybe I *was* the target when Keith died, or maybe it was just a random drive-by and Keith truly was an innocent victim. Maybe Keith knew none of this stuff. That last night he said he was torn up about something personal and ethical, but maybe it was just his girlfriend's death. I know I wouldn't be able to think straight if anything happened to you. What if we're seeing crimes where none exist because that's what we've both been trained to do? What if there's some logical explanation? I'll admit it's a remote possibility, but what if?"

Before Hulan could say anything, David held up a fourth finger. "Four, I confront Henry and he tells me: (a) it's none of my business, or (b) his company doesn't have internal practices that are up to my standards, but so what? I go to Sun and he admits to crimes galore. Whatever he says is *still* privileged information."

Hulan waited as David thought. At last he said, "Again things are complicated by representing different clients doing and wanting vastly different things. In the U.S. we have a couple of exceptions to privilege. One is the crime-fraud exception, which is if you think your services are being used to help commit a crime—meaning if you have *actual knowledge* that a crime or fraud is occurring—then you can come forward. The problem is that I don't have actual knowledge of that."

"What about the machinery?"

"One machine, one injury. Maybe Xiao Yang didn't know how to use it properly. Maybe she was tired. No, it's not enough on its own. It's probably not even a crime. Anyway, Knight isn't using my services to do anything, and my client has no knowledge of the problems with the machinery. I could try and get Henry to admit he's injured, dismembered, and murdered employees. He's not a client, but even if he was, I'd be compelled to protect others. Besides, do you honestly believe he'd admit such a thing?"

David didn't wait for an answer. Instead he moved to a second option. "I can try to withdraw as counsel for Tartan and Sun, but I still wouldn't be able to say anything, because privilege goes with the firm. Finally, I have to remember that there's a financial transaction going on. Knight International is a publicly held company. The Securities and Exchange Commission expects the lawyers to sign off on the truth of the disclosures of a company in the event of a sale. Maybe I just won't be able to sign."

"What about Sun?"

"I don't know, but I think I need to find someone who really understands the subtleties of Chinese law." He sank back down on the bed. "It seems to me I can either let it all go, in which case I'd have abandoned any personal integrity that I ever had—"

"Or you could go to the press—"

"Pearl Jenner?" David asked, shocked.

"The *New York Times*. The *Washington Post*."

"That only happens in the movies. This is real. I can't go to the press. I'd lose all control of the situation, and it would be totally unethical. If this is something more and somehow Tartan or Sun is connected to the deaths of Miaoshan, Xiao Yang, or Keith—I'll lose my license to practice law, for I will have violated the law's most sacred trust." He seemed at a loss for words, then added, "And if *any* of this stuff is true, it's going to be dangerous. We'll be dealing with people who have no compunctions about killing."

"What should I do?"

"Are you asking as an investigator or as the woman I love?"

"I don't know," she admitted.

His first suggestion seemed banal given what was at stake. "Look up everyone's travel schedules. At least we'll know where everyone was on the crucial dates."

"Including Sun's?"

"I know you'll do that whether I ask you to or not. It's your job."

"Okay then, I'll do the travel inquiries as soon as we get back to Beijing."

"And Miles will arrive there tomorrow afternoon. He's nothing if not a good lawyer. He'll know what to do." His meaning was clear to both of them. David would be able to confide everything to Miles because Tartan and Sun were firm clients. He kept his gaze steady on her to gauge her reaction to his next question. "Can you go back to the factory tomorrow?"

"I'd already planned on it," she said.

"We need to know more about Miaoshan, about the way she was speaking to the women, about what she really had in mind with her inquiries. Did she love any of those men? Did one of them fit into her future plans? You can also watch and ask about Aaron Rodgers." He hesitated, then added, "If you smell anything . . ."

David saw his apprehension mirrored in Hulan's eyes as she put a hand protectively over her stomach. "I'll get out somehow." Her face made a subtle adjustment as she buried her feelings, then said, "I also want to see Suchee again. As soon as I'm free to leave, I'll go to the farm." Then she asked, "When's our flight?"

"Henry said we should all meet at the airport at five o'clock."

Thinking aloud, she said, "I'll have Lo pick me up at Suchee's at four; then he can drop us at the airport before driving back to Beijing. Wait! Can you even have me with you? Is that ethical?"

"I won't let you ask any questions."

"Agreed."

"How will you introduce me?"

"As my fiancée," he answered. "But I mean it, Hulan, no questions. No investigating in front of me."

She agreed to his terms, then asked, "Where will you be tomorrow?" He smiled grimly. "Randall Craig and others from Tartan are arriving tonight. Tomorrow there's some sort of celebration; then we have more meetings before flying to Beijing." He thought for a moment, then added, "I'll try to talk to Randall first thing in the morning. Later I'll try to see Sun. You never know. He may just tell me what's happening."

They had a plan, but they'd left much unsaid. For both of them there was no question that they should go forward no matter what the physical, psychological, or professional danger. But they were on separate tracks now, on opposite sides. The more they pursued their own investigations, the more obvious they would become. The more they asked questions, the more likely they would be targeted just as Keith and Miaoshan had been.

# 15

THE NEXT MORNING BEFORE DAWN, INVESTIGATOR LO drove Hulan out into the countryside and left her by the side of the road, where she found a rock on which to wait. Even before the pink streaks of dawn had faded into the dull white of day, the family that worked this tract of land emerged and began the long, slow process of watering the field. The mother, wearing a wide-brimmed, conical straw hat, carried a pole across her shoulders from which two buckets of water were suspended. The father and son each used a ladle to scoop out the water and carefully pour it on the roots of the individual plants.

The air stirred not at all this morning, and Hulan felt already that she was sitting in a steam room. Still, people went on with their lives, slowly but with increasing numbers appearing on the road's horizon. Some pushed wheelbarrows piled high with corn. Others pedaled past with baskets of produce strapped to the sides of their bicycles. But most carried their goods in large baskets lashed to their backs. One man was dwarfed by the load of hay he carried that rose a good five feet above his head and stretched out another couple of feet on either side of him. His back was bent double from the size if not the weight of his load, which bounced with each step.

At 6:30, as several unencumbered men walked past, Hulan stood and joined the parade. A few minutes later she reached the Knight compound. Each time she came here she marveled at how it rose up out of the landscape and stood starkly against the red soil and the hot white sky. Outside the gates over a hundred men milled about. As she had done yesterday evening, she drifted into the center of the crowd.

The gates opened and the men surged forward. Hulan felt herself pushed along. Once inside the compound, she stuck with the men as they walked to the warehouse. At the last moment she drifted apart to stand in the shadow of the Administration Building and take her bearings. Unlike the day before, this morning there was a lot of activity in the courtyard. Some of the men who'd entered the warehouse immediately reappeared with poles which they stuck into pre-set holes in the ground, while others began unrolling canvas for the canopy which would shade the hand-over celebration.

At quarter to seven the women began leaving the cafeteria. Seeing Peanut, Hulan swung into step with the young team leader. "I was scared you wouldn't come back," Peanut said. Then she took one of the two smocks that were draped over her arm, handed it to Hulan, and added, "Here, put this on quickly."

The two women slipped the pink material over their arms and buttoned up. Hulan tied her matching bandana over her hair.

As they wound through the Assembly Building's maze of corridors, Hulan whispered, "Can I ask you something about Miaoshan?" When Peanut nodded, Hulan asked, "You said she was a troublemaker. What did you mean by that?"

Peanut slowed, turned her head, and looked up at Hulan. "Always you are asking questions! What are the men doing? How do you get out of here? Now you ask about someone you never met. Why? Did the foreigners send you inside here? Is that why you were able to leave last night and sneak back in so easily? Am I going to lose my job because I helped you?"

"No, no, and no."

Someone behind them called out, "Hey! Hurry up! We don't want to be late because of your slow walking!"

Hulan and Peanut picked up their pace. Hulan leaned her head toward Peanut's and spoke softly. "Remember when I came into our room the first time and you said no one wanted that bunk because of the ghost spirit? Since I slept there, I can't stop thinking about this girl. Even now she troubles me."

"Because her ghost spirit is the same as her live spirit. Miaoshan only brings trouble to people."

"Did she report others for their transgressions or complain to Madame Leung about the other women?"

"You are going in the wrong direction," Peanut said. "It was the other way. All the time she is complaining to *us* about the machines, about the long day, about the food we eat. She says to us, 'We can go on strike. We can make the company improve things.' All the time she is pestering Madame Leung and reciting all of the things that are bad in here. You know what she says? That our toilets are not good. I can't understand that. In my village no one had a toilet inside the house. In fact, I had never even seen a toilet like this until I came here. When I first saw those things, I didn't know what to do. One of the women had to show me."

They turned a corner and Hulan saw the entrance to the factory floor.

"I'll tell you something else," Peanut said. "You don't know many people here yet, but everyone is nice. Even so, I can tell you that every-one—even the mothers and the older women—were happy when Miaoshan died, because we were all afraid of her words. What if we had gone on strike? What would have happened to us if we all lost our jobs?"

Entering the factory, Hulan saw Tang Siang already in position before the conveyor belt. Her face was slightly swollen from lack of sleep and her hair had not had the benefit of a brush. She didn't look happy.

At seven the bell rang, the machines cranked to life, and work began. The three women worked silently side by side, shoulder to shoulder. In such close proximity and in such a hot room, Hulan couldn't help but notice the smell of sex that radiated from Siang. She didn't seem inclined to talk. Peanut sensed this and bent her head to her work, expertly threading the hair through the doll heads. Although Hulan had many questions she wanted to ask, she followed Peanut's lead. Fortunately, Hulan didn't have to wait long before Siang broke her silence.

"Well, Peanut, aren't you going to ask me about Manager Red Face?" Siang petulantly demanded at last.

Wordlessly Peanut scooped up another head and began jabbing.

"This I know," Siang said. "He is a man like any other. He talks sweet words until he gets what he wants, then talks some more when he wants it another way. I tell him I'm not a gutter girl, but he wants to do gutter things. He says, 'Miaoshan does this for me. You do it too.' Miaoshan, Miaoshan. Always I'm hearing that name. It makes me crazy!"

"But you knew he had sex with Miaoshan before," Peanut said. Her tone was so matter-of-fact that Hulan could almost forget that Peanut was only fourteen.

"You think I don't know that every penis that has been inside me has already been inside Miaoshan?" Siang asked bitterly. The question required no answer, so Siang went on. "You're still young, Peanut. It's good for you to be safe in here. You wait for your father to arrange a marriage for you."

"I am hoping for a true-love marriage," Peanut said wistfully, her voice barely audible over the machinery.

"True love?" Siang spat out. "Look around this room and tell me if there is a single woman here who has experienced true love."

"I have," Hulan said. "And I know you have too. I've seen you with Tsai Bing."

"Tsai Bing?" Siang sputtered. Then resolve crept into her voice. "Let me tell you something about Tsai Bing. Remember that day you found us in the cornfield?"

Hulan said she did.

"You asked him about the baby and he blushed. I hadn't known about that."

"You mean about the baby?" Hulan queried.

"No, that he was still having sex with Miaoshan even when he told me that he only loved me and that we would find a way to get married."

Hulan was in no way prepared for what Siang said next.

"He had sex with her," she continued sorrowfully, "even after I told him about seeing her with my father."

Next to Hulan, Peanut sucked air in through her teeth.

"So now you have sex with the manager to get back at the one you love." Hulan eased her voice over her words, erasing anything that might be taken for judgment.

"No, I let the manager put his organ in me so I can get promoted and make more money. The only way Tsai Bing and I will ever be together is if we leave Da Shui Village. The only way that will ever happen is if we have money." Siang brought her shoulder up so she could wipe away a tear. "A night or two with a foreigner is a small price for a lifetime."

But looking at Siang, whose toughness was as thin as a sheet of gold leaf, it seemed a very high price.

The morning wore on. The temperature in the room quickly rose over a stultifying forty degrees centigrade. Around them conversation dwindled to nothing as the heat and humidity drained the last bit of energy from the women who had already worked more than fifty-six hours this week. Hulan welcomed the relative silence from human voices. She had asked as many questions as she could today without drawing excessive attention to herself. Peanut's queries about what Hulan was doing here only reminded her of how transparent her mission was becoming. Similarly, she could not continue her conversation with Siang. The girl had shut herself off, working with her head bent and her shoulders slouched except for those times when Aaron Rodgers swung by on his rounds and she plastered a fake smile on her face.

Hulan—her hands bandaged, her stomach queasy, her shoulders aching, her head pounding from the heat and noise from the machines— made her mind focus on the enigma of Ling Miaoshan. Last night Guy Lin hadn't mentioned anything about a strike. Would Miaoshan have kept that information from him? Could Miaoshan have thought up the idea of a strike by herself? Could she have then moved forward, organizing, cajoling, *frightening* her fellow workers into following her without outside help? And if someone had helped her, who and why? Maybe this someone hadn't helped her at all. Maybe he—and knowing what she did about Miaoshan, Hulan had no doubts that it would be a he—had used her as a way to foment unrest for some reason that wasn't yet clear.

As Hulan circled around these ideas, she kept coming back to Miaoshan's promiscuity. To use the coarse words of the local Public Security captain, it seemed true that Miaoshan had spread her legs for any man with a beating heart. From the beginning of time there had been women who had used sex as a method of survival, as a way of getting what they wanted, as a means to an end. But also from the beginning of time there had been women who had been victimized, used, and tossed aside when their novelty wore off or they became diseased or old. Was Miaoshan the manipulator or the manipulated?

*　　*　　*

David's first obligation was to speak to Randall Craig. At seven, he called the hotel operator for Randall's room number, but was told that Mr. Craig hadn't checked in until late last night and had asked that no calls be put through. At eight, he tried again. Randall Craig picked up on the first ring. David asked if they might have breakfast together. Ten minutes later, David was in Randall's spacious suite with a view overlooking South Xinjian Road. David had a duty to tell Randall about the problems that could be of concern to Tartan Incorporated. At the same time, David needed to protect his other client, Sun Gan. If David believed Sun was innocent—and the simplicity of the code more than anything made that a strong possibility—then he had to try to flesh out the truth to help the governor.

By the time the continental breakfast arrived, David had run through his concerns about the sale, outlining the alleged dangers on the factory floor, the use of child labor, and—without using names—the possibility that bribery had occurred.

Randall Craig listened patiently, occasionally taking sips of coffee or breaking off a piece of croissant. When David finished, Randall said, "Why hasn't this shown up in the reports?"

"I don't know," David answered.

"Well, look, the due diligence was already done by your predecessor. I'm willing to stand by Keith's reports."

"But they're wrong. If this information—any of it—comes out, then Tartan will be exposed to various lawsuits, not to mention criminal proceedings."

"Let's deal with the bribery issue first," Randall said. "I assume old man Knight is the one you think is paying out. Who's he paying?"

"I can't say," David answered. It wasn't a lie exactly, but it was vague enough to keep his other client protected.

"Is there any danger of it coming out before the sale?"

"There's an American reporter who's on to the story."

Randall sighed. "Pearl Jenner, I suppose. Have you talked to her?"

"Last night."

Randall nodded sympathetically. "When I checked in, I had about a dozen messages from her. But she's been sniffing around for a long time and hasn't been able to find anything of substance. What'd she say? Did she have names to go with the bribery?"

David was fully aware that Randall had let slip an important piece of information: Even before David walked in the room, Randall Craig had known there were problems and that a reporter was here in Taiyuan ostensibly to cover the sale. David's senses, which were already working at full tilt, jumped another notch.

"She doesn't know any names," David said. "She may not even know of the bribery, but she's aware of some of the other problems. . . ."

"The way your predecessor explained it, if there's been wrongdoing in the past, we're not responsible. If it happens in the future, we are."

David leaned forward in his chair. "I think the Knights lied on their disclosure forms."

"About the bribery?"

"About the child labor, about the working conditions . . ."

"My position is, I don't know about all that."

"But you do."

"And how's the government going to know?"

"I have to disclose it to the SEC."

"You could do that," Randall acknowledged, "but what's the point? It's better just to let the sale go through as is. Tartan's shareholders will be happy. The Knight shareholders ought to be thrilled too. What's done is done. I say let the old guy retire gracefully."

"I still think we have to disclose."

"You know what would happen to a guy like Henry Knight? Maybe he'd pay a fine. On the other hand, maybe the Feds would send him to a country-club jail. He'd be in good company for a few months, and then he'd go back to his retirement. But in the meantime you will have hurt his son, and we're counting on Doug for continuity."

"And what about me?"

"What about you?"

"I have a legal obligation to file the papers properly. If I don't, I'm leaving my law firm open to prosecution."

"You do what you gotta do. But remember this, you'll have a clear conscience, but you will have wrecked havoc on a lot of people's lives and for what? Once Knight Senior's out of the game, we clean up the company's internal problems."

Randall's tone sounded suspiciously practiced. David felt the need to remind Randall that Knight's crimes could come back to haunt Tartan.

"My job here is to perform the due diligence and—"

"No," Randall shot out sharply. "That was Keith Baxter's job, and he did exactly as we wanted. Your job is to make sure the acquisition contracts are signed on Sunday. I'm not hearing that."

"What if the women who've been hurt come forward?"

Randall Craig shrugged. "I'd say that sometimes there are little blips on the radar screen, but that they never amount to anything. Put another way, we've got five factories in and around Shenzhen, and we haven't had any problems."

"China's laws are changing."

Randall grinned and spread his hands wide. "Not fast enough. And besides, who's a Chinese judge going to believe? A peasant woman or two or a big American conglomerate that employs thousands upon thousands of men and women, that has been responsible for increased prosperity in various provinces, and that has the backing of high-ranking officials in the government?"

"A court might think differently if it had documents to back up what the women said."

Randall's demeanor suddenly changed. "What documents are those?"

"A young woman smuggled them out. She planned on giving them to Pearl Jenner."

"But she didn't?"

"No. She's dead, murdered, I believe."

"Is there an investigation into her death? Is there anything that can tie her to us?" Randall asked.

"Those are two questions. The answer to the first is not officially. The answer to the second is I don't think so."

"Then we have nothing to worry about."

"What about Keith's death?"

"I understood you were the target there."

"I have reason to believe I wasn't."

Randall sighed. "Miles thought this might come up—some kind of post-traumatic stress thing. Look, I'd like to help you through this, but the fact is I'm not trained for it. Miles will be in Beijing tomorrow. Cry on his shoulder." Randall glanced at his watch. David was supposed to take the hint and leave. When he didn't, Randall asked, "What?"

"What you just said is so out of line, I hardly know what to say."

"David, you represent me and my company. Focus on that. If there's another matter I should know about . . ." He eyed David curiously, as if sizing him up. "Have you seen those papers you mentioned? Is there something in them that I should be concerned about? If Pearl Jenner doesn't have them, then where are they? Are we going to be black-mailed?"

David couldn't answer all of these questions without putting Suchee in possible jeopardy. Instead he said, "I don't think anyone has plans to blackmail you. As far as what's in the papers, they show that the factory building wouldn't be safe in a fire. There aren't enough exits and . . ."

Randall grinned again, clearly relieved. "That's nothing. We install another door or two. No problem."

David couldn't believe what he was hearing. "The child labor and the rest of it?"

"How can I say this except bluntly? Tartan is already aware of those issues. Women getting hurt? Chemicals? Why do you think we've been in China for the past twenty years? It's because we can get away with a lot." Randall rose to signal the end of the meeting. He opened the door, then, seeing David's appalled look, said, "Don't look so shocked. China's helped build Tartan to what it is today—a billion-dollar company. Don't lose sight of that or your potential place in it."

He clapped David on the shoulder and fairly pushed him out the door. "Forgive me, but I've got to get out to Knight. We've got a full schedule today." And he shut the door in David's face.

Furious, stunned, outraged, David walked back to his room. Every-thing Randall had said was true. Even if David stepped forward—and he was cognizant of all the problems that would cause him personally—it would only be a fleabite on the corporate butt of Tartan. Still, he couldn't allow the sale to go through as it was laid out.

Back in his room, he once again called down to the hotel operator and asked to be put through to Henry's suite. When no one answered,

David called Knight International. A receptionist with a lilting voice informed him that Mr. Knight wasn't at the compound nor was he expected until eleven when the festivities would begin. "What about Douglas Knight?" David asked.

"No, sir, he isn't here either. Perhaps you should try the hotel."

David called back down to the hotel operator and was transferred to Doug's room. But he wasn't in either. David went to the hotel dining room, hoping that the Knights would be having breakfast. They weren't, so he went back upstairs.

He waited a half hour, called again at the compound and the hotel for both father and son, but they were still unreachable. David began to pace, checked his watch, then sat down and punched in what felt like dozens of numbers. If it was 9:00 A.M. here, it would be 5:00 P.M. yesterday in Los Angeles. Miles Stout's secretary answered the phone and verified that Miles had left the city. "He'll be arriving in Beijing tonight your time. He'll be at the Kempinski if you need to talk to him." David thanked her and asked to be transferred to the voice-mail message center. He tapped in his pass code and waited. He had six new messages.

The first was from Miles, who repeated almost word for word what his secretary had just told David, adding, "I'll be half dead by the time I get to the hotel, but maybe we can have breakfast together. I'd like us all to be on the same page when we meet with Randall and his people." Next, David heard Rob Butler's voice asking how things were going in private practice, informing him that there'd still been no progress on the Rising Phoenix investigation, and reminding him that if David needed anything to be sure and call. "You know, Carla's always wanted to see the Great Wall," Rob said. "Maybe we'll come out for a vacation and you can show us the sights. Anyway, it'd be a great way to get in a game or two of tennis. Do they have tennis courts out there? Send an e-mail if you can." Eddie Wiley left a message saying that the downstairs toilet had backed up and was there a plumber that David used.

Interspersed among these calls were three from Anne Baxter Hooper. At the sound of her voice, David conjured up Anne's grief-stricken face. "The operator at the U.S. Attorney's Office told me I could reach you here," she said. "I must say, I'm surprised to hear that you made that move. Well, give me a call." She spoke her number carefully, then added,

"I really want to talk to you. You can call collect if you want."

The second message said simply, "This is Anne, Keith's sister. Please call." In the third, which had come in just that morning, she sounded impatient. "Since my brother died, I've left you several messages. I'd appreciate a call back."

David erased the messages and hung up the receiver. He thought about the day of the funeral and the accusation in Anne's eyes. At the time he had thought himself to blame for Keith's death, but the picture had changed. How much should he tell her about her brother? Was it better for her to know the truth or continue to believe that her brother had been an innocent victim? And what was the truth anyway?

David dialed Anne's number in Russell. The phone rang four times, then was picked up by the answering machine. Anne's two children spoke in unison. "You've reached the Hoopers. We're not in right now, but leave a message and we'll call you back, back, back!"

After the beep, David said, "Anne, it's David Stark. I only got your messages today. I'm in China and it's a little after nine in the morning. I'm in a hotel and I'm going to be leaving soon, but I'll be back in Beijing tonight. I'll call you as soon as I can."

David hung up and resumed the pacing he'd started last night, which only exacerbated his feeling of being ensnared. He stopped, searched through his papers, found the number for Governor Sun's office, and dialed. The woman who answered didn't speak English. But after repeating Sun's name several times, he was transferred to Assistant Secretary Amy Gao. When David said he urgently needed to see Sun, Amy asked him to come straightaway. "Governor Sun has several appointments this morning," she said, "then he's going out to the factory. After that we're flying back to Beijing. Still, I know he'll make room for you."

David packed Sun's papers in his briefcase, went downstairs, and found Investigator Lo ready with the car. They rode a few blocks down Yingze Avenue and stopped at the guardhouse of an official-looking compound. On the gate was a plaque with red and gold Chinese characters announcing that this was the headquarters of the provincial government. A Chinese flag flew from the building's roof. The guard, armed with a machine gun, wore the drab green uniform of the People's Liberation Army. He eyed David in the backseat as he phoned the main building. Once he got the okay, he had Lo sign a check-in sheet, then waved them through.

Inside, the walls were a dirty beige and the floor was composed of gray stone. Lo went to the desk and explained that David was here for Governor Sun. The woman made a call, rattled off a few high-pitched phrases to the investigator, and pointed at the straight-back chairs that lined an adjacent wall.

"She says you are to wait here and I am to wait outside," Lo explained. "Someone will be with you shortly." Before David could say anything, Lo exited the building. David did as he'd been told. Five minutes turned into fifteen. Despite the open windows and the fan whirling overhead, the room was desperately hot. Every few minutes someone opened a door, peeked out, stared at David, then closed the door again.

Finally Assistant Secretary Gao emerged, her high heels clicking efficiently on the stone floor. She wore a light suit and somehow managed to look cool. "I'm sorry to keep you waiting, Mr. Stark. I was not told of your arrival until just now."

David found this unlikely.

"Please come with me."

Again David obeyed.

But instead of going to Governor Sun's office, he was led into Assistant Secretary Gao's. "Please be seated," she said. She sat down behind her desk, pushed an intercom button, and spoke a few words. A minute later a pretty young woman arrived with a thermos and cups. After the tea was poured and the girl left, Amy asked, "How can I help you?"

"I need to meet with Governor Sun."

"What is this in regard to?" she asked earnestly.

"He has asked me to represent him on some matters. I'm here to go over them with him."

"I'm familiar with all of the governor's affairs. Please feel free to discuss them with me."

Hulan had often talked about Chinese bureaucracy and how it was designed to move sluggishly, create the most paperwork, and aggravate, thereby controlling the petitioner. No wonder *guanxi*—connections— were so important. People did anything they could to circumvent bureaucratic layers and go straight to the top, whether in a hospital emergency room or in a business situation such as this.

"With all due respect, Assistant Secretary, I think it prudent to wait for Governor Sun."

"I believe Governor Sun himself told you that if you had any problems you should speak to me. That is my job and I'm here to help."

How tempting it was to just open his briefcase, toss Sun's documents on Amy's desk, and ask her what they meant. She was bright. Like most women in similar positions, she probably did more work and knew more about Sun's affairs than he did. Still, if Sun had committed a crime, then David would be violating China's judicial code in discussing these affairs with the assistant secretary.

"I'll just have to wait for the governor."

"Then you'll have to wait a long while. He has already left for Knight International."

"But you said that I should come right down and I'd be able to see him."

"Unfortunately, he was unable to delay his departure. Mr. Knight wanted to meet with him before the ceremony started. If you'd gotten here earlier, then perhaps he would have been able to see you." She glanced at her watch, then offered helpfully, "You're going to be late if you don't hurry. I'm sure you don't want to miss anything."

"I've been sitting out in your lobby for the last hour," David said coldly.

"This is unlucky, but as I said before, I didn't know you were here." In light of the two phone calls that had announced his arrival, as well as the numerous people who had taken a gander at him, this seemed disingenuous at the very least.

"And, I might add, as I was sitting there, I didn't see Governor Sun leave the building."

Amy smiled at David in a pitying way. "Attorney Stark, surely you don't believe that a building such as this would only have one exit." She paused, then added, "Perhaps if you come back on Monday or Tuesday, the governor will be able to accommodate you." She opened the top drawer of her desk, pulled out an appointment book, opened it, and looked at David expectantly.

Again, this kind of runaround was common in China, but it wasn't common to David. Not only was he used to appointments being met—certainly as an assistant U.S. attorney he was accustomed to being treated with respect—but he was feeling very much at the mercy of circumstances. So, he did the one thing he shouldn't have. He lost his temper.

He stood, leaned over the assistant secretary's desk, and said gruffly, "Tell your boss I'll see him later. Tell him it won't be so easy for him to avoid me. Tell him . . ." David looked down at Assistant Secretary Gao. She looked frightened, and he wondered just how far he could or should go. He wanted the urgency of his message relayed, and he wanted to guarantee a prompt response. The only way to do that was to shade the truth. "Tell him I understand what he was doing. Tell him I have other documents that will be of great concern to him."

David didn't wait for a response, sensing that the impact of his words would be greater if he walked out. Once he had left, however, he felt anxiety bubbling up in him again. Miss Gao was young and, for all he knew, inexperienced. What if she didn't understand the seriousness of his words? What if she dismissed him as just another rude American? As David stepped back into the sweltering heat, he knew he'd done the best he could given the circumstances. But after the revelations of last night, he'd hoped to grab the loose ends, examine them, make sense of them. Instead it was quarter to eleven, he was sweating like a pig in a government courtyard, and all that he'd accomplished was a conversation that by Chinese standards could only be considered ill-mannered and lacking finesse.

# 16

B Y THE TIME DAVID AND INVESTIGATOR LO REACHED THE compound, the festivities were in full swing. A podium, dais, dance floor, and seating for two hundred had been set up under a canopy. Balloons swayed in the hot air. Streamers billowed from poles, and posters of Sam & His Friends stood on easels in a semicircle next to the dais where Henry and Doug Knight sat with Governor Sun Gan and Randall Craig. Music played from loudspeakers, and on the dance floor a group of about twenty girls dressed in colorful costumes came to the end of an acrobatic routine. The audience, which seemed to be made up almost entirely of Chinese women, politely applauded.

Sandy Newheart saw David and waved him over to the front row. As David sat down, Sandy whispered, "You're late."

"Sorry," David said. "It couldn't be helped."

The performers gathered into a little group. One of the girls stepped forward and in a loud but melodious voice announced that they would now sing a few American songs, all favorites of President Jiang Zemin. An instrumental introduction blared through the loudspeaker, and a moment later the girls were singing "Row Your Boat" in ever more complex rounds.

Sandy inclined his head toward David and said under his breath, "Practically every goddamn meeting has to have this rigmarole. Hero music. Firecrackers. Out-of-tune marching bands. Twenty-seven thousand verses of 'Jingle Bells.' Then an exchange of gifts. Then speeches. Meanwhile everyone here is roasting to death."

"Then why do it?"

"Custom."

"For Knight?"

"Hell no. It's a Chinese custom."

"Knight is an American company."

"So? This is how it's done over here. At least that's what that grease-ball Sun says. And whatever he says, old man Knight'll do it. He's into this shit."

The last strains of the tune faded, and the girls broke into a spirited rendition of "Jingle Bells."

Sandy looked over at David and raised his eyebrows. "I told you. It's a hundred and fifty degrees in the shade, and they're singing about snow."

"Are they employees?"

Sandy shook his head. "They're a local performing troupe. I've probably seen them five times in the three years I've been here."

David jerked a thumb back over his shoulder. "And them? Are those all of your employees?"

"You kidding? No, they're just the women from the Administration Building."

"Why aren't the others here?'

"Henry wants a show, not a convention."

This was the first time David had been alone with Sandy. With Henry Knight he played the sycophant, but alone he seemed not only disillusioned but like he wanted to complain.

"Sandy, what are you going to do after the acquisition?"

"When the old man asked me to come out here, I thought it would be a big adventure. But look at this place. It's a hellhole in more ways than one. As soon as I got here, I called Henry and said I wanted to go home. But Henry was sick, so what could I do? He said he needed me to make Sam & His Friends a reality. The deal with the studio had been cemented and the prototypes were ready. Henry practically begged me to stay on until we'd gotten the first line out. Toys are a crazy product. You do a hundred lines and if you're lucky—really lucky—one hits. Well,

Sam hit. I've been with Knight for fifteen years, and we've never had anything like this craze. I've tried to look at it as my big opportunity."

The girls had now broken into four groups and were skipping in little circles, imitating horses drawing sleighs. Sandy wiped the sweat off his face and neck with a handkerchief, and said, "I've given the company fifteen years, and now they're selling. For all I know, I'll be out of a job by the end of the month. The only good news is that I'll be able to leave this godforsaken place."

The girls finished their song with a loud "Hey!" They bowed to the audience and to the men on the dais, then walked in a straight line off the dance floor. Henry Knight, beaming and clapping, stood and walked to the podium.

"Thank you, Number Seventeen Shanxi Province Acrobatic Company! You have, as always, done a beautiful job. Let's all give them another hand!" He stepped aside and continued to clap, while Madame Leung translated his words into Mandarin. Behind David the women increased their applause. Henry resumed his position. "Today we have with us Randall Craig from Tartan International. Very soon I will turn the company over to him. But don't worry. My son will be here, and things will continue on as smoothly as they have since we opened."

As Madame Leung translated, David glanced over at Sandy. He could read nothing from Sandy's expression, except perhaps boredom.

Henry continued, thanking Governor Sun Gan for years of help. Sun stood, bowed, accepted a loud round of applause, then sat down again. Then Henry launched into an introduction of Tartan, but it was so hot even under the canopy that David doubted anyone was listening. Finally Randall Craig stood and joined Henry at the podium. They shook hands, then motioned for Sun to join them. Just as Sandy predicted, there was a three-way exchange of plaques. At twelve sharp the ceremony ended. Military marching music came blaring out of the speakers, and the women in the audience quickly left their seats and hustled back to the Administration Building. The sweating Knight contingent was introduced to the equally sweating and wilting Tartan contingent; then Henry announced loudly, "Everyone please follow me. It's time for lunch and something cold to drink."

The group entered the Administration Building and went to the conference room, where, as Henry had promised, lunch was laid out. There were soft drinks with ice (made from sterilized water, or so Henry said), potato chips, and a platter of sandwiches. Looking around, David saw Governor Sun deep in conversation with one of the Tartan people. Henry, Doug, and Randall grabbed plates and took spots at the table. This lunch would be immediately followed by a tour of the compound—a sanitized tour, David was sure of it. As much as he wanted to ask these men questions, he was simply going to have to wait for a more private opportunity.

At one o'clock the bell rang in the factory. Before the machines had fully wound down, the women began filing out of the room. Hulan, Peanut, Siang, and hundreds of other women emerged out into the sunshine and headed back toward the dormitory. The festival was over and so completely cleared away that, except for a few eddies of spent firecrackers that had yet to be swept up, the courtyard seemed back to normal. Hulan had expected an air of release, but the women just seemed tired after their week's work. Once inside, Siang ducked into her room, while Hulan and Peanut continued on to theirs. Hulan pulled out the bag she'd brought with her on Thursday and slung it over her shoulder.

"Where are you going?" Peanut asked. "I thought you weren't from here."

"I'm not, but you know I have a friend in the village. I can stay with her."

"I wish I had somewhere to go," Peanut said as she stripped off her pink smock, threw it on the floor, and climbed up to her bunk.

"At least you can come to the village," Hulan said. "Get a bowl of noodles, walk around."

"I've seen that village. What's there? Nothing I haven't seen a hundred times before in my own village. No, I'd rather stay here and save my money." Peanut sighed and rolled over to face the wall. "See you later."

Hulan stared at Peanut's back, knowing that she probably wouldn't be returning. "Okay," she said, then added, "take care of yourself."

Without turning, Peanut held up an arm and waved as if to push Hulan out the door. "Yeah, yeah, yeah."

Back in the courtyard, the men who worked in the warehouse waited for the gate to open, while about fifty women and girls boarded the bus, their attitude very different from those left behind. Going back to their families, if even for a day and a half, gave them a buoyancy, a sense of expectation. Hulan took the seat next to Siang, and the bus drove out of the compound. Neither spoke and Hulan chose not to push it.

Just outside Da Shui Village several barefoot children waited for their mothers. After a flurry of hugs, they set off toward their homes, perhaps stopping at the meat shop to pick up a few slivers of pork with their hard-earned salaries. Siang said good-bye and turned down one of the alleyways. Hulan adjusted her bag on her shoulder, then hurried back onto the road.

A half hour later, she cut down into a cornfield. She called out that she was there, and Suchee called back so that Hulan might come toward her voice. A minute later they were face to face. Suchee's shirt was wet with sweat, and her face was streaked with the red earth that had dusted up as she'd hoed a furrow.

"I go back to Beijing today to follow the story," Hulan plunged in. "Before I leave, I want to see Miaoshan's belongings from the factory and ask you a few more questions."

Suchee set down her hoe and led the way along the furrow back to the house. From under Miaoshan's *kang* Suchee pulled out a small, unopened cardboard box. "The factory sent a message to me through the men in the village that I should go and pick this up," Suchee said, holding the box on her lap. "I haven't opened it." Her lips trembled, then she brusquely set the box down and went outside.

Hulan found a knife and slit open the tape that held the box closed. On the top was folded a black miniskirt and a little lace blouse. The label said THE LIMITED, and Hulan had a vague memory of that chain of mall stores in California. She set these aside and pulled out a pair of Lucky Brand jeans and a T-shirt with a Wal-Mart tag. She'd seen these T-shirts before, since they were manufactured in China and often pirated out of factories by employees or the seconds were sold off in free markets, but the jeans brand was new to her and she wondered where they'd come from. Unzipping a toiletry bag, Hulan found a toothbrush and toothpaste, a hairbrush, gel, and hairspray, Maybelline mascara and eye shadow, and a bottle of White Shoulders perfume. Then she flipped through several glossy magazines filled with colorful photographs, looking for hidden papers or notes but encountering none. Some underwear littered the bottom of the box. Tucked into the sea of cotton was something wrapped in tissue and tied with silk ribbon. Hulan opened the package and found a bra and panty set of pink silk edged with black lace. Things like this could certainly be found in China, but not in Da Shui Village or even Taiyuan. Hulan looked for the label and read NEIMAN MARCUS.

Hulan repacked the box and slid it back under the *kang*. She went outside, stopping at the shed to pick up a hoe, and waded into the field to find Suchee. Once she reached her friend, she eased into the space next to her and began working the soil around the base of the corn. She hadn't done this in more than twenty years, but the movement came back to her as though it had been yesterday—the chop into the soil, the quick jerk to lift it up, and then going back into the mound to aerate. Occasionally she bent down to pull out a weed. Soon sweat ran down her face, and the hand that had been punctured throbbed. Her shoulders, already sore from the factory, burned from a combination of her exertions and the sun's rays coming through her cotton shirt. She knew her discomfort was compounded by her pregnancy, but at the same time realized that peasant women never stopped working for such an insignificant reason. At the end of the furrow, the two women crossed over to the next row and bent once again to their labors. Hulan's mind was filled with questions she wanted to ask, but she was reticent, not knowing how to bring up Miaoshan's sexual activities. But soon enough Hulan lost awareness of proper conduct, time, and even of the heat as she glided into the ancient rhythm of human and soil.

Two hours later, as they reached the end of yet another row, Suchee stepped out of the field to where she'd left a basket. She set down her hoe, squatted down on her haunches, and motioned for Hulan to join her. Suchee reached into the basket and pulled out a thermos. She poured hot tea into the tin cup that served as the thermos top and handed it to Hulan. The bitter green liquid cut through the dust that coated her throat. She gave the cup back to Suchee, who noisily sipped the last of the liquid, then refilled the cup.

Hulan looked at her hands. On Thursday morning her hands had been those of a Red Princess and an investigator at the Ministry of Public Security—smooth, pale, with tapered fingernails. After three days in the countryside her hands were scratched, her nails cracked and ragged, and her palms a mass of broken and unbroken blisters. The bandage that covered the deep gouge was caked with dirt but still protected the wound, which hadn't stopped throbbing. Hulan longed for the cool shower she knew awaited her at the hotel, at the same time realizing that Suchee would never waste water on such a frivolous luxury. Hulan remembered back years ago to the Red Soil Farm and how in the morning people would wash their faces and brush their teeth in the communal water trough, then return at night to wash their hands, faces, feet, and teeth in the same water, which was changed only every three or four days.

"You have questions about Miaoshan," Suchee said at last, "but your manners keep you from asking them. You should know that the customs regarding visitors and etiquette no longer matter to me now that my daughter is dead."

"I've heard things about Miaoshan that trouble me," Hulan said. "You say she was to be married, and yet I hear of other men."

"There were no other men. Miaoshan loved Tsai Bing."

No mother wanted to hear what Hulan was going to say, but she relied on the fact that Suchee had insisted that she wanted the truth at whatever the cost. "I have met a man, Guy Lin, who says he is the father of Miaoshan's baby. I believe him. Did she ever mention him to you?"

Suchee turned her head away to face into the green of the field as though she had not heard.

"There is also a girl at the factory who says that Miaoshan was meeting with a foreigner." Hulan had used a euphemism, but the meaning was clear. "I believe this girl, especially when I add it to what I found among Miaoshan's belongings. You said that Miaoshan dressed like a foreigner. I hadn't thought this that important. So many of our young women—no, so many women in all of China—now dress to copy Westerners. But I was thinking of the clothes that we make here to look like clothes from the West, not the real thing. Even in Beijing I would have trouble finding the type of *nu zai ku*—'cow boy pants'—that Miaoshan had."

Suchee opened her mouth to speak, but Hulan held up a hand to stop her.

"There is more. In the box in your house I found perfume, panties, and a bra. These are not from our country. These are foreign. You might even say corrupt. There can only be one explanation: The foreigner gave these things to Miaoshan. I have a guess about who this was. Did Miaoshan ever talk to you about Aaron Rodgers?"

Suchee shook her head, but still kept her eyes averted. Her fingers began to fret the hem of a pant leg.

"What about Manager Red Face?" Hulan asked.

Again Suchee shook her head.

"Another name has also come up," Hulan continued. "It is that of your neighbor Tang Dan."

Suchee slowly rotated her face to Hulan. Her eyes were filled with pain and anger. "*That* is a lie."

"Tell me," Hulan said.

"Tang Dan is my neighbor. I was a friend of his wife's. She helped me when Miaoshan was born."

"But Tang Dan is a widower now."

"Yes," Suchee acknowledged, "and perhaps for that reason he is looking for a new wife."

"Miaoshan?"

Suchee chortled. "Tang Dan is old enough to be Miaoshan's father."

"Which would only show his strength and virility in the village."

"And that is why he has asked *me* to marry him?"

Hulan was not surprised by the news. "How many times have you said no?"

"He asked me for the first time five years ago, just as Miaoshan finished middle school. I considered it. Tang Dan is a wealthy man in our county. Our lands would have been consolidated. I thought this would give Miaoshan a better opportunity to continue her education. You always said that an education was important for women. Remember how you taught me my first characters? Then, after the Cultural Revolution, people came to our village with a new campaign. It wasn't the usual political campaign that we had all grown so accustomed to. No, this time it was a campaign to educate women. Shaoyi encouraged me and I was one of the first women from our county to join. We began with Chinese, but very soon they introduced us to English ABCs. The government said it was important for us to learn the foreigner's language as well as our own. I thought, if this is so, our country must truly be changing. And if it is changing, then Miaoshan must be a new kind of girl for our new country."

All this seemed very far off the track, but Hulan let Suchee continue for now.

"Very few children in this area go on to high school, because they're needed on the land," Suchee said "But Miaoshan was never much for physical work, and my place is so small that I really didn't need her help every day. Of course, I could have used her hands for watering, but she complained so that I thought she was just like her father. She was born to be a scholar, not a peasant. For her ninth-grade year she was one of only two children from our village accepted to high school. She accomplished that on her own. We didn't need Tang Dan for help, but this didn't stop him from asking if we needed it. Four years later, when Miaoshan graduated, I once again considered accepting Tang Dan's proposal. I don't know if you can understand this, Hulan. When I say he is wealthy, it may not seem so to you by your counting, but he is the first man in our county to become a millionaire."

Hulan told Suchee that Siang had said her father *wasn't* a millionaire.

"Tang Dan isn't going to discuss his business affairs with his daughter," Suchee insisted.

"But he would with you."

Suchee grunted. "I have been alone here for many years. I have relied on no one. I have raised and slaughtered animals. I have bought my own seed and tilled my soil. I have hired people to help me during harvest, but I have sold all of my produce myself. Tang Dan and I understood each other."

"So you discussed his money?" Hulan asked skeptically.

"Liu Hulan, look around you. There is nothing here but hard work. Oh, people can go to the village and watch television in the café. Some people, like Tang Dan, even have their own television sets. But what do half-naked American girls bouncing their big breasts in their *bi ji nis* have to do with me?" Hulan understood that Suchee was talking about *Baywatch*, a show very popular in China for its bikini-clad actresses. "For young people like Miaoshan, Tsai Bing, and Siang, they see a paradise that they want to be a part of. For old people like me, I think it only makes people dream of things they can never have."

"You're not old."

Suchee frowned and said, "We are the same age, yes, but look at you. You are just starting your life. I am ending mine."

Hulan could have denied all this; instead she asked, "What about Tang Dan?"

"For many years—since his wife's death and Shaoyi's death—we have met. It has only been talk, and most of that has been about our regrets. Tang Dan and I grew up in the same area, but our lives were almost as different as yours and mine. Even though we had both been born after Liberation, our families had held on to old ways and customs, as was the case in the countryside. As a boy he was well fed and spoiled. As a girl I was seen as merely a visitor to our family home. My father treated me very badly. I wasn't given food or a place to sleep in the house. My mother could do nothing about it, because she had been sold to my father by her father for only a few *yuan* during a famine. When the Cultural Revolution came, everything changed."

Having heard Siang's version of these events, Hulan listened carefully for any discrepancies, but the story was still the same. Tang Dan's family had been destroyed, and he'd spent years in a labor camp.

"But for me those early years of the Cultural Revolution were glorious," Suchee continued. "I couldn't imagine being so happy. I was sent to the Red Soil Farm to teach people like you. I was away from the suffocation of the village. I was fed. I remember how the city kids complained about the food, but that was the first time in my life that I'd had three meals in a day, and that happened every day, week after week, month after month. Then everything changed again. By the end of the Cultural Revolution, I was married to someone with a bad record and Tang Dan had his own black mark. So for the first time Tang Dan and I had something very much in common."

Suchee described their lives. The birth of children. The cycling of the seasons. The famines and droughts. The deaths of their spouses. And the never-ending drudgery of eking a living from the soil. But unlike Suchee's farm, Tang Dan's land had flourished beneath his hard work. "I try to keep up with my land," she explained. "The soil is good, but it's hard for me to do the watering alone. Since he got rich, Tang Dan has been able to hire many men to help him with his watering and caring."

All this hadn't stopped the villagers from gossiping about the Tangs. "They said the Tang family hid its gold and only dug it up again when they knew it was safe. What nonsense!" Suchee sniffed indignantly. "I saw him work. The Tsai family saw him work. His wealth comes from his own efforts, but it is something that he doesn't discuss, not even with his own daughter." Suchee hesitated, then added, "Especially with his own daughter."

"Why?"

"For two reasons. First, like so many young people in our village, she has become greedy for the outside world. Tang Dan doesn't want to pay for such foolishness! And second, he has been negotiating with a family for almost two years now over a bride price and dowry. He doesn't want to pay more than he has to."

So many of these customs were outdated, even forbidden, but that didn't stop them from persisting in the countryside far from the watchful eyes of the central government.

"You would have married Tang Dan for love or because he was rich?" Hulan asked.

"Love? I have great respect for Tang Dan and I would have done my woman duty, but the only reason I would have married him was because I thought he would send Miaoshan to English teacher's school or maybe to Beijing University."

Taken aback by this revelation, Hulan asked, "Could she have qualified?"

Suchee went back to fretting the hem of her pants. "She didn't apply. She said she would do it on her own with no help, which was a good thing, because as soon as Miaoshan graduated, Tang Dan no longer asked me to marry him and I couldn't very well ask him."

"But he *has* asked you again."

Suchee nodded. "Since Miaoshan's death he has asked me several times. He says I shouldn't be alone. He says that once Siang is married away to another village, he will be completely alone too. But I have said no. He says it's okay if we don't have sex. He understands that I grieve for my daughter. But I still said no. Last night when you were here, he said that he would buy my land. That way I could leave this place of unhappy memories. He said he would pay me enough that I could move to Taiyuan City and be comfortable for the rest of my life. I thanked him for his friendship, but I had to say no to that as well. I'm an end-of-the-liner now. All I have left are my memories. The good ones and the bad ones are here, not in Taiyuan City. To leave this place would be to say good-bye to my life."

What was brutally obvious to Hulan seemed invisible to Suchee. During the period that Miaoshan had come home, Tang Dan had probably turned his full attention to her. For whatever reason, she'd rejected him. Now that Miaoshan was gone—and the thought that Tang Dan might have killed Miaoshan for refusing him weighed heavily on Hulan's mind—he once again zeroed in on Suchee. Miaoshan was beautiful and young, and, as Hulan had already said to Suchee, that was reason enough for any man of a certain age. But what was his interest in Suchee? The saying went: A family without a woman is like a man without a soul. But Tang Dan, as a millionaire, could have any woman he wanted. He could even buy a young girl from a neighboring province to prove his virility to the village. Why then would he chose a prematurely aged peasant who didn't have many years left in her? The only answer, it seemed to Hulan, was that Tang Dan wanted something from the Ling family. Hulan decided to tuck this line of inquiry away for now, as she had other, more important questions she needed to ask about Miaoshan.

"Your daughter was trying to organize the women in the factory," Hulan pressed on. "Did you know about that?"

Cicadas whirred about them. The air hung thick as porridge.

"She wanted the women to strike for better conditions," Suchee acknowledged at last. "That—and not some man—is the reason she stayed at the factory on weekends."

"You knew this, but you didn't tell me?"

"I thought if you knew my daughter was a troublemaker, you wouldn't come. It is your job to punish troublemakers, not help them."

Hulan didn't know how to respond to the truth of her friend's statement. Instead she said, "I need to know exactly what Miaoshan was doing."

"I'll tell you what I know. Miaoshan was smart, smart like you. But she didn't have your opportunities. I was proud of her, but that was never enough. 'A mother is supposed to be proud,' she used to say. 'What does it matter if you are proud of me?' Do you know the old proverb, 'He who has a mind to beat his dog will easily find a stick'?"

Hulan hadn't heard it, but she understood the meaning. Miaoshan had been an angry person who had wanted to strike out. But as a poor but intelligent peasant girl, she had little opportunity either to use her brains or to strike out. Knight International gave her the chance.

"She would come home and say things. *'Fight selfishness! Puncture the arrogance of imperialism! Repudiate revisionism! It is right to rebel!'* Oh, the slogans I heard! They cut into my heart like shards of glass."

"But those are slogans from the Cultural Revolution. Did you teach them to her?"

"Me? Never! I wanted to forget those days."

"Then where did she learn them?"

"I don't know."

"The factory? At school? From your neighbors? From Tang Dan?"

"Maybe from one, maybe from all. I don't know. But I can say this, those words frightened me, not just because of their content but because she was willing to change the meaning to suit her own purposes."

"How do you mean?"

"'A tree may wish to stand still, but the world will not subside,'" Suchee quoted.

"I remember that one. Mao meant that class struggle was unavoidable. She must have been thinking of the American owners."

"Exactly, but what scared me was that she saw herself as the wind, a wind that was so strong she would be able to blow the others along with her." Suchee repacked the thermos, stood, and picked up her hoe. "My torment is that I always viewed Miaoshan with mother eyes. Since I saw her hanging before me, I have cursed myself for refusing to see her as she truly was. My blindness prevented me from guiding her away from danger. In the end I failed as a mother, because I couldn't protect my child." With that, Suchee disappeared into the wall of green, leaving behind her a wake of rustling stalks.

Hulan didn't move. Her mind wrestled with this contradictory girl. By all accounts and on the evidence of her own belongings, Miaoshan had become increasingly Westernized. But what Suchee had just told her made Miaoshan sound like a fervent Communist of the old school. Had one of these personifications been an act? If so, which one was the real Miaoshan? In a way it didn't matter, because even with these contradictions the character of Miaoshan was emerging. In fact, Hulan understood the dead girl intimately, because at one time in her life she had been like Miaoshan. Years ago Hulan had been consumed with political fervor, with grievous consequences. Miaoshan too had been filled with a Communist zeal that could also be dangerous in the new China. She had gone to the factory and immediately understood that she could profit from it. Today Hulan could see from the wisdom and pain of time that those windows of opportunity were rare and dangerous. Like Hulan, Miaoshan had been smart and beautiful. But Miaoshan had an extra attribute: the ability to make herself beautiful for a wide variety of men with whom she could be quite persuasive. Now the question was, which of Miaoshan's amorous or political manipulations had gotten her killed?

The persistent honking of a car horn snapped Hulan back to the present. She looked at her watch, realized how late it was, then ran through the fields until she reached Suchee's little compound, where David and Investigator Lo were waiting for her.

"Where've you been?" David asked. "We've got to get to the airport."

"I'm ready," she said.

David and Lo exchanged looks that said otherwise. "You're, ah, dirty?" David said, giving up any pretext of diplomacy.

Hurriedly Hulan drew water from the well, dipped her arms in the bucket, rubbed them as clean as she could, and splashed water on her face. She threw the filthy water out on the ground and drew up another bucket of water. "Investigator Lo," she called out as she tipped her head over, "get my bag out of the trunk and put it in the car." She poured the rest of the water over her hair, shook it out, then smoothed her hair back from her forehead. "Okay," she said. "Let's go."

She called out a hasty good-bye to Suchee across the fields, then got into the car next to David. Lo stepped on the gas and they squealed down the dirt road in a cloud of dust. While Hulan rummaged through her suitcase, David recounted his pointless day. He hadn't been able to speak with Sun. The tour of the Knight compound for the Tartan entourage had gone well, meaning no cafeteria, no dormitory, and the factory itself was completely deserted. As for his conversation with Randall Craig, his other client, all he would say was that it had gone badly.

By the time he was done, Hulan had spread out on the upholstery between them a brush, a hair clip, a pair of sling-back sandals, and the silk dress she'd worn last night. "Investigator Lo, keep your eyes forward," she ordered, then slipped out of her dirty clothes and into her dress. With her hair slicked back and held in place with the clip, she looked quite chic.

# 17

T HEY PULLED INTO THE AIRPORT AND WERE WAVED
through to where two small private jets waited. Randall Craig and
his minions had already boarded Tartan's company plane—a Gulfstream 4—and were waiting for permission to leave from ground control. Two men—both Caucasian—were doing the final walk around the
other plane, a Gulfstream 3. One of them stepped forward and said,
"Welcome, Mr. Stark. We've been waiting for you. Why don't the two of
you go on board? Mr. Knight says you can fly with him. Just leave your
bags here. We'll take care of them."

As the plane carrying the Tartan folks taxied out onto the runway,
David and Hulan made plans for Lo to pick them up the next morning at
Hulan's house. With that, they said good-bye and climbed the narrow
stairs into the G–3. The air conditioning was on full blast, and Henry
looked relaxed and comfortable in a roomy chair upholstered in soft-
cream leather that he swiveled toward them.

"Henry, this is my fiancée, Liu Hulan."

Henry shook Hulan's hand. "A pleasure to meet you," he said. He
gestured about him. "We don't have a lot of seats, but you can have your
pick since Doug and Sun decided to go with your employers."

The jet had been customized to suit its owner. The use of polished
brass, teak, and mahogany imposed an almost nautical feel. The subtle
shades of cream and beige in varying textures and textiles gave an over-

all impression of luxury. It was a far cry from the stripped-down, utilitarian CAAC planes that Hulan was accustomed to. The casual elegance, roominess, and comfort that the small plane offered impressed even David.

Henry beamed at them. "I've had her for three years. You have to figure you only live once."

The two-man crew came on board. The pilot went straight to the cockpit while the copilot came back to check on the passengers. "You been on a small bird like this before?" When David and Hulan said that they hadn't, the copilot went through a few of the safety features, which weren't all that different from commercial jets. Then he opened a cupboard by the front door. "We've got a fridge in here stocked with drinks—Coke, mineral water, wine. We've got all kinds of snacks—M&Ms, chips, cheese and crackers. This is a short flight and I'll be busy up front, so just help yourselves to anything you want."

A few minutes later, they reached cruising altitude and David had Henry where he wanted him—alone. The rules of confidentiality required that anything that involved Governor Sun or David's other client—Tartan—was off limits. On the other hand, he was on this plane on behalf of Tartan. It was his duty as a lawyer to investigate anything that might be potentially harmful to the conglomerate.

"I'd like to go over a few things with you, Henry."

The older man looked up from his book, and David began outlining his concerns: He'd heard a report that not one but several women had received injuries in the factory. Additionally, it was a mistake to use the word *women*, when many of the employees were girls of twelve, thirteen, fourteen. He'd heard that the company might be using unhealthful chemicals. As David ran through all this, he kept his eyes steady on the older man to gauge his reaction. It appeared to be total bewilderment. At last Henry said, "What you say is wrong."

"Tell me how," David said. "Prove it."

"How can I prove something never happened or just plain isn't true?" Henry asked. "Just today we took the Tartan team on a tour through the compound. You were there, David. Did you see anything that looked bad?"

"We saw the Administration Building. You showed Randall and the

others the final assembly area and where the products are shipped. We
didn't go into the dormitory—"

"We have strict rules about that. No men allowed. I want the women
who work for me to feel protected. You don't know where they've come
from, what they've escaped—"

"And when we went in the room where the products are actually
manufactured, the women were gone and the machines turned off. . . ."

"I don't like your insinuations."

David repeated his accusations, this time in an even rougher tone.

"I've already told you," Henry said, his voice rising. "I run a clean
shop. I've done that my whole life. So did my father."

"Mr. Knight," Hulan interrupted, "I've been in your factory, and
what David says is true."

Henry looked from Hulan to David and back again, horrified by the
implications. "Tartan sent you in?"

"Hulan," David said, "we had an agreement!"

She ignored him and answered Henry.

"No, I'm an investigator for the Ministry of Public Security. That's
like your FBI. I went to your factory as a favor to a friend. The police said
a girl committed suicide, but her mother—my friend—believes it was
murder—"

"Your friend is the mother of that poor woman who jumped off the
roof?"

"No, the death didn't happen at the factory."

"Then what does it have to do with me?" Henry demanded. "You
can't blame everything on me. I haven't done anything."

David cut in. "Hulan, this is way out of line."

She turned her dark eyes on him and willed him to believe that she
wouldn't violate his trust by bringing up the bribery accusations. "I
believe our agreement meant no questions involving your clients. Mr.
Knight is not your client."

Before David could continue his argument, Henry said, "Let her
speak. I want to hear what she has to say."

Hulan edged forward on her chair so that her knees were almost
touching Henry's. Slowly she unwrapped the Band-Aids that covered her
fingers and the gauze and tape that covered the puncture in her left

hand. She turned her palms up and laid them gently on his lap. "I've worked at your factory for two and a half days. Look at my hands. What's happened to them . . ." She shrugged. "These are minor injuries, skin scratches, but they are injuries nevertheless."

He picked up her hands and looked at them. The gash looked inflamed, and a little fluid oozed from between the stitches. Henry slowly raised his eyes to meet Hulan's.

"How did this happen?"

"I was assigned one of the easier jobs. I insert the hair into the heads of the Sam dolls."

"That shouldn't cause damage like this," he said, and Hulan saw in his eyes the gradual and painful acceptance of *a* truth if not *the* truth. That look, she believed, was not something that could be faked.

Still holding her hands, he said, "They told me I shouldn't go in there when the women were working. They said it would distract them. I figured it's China. I have to do what's best for the workers." Henry dropped her hands, toughened his face, and turned to David. "You come to me with this information now, on my plane. Why not do it at the factory, where we could go and see for ourselves?"

"Because I only believed it as of last night and this morning there wasn't a chance."

Henry stood and took a couple of steps toward the cockpit. "Let's go back. I want to show you you're wrong."

"The women won't be working," David said. "It's their day off." He glanced at his watch. They didn't have much time before they reached Beijing and Henry was whisked away for more meetings. "You've made claims and presented affidavits to Tartan, which—despite your denials—I believe are inaccurate. You're supposed to sign the final documents for the sale tomorrow night after the banquet. As Tartan's attorney, I can't force you to do right. I can't force you to confess. But you've built this company." He gestured around him. "You've created a nice lifestyle for yourself, which will only improve after the sale. You've also established a reputation by building on your father's record. So I want you to think, *really think*, about what will happen when this stuff comes out after the sale, because it will. If Knight is involved with the things I believe it's involved with, you'll be looking at criminal fraud charges. Think about what that will do to your reputation, your son, your family. I suggest that you speak with your attorneys."

"You know I don't have them," Henry said.

"Of course you do, and now is the time to use them."

Henry twisted in his seat.

The copilot came back and announced that they were beginning their final approach into Beijing. "You know the drill," he said cheerfully. "Fasten those seat belts. We'll be on the ground in ten minutes." Then he ducked back out again. But his appearance had broken the flow of the conversation. Henry turned his face to the window and looked out over the heated fields that surrounded the airport.

On the ground, a small red carpet had been rolled out and three limousines waited. Without a word, Henry left the plane. As David and Hulan walked down the narrow stairs, the copilot quickly unloaded the bags. Henry grabbed his, walked to one of the limos, opened the door, said a few words to the occupants, and slammed the door shut. As that car pulled away, Henry went to the second limo, checked to see who was inside, then got in. A minute later only one car remained. The copilot threw the bags in the trunk, tucked David and Hulan into the spacious backseat, and said good-bye. Hulan gave directions to her *hutong* neighborhood, and soon they were speeding along the expressway. Not knowing or trusting the driver, they didn't speak. But even if they could, what would they have said? Henry had been adamant in his denials.

The next morning when David left Hulan's compound, he found Lo leaning against the front fender of the Mercedes. Lo looked tired, but he'd obviously made it back to his apartment for a shower and a change of clothes. He was in the city now and under the watchful eyes of his superiors at the MPS, so he'd put away his short-sleeve cotton shirt and loose slacks in exchange for his customary ill-fitting dark suit. They headed east along the Third Ring Road paralleling the last remnants of the city's ancient moat toward the Kempinski Hotel.

As David pushed through the hotel's revolving doors, he could hardly believe that he'd met Miss Quo here just ten days ago to go office hunting. He passed through the luxurious lobby and into the dining room. The breakfast buffet was in full swing with businessmen—distinguishable by their suits or the convention badges pinned on their shirt pockets—and a handful of tourists, who, no matter what part of the world they'd come from, had peeled down to the bare essentials of shorts, T-shirts, and sandals. The buffet offered an international cornucopia of delights: miso soup and sushi for the Japanese, dumplings and noodles for the Chinese, fruit and musli for the health-conscious, and eggs, bacon, sausages, and a variety of cold cuts for the Americans, Australians, Brits, and Germans.

David spotted Miles Stout at a window table reading the *International Herald Tribune*. Miles stood when David reached him and shook his hand. "Come on," he said. "I'm famished." While Miles waited in line for an omelet to be made, David took a glass of orange juice and a muffin back to the table. At the next table five Germans huddled together over papers and food. At another two businessmen—one French, the other Scottish—tried to work out a joint-venture deal with a group of obviously uncooperative Chinese. Across the room he saw two PLA generals come back from the buffet with plates piled high with nothing but kiwis. They each took one, sliced it in half, and began scooping out the luscious and expensive pulp with their spoons. Outside the window was a man-made pond with a footbridge and manicured paths. Beyond that lay the Paulaner Brauhaus, where on hot summer evenings visiting Germans met their Chinese guests for foamy steins of beer and traditional plates of pickled herring, grilled pork knuckle, and Nuernberger bratwurst.

When Miles returned to the table, they exchanged the usual chitchat on the rigors of the transpacific flight. Then, before David could say a word about the Knight sale or his suspicions about Sun, Miles said, "I had several messages from Randall waiting for me when I arrived last night."

"I would imagine he's concerned—"

"David, shut up and listen." Miles's voice was sharp. "I don't like hearing that one of my attorneys has pissed off my biggest client."

David's jaw tightened. "It's my job to advise Tartan," he said. "I've found some things in this acquisition that could cause Tartan considerable harm down the line."

"You're new to this deal—"

"That's right. I've been working on it for just a few days—"

"And you don't know anything about it—"

"What I was going to say," David raised his voice, "is that in those few days I've found things that Tartan's accountants, Keith, and even you missed."

"Like what?"

David was ready with his list: bribery, personal injuries, unsafe labor practices, child labor. Miles cut him off.

"Except for the bribery, I heard all of this from Randall last night. These accusations are thoroughly ridiculous."

"Let's say Sun's innocent. That still means that someone at Knight is playing with the financials."

"I'm telling you, David, the financials, the disclosures, the whole works, have been done perfectly, and I'm not going to let you ruin this deal."

"I'm not trying to ruin the deal! I'm trying to protect Tartan!"

"There's seven hundred million dollars on the table. That may sound like a lot of money—and it is—but the real money will come with the purchase of Knight's technology—"

"You want it in pure monetary terms, okay," David responded. "The risks—past, present, and future—will travel from Knight to Tartan with the sale. Do you really want to expose the firm's biggest client to that?"

Miles glared at David.

"Let's go back to Henry," David tried reasonably. "Have him provide an indemnity backed by a letter of credit saying that Knight assumes responsibility for everything that's happened in the past. Or we could have Tartan buy Knight's assets but not the company. Either way, once the deal is done, Randall can have a press conference where he unveils a plan to correct any past mistakes and obliterate any future ones."

"It's too late. The contracts are due to be signed tonight."

"Then I'll have to withdraw from this matter."

"Withdraw if you like. You can even leave the firm if you like, but confidentiality stays with the firm. You won't be allowed to repeat any of this to anyone."

"What about the FTC and the SEC? I have an obligation to disclose economic fraud that would lead to economic risk to the shareholders of a public company."

Miles gestured around him. "Do you see any of those people anywhere around here? David, get serious. Who's looking? Who cares? This
is a business deal like any other that's happening in this room right now.
Henry and Randall are just a couple of men trying to make a profit—no
harm, no foul so long as no one's looking, and they aren't."

"You're right," David conceded. "Maybe no one's looking, and what
Henry and Randall do behind closed doors is none of my business. But
Tartan *is* a publicly owned company. It's a conglomerate made up of
many shareholders. I would also point out that if, as a lawyer, I'm aware
that the information that's being provided regarding the sale of one publicly owned company to another is false, that I *and* the firm can end up
with civil and criminal liability."

"Are you saying you're willing to bring down the firm—literally hundreds of lawyers, secretaries, and paralegals, as well as their families—
because of these ludicrous charges?"

"I've already told you. It doesn't have to go that far. We go back to
Henry—"

"No!" Miles slammed his fist on the table. There was a momentary
silence in the restaurant. Then everyone went back to his or her deals.
Miles quickly composed himself. He kept his voice low and steady as he
said, "Even if you go public, no one will believe you. I mean, look at
yourself, look at your history. Three months ago you come over here and
everywhere you go you find death. Even when you come back to L.A.
death follows you. You lose a friend, an FBI agent no less. It's tough and
it's public. But you seem to get over it. Then one day you go out to dinner with a friend and the poor guy gets killed right before your eyes. He
dies in your arms. It's tragic. It's also quite public. Given the circumstances, no one should be surprised that you'd eventually have *some*
reaction. It's called post-traumatic stress disorder."

David stared at his partner in disbelief. This was the same language
Randall Craig had used last night, only worse.

"Naturally," Miles continued, "at the firm, where you have a long
association, we were terribly concerned. So when you left the government—or were you asked to leave?—we at Phillips, MacKenzie & Stout
felt that at the very least we could bring you back into the fold."

"That's not how it happened."

"It's your word against ours—"

"Madeleine Prentice and Rob Butler won't back your story."

"Yes, but they're federal employees, and who believes anything the government says? Do you? Most people will just think that the government was smart to get rid of you before you went postal on them."

Miles had always been smooth, and he'd obviously prepared for this conversation.

Suddenly something Hulan had said in their hotel room last night fully registered. "You asked me back to the firm knowing that if I found something, if this moment came, that you'd be able to deflect any unpleasantness that came up by using your twisted version of the facts."

"They may be twisted," Miles acknowledged, "but you have to admit they'll work."

"What about the press?"

"Again, who's looking?"

"Pearl Jenner from the *Times*. She's here in China."

"I know, but her take on the story is over. She's written her last piece. Now that Keith is dead, the investigation is over."

There was a lot of information and misinformation in this last exchange. There had never been a government investigation, but Miles didn't know that, and Pearl's story was far from over. If anything, this gave David a shred of hope. Maybe Pearl—as unpleasant and untrustworthy as she was—would come to the truth of the story on her own. If she exposed it, he'd be absolved of any professional misdoing in regards to Sun. As far as Tartan's acquisition of Knight, he could always say he was new to the matter and hadn't yet come across any malfeasance. Or, if worse came to worst, he could fall back on Miles's warped plan: David had been stressed personally and professionally. This, coupled with culture shock and jet lag, had resulted in a momentary lapse. He'd taken all the evidence—the financial reports, the governmental forms, even the modified tour of the factory—at face value, assuming that the work had been done correctly by Keith and the firm. He'd been as swindled as the public.

All of these thoughts flashed through David's mind in a second. With his cards played close to his chest, he tried to get more information from Miles.

"You've known all along about this stuff with Knight, haven't you?" David asked.

"You're just like Keith, flying off the handle with these crazy allegations," Miles chided. "I guess the added stress of being back in China has triggered a lot for you. Of course, that's the exact reason that no one would blame you if you quit, although I doubt you will. Still, the stress has been terrible, really beyond what any normal person should be expected to endure."

As Miles spoke, David realized that his partner had stayed only with his own game. He hadn't anticipated David's question nor had he played out any scripts other than his original David-will-take-the-fall-and-be-blamed-or-not-blamed-for-reasons-of-post-traumatic-stress-or-some-other-bullshit scenario. David quietly allowed his optimism to rise.

A waitress set the bill on the table. Miles signed the check and gently closed the leather cover.

David doubted he'd get a straight answer, but he asked his question anyway. "Is this just about money?"

Miles laughed. "Everything's about money, David."

"Should I consider that a confession?"

"You can call it whatever you like," Miles said, "and you can think whatever you want." He leaned forward confidentially. "But you don't have one scrap of proof." Then, "Better yet, no one will ever believe you—not in the firm, not in the U.S. Attorney's Office, not even in the press." Miles pushed back his chair and stood. "Now, I need to get upstairs and call Randall Craig and tell him he has nothing to worry about." He took a couple of steps, looked back, and said, "Oh, and see you at the banquet."

At about the same time that David was sitting down with Miles, Hulan was on her Flying Pigeon, pedaling to the Ministry of Public Security compound. It had been many weeks since she'd had the luxury of being alone this way. Around her, young women were stripped down to miniskirts and pullover tops that daringly showed their belly buttons. Men wore baggy shorts and sleeveless T-shirts. Street vendors sold ice sticks, cold drinks, and slices of watermelon. The air was hot, humid, and smoggy. As she passed Tiananmen Square, she saw heat shimmering off the concrete expanse and several busloads of foreign tourists looking dejected.

Since this was Sunday, the MPS bicycle park was nearly empty and no one was playing basketball in the courtyard. Her shoes echoed on the stone floor of the lobby, and she saw no one as she climbed the back stairs and went down the hall to the computer room. One after the other she tapped in the names of several Americans: Henry Knight, Douglas Knight, Sandy Newheart, Aaron Rodgers, and Keith Baxter. Almost as an afterthought she added Pearl Jenner, Randall Craig, and Miles Stout. She wished she could add Jimmy, the Australian guard, to the list but she didn't know his last name. She waited while the computer processed the names, then visa and passport numbers appeared on the screen. Once she had these, she had no difficulty in accessing dates for entry and exit from China. She printed out the information on separate sheets of paper, then repeated the same process, only this time typing in the names for Governor Sun Gan, Guy Lin, Amy Gao, and, finally, Quo Xuesheng, David's assistant.

Hulan studied the sheets of the Americans first. Henry's official record began in February 1990, although she knew he'd first come to China during the war. (There was nothing peculiar about this. Many records had been lost during the formation of the People's Republic, and besides, Henry had been a member of the U.S. military.) By the end of the summer of 1990 he'd established a regular pattern—a trip each month with a one-week stay. She guessed that this was the period during which he negotiated for the land and set up the venture. Then there was a long absence, which reflected Henry's convalescence. Since the factory opened, his visits had been limited to two or three per year. This last year he'd only come out twice, and only one of those times did the record show a visit to Taiyuan. Just at the time that Henry's visits dropped off, Doug Knight had increased his. Sandy Newheart's travel plans centered on the Christmas holiday, when he flew home for a month. She skimmed the dates for Miles and Keith and saw that the frequency of their visits had increased as the sale to Tartan approached. Randall Craig had come to China numerous times, beginning back in 1979, but Tartan had several factories in Shenzhen so this too was predictable. The real surprise was Pearl Jenner. The reporter—who'd said that this was her first trip to China—had lied. The record showed that she had been here ten times during the last fifteen years.

Hulan shuffled through the papers until she found the information on her compatriots. Guy Lin had traveled abroad only once, just as he'd said. Miss Quo, the young Red Princess, had seen more of the world than most Chinese. During the four-year period from 1988 to 1992 she had returned to China only twice, both times in December. Hulan recalled that Miss Quo had been educated at Barnard, and like Sandy Newheart had only come home for Christmas vacations. After her return to China in 1992, she had gone on several trips—to Switzerland, to Singapore, to France, even to Brazil. But none of this seemed out of line. As a Red Princess, Quo Xuesheng was by definition a jet-setter.

Finally Hulan turned her attention to Sun Gan, who had traveled back and forth to the U.S. quite frequently, often staying for long periods of time. His assistant, Amy Gao, had accompanied him on several of these excursions. What surprised Hulan was not so much the frequency of these trips—of course he'd travel to Los Angeles, San Francisco, Detroit, New York, and Trenton to drum up business for his province—but the duration of those stays. Government officials were always looking for trips abroad. They enjoyed going to Disneyland and seeing the other exotic sights of America. But they also had to be careful how those visits were perceived back in China. Power and ideology were fluid here. What might be considered beneficial to the country today could be deemed harmful tomorrow. Many times during the last fifty years, people—especially Party officials—had gone too far to one side, had bought one too many suits in Hong Kong, returned with one too many UCLA sweatshirts, or had held one too many parties with western rock 'n' roll, and were suddenly mocked, denounced, jailed, or eliminated. As a result, most cadres now kept their visits abroad short and to the point. They also traveled in the company of others. No one in government was immune from this. Even Hulan had had a watcher during her last trip to America. In turn it had been Hulan's unspoken responsibility to watch her watcher. The government wanted to make sure that no one defected, that secrets weren't told, and that any acts of impropriety would be recorded and stored away in the government's secret personal files for future use.

Hulan gathered up the papers, knowing that she would have to look at them more closely later, and left the computer room. She walked up a flight of stairs to Vice Minister Zai's office, hoping that even though it was Sunday he'd be there. He was. He looked up from his paperwork, and she couldn't help but see the subtle look of triumph that passed over his features. It was as though he had said aloud, *I told her to come back and she obeyed.* But then, seeing the expression on her face, his eyes narrowed and he asked her to sit.

"I'm afraid you're going to tell me you haven't finished with your personal investigation," he said.

"You're correct, Vice Minister."

He waited for her to speak again. When she didn't, he drummed his knuckles on the table, thinking, then stood. "It is hot in here today, Investigator Liu. Come, let us get some fresh air."

They left the compound and walked around the corner to Tiananmen Square. Despite the fact that this place was important to the government, it was really quite barren. The Forbidden City anchored one end, Mao's mausoleum sat at the other. The Great Hall of the People and the Museum of the Chinese Revolution flanked the other two sides of the square. The concrete square spread out vast and hot under the unrelenting sun. If Hulan and her superior kept to themselves, strolling through the middle, their conversation would be private.

Zai stopped finally, gazed about at the impressive buildings, and said, "You want me to do something." When she nodded, he sighed and said, "Only with you would a suicide turn into something more."

"I'm sorry, uncle. I didn't choose this outcome."

He sighed again, more deeply this time. This was going to be worse than he thought. "What do you have?"

"Has Investigator Lo spoken to you yet?"

Zai frowned at the woman before him. How like her to confront him with the person he'd assigned to watch her. Zai said, "Lo is with your David this morning. He has been disappointingly secretive in his reports the last few days. As you can imagine, this gives me even greater cause for concern."

"Your Lo is a good man."

"You say that today because he is obeying you. Tomorrow he may once again return his loyalties to me . . . or someone else. Don't trust him too completely."

"Him or anyone else," Hulan agreed, echoing a lesson that Zai had hammered into her since she was a child. But all this was almost pro forma banter to keep them away from what they both knew had to be a dangerous subject. As an inspector, she didn't have to observe the rigors of privileged information that David adhered to. In fact, in China she had an obligation to expose what she knew or suspected. On the other hand, David was her lover and the father of her child. While the Chinese law was vague about what he could and could not say about his client's activities, she didn't want to do anything that would harm his career or reputation.

She began by telling Zai how she'd infiltrated the factory. She spoke of the harsh working conditions and showed him her hands. But Zai, who'd spent many years at hard labor, was not terribly impressed. "Don't be so naïve," he said. "You haven't worked with your hands in more than twenty years. Of course you would have blisters and scratches."

Then she said that she'd met a man who'd been in love with Miaoshan. Now for the first time Hulan hedged on the facts, taking them out of order and implying something for which she did not yet have concrete proof. "This man mentioned that Miaoshan had papers that were proof of bribery of an important official. I saw those papers, which did indeed show large amounts of money being deposited in various accounts."

"Who was receiving the money?"

"I believe it is Governor Sun Gan," Hulan said. It was true she believed this statement, but she didn't know it to be a fact. As air came out in a tight hiss through Zai's teeth, she continued, "I came in today to look up his travel record." She handed the piece of paper with Sun's data to Zai. He hesitated, not wanting to touch it. Then, with his forehead deeply creased, he took the paper and read.

"When I saw this I came to you," Hulan went on. "Doesn't it seem strange that his trips abroad, especially to the U.S., lasted so long?"

When Zai looked up, it seemed to Hulan that he had aged. They both knew how dangerous this was. Sun was a popular politician, and there had been no mandate from above to bring him down.

"I would like to see his *dangan*," Hulan announced. "How is he able to travel so freely? Where does his money come from? Who protects him? How did he get to where he is today? What is the government's plan for him? There is so much I need to know, so I can decide whether or not to act. Obviously I will be careful," she added, taking full responsibility if anything should go awry. "Obviously I may be completely wrong."

"What does this have to do with the death of your friend's daughter?"

"I don't know yet, but the leads in that murder have brought me here."

Zai looked down at Sun's exit and entry record again. After a moment he looked up, nodded, handed the paper back to Hulan, and walked away. After a few paces he stopped and looked back at her. "Are you coming?"

Once back in the compound, he told her to wait in his office. A half hour later, he rejoined her. In his hands he held a large manila file. He sat down and wordlessly pushed it across the desk. He watched her open it; then he turned away and went back to work of his own.

Hulan began to read. Sun Gan had been born in 1931 of the Western calendar in a village outside Taiyuan. The Communist Party had already been in existence for ten years, and Sun was blessed with a pure peasant background. He was still just a little boy during the Long March but was old enough to remember the atrocities of the Japanese invasion of 1937. By 1944 Shanxi Province was firmly in Japanese-Occupied China. A few Americans came into the territory either as spies or had parachuted in when their planes were shot down during the occasional bombing mission. After the Japanese surrender American marines made up a new presence in Taiyuan.

At thirteen years old Sun Gan had apparently been a bright boy and very involved in his village's Communist party. (His third uncle had gone off to join Mao's troops many years before). He also had an affable personality—a trait he still carried to this day, Hulan noted—and had easily become the mascot for a group of American GIs. Hulan suspected that although this camaraderie had been less than innocent—he'd been sent by local cadres to see what he could make of the foreigners and their intentions—it would probably prove to be nearly devastating during the Cultural Revolution. But that, she supposed, was getting ahead of the story.

This early work came with a reward—a position in the People's Liberation Army. During the winter of 1948, when Sun was only seventeen years old, he participated in the massive and decisive battle of Huai Hua against the Guomindang in neighboring Anhui Province. It was here that Sun performed several heroic acts, which were detailed over several pages. He could have stayed in the army—which would have meant that today he would have been a very high-up general, rich and powerful—but Premier Zhou Enlai had personally asked the young man to go back to Shanxi.

Sun first served the people as a rural cadre in his home village, working as a team leader, then brigade leader on one of the local communes. In 1964 he was elected to the Taiyuan City People's Assembly. During the weeklong gathering a wide variety of subjects had been covered, including the imperialism of the West, how to increase wheat production, and the importance of advancing industrialization. Even though discussions sometimes grew heated, Sun had kept quiet. Two years later, Mao unleashed the terrors of the Cultural Revolution. For many months Sun's reticence at the People's Assembly protected him; he hadn't said anything, so his words couldn't come back to haunt him. But eventually some of his subordinates in his home village, where he had risen to brigade party secretary, saw an opportunity and took advantage of it. They remembered that back during the war Sun had been friendly with American servicemen. He had acquired a taste for their expensive cigarettes, decadent style of dress, and barbaric language. As a result he was made to wear the usual dunce cap, kneel in broken glass, and get castigated in the public square.

But this was nothing! Hulan thought. Given his American connections, this punishment had been extremely lenient. Why? The few village cadres who managed to escape the wrath of the Cultural Revolution were typically the ones who were the most corrupt and wielded the most power. Had Sun been one of these? Had he bought his way out of trouble?

Whoever had written the comments on this page seemed to hear Hulan's questions many years later and had written the answering characters in a finely trained classical hand: "Brigade Leader Sun Gan has a visceral understanding of the old saying which goes, Once you eat from someone, you will have a soft mouth toward that person; once you take from someone, you will have soft hands toward that person. Because Sun has shown himself to be someone who will not accept or pay bribes in any form, nor has he abused his power during this time of darkness, I believe he is a candidate for advancement."

Within a month Sun had been promoted from rural cadre to national cadre, where he earned ninety *yuan* a month. The next year he rose to deputy chairman of the City Assembly. In 1978 he was sent to Beijing as a representative for the Third Plenum of the Eleventh Party Congress. In 1979, when China opened up fully to the West again, Sun was on one of the first provincial delegations to travel to the United States. Security was tight, but Sun acquitted himself well, earning the respect of his fellow travelers as well as his hosts. By 1985 Governor Sun—responsible now for his entire province of Shanxi—was flying across the Pacific with some regularity. By 1990 he had an additional office and apartment in the Zhongnanhai compound in Beijing awarded him by the government for his contributions to the country, especially his home province. His continuing travel to the U.S. was not only sanctioned but encouraged. As a bureaucrat in 1995 observed: "Governor Sun Gan has impeccable contacts in the West. With these he has brought prosperity to his home province. We must continue to encourage him, for with his help we will build China into the most powerful country on the planet. By the year 2000 Sun should be permanently in Beijing." This pronouncement, like the one during the Cultural Revolution, seemed to have two immediate effects.

First was an even more thorough check of his background and personal habits. The *dangan* noted that while Sun had never married, he was not known to be a homosexual, nor had he engaged in any illicit affairs with the opposite sex. He lived in the governor's house in Taiyuan, where he kept his staff to a minimum. His maids said that his needs were simple, that he did not abuse his authority, and often made his own bed in the military manner. He did not have a history of drinking or gambling, and was known to be very loyal to the Party. These things continued to make him a good candidate for travel, since he could not be compromised through sex, money, or political persuasion. Attached to this addendum was a list of the banks where Sun kept his money, as well as recent balances. Like Hulan and almost everyone she knew, Sun kept some money in American banks. But Sun was not a Red Prince, and the amounts didn't seem inordinately excessive. This record, dating from 1995, didn't reflect the large deposits that Miaoshan's papers showed, but then the Knight factory had opened just that year. Nevertheless, Hulan jotted down the names of the banks and the account numbers, hoping she could eventually connect them to deposit records.

The second effect, and more obvious to Hulan, was that she could trace her knowledge of Sun to 1995, the year the unnamed bureaucrat had written his recommendation for Sun's future in the file. As if out of nowhere, Sun had appeared one day in the national press. His every move and comment were covered. He posed for photographers, chatted up perky female reporters, and engaged in public discussions about economic policy, the countryside, and the next century with school children, peasants, even members of the Party Congress. That he had surpassed all expectations and on paper looked to be a good guy didn't alter the fact that people very high in the government had moved him into position. His success was assured, which was why some bureaucrat had unwittingly allowed Sun a free ride.

Hulan closed the file and pushed it back across the desk. Her mentor looked up from his work. She could see him trying to read her expression, but she kept her face impassive.

# 18

WHEN HULAN GOT HOME, DAVID WAS SITTING AT THE kitchen table with several three-by-five cards spread out in two rows before him. As she approached, he put a finger on a card and slowly slid it across the table and up into the top row. Then he repeated the process; only this time he moved a card down from the top row to the bottom row. He didn't look up, not even when she put her hands on his shoulders and began to massage his tense muscles.

"I learned a lot from Miles," he said. "None of it good."

She stopped massaging and sat down next to him. "Tell me," she said, and he did.

With each piece of information he pointed at a matching card. "I've been looking at these since I got back, trying to figure out what happened when. Randall Craig said he knew about conditions at the factory; Henry Knight says they're a complete fabrication; you tell me they may not even be prosecutable in China. Miles practically admitted that he knew that the Knights' disclosures were false; Henry says that they're accurate. When Miaoshan died, she had in her possession documents that suggest that Sun may have accepted bribes; he gave me something that might be related. Then there's Pearl Jenner. She too is a walking contradiction. She knows some things but seems totally ignorant of others. The pieces have to fit together, but I still don't see how."

"Maybe you should try a different approach." Hulan picked up the stack of cards and wrote on a few new ones. When she was done, she laid them out in two columns, leaving an area in the middle empty. On the left were the various crimes; on the right were the names of people that were suspicious. Then she went back to her scribbling.

A moment later she looked back at the two columns and began setting down the new cards. "I am looking for a match, but I also don't think we can separate crimes and criminals from jurisdiction, because I think they're interrelated."

Once her three columns were completed, Hulan surveyed her handiwork.

| | | |
|---|---|---|
| Miaoshan (murder) | China | — |
| Keith Baxter (murder) | U.S. | — |
| Xiao Yang (murder) | China | Aaron Rodgers |
| Paying bribes | China/U.S. | Knight International |
| Accepting bribes | China | Sun Gan |
| Illegal working conditions at Knight | — | Knight |
| Illegal filing of papers to FTC & SEC | U.S. | Tartan/Knight (Phillips, MacKenzie & Stout) |

Hulan realized how desperate David was when he didn't automatically strike Sun Gan off the chart and that he'd let down his guard enough to let drop that Miaoshan's papers and Sun's papers were similar.

"Why are you so sure about Aaron Rodgers?" David asked. "He was really shaken up when Xiao Yang died."

"He was the last person to see her alive, and everyone else was in the meeting with you," Hulan answered. "I'd also like to put Aaron down for Miaoshan's murder. He was having an affair with her. Maybe she made one too many demands on him. The fact that she had the papers would have meant nothing to him, which explains why he didn't take them." Hulan put a finger on the last card and asked, "What do you think Miles meant when he was talking about Keith? Do you think Keith had found what we've found and told Miles?"

"Miles made it sound that way, but I'm not sure."

"Tell me again what he said about you and Keith."

"Which part?"

"About when Keith died . . ."

"Miles said that I went out to dinner and 'a guy' gets killed in front of me, that he died in my arms in public," he said.

"Right, and that people would think you'd suffered from post-traumatic stress and had made up all this stuff," she said, motioning to the cards.

"He made it sound like the firm had done me a big favor, like hiring back some brain-injured person as a way of doing the right thing."

"But actually he wanted you back in the fold, where he could control you in case you decided to pursue Keith's death while in the U.S. Attorney's Office."

"I think so."

"So, do you think that the others in the firm know what Miles is up to?"

"I can't imagine it. They're good people."

"Then let me put it this way: How much money will the firm make from the deal?"

"About a million, but a lot of that goes toward overhead . . ."

"I know it's not much in a law firm," she agreed, dismissing the idea. Then, "I want to know if Miles is the only one behind Keith's murder or if they're all in on it."

David looked back down at the chart, then, keeping his voice light, said, "I don't see that as an alternative here." He peered over at Hulan and asked, "You're not serious?" When she didn't respond, he said, "I worked at the firm for years. You and I met there, for Christ's sake. Was there anything that *ever* made you think that they were engaged in criminal activities?"

Hulan shrugged. "Times change. Maybe they got greedy."

"But murder! Come on! I don't think Phil or Ralph or Marjorie would go out and kill one of their own partners."

"What about Miles?"

"He's an asshole. But a murderer? The man lives in Brentwood. He's got a couple of kids. He's well respected." Seeing Hulan's smirk, David stopped. He had to smile himself. "All right, so that matches the description of another Brentwood resident, but really! Miles is purely white-collar. I don't see him getting blood on his hands."

"And the other stuff?" she asked, pointing at the card that corresponded to the filing of the paperwork to the FTC. "Could the others be involved in the fraud?"

When David shook his head no, Hulan picked up that card, crossed out Phillips, MacKenzie & Stout, and wrote in its place David, Miles, and Keith.

"*That* makes me feel so much better!" David said.

A strand of Hulan's hair came loose and fell across her cheek. David smoothed it behind her ear.

"You haven't told me what you found out," he said.

She quickly summarized her morning's activities and showed him the travel records. At the end she said, "So like you I'm looking at contradictions. Sun had contact with Americans and yet wasn't punished for that during the Cultural Revolution. Or I should say that his punishment was mild. Kneeling in glass, a few struggle meetings, are nothing. I would have expected ten years of reform through labor."

"Maybe he was lucky . . ."

"His file also says that he hasn't accepted bribes, but we have circumstantial evidence that he has, which is why his name's on the chart," she said, pointing at the card. "But does someone's essential nature change?"

"Everyone says that Sun is good. His power is based on the premise that he's honest."

"Power may be the key word. Power corrupts, and my government is by definition corrupt," Hulan admitted.

"You said it, not me. But, yes, China does have a little problem now and then with corruption."

"Is that what happened to Miles?" Hulan asked.

"Power, money, for him I think they're synonymous."

"And Henry Knight and Randall Craig?"

"My country was built by corporate and industrial bandits. We glorify people who've pulled themselves up by their boot straps by any means possible."

They sat silent for a few minutes, then Hulan asked, "What are you going to do now?"

"I'm going to go for a run, take a shower, put on a suit, and go to the banquet."

"What about Miles?"

"What about him? He said I could quit. I won't." David hesitated, then repeated himself, this time with more conviction. "We're going to that banquet. We're going to put smiles on our faces, act charming, and hope one of the players slips. When and if one does, I want to see it."

"Then I suppose I'd better figure out what I'm going to wear." She stood and smiled. This was the closest she'd felt to him since they'd looked at Miaoshan's papers together, for he was finally speaking to her as a trusted lover again rather than an inspector. She smoothed her hands over her slightly swelling belly. "I hope I have something that fits."

It was an intimate thing to say, and as David grabbed her hand, brought her close, and looked into her eyes, she thought he might respond in kind. But he had something else on his mind. "Did you tell me everything?"

She felt the professional wall come back down between them. She met his gaze squarely. "Did you?"

"Yes," he said, though he'd left out the way Miles had implied much more clearly than Hulan surmised that he might have had something to do with Keith's death. But David couldn't bring himself to believe it. David knew Miles, played tennis with him, was his law partner. The idea that Miles was a murderer was inconceivable. But if on some chance it was true, then David would have to deal with it in his own way. He couldn't allow Miles to become a victim of the Chinese legal system.

"I told you everything too," Hulan said, though she'd withheld the names of Sun's banks in China and abroad. That information would be useless to David. In America he'd need a court order to gain access to Sun's accounts. But David was in China, and besides, he would never use a court order against his own client. To Hulan, however, Sun was nothing but a suspect. If she had to, she'd use, to quote David, any means possible to bring Sun to justice, even if that ultimately meant betraying David's trust, because . . . Because it was in her nature to put duty first—whether on the Red Soil Farm or here in Beijing—before matters of her own heart. She couldn't allow herself to forget that again.

The silence lingered between them, then David said, "That's good. We don't want any secrets between us."

Hulan pulled away. "I'd better get ready."

The Beijing Hotel was the oldest of the grand hotels in the city. It sat at the end of Wangfujing Street where it intersected with Chang An, the imperial boulevard of Eternal Peace. The Beijing was a venerable dowager that had seen it all. Today she was comprised of three wings, each representing a different incarnation. The oldest dated back to the days when she was the Hôtel de Pekin, a French-owned establishment originally designed to appeal to decadent and cosmopolitan foreign guests. The west wing had been built in the fifties for the more severe requirements of Soviet visitors. The newest wing, the "Distinguished Guests Building," attempted to serve the needs of today's most demanding guests—foreign and Chinese. Although not as popular with Americans as some of the new hotels that had sprung up around the city, the Beijing's location—within walking distance of Tiananmen Square, the huge governmental edifices that bordered it, and the ancient Forbidden City—made it a preferred venue for business meetings and banquets for officials and dignitaries.

The banquet was scheduled to start at six. Although Tartan and Knight were American companies, Chinese custom would prevail since Governor Sun and a few low-level ministry officials would be in attendance. This meant that the banquet would start *promptly* at six and end *precisely* at eight. However, this was not the only event taking place at the Beijing Hotel on this particular evening, as Hulan and David discovered when Investigator Lo attempted to drop them off. Several limousines and Town Cars clogged the entrance, depositing parties of young people, men in business suits, and entire families. As Lo edged forward in the line, he suggested that these people might be here for wedding banquets. This assessment was verified as they reached the entrance and saw a couple of men with video cameras capturing the arrivals for wedding tapes.

David and Hulan edged past the video crews, who jostled to get shots of everyone entering the building. Once inside, they looked around the bustling lobby until they found Miss Quo, who'd been invited as part of the permanent staff of the Beijing office of Phillips, MacKenzie & Stout.

Unlike the typical law firm underling who adhered to modestly priced, conservative styles, she was dressed this evening in an elegant black slip dress bought off a couture runway in Paris. Yet it was Miss Quo who gushed over Hulan's outfit—a summer dress made from silk the color of a ripe persimmon. Over this Hulan wore a handmade short-sleeve jacket woven from the thinnest strands of rice straw. These clothes, like so many of Hulan's, had come from her mother's trunks and dated back many decades to a period in China when wealth meant time and luxury, refinement and grace, no matter what the temperature.

David and the two women walked up the sweeping staircase to the second-floor banquet rooms. Knight had followed Chinese tradition by booking two connected rooms—one for sitting, one for eating. Outside the door, Henry was speaking intensely to his son. As David and Hulan approached, they heard Doug's reply.

"Dad, I've said it a hundred times today," he said impatiently. "If you want to cancel the sale entirely, fine. We fix everything and move forward, but . . ." When he noticed that the others had arrived, his voice changed. "David, good to see you. You have a nice flight up?"

Henry stared from his son to David and back again. Just as he was about to say something, Miles poked his head through the door and said, "I wondered where you two had gone. Oh, and here's David and Hulan." Miles gave Hulan a hug and kiss, then said, "It's been a long time. You're more beautiful today than when I last saw you. No wonder David's turned his world upside down to get back to you."

During this exchange David watched as Doug took his father's elbow and led him back into the room, but not before Henry looked back over his shoulder at David, a worried look on his face. Then David's attention was drawn back to Miles, who was shaking his hand, smiling warmly, and saying sotto voce, "I knew you'd come around."

Together they entered the sitting room, which was lined with thirty overstuffed easy chairs upholstered in heavy gray wool with tatted antimacassars on the arms and headrests from which a vague smell of mothballs wafted. On the walls were a series of landscape scrolls, each showing a different season.

Whereas in the U.S. the cocktail hour was designed for casual mingling, this portion of a Chinese banquet was carefully scripted, with the bigwigs on the north and south walls communicating across the expanse of the room in formulaic sentences. As a result, where people sat was carefully strategized according to rank and importance.

As if nothing had happened, Randall Craig rose from his chair, greeted David warmly, shook hands with Hulan and Miss Quo, and began introducing them to those already seated. Governor Sun, as the highest-ranking official, sat in the middle chair against the northern wall. To his left sat Henry Knight, while on his right was Assistant Secretary Amy Gao. Flanking out from them and lining the walls to Sun's right and left were officials from several government entities. By the time these introductions were done, Miss Quo had taken a chair far from the middle along one of the side walls, thus showing her very low rank.

Somewhere above the middle of the west wall, Randall began to introduce David and Hulan to Nixon Chen, who was representing one of the government agencies.

"No introduction necessary, Mr. Craig," Nixon said, jumping up and pumping David's hand. "We are old, old friends! I have known Liu Hulan my entire life, and David from my years in America." In answer to Randall's unasked question, Nixon rattled on. "Like Liu Hulan I was sent to America to study. She was there for many more years than I, but for some of those years we were in the same place."

"Phillips, MacKenzie had an innovative program," David explained to Randall. "Almost as soon as Nixon—President Nixon—opened China, the firm started hiring one or two Chinese law students who were studying in the States each year as summer clerks or even as associates. As you can see, the program had long-term benefits. People like Nixon here returned to China and have risen to positions of power."

"Not anymore," Nixon said with feigned indignation. "Now that you've come, you'll put the rest of us Chinese attorneys out of business."

"I doubt that."

"Really? Look what's happened to my business for Tartan. You don't know this, Mr. Craig, but I've done a lot of work for your company. Until now Miles always sent me your China matters, but no longer. Now he has a 'big gun' in Attorney Stark."

"Don't believe everything you hear," David warned Randall. "Attorney Chen is one of the highest-paid lawyers in all of China." Then to Nixon he added, "I recall you said that you bill like New York lawyers."

Nixon patted his ample waist. "Beijing is the third most expensive city in the world. I have to take care of myself and my hundred employees. We want to live the high life! Given that, I should bill even more than I do."

Randall Craig seemed to lose interest in the small talk and edged back to his chair, which stood directly across the room from Sun. This south wall was home to the Tartan entourage. Since Doug Knight would be staying with Tartan after the sale, he too was on this wall, seated to Randall's left. To Randall's right was Miles Stout. David caught his eye. The senior partner gave a subtle nod to the two chairs next to him. Hulan and David crossed the room and sat down. They had been placed on a wall of equal importance to Sun and firmly in the Tartan camp.

It was going to be a long night.


At six-thirty exactly, the party began moving to the other room. Governor Sun sidled up to David and, slowing his pace so that the others would pass them, asked in a low voice, "Have you had a chance to look at the papers I sent over?"

"Yes," David answered stiffly. As much as he tried to believe in his client's innocence, he was becoming increasingly convinced of his guilt.

"We need to talk—"

"I tried to see you yesterday. I was told you were unavailable."

A frown creased Sun's face, then instantly smoothed away. "I'm sorry if it was an inconvenience. Tomorrow I will come to your office at ten. Is that okay?" But Sun didn't wait for a response. Instead he raised his voice and said affably, "David, tonight you are in for a treat. The Beijing Hotel always provides a fine banquet." He gestured with his arm into the dining room, and David entered.

The room had been set up with three tables of ten place settings apiece. Name cards marked each seat, so that decorum would be maintained. David and Hulan were seated at the head table with Governor Sun, Randall Craig, Miles Stout, Doug and Henry Knight, one of Randall's minions, and a vice minister from COSCO, the largest shipper of merchandise out of China. Nixon Chen had also made the cut.

Unlike Chinese restaurants in other parts of the world where the food was served family-style in the middle of the table, banquets in China were presented course by course on individual plates. The first dish offered three cold selections—shredded jellyfish, cold steamed chicken, and a few thin slices of barbecued pork. Accompanying this was a glass of *mao tai*, a fiery and fierce liquor. Almost immediately the sense of conviviality rose in the room.

Within minutes, David could understand why Nixon Chen had been placed at this table. Nixon was jovial and irreverent. He led the toasts. He yammered on in flowery terms about his law firm ("The best and most profitable in all of China"), about David's return to China ("You think I'm joking when I say you will steal my business! Everywhere I go people say to me, I only want that new American lawyer. Isn't that right, Governor Sun?"), about David and Hulan's true love ("A love that has spanned two continents, two decades, and an ocean"). He entertained the table with his recent dining exploits. He still frequented the Black Earth Inn, where other former Phillips, MacKenzie associates met once a week for a meal and to network, but he'd also found a new place that he was quite fond of. "Like the Black Earth, the Autumn Jade Western-style Food Restaurant is also a nostalgia restaurant. I'm not talking about one of those nightclub places like they have in Shanghai—all gangsters and beautiful femmes fatales. No, this one is from my parents' generation. The Autumn Jade celebrates the fifties and our relationship with the Soviet Union. I tell you, until I went there I had never had food like that. It is nice if you want a retreat from the luxury life. You understand my meaning?"

Nixon's main interest was Governor Sun. It turned out they had met before, and they bantered easily about mutual friends and business acquaintances. But Nixon never let well enough alone.

"Every day I go to my office building I think to myself, no one can believe I have climbed so high. Every day I remember back to the Cultural Revolution and my years on the Red Soil Farm with Liu Hulan. Are you familiar with that place, Governor Sun? It is in your home province of Shanxi, not too far from Taiyuan."

"Attorney Chen, many people remember the Red Soil Farm. It was a model in our province and a place where I took many visitors."

Nixon snorted. "We never saw you, right, Hulan?"

"And I don't recall meeting you either, Attorney Chen," Sun said.

"How could you?" Nixon queried. "You were one and we were one thousand. Besides, we were too busy working in the fields under that sun of yours."

"*That sun,* as you call it, belongs to all of us," Sun responded smoothly. "And, as much as I like Beijing, I find the heat as harsh here as in the countryside. Only here you see no blue sky, only haze, coal dust, and Mongolian dust." Sun turned his attention to Hulan. "Now I understand who you are, Miss Liu, or should I say Inspector Liu?" Sun addressed the table. "Did you know that our beautiful companion tonight is the daughter of a very famous man in China and Miss Liu herself is a notable person in her own right?"

Doug asked the question that some of the Americans were wondering about. "What are you, then? A policewoman?"

Nixon Chen laughed. "Policewoman? Ha! She is with the Ministry of Public Security. Do you know what that is?" When Doug didn't answer, Nixon elaborated in his oddly colloquial English. "You don't want to know! It's like the FBI or KGB. Liu Hulan is one of our best investigators. Little fish, big fish, they are the same to her. She reels them in, slits them open, and sets them on the steamer. With Liu Hulan you are cooked!"

As Nixon spoke, David casually observed the others' reactions. Sun seemed indifferent, as did Randall Craig. Henry stared at his son, while Doug tried to look everywhere but at his father. In fact, it seemed to David that Doug had tried to catch someone's eye at the next table, but David couldn't see whose. Miles's fair complexion looked sunburned, but his expression was the same one he presented in the courtroom—coolly unconcerned. And Hulan, well, she looked amused.

"I'll tell you where she learned that," Nixon continued as a second course of sautéed squid arrived. "On the Red Soil Farm. There was no forgiveness there."

"Those were dark days for all of us," Sun said.

Hulan, who'd read Sun's *dangan,* knew that this wasn't the case. "But you were only a visitor to the Red Soil Farm, while we—and others like us—had to live and work there or at places like that," she said.

"Or places that were worse, like hard labor camps," Sun said knowingly.

"Anyone who reads a newspaper or watches television knows that my father spent time at the Pitao Reform Camp in Sichuan Province," Hulan said. "For some people, like my father and myself, personal stories of misdeeds and good works, of sacrifice and punishment, are very public. For others . . ." She let her voice drift off, hoping that Sun would accept the challenge.

But Sun was a politician. In his career, success was tied to the ability to deflect difficult questions. "The media is a game we must play, Inspector. I think many of your problems have stemmed from your inexperience. You let them say what they want about you. You never fight back. You do not wear a smile on your face. You don't work behind the scenes to build friendships. And so you react when you should be ruling what is said."

"That's a Western view," Hulan observed. "I think you've seen too many western movies!"

"You're absolutely right," Sun agreed cheerfully. "You want to know when I saw those movies? It was at the end of the war with Japan. They had them for the American soldiers who came to help us. Remember that, Henry?"

Henry barely nodded.

Sun continued. "Later I saw other western movies, and I'll always remember them for the way that people stood strong for what they believed in. Such an American trait, don't you think? To be unafraid to speak your mind, to believe in the human right to grow and change and be free?"

"It is words like that that make you very popular in China," Nixon said.

"It is words like that that we all want to follow," Sun clarified.

"This is why you are at the center of power," Nixon went on.

Sun tipped his head, modestly accepting the compliment. "But this isn't America. I can say many things today and tomorrow who knows?"

"Maybe tomorrow will bring even greater freedom. You can't turn back the clock," Nixon said.

"I just want my province to prosper and improve the quality of life for my people."

It was pure political talk, and Randall Craig, like many of the others at the table, was caught up in the sentiment. "It is people like you who will make China great in the next century."

"But, Mr. Craig, it is people like you who will make that possible. When you bring money to people, it changes their lives."

Hulan glanced at David. Was this the first parry in a new relationship that would be based on illegal money changing hands? David in turn shot a look across the table to Miles, but the senior partner was smiling and acting every inch the part of the great facilitator. Then David's eyes drifted over to Henry. This man, usually so light-hearted, had grown increasingly dispirited through dinner.

# 19

M ORE DISHES WERE BROUGHT OUT: STEAMED CARP, STIR-fried egg with sea cucumber, shredded ox stomach stew, Beijing duck, bird's nest soup, and finally rice. Then more tea, more toasts with the *mao tai*, and a few sweet dumplings for dessert. Sun, as the highest-ranking official, signaled the end of the evening by pushing his chair back from the table exactly at eight. The other Chinese in the room immediately stood. Everyone quickly moved back to the sitting room.

During dinner a rectangular table had been set up in the middle of the room with two chairs on each side. At each seat ceremonial pens made from colorful cloisonné waited to be used. A red banner strung between two poles read KNIGHT BECOMES TARTAN. A photographer was on hand to record not only the signing of the agreement, but also take other posed shots of the people from the Chinese ministries and bureaus before the official signing.

Finally the time came for the four principals to take their seats. Miles and Randall sat on one side of the table, Henry and Doug on the other. David and Miss Quo, who would take notes, took seats just behind Miles and Randall. Governor Sun and Amy Gao sat behind Henry and Doug. The others clustered around while the photographer continued to shoot film.

"Well, Henry," Randall said, "let me first thank you for all of your hospitality here in China. You have certainly made us feel welcome. And now we come to the culmination of months of talk and hard work."

Miles ceremoniously brought out the final contracts from his brief-case. Miss Quo stood and distributed copies to the people seated at the table.

"Henry," Randall said, "I think you'll find everything in order."

But Henry, who'd been so quiet during dinner, just stared at the contract. His face was tinged gray.

"Henry?" Randall asked.

"Dad?"

Without moving his head, Henry turned his eyes to his son. "Doug," he said, "I need to speak you outside."

"Henry, can't it wait?" Randall asked, all friendly concern, as the two men stood.

Henry came around the table, tapped David on the shoulder, and jerked his head toward the door.

As David rose, Miles said in his most senior partner everything-is-under-control voice, "Whatever the problem is, David, I trust you to take care of it right now."

David nodded and followed Henry back into the dining room, where the waitresses were clearing the remains of the banquet. Henry said, "David, I've tried talking to him, but he doesn't seem to understand the seriousness of the situation. Maybe he'll listen to you."

But before David could speak, Doug said, "That's not what happened. I listened and I told you that it's not as bad as he made it sound."

"You still haven't told me how bad," Henry pressed.

Doug shrugged. "We've had some accidents. Some of the women have quit."

Henry grabbed his son's arm and squeezed. "How bad?"

"Bad," Doug admitted. He looked the picture of a contrite son. Only this time the boy in question was forty-something and he'd been caught with more than a few *Playboys* tucked under his mattress.

Henry's face crumpled in disappointment and horror. "Why didn't you tell me before?"

"We went over this a thousand times today, Dad. I was ashamed."

The dining room door opened, and Miles stepped into the room. "Is there something I can help you with?"

Henry said, "I've just asked my son a question. I'm waiting for the answer."

Doug hurried on. "You were back at home, I was out here, and I didn't want you to worry. I knew you wanted this sale and I wanted you to enjoy your retirement, so I thought we'd just hang on. If I could keep this a secret from you, then I knew I could keep it a secret from Tartan, for several months at least."

"Let's go back to the other room," Miles tried placatingly.

Henry stayed focused on Doug. "Do you have any idea what would have happened if the sale went through tonight and tomorrow Tartan discovered what was happening? And what about our shareholders?"

David knew for a fact that Randall Craig already knew some of what was going on in the factory and didn't care. As for the shareholders . . .

Doug said, "The sale's what I've been counting on. With the influx of cash we'll be able to remedy all of our problems."

"That's right," Miles soothed. "Don't worry so much, Henry. Everyone's nerves get frayed at the conclusion of a big deal like this. And we all appreciate that Knight International is your baby. It's just eleventh-hour jitters."

"He's right, Dad, the sale *has* to go through. We've all worked so hard!"

Henry looked questioningly at David, but Henry wasn't David's client.

Miles, sensing Henry's indecision, put a companionable hand on the older man's shoulder. "Come, Henry, come back to the table. Once we get this over with, you'll feel a lot better."

Miles led Henry back to the dining room, where the Chinese bureaucrats looked unconcerned. Last-minute negotiations and delays were the norm. Miles, Doug, and his father resumed their seats. David remained standing, positioning himself so that he could see the whole table and not just the back of Miles's and Randall's heads.

"Is everything all right?" Randall asked.

Henry nodded.

"Good," Randall said. "Miles, we're all familiar with the terms of the sale, but maybe you should take us through them one more time."

David watched Miles weigh the possibilities. If he'd so easily convinced Henry to come back to the table, then maybe Henry would sign right away. But one look at Henry made that seem a dicey proposition.

He was slumped in his chair, staring blankly at the papers before him. David caught an almost imperceptible nod as Miles made his decision. "The first three pages are mainly boilerplate," Miles began, "so if you'll all just turn to page four."

Henry slowly reached out, picked up the papers, and flipped them over to the page Miles had ordered. The reading began. Several of the Chinese glanced at their watches. This was not part of tradition and very rude of their hosts to expect them to stand through this.

A half hour later, they came to the signature page. Randall picked up his pen and signed the original. Miss Quo picked it up and set it in front of Henry. He put the nib of his pen on the signature line, then just as easily lifted it. "I'm sorry, but I can't sign."

"Come on now, Henry," Randall said pleasantly. "Sign and it will all be over."

Henry pushed the contract away. "No."

Murmurs rippled through the room as the Chinese who understood English translated this latest development to those who didn't.

"If this is a last-minute plea for more money, I can tell you that you're way off base," Randall said.

But Henry just sat there.

"Look, Henry," Randall said, "we all know that you love China and think her ways are great. But using Chinese delay tactics is going too far."

Hearing this, a couple of the representatives from the Chinese ministries abruptly left the room. Sun and Amy Gao exchanged looks but kept their seats.

"It's not that. I'm just not prepared to sign at this time."

"Dad!"

"You can't back out now, Henry," Randall said.

"I just did."

"Doug," Randall said, "try talking some sense into your father."

"Dad, do it and it will be done," Doug implored.

Henry shook his head. "Not at this time."

"Look, seven hundred million is a lot of money," Randall said. "I can't guarantee that it will be here tomorrow."

"Then we'll see what happens tomorrow," Henry said. With each word his resolve seemed firmer.

Randall turned to his lead attorney. "Miles?"

Miles sighed heavily, then curled his lips into a disappointed grimace. He held up his hand and shot out a finger. On what was obviously a pre-arranged signal, the two minions from Tartan rose and began circulating around the room, whispering discretely to the assorted guests that Tartan and Knight were pleased that they had come and they hoped to see them again sometime soon. The rest of the Chinese took their cue and hurriedly left. Amy Gao's heels tapped smartly as she followed Governor Sun. Nixon Chen lingered for a moment, gazing appreciatively at the center table as if memorizing the spectacle for future tellings. Then he bowed formally, swiveled on his heel, and left the room.

One of Tartan's men approached Hulan. "Miss Liu, you'll have to leave as well."

Hulan glanced at David. He nodded and said, "I'll see you downstairs."

As soon as the door closed behind Hulan, Miles said, "I'm sorry to say I anticipated this moment, so of course we're prepared with some alternatives. The easiest thing to do is something my partner suggested. David thinks everything could be resolved if you sign an indemnification letter."

If Henry had read between the lines of that statement, he might have understood that Miles and Randall were aware of problems in the factory. But Henry was not an attorney, nor did he have one present to intervene on his behalf.

Still, anticipating that Henry might see through this, Miles went on. "We understand that this is a family business and that you're quite attached to it. So a second alternative would be for us to buy only your company's assets. You would keep the name of Knight International, and we would purchase your factory and your toy lines." David understood, but again no one was there to tell Henry that in buying only the assets, Tartan would be absolved of any previous wrongdoing.

"Finally, there's a third alternative. We go for a hostile takeover."

"You can't do that," Henry said smugly. "Fifty-four percent of Knight's shares are owned by my son and myself."

Miles shook his head in mock sadness. "As soon as the market opens Monday morning New York time, we're prepared to offer forty dollars for every share that's been selling at the already inflated price of twenty. This, combined with the twenty-two percent that your son has agreed in principle to sell us, will put us in the majority position in forty-eight hours."

"Doug?"

"Just sign the papers, Dad. Like the man said, seven hundred million is a lot of money."

Henry's eyes turned hard, and he turned back to Randall. "When did this happen?"

But Miles answered for his client. "Yesterday on the flight from Taiyuan to Beijing. We confirmed everything this afternoon."

"You bastards," Henry said between gritted teeth.

"Henry, don't take it so personally," Randall said gently, playing the good cop to Miles's bad. "It's only business."

"Knight International has been my life. It's been my family's life."

Randall shrugged. "Then you should have thought of that before. Our offer is still on the table. We're ready to buy. But if you won't sell, then we have to go another way. It's your choice."

Silence fell over the room, with all attention focused on Henry. Then he said, "I have some thinking to do. Give me till the market opens."

"Agreed," Randall said. "I'm off to Singapore tomorrow. Miles and Doug will go back to the factory and wait for your decision there, but don't misunderstand me. I don't need your agreement on this. We'll go ahead with or without your approval. You can call it a merger, you can call it a sale, you can call it a hostile takeover, but in forty-eight hours Tartan will own Knight."

Henry nodded again, then stood. He looked at the faces in the room as if measuring them for the first time. Then his eyes settled on his son. "Doug, let's go." When his son didn't move, Henry's face and body sagged in further disappointment. Then he turned and walked toward the door.

"Any way you slice it, Henry," Randall called out after him, "you're out."

The words stopped Henry in his tracks. Then his back straightened, and without another word he left the room. Once he was gone, Miles said, "I think that went well. I bet he comes around by tomorrow."

Randall added, "Doug, I think you should go after him. Work on him. Make him understand. Whatever's happened in the factory is no concern of ours. We're happy to rectify his problems. You accomplish that, Doug, and I promise, I'll never forget it."

Doug didn't say a word. He simply stood and left the room to follow his orders.

"That Doug's a good soldier," Randall observed. "He's just stupid enough to obey without question." He looked around. "Let's get out of here. I'm bushed."

Making a point to ignore David, Randall, Miles, and the Tartan entourage left together.

David stayed in his chair, deep in thought. *Miles Stout and Randall Craig had prepared for this evening in exactly the way it played out.* They'd been at least one step ahead of David all along. More important, this only confirmed that they didn't care about the factory's problems. They'd been aware of them—as Randall had said—and were going ahead full bore. For David, the question was, what happened next? In one sense the hostile takeover solved some problems, because David wouldn't have to worry about illegally filed SEC or Foreign Corrupt Practices papers. As for what had happened in the factory, Henry Knight would be off the hook and David could get clear of this mess with a clean, if slightly tarnished, conscience. This still left the bribery and the deaths of Miaoshan, Keith Baxter and Xiao Yang. But it wasn't David's job to prove Sun's guilt, and there wasn't a scrap of proof of murder, only theory. If in fact those had been murders, whoever had committed them could walk away and there was nothing that David could do about it.

He went downstairs and found Hulan leaning against a pillar, staring into the bar. When she saw him, she took his hand and pulled him behind her. "Look," she whispered and gestured with a slight tip of her head into the bar's darkness.

Whatever relief he'd felt moments before evaporated when he saw sitting at a back table against the wall Pearl Jenner and Guy Lin, who looked as miserable as ever in a loose suit that hung baggily on his thin shoulders. They were talking to another man.

Hulan said, "While I was waiting, I took a walk. I thought I'd take a peek at the weddings. Just curious, you know. But, David . . ."

"They followed us to Beijing," David said, stating the obvious.

"It's much worse than that," Hulan said. "They're talking to a reporter from the *People's Daily.*"

"How do you know?"

"Bi Peng has written the worst articles about me and my family. Whatever he writes, the others follow."

David groaned, then asked, "Do you know what they're talking about?"

"I didn't go in there, if that's what you mean."

"Have they seen you?"

Hulan gave him a look which conveyed something along the lines of: *Have you forgotten what my job is, you idiot?*

Inside the bar the three rose. Bi Peng threw some money on the table. When he turned, David and Hulan could see his big smiling teeth. The trio came forward; David and Hulan edged around the pillar, staying out of sight. As Pearl passed, she said, "We're staying at the Holiday Inn on Beilishi Lu. If you need more information, just call. I'll be happy to answer any other questions."

David and Hulan spoke little on the way back to the *hutong.* Hulan was pale with fatigue, and David felt wrung out, exhausted from travel, mind-numbing puzzles, and the stress of not knowing what would happen to his life. Once they reached Hulan's home, they stopped for a moment to look at the three-by-five cards that she'd written earlier today. There was nothing to add or change. They went to the bedroom, peeled off their clothes, and slipped under the sheet.

Hulan curled into David's shoulder as he filled in what had happened after she and the others left the room. He understood that parts of this story, because of the way she'd exposed her father's criminal actions, would be especially painful to Hulan, but there was no point in trying to protect her. She was in this with him, and maybe her own experience would provide insight into what had happened. When he came to the part about Doug selling his father down the proverbial river, David felt Hulan press herself even closer into his chest. He tightened his arms around her in response.

"What would make Doug do that?" she asked. "What does he get out of it?"

"Money, I suppose."

"But to do that to your own father? It's too cruel. There must be more about them that we don't know, something in their past that would make Doug want to disgrace his father."

"I don't think so. They're just Americans from New Jersey. There's nothing life-threatening in that, and I don't take Henry for one of those secretly abusive fathers."

"What do you think he'll do?"

"About the sale?"

"That, and about his son. If his son wants the sale that much, will Henry let it go through?"

"I don't know."

"You're going to be a father," she said. He could feel her body tense against his. "What would you do if our child tried to ruin you?"

"That won't happen," he said, trying reassurance.

"But if it did," Hulan insisted, "what would you do?"

He nudged her away so he could look at her face. Even in the darkness of the bedroom, he could see it was taut and anxious. He put his hands on her cheeks and kissed her. "Our child will never do anything to harm us. I'm not saying he won't torture us with worry or drive us crazy when he's a teenager. But he'll have two parents who'll love him, and nothing will ever change that."

"What if it's in the blood—"

"And even if for some strange reason," David spoke right over her, "he grows up to be some mad rapist hatchet murderer, I will always love him and his mother no matter what."

Hulan buried her head back into his chest.

After a moment she said, her voice brave, "Who says it's a boy anyway?"

They were awakened several hours later by the front gate buzzer. Hulan got up and put on her robe. David pulled on jeans and tennis shoes. Together they made their way through the various courtyards, lit only by the beam of Hulan's flashlight. She pulled back the bolt to the front gate, opened the door a crack, and found Governor Sun Gan standing on the step. Hulan opened the door just enough to put her head out into the alley. She looked both ways. The alley was deserted, but in another hour her neighbors would begin to rise with the pre-dawn light. She held the door open and said, "Come in."

Sun stepped over the old imperial threshold, saw David bare-chested in his jeans, extended his hand, and said smoothly, "I'm sorry to call so late. I hope you will forgive me."

David shook the governor's hand, and together they followed Hulan back through the courtyards to the main living quarters. Hulan motioned for Sun to sit, then put water on for tea. Sun watched Hulan, then leaned forward and whispered to David, "I think we should speak alone. I'm not here as a guest but as your client."

Hulan nodded, and David and the governor ducked outside to sit on two porcelain stools close enough to the house so that they might have light from the window.

"Have you had a chance to look at what I sent you?" Sun asked.

"Yes," David said cautiously, ready for the confession he didn't want to hear.

"They show deposits in the bank accounts of several businesses."

"I know."

"Those papers were sent to my office here in Beijing along with a note suggesting I check my personal accounts. The accounts on those papers are the same as my personal accounts. I think someone is trying to make it look like I've accepted payments from Knight."

"And you're saying you haven't?"

Sun let his breath out heavily. "Those are not my accounts. They aren't my papers. And that certainly isn't my money."

"It's a little late for an outright denial—"

"You have to believe me!"

David regarded Sun. Any pretext at his being a polished politician was completely gone now, but it could have been an incredible act.

"If they aren't your accounts, whose are they?"

"What I mean is, the numbers match my accounts, but the balances are not mine. *That's* the problem. I want you to know that I went to my bank here and wired my banks in America. My accounts show the proper numbers." He unfolded several pieces of papers. "See? These are my accounts and my actual balances. You can use these to prove my innocence."

But instead of looking at the papers, David glanced at his watch. It was 3:10 in the morning. "I thought we had a meeting tomorrow at ten. Couldn't this charade have waited until then?"

"Charade? What is that word?"

"Didn't you send me those reports so that when I discovered that you'd accepted bribes—and not just a little bit of money, but hundreds of thousands of dollars—that I wouldn't be able to turn you in because you were my client?"

"Is that what you think?"

"Isn't it the truth?"

"No." Sun thrust his papers at David. "Just look at these."

David took them reluctantly. From the light of the window he could see that Sun's balances were quite modest. "This means nothing to me," David said. "You could have moved the money—"

"But I'm an honest man."

"Then you've never accepted money from Knight International?"

"That's right."

"Then how do you explain papers with Knight's letterhead and a list of businesses with your account numbers? How do you explain how there's another set of papers showing other deposits and your name spelled out in code?"

"If I were guilty, would I come to you?"

David didn't answer the question. Instead he said, "When I first got here and opened my office, I was surprised at all the extra fees I had to pay as a foreigner. Are you telling me that you have never received money from Henry since he decided to open the factory?"

Sun looked at him in bewilderment. "I never took money from Henry, except . . ." A tortured look crossed his face, and he moaned in anguish. "But it wasn't a bribe. I took money, yes, but it was a fee paid straight to the contractor through me. I wanted Henry to have someone good. No delays. No bad materials. How was Henry going to find a reputable construction company? So I interviewed people, I got recommendations, I went out and looked at various work sites—some under construction, some completed. When I found the right company, I negotiated the contract and Henry's money was the first payment. I did all this as a friend. I received nothing, not one of your American pennies."

"Can you prove it?"

"Brilliant Construction is in Taiyuan. You can call them when they open. They'll have the records." Seeing David's skepticism, Sun said, "I'm telling you the truth. Why would I lie?"

"To cover up the other payments."

"That is not my money!"

There was a gentle tapping at the window. David looked up. Hulan had a tray with teacups and tea. David nodded and she brought it out, set it on the table, and left.

"Someone is trying to frame me," Sun said.

"Who?"

"Henry, but why would he do that to me?"

The conversation had become circular.

"Let's assume for a minute that what you say is true," David said, changing tactics. "What would someone get out of it?"

"I don't know why Henry—"

"Forget Henry. Look bigger, smaller, wider. Who out there would do this to you and for what gain?"

"To destroy me."

David shook his head impatiently. "That doesn't mean anything. That's vague. Why? *Why?*"

"I don't know."

The more Sun denied the charges, the more David was convinced of his guilt. David said, "I want you to understand that you can find another attorney—"

"I want you."

"Look, I don't know enough about Chinese law. This is a Chinese problem and you're in serious trouble."

"I'm aware of that." For the first time a small smile came to Sun's lips. "Attorney Stark, you haven't asked me why I came here in the middle of the night. I'm here because I am trying to avoid being arrested."

David looked at him in shock.

Sun seemed glumly pleased at David's reaction. "Someone has spoken to the press. Tomorrow there will be an article. I'm in it. You and Liu Hulan are in it. I'm not sure of all the details, but my friends say it's very bad."

David opened his mouth to speak, but Sun cut him off. "I don't want to be arrested in Beijing. I don't want to be arrested anywhere in China. As you perhaps know, justice moves very quickly here."

David did know. A trial with few if any defense witnesses, sentence, and punishment within a week. If Sun was found guilty of corruption, he would be executed and his family would be billed for the bullet.

"But if I'm to be arrested," Sun continued, "I'd prefer to go—"

"No, don't tell me! If you tell me, I might be obligated to tell the authorities, because I don't know if my American privilege will be respected here."

"What about Liu Hulan?" Sun asked. "She works for the MPS."

"You are my client," David said. "What we've spoken about is between us."

Sun looked out into the darkness. "I've worked my whole life to better myself, to better the lives of the people of China. I sit here now and I'm lost. I have friends in the government who are protecting me, but even they are sometimes powerless against outside forces. Still, I'm grateful to them. But there is another kind of friend, someone who is close to your heart, who understands you, who you would give your life for. I thought Henry was that kind of friend." Sun shifted his gaze back to David. "I know you're an honest man. I know your reputation and what you've done for China in the past. These things that are on those papers are a lie. I don't know how to prove it to you, but I hope you can accept my word." Sun took a last sip of tea, then stood. "I should go before it gets light."

David saw Sun to the front gate, where he mounted a bicycle and began pedaling. When the governor disappeared around the alley's corner, David locked the gate and made his way back to the last courtyard. Hulan sat at the little round table. Her bandaged hand rested palm up before her. She looked tired, more tired perhaps than he had ever seen her. Weren't pregnant women supposed to need, want, and get a lot of sleep? He thought he could remember reading something like that or seeing it in a movie.

"He's innocent, isn't he?" she said.

"My logical mind says he can't be, but when he speaks, I want to believe him."

"He's a politician," Hulan reminded him. "You're supposed to believe him."

"He also gave me these." David handed Hulan Sun's bank records. In his mind they proved nothing, but he had a duty to turn evidence over to the authorities if it might help his client.

Hulan saw that the names of these banks matched those in the *dangan* and that these were official documents dated yesterday, but she said none of this. Instead she picked up the index card that had Sun's name on it and corresponded to the columns which read ACCEPTING BRIBES and CHINESE jurisdiction. Without saying a word, she tore the card into pieces and put them in the trash. Then she said, "I need some sleep." With that she left the room, leaving David to stare at her chart and wonder if she really believed Sun was innocent.

# 20

MONDAY MORNING DAWNED HEAVY AND HOT. HULAN dressed in a loose-fitting suit of pale green pongee. Since she was going to the MPS, she carried her weapon under her jacket. She still felt tired, and she went about her morning activities quietly. At 7:30 she left the compound, got into the backseat of Lo's black Mercedes, and drifted back to sleep for the short drive to headquarters. As she walked through the lobby and upstairs to her office, the temperature seemed worse than ever before. The dinginess of the walls and the lack of light made the heat all the more oppressive.

She went straight to Zai's office. Vice Minister Zai was already at his desk, and it occurred to her that perhaps he'd spent the entire weekend there. The tea girls hadn't come in yet, so Zai poured the tea from his thermos himself. Hulan took a sip and felt its heat radiate through her body and produce a fine sheen of sweat on her face. This was exactly what tea was supposed to do. Sweat was nature's way of cooling the body. But today, instead of giving any relief, the tea only added to her discomfort.

"You recall the file of which we spoke yesterday?" Hulan said. When Zai nodded, she went on, "I would like to see it again."

They were inside, where anyone could be listening, and yet Hulan—though her words were ambiguous as to whose file she wanted—had broken the protocol with which she and her mentor usually communicated. But Zai didn't question her motives or even ask her to step outside for a walk. For her to show such a lapse must mean that she needed Sun's *dangan* urgently. He left the room and came back a few minutes later. As he'd done the day before, he placed the file in front of her, but instead of turning away he watched as she opened it and read. Sometimes she would pick up a piece of paper and hold it up to the hazy light coming through the window or she would set out two pieces of paper side by side to compare them. She worked silently and Zai didn't ask any questions. After a while he went back to his own work, and the two of them worked in companionable silence.

At nine sharp, Zai's support staff arrived. A pretty girl came in and refreshed their tea, bowed, and left again. A few minutes later another girl entered carrying his morning newspaper, and Zai instantly felt the change in her demeanor when she saw Hulan. It was true that Hulan had never been considered as just one of the workers. She was different from them by education, money, and political position. As a result she had always been seen as an outsider, and when Zai considered this he thought that this separateness above anything was what made Hulan so good at what she did. Still, this morning Zai's assistant stared at Hulan with more than the usual curiosity. After the girl left the room and he picked up the *People's Daily*, he understood why.

He cleared his throat. "Inspector Liu," he said formally, knowing without doubt that someone would be listening given the circumstances, "have you seen this morning's paper?"

"No, uncle, I haven't," she said without looking up. "You know I try not to read our papers. I have learned from personal experience that what they say is not necessarily true."

Zai stared at his protégée. She was speaking to him with her mouth, but her words were clearly for the others—if they were listening. He realized then that she'd come here for two reasons. The first was that she had a legitimate reason to look at Sun's file. The second was that she suspected something was about to happen and wanted to get her position on record with the people who'd be monitoring their conversation.

He pushed the paper across the desk and watched as she looked at the four photographs that blotted the front page. The first had been taken last night and showed Governor Sun, Henry Knight, and Randall

Craig. The second showed the Knight factory. The third was of a Chinese woman—a foreigner from her dress, haircut, and know-it-all expression. In the article Zai had read that this Pearl Jenner worked for an American newspaper and was spoken of in glowing terms as a true friend to China, who'd come back to the motherland to help her countrymen rid themselves of corruption. The last was that same grainy photo of Hulan and David dancing at Rumours Disco that newspapers across China had used when the propaganda tide had shifted against her. Rumours was in the Palace Hotel and reputed to be owned by generals from the People's Liberation Army. Only a handful of people on the globe knew that Hulan's last big case had at its heart the smuggling of nuclear components. Those smugglers happened to be some of the same generals who owned Rumours. These were men who, with the exception of a couple of scapegoats, had avoided prosecution. Still, they had lost a lot of money, and they did not forgive easily.

Hulan picked up the paper. Unlike the others who were listening, Zai had the benefit of watching Hulan's reaction as she scanned the article. Immediately he saw her brow furrow as she read the allegations: Knight International was harming Chinese citizens. Another American company, Tartan, was prepared to buy Knight to further this activity. The deal was being shepherded by Governor Sun Gan, who was reputed to have accepted bribes. The proof? The newspaper printed a copy of one of the pages of numbers that Guy Lin had tried to show them in the bar of the Shanxi Grand Hotel. It was a page from Miaoshan's papers and the reporter, Bi Peng, had deciphered the SUN GAN code. Sun's arrest was pending, but it was a forgone conclusion that he would be caught soon. Representing Sun was American attorney David Stark, which suggested just how corrupt the governor was.

Hulan winced, and Zai knew she'd come to the section where Pearl Jenner was quoted as saying, "Inspector Liu Hulan and a certain Miss Quo Xuesheng are responsible for introducing Mr. Stark to Governor Sun. These two women—both Red Princesses—obviously stand to profit from their affiliation with Sun and Stark. It is no wonder, then, that Inspector Liu has tried to bury the facts of Sun's misdeeds and Stark's cover-up."

Hulan set the paper down in disgust. The government controlled the newspaper and this story wouldn't have appeared if Hulan didn't have powerful enemies, but it was also true that Bi Peng had it out for her. This time the reporter had surpassed himself. By tonight this news would be on television. By tomorrow it would go out across the country. It might take two or three days to reach deep into the countryside, but these lies would get there eventually.

On the other hand, Hulan also had some powerful friends. It was to these unseen people that she spoke now. "Attorney Stark is innocent of these unfounded charges. I am also innocent. Miss Quo comes from one of the Hundred Families. To suggest that she would do something like this for money is ludicrous when she could practically buy Knight International herself."

Zai didn't say a word.

"In many ways I'm most concerned with these lies about Governor Sun. As you know, Vice Minister, I've been curious about him. I'm an investigator of facts. My job is to look for criminal activity. I think that I've done a good job over the years. But as I look at his personal file and as I've talked to him, I see nothing to suggest that he would be guilty of any acts of bribery. Still, I believe we're being manipulated into thinking he's to blame."

"Nevertheless, if he has run away, then we must find him."

"Of course, Vice Minister. Have you already authorized this as it says in the paper?"

"I will authorize it now."

"Good," Hulan said. "When we find him, I'm sure that he'll be able to clear away all ambiguity." For the first time since she'd entered his office, Zai heard the deceit in her voice. But would the others, who didn't know her as well as he, hear it as well?

Hulan stood. "Thank you for your time, Vice Minister. I will keep you informed of my activities."

Zai followed her out the door, past the cluster of chattering assistants, down the stairs, and into the parking lot. They stood in the middle of the courtyard and hoped they wouldn't be heard.

"Are you so sure of what you said, Hulan?"

"I'm sure that David, Miss Quo, and I are innocent. I believe that Governor Sun is being set up. But why and by whom I don't know."

"Maybe it's politics. He may be too popular and they want to bring him down as they have done to you."

"Um, perhaps."

"What is it?"

"Someone has doctored his *dangan*."

Zai recoiled. "This can't be!"

"In some sections the paper doesn't match. In others it appears to be the same person making the report, and yet the calligraphy is subtly different. I only have my bare eyes, but I think a lab would be able to verify my conclusions."

"They've put damaging information in it?"

"Just the opposite. His file reads as thought it were for Mao or Zhou. It's perfect. Every place that you'd expect to find criticism is only praise. He was not targeted during the Cultural Revolution, yet I *know* that the people in and around Taiyuan were very harsh and cruel."

"Why change his file to make him look good if they're going to accuse him of corruption so publicly?"

"This is exactly the question I'm wondering."

Zai contemplated Hulan. He admired her fortitude, but always worried that it would get her into trouble.

"Tell me this," he said. "Do you still believe this has something to do with the death of your friend's daughter?"

"Yes, and what Bi Peng wrote about the Knight factory is true. It's all linked."

Zai grunted. This was not what he wanted to hear.

"I think you should leave the city," he said at last.

"I'm going back to Da Shui Village. I think the answers are there."

"No!" he rapped out. "I was thinking you should go to Beidaihe and stay with your mother. It might remind people who you are." He thought for a moment, then said, "Better yet, go to Los Angeles. If you remain here, I don't know what will happen. Our anti-corruption policies are very strong now. If they demand your arrest, there's nothing I can do. The best thing for you to do is leave. Do you have your visa ready?"

"Of course, always." As a Red Princess she was always prepared to leave on a moment's notice. It also went without saying that she had plenty of cash—Chinese and American—hidden at her house.

"Go with your David to the United States," Zai said. "Take Lo with you. He'll always be able to reach me. I'll take care of your mother. I'll bring her to you as soon as I can." He put his hands on her shoulders. "You should never have come back here. Not in 1985 and not three months ago. It's time you realized your life lies elsewhere." He released her, looked around, and signaled for Lo and the car.

He stood on the hot asphalt and watched as the Mercedes left the compound. Then he headed back to his office, where, as soon as he had made the proper calls to ask that Sun be arrested and Miss Quo picked up, he would have to decide just how long he could wait before he ordered Hulan's and David's detainment.

When Hulan, hot and feeling exhausted, entered the small reception area of David's office, she saw Miss Quo crying into her hands. Hulan put an arm around the young woman, said a few soothing words, and escorted her into David's office. He was perched on the edge of his desk, staring at the television. Pearl Jenner, wearing a sky blue suit, was on the screen, her face twisted into a look that somehow managed to convey outrage and pleasure. She was clearly enjoying her newfound celebrity. She spoke in English while a Chinese woman's voice translated over the broadcast.

"Pearl's been busy this morning," David said. "How long before we're taken in for questioning?"

David had used tame Western words for what could be hell in Beijing, but his worried look told Hulan that he wasn't taking this lightly. But before she could answer, she needed to know how far the story had gone. With Miss Quo still weeping, David ran through events to this point. He'd come to the office and found Miss Quo sobbing over a copy of the *People's Daily*. They turned on the television and learned more. Reporters and the local police had gone to Governor Sun's Taiyuan home and to his Beijing apartment, but he was in neither place. Between the time that Hulan had left the ministry and now, Vice Minister Zai had sent out a spokesperson to announce that the country should be on full alert for Governor Sun. He might try to leave the country, or he might try to disappear into the interior. People should report any strangers to their Neighborhood Committee or local police.

This had been followed by clips showing Sun at banquets, cutting ribbons at commercial fairs, and striding across cultivated land as peasants trailed along behind him, while the anchor discussed the acts of bribery and corruption. "This all seemed innocuous enough," David said, "but then the stories and with them the images shifted. Suddenly there was Sun clinking glasses with a Caucasian, posing with Henry and others before the Knight compound, and moving through a crowd, shaking hands and pressing the flesh as if he were a presidential candidate working his way through New Hampshire."

Unlike the U.S., where journalists were supposed to use the word "alleged" in connection with supposed crimes, the Chinese reporters had made no such attempt. Sun was portrayed as an enemy of the people, a man who was willing to sell China to the lowest and most corrupt bidder in the world—the United States of America. Randall Craig of Tartan Enterprises and his entourage had left the country. (That they'd gone to Singapore on a previously arranged trip was not mentioned.) The government promised a prompt inspection of the manufacturing giant's factories in Shenzhen.

David paused in his recitation when a visa photo of Henry Knight flashed on the screen. As the television anchor spoke, Hulan translated: "We opened our doors to this man. He has paid bribes to Governor Sun Gan and who knows whom else since he has come to our country. The government suggests that he be expelled at once. The American embassy has made no official statement regarding either Knight or Tartan. America is a strong country, but we are strong too. China will not allow any bad fellows on her soil."

But the story didn't end here. Quo Xuesheng, David's assistant, translator, and secretary, was shown in a tight evening dress getting out of a limousine. "Is Miss Quo, daughter of Quo Jingsheng, the victim of these Western influences, or is she one of the co-conspirators? Her father, who is a well-respected member of our government, has been unavailable for comment, as he is in the United States on tour." In other words, the press, for now, was withholding judgment on Miss Quo. They might have to wait a day, a month, even a year or more before the government made its final decision on her and her father. But that didn't offer any solace to Miss Quo, who continued to weep.

And of course, those few grainy clips of David and Hulan dancing many months ago in the Palace Hotel appeared on the screen. More surprising was a shot of Hulan and David getting out of the Mercedes just last night in front of the Beijing Hotel. One of the video men who'd been there to record the arrivals to a wedding banquet had probably opened the morning paper, remembered the mixed-race couple from the night before, replayed the tape, found their faces, and had promptly gone down to China Central Television hoping for a little remuneration. However, the anchor gave the film a rather more sinister interpretation, reporting that her station's cameras had spotted Hulan and David as they went in for a clandestine meeting with Henry Knight and Governor Sun. (Hulan supposed that all across Beijing the handful of people who had been at the banquet were hoping that *they* hadn't been filmed by the wedding video crews, that the other shots taken by the official photographer wouldn't be released, that their names wouldn't arise in this mess.)

Once again the good and bad of Hulan's family background were dredged up. Reporters suggested that Hulan had been tainted by the West, by David, and by Governor Sun, who was of the same generation as Hulan's father. The implication was that if Sun and Hulan's father had been friends, then they were both equally wicked. If they were corrupt, then Hulan was without question corrupt as well. It wasn't a matter of what was false but rather what parts, if any, had been true.

"Where do they get this stuff?" David asked when Hulan stopped translating.

"This wouldn't happen if there wasn't agreement somewhere high in the government."

"But I don't understand why they would do such anti-American stories," David said.

Hulan looked at David in surprise. What did he think was happening here?

David tried to clarify what he meant. "I thought it was anything for profit. Business relations with foreign countries should be preserved no matter what the cost."

"Come on," she said, her fatigue deteriorating to impatience. "With China and the U.S. it's always the same. One minute they're friends; the next minute they're enemies. These things have little to do with us or even how things really are."

David thought back to his country's yearly hullabaloo over whether or not to give China most favored nation status and the ongoing conflicts over human rights while at the same time investing billions of dollars. These thoughts brought back the conversation they'd had with Pearl Jenner in the bar of the Shanxi Grand Hotel. All of that work she had talked about—the manufacturing of toys, computer chips, clothes—all of that went on even as American politicians beat their chests about China's unfair trade practices, its selling of nuclear technology to rogue nations, and its attempts to influence American elections. It was part of the American psyche not to look at the shades of gray in the big picture.

"We're so close-minded," Hulan said, as if reading David's mind, except that she was speaking of her own people. "The Chinese were the first explorers. It is said that we were the first ones to the Americas. We had fleets going across the Pacific, exploring, trading, but we looked, we saw, then we came home, shut the door, and built our walls even higher. I listen to these people on the news . . ." She shook her head in disgust. "They speak with smiling faces and tell one story as though it were true, but tomorrow they may have a completely different agenda to sell. One day we're forbidden to use the Internet; the next we're encouraged to use it. The day after that? Who knows? We might be forbidden again. Yesterday, every time a new deal was signed with an American company, these same reporters were covering it as though it was a great gift to China. Today those same deals are stained. Tomorrow, you may still see the deal with Tartan and Knight go through. If it does, these people will be doing stories about how the factory is bringing prosperity to the countryside. Three months ago you were our new friend, our hero; today you are once again a suspicious foreigner."

"How do you stand it?"

"How do you?" she asked back. "It's not so different in the U.S. Here our 'truth' is usually political propaganda. In the U.S. propaganda is disguised as 'truth.'"

Pearl Jenner reappeared on the screen. "I'm an American by birth," she said, "but I felt it was my duty as someone of Chinese blood to step forward. In America freedom of the press is a Constitutional right. It's our duty to expose wrong. That I have been able to help my ancestral homeland . . ."

Hulan shook herself. What were they doing sitting here, watching television, and having a chat about Sino-American relations? It was only a matter of time before Hulan was arrested. David could probably get her to the U.S. embassy. Rob Butler might be able to finagle political asylum, but this all seemed a pipe dream. Because if they came after Hulan, then they'd come after David too. In the meantime Sun would be tried and executed. Miss Quo, innocent of all charges, would also face prosecution. Henry Knight and Tartan would settle their differences, and tomorrow newspapers in China and the U.S. would talk about the acquisition, about the money that had changed hands, about the profit that would be made. No matter what, Hulan and David shouldn't be wasting time. They needed to get moving. But it wasn't so easy to leave Beijing if the government was looking for you. More than a half million of the city's citizens were engaged in watching. Intersections with traffic lights had cameras to track cars through the city. There were ways around these devices. Certainly David and Hulan had gotten out of Beijing once before when the stakes had seemed as high. But it wouldn't be so easy this time.

As all this ran through Hulan's mind, Miss Quo had continued her sniffling. Hulan crossed to her and patted her hand. David too had been lost in thought, and suddenly he said as he pushed himself off the edge of the table, "I've got to try and reach Miles. This whole thing has gotten out of hand." Without moving, Hulan watched as he picked up the phone, dialed, and asked for Miles Stout's room.

"I called my father in California this morning," Miss Quo said to Hulan. "I told him not to come home. He has money there. He'll be okay. But Mama and me?" Two new rivers of tears sprang from her eyes. "I've brought disgrace upon our family. My father will be abandoned in a foreign land. I'll go to jail. Mama will die all alone." An idea suddenly came to her, and she quickly stood. "I have to run away. Maybe I can leave the country. Dissidents do it. Maybe I could too. I have money. Pay a little here. Pay a little there. I could be in Vancouver by tomorrow." The young woman quivered in terror. "I don't want to die."

Hulan felt sorry for the girl. She'd been raised in a house of privilege. She'd never known hunger or suffering. She was too young to have experienced the Cultural Revolution. Instead she'd partied, swilled champagne, gone to karaoke bars and nightclubs, dressed in designer clothes, traveled the world. In an hour her whole life had fallen apart in a way she could never in her worst nightmare have imagined.

"Did you do anything wrong?" Hulan asked gently.

"They say I did."

"Do you think you did anything wrong?"

Miss Quo shook her head.

"Then you have nothing to be afraid of."

In the background Hulan heard David raise his voice. "Listen, Miles, you can't do that. You need a vote from the full partnership."

Hulan felt a tap on her arm. It was Miss Quo. "I was asking you, how can you say that? Don't you know what they'll do to you?"

"Yes, but I also didn't do anything wrong."

Miss Quo's eyes widened. "You're not going to stay here, are you?"

Hulan glanced back at David. He gripped the receiver so tightly that his knuckles had gone white. "Special circumstances?" David shouted into the phone. "What are you talking about? When I explain to the partners what's been going on over here . . ."

David was talking like he was going to get out of China, but they'd never go anywhere but jail unless they got moving. The more Hulan eavesdropped on David's conversation and the more she talked to Miss Quo, the more she wanted to go home and wait it out. She was too tired to run. Her arm throbbed, her body burned, and all she wanted was to lie down under a cool, wet cloth and sleep. She registered David's anxious look and thought he understood what she was thinking, but the words that came out of his mouth were all wrong.

David slammed down the phone. Without explanation he began issuing orders: "Everybody up! Let's get out of here. We're going to the American embassy!" When Hulan and Miss Quo didn't move, he barked, "Now!"

Miss Quo jumped up. Hulan slowly drew herself to her feet as David threw a couple of things in his briefcase and Miss Quo scurried about looking for her purse and . . . What was she jabbering on about? Her umbrella? Then someone pounded on the door, and the others froze in place. Hulan thought it was one of the funnier things she'd ever seen, but the look of horror on Miss Quo's face trapped the laughter in her throat.

"Why didn't you tell me about Sun and the bribery?" Henry Knight demanded, as he finally burst through the door. "Did you know all along this was brewing? Did you know he was going to be arrested?"

David, briefcase in hand and ready to flee, asked, "Has he already been arrested?"

"Now, how in God's name am I supposed to know?" Henry queried, dramatically throwing himself into a chair.

David just looked at the man.

Henry began to take in the scene: Miss Quo in her pink Chanel suit, eyes swollen and red, her bag over her shoulder and an umbrella in her hand; David looking rumpled, harried, with his briefcase in one hand and his laptop in the other; and Hulan swaying there as if she were ready to keel over for an afternoon siesta except it was only 10:30 in the morning.

"What's going on here?" Henry asked.

"In case you don't know it, Sun isn't the only one who's in trouble," David answered. "I've been named, as have Miss Quo and Miss Liu."

"Well, I know *that*! But you aren't going to turn tail and run away like scared dogs, are you?"

"That's precisely what we're going to do."

"But you have a duty to your client."

David didn't have time to talk with Henry about this. He looked at the two women. "Come on, let's go."

They made for the door, but Henry jumped up and blocked them. "If Sun's arrested," Henry said, "he'll be executed. His death will be on your head."

"If he's arrested and I go down to the jail to help him, I'll probably be arrested too. If I'm lucky, I'll simply be expelled from the country. If not—"

Henry grabbed David's shirt. He was a small man but wiry and tough. "You've got a duty, boy. The man's innocent."

"Like you're innocent of illegal practices in your factory? Like you're innocent of paying off Sun?"

Henry shoved David away. "Do you realize that at this very minute

my son is selling my company out from under me? That vulture Randall
Craig and your partner Miles Stout are trying to rip my life away from
me, but I'm not going to let them. I'll use every penny I've got to keep
them from getting Knight. What's happened there, if it's to be believed, is
terrible. But I've got money too, and I've got people in New York poised
to buy the stock. If Tartan wants war, I'll give it to them. Because I'm
telling you right now, whatever happened in that factory before is ending. The past record won't matter anymore—"

"Of course it will, Henry. It's the key to everything. Tartan wants
your company for the very abuses you insisted you didn't have. And
your pal Sun has moved the whole thing along. Now," he added force-
fully, "we're leaving."

"What if I told you I knew where Sun was?"

David motioned at the walls around him. "I'd say you'd better be
careful where you say that. I don't think the Chinese will take kindly to
your hiding a criminal."

"I'm not hiding him, but I know where he is, and . . ." He once again
grabbed David's shirt, pulled him very close, and whispered, "I've got a
plane."

The phone rang. Miss Quo stared at it. When it rang a third time, she
picked it up. "Phillips, MacKenzie & Stout," she said, taking a stab at a
cheerfulness she didn't feel. The voice on the other end spoke for several
seconds with Miss Quo nodding. "Please hold," she said at last, "I will see
if he's in." She held the receiver out to David. "It's for you."

"I don't have to take it. I no longer work for the firm."

"She's calling from America."

"Oh, Jesus," David said, "Jenner must have sent her story out on the
wire. We're probably all over the papers in the States too. Just say no
comment."

Miss Quo shook her head. "No, it's a woman from Kansas. She says
she's been trying to reach you for a long time."

# 21

D AVID MOVED SWIFTLY TO THE PHONE. "ANNE?"

After a long-distance delay, Anne's voice came floating over the line. "Is this David Stark?"

"Yes."

"I've wanted to talk to you and apologize for how I acted at my brother's funeral. I think anyone would have been upset. But when we heard the circumstances—that he'd been killed instead of you— well, I, we . . ."

David listened impatiently while Anne struggled with her apologies. He was chafing to go. Yet these few seconds gave him a chance to take stock. Where was Hulan? She'd been awfully quiet. His eyes scanned the room. Henry was still at the door, ready to bar it again if they tried to leave. Miss Quo was looking nervously out the window. And Hulan had sunk into a chair and appeared to be dozing. The skin on her neck and arms looked pale, while two bright blotches of color heightened her cheeks. A new and completely different wave of concern swept over him, but he tuned back into the phone call as he began registering Anne's words.

"I thought he'd gone to you for help. I thought, now isn't that bad karma? I mean, you go to someone for help and you end up getting killed. That's why I was so rude."

"He didn't come to me for help," David said. "I invited him to dinner. I wanted some information—"

"I know that now," she said. "But at the time I was only going off what Keith had told me. He called me that day. We were very close, and whenever he had a problem he'd call. He was troubled. He said he was going to meet a friend, someone he could talk to. He had dinner with you, so I just assumed that . . ."

As on the day of the funeral, David felt that there was no reason to ruin the Baxter family's memories of their son and brother. "We just had dinner—"

"I know, I know. All I'm saying is that when I saw you at the funeral, all I could think was that you hadn't helped him. I'd told him before to go to the FBI. He'd laughed at my ignorance. He said he didn't need the FBI; he needed the State Department. Then he told me that he had friends down at the U.S. Attorney's Office who might put in a good word. But he didn't go to you."

No wonder Keith had acted so strangely that night. He was ready to throw away his career by going to the feds to rat on his client. "Was it about what was happening with the Knight deal?"

Even over the thousands of miles David heard Anne's deep sigh. "It was about his girlfriend. She was Chinese. He wanted to bring her over here. He thought political asylum might work."

David couldn't believe what he was hearing.

"Anyway," Anne continued, "that day at the funeral I was angry at you for not helping him, but actually it was someone else. I met him there."

There was only one person at the funeral to whom Keith might have gone. "Rob Butler," David surmised.

"That's right. He came up and introduced himself. He said he'd tried to do what he could for my brother. Do you think he tried to help?" Anne asked.

David thought back to his last meeting with Rob and Madeleine. He'd asked them point blank what they thought about Keith's death. They both said that they thought it had been a botched attempt by the triads to kill David. He'd also asked if Keith was under investigation. Again, both Madeleine and Rob had said no. Why hadn't Rob mentioned Miaoshan? (It *had* to be Miaoshan.) If he thought she was eligible for political asylum, it must have been because Miaoshan could offer something—the proof of the Knight-Sun bribery. Would Rob have lied to David? And for what reason? Keith was dead. The girl was also dead, and her papers were in China. There was no case without evidence. Most important, had Keith used Miaoshan to circumvent getting in trouble himself? He offers up the girl, lets her hand over her information about Sun and Knight, and he walks away clean?

"Hello? Are you there?" Anne asked.

"I'm sorry," David said. "I was thinking. I have so much to ask you, but . . ." He saw Miss Quo staring out the window. She didn't seem to be panicking. "Things are a little crazy here."

"That's okay," Anne said. "Before you ask me anything, let me explain the real reason I'm calling. My brother sent me some papers before he died. They were here when we got back to Russell. I don't know what they are, but he put a note on them. 'If something happens to me . . .' Can you imagine what it's like to get something like that in the mail? My brother was dead! It's been like some horror movie, only we can't turn it off or walk out of the theater."

"What are they?" David asked, although he already suspected what they were.

"Pages and pages of numbers. They don't mean a thing to me, but in the note he wrote that they were a key."

*A key?* Miaoshan had her set. Sun had his. Now it appeared that Keith also had his own set. Could it possibly be a key?

"Anne"—he tried to put as much conviction into his voice as he could—"about the papers . . ."

"You're going to tell me about the girl and how Keith wanted to marry her."

No, he wasn't, but he let it go for now.

"We're from Kansas," Anne went on. "We don't see a lot of Asians where we live. But our feeling was that if Keith was in love, that was his business. We'd do our best to welcome this Meow-meow. Even her name was foreign to us. I mean, it wasn't really Meow-meow, but it sure sounded like that to my dad, so that's what we've been calling her around here. Anyway, you can see why we thought it was a good thing they'd be living in L.A. They have all sorts of people out there, and they wouldn't have stood out so much."

David and Hulan had known that Miaoshan was having an affair with an American. They'd thought it was Aaron Rodgers—and maybe she'd still had an affair with him—but Keith was who mattered. He must have met her during his regular pre-sale visits to Knight International. Keith and Miaoshan? Why hadn't David seen that from the beginning? When Miles had said Keith's girlfriend wasn't from L.A., David had assumed that she'd been a hometown girl. That image fit with what he knew about Keith. Even now it was hard to imagine his friend, who was overweight and in his late thirties, with an eighteen-year-old Chinese factory worker. Of course, things like that did happen. It was called a mid-life crisis. The manipulative Miaoshan must have seen Keith as incredibly gullible. And she'd pushed at that gullibility by asking for and receiving all kinds of gifts—the fancy underwear, the jeans, the makeup, the . . . Suddenly he remembered the sickening sweet smell at the funeral and what Hulan had said about Miaoshan's bunk.

"Do you wear White Shoulders?" David asked Anne.

"Yes, my mother and I both do," she answered, surprised.

"Keith must have had it bad." It slipped out before David could stop himself.

"He was head over heels," Anne said. "My parents and I hadn't seen him—I mean, we only talked to him on the phone or over the Internet, but you know what I mean—that lovesick since eighth grade when he'd gone gaga over Maryellen Sanders. He was calling me all the time, wanting to know what he should get her. I even bought a few things for her myself. And she must have felt the same way. Meow-meow gave Keith all sorts of things."

"Like the papers," David concluded. "Anne, can you fax them to me? You probably don't have a fax, but you could send them at Kinko's. Do you have a Kinko's in Russell?"

"I don't have to go looking," Anne said, a tad indignantly. "We may be in Kansas, but I still have a fax machine. Here, hang on. I'll send it through. Give me your number."

David gave it to her. Anne said she was going to put down the phone for a second and would be right back. He heard the thump of the phone hitting what he'd imagined was a quaint kitchen counter and realized, given his many misconceptions about Anne and her life, that she was probably in her fully outfitted office. A minute later, Anne picked up the phone.

"It's not going through. Give me the number again."

David repeated it, then Anne said, "Yeah, that's what I dialed. Twice. Check your machine."

He went over to the fax. Everything looked fine. Miss Quo came away from the window and doubled-checked. It was plugged in; there was paper. Then Miss Quo picked up the line. She paled. "It's dead," she said.

"We need that fax!" David exclaimed.

"I've got a fax on my *you know what*," Henry said, motioning to the walls. "I'll get you your fax, if you come with me to Taiyuan."

But Henry didn't need to resort to this kind of bribery. If Anne really did have a key, then maybe this would all become clear. It was a risk, but at this point everything was a risk.

"Give me the number," David said.

Henry did, and David in turn recited it to Anne. When he was done, Henry added, "Tell her to wait awhile. I've got to get my guys together and the electricity on before we can receive."

David passed on Henry's comments, then said, "I don't want to sound melodramatic, Anne, but if anything happens to *us*, will you get those papers to Rob Butler? Tell him . . . Tell him . . . Anne? Anne?" But the phone had gone dead. The line had been cut.

David set the receiver back in the cradle. He tried to maintain some semblance of calm, knowing that fear would dull their senses. "We really need to go," he said.

They gathered up their belongings and headed for the door. David looked back. It had been a nice office and a nice attempt at a new life.

Quo Xuesheng still held her post at the window.

"Miss Quo?"

She turned to face him. "You go ahead."

"Don't be foolish," Hulan said harshly. David realized it had been a long time since he'd heard her voice.

Miss Quo straightened her shoulders, crossed the room, and took Hulan's good hand. "You're right. I shouldn't run away. I've done nothing wrong. Thank you, Inspector, for giving me courage. I'll tell my father that you have, as always, been a good friend to our family."

David wanted to argue with her, but determination had formed as hard as stone just under his assistant's blotchy and swollen skin.

"Go on," Miss Quo said, walking back to the window. "I'll stay here. When they come, I'll tell them something."

It was a vain hope for delay. With the phone lines cut and the possible monitoring of the office, their movements were probably already known, which might make this whole venture futile.

"Good luck," David said, then closed the door behind them.

Henry wanted to take his car, but Hulan overrode him and they piled in with Investigator Lo, because she thought the small insignia on the car might give them some authority. (On the other hand, if the cameras that were set up at the major intersections were already alerted to look for them, then they would be exceptionally easy to follow. But Hulan decided it was a risk worth taking.) As soon as they were in the car, Hulan handed Henry her cell phone. He spoke elliptically, saying that he'd like his crew to get the electricity running, hoping they would interpret that to mean they should get the plane fueled and ready as he'd be leaving town shortly.

Then, as they headed across town, making for the expressway that would take them to the airport, David reported his conversation with Keith's sister. When he came to the end, Hulan, who'd revived slightly, said, "Suchee—everyone actually—kept saying Miaoshan wanted to go to America. I thought it was a dream for her, an unrealistic dream. Peasants never leave. It's even hard for them to get away from their villages and go to a big city, so how could she ever think she would get to the U.S.? But obviously she had a plan."

"Do you think she loved Keith?"

Hulan thought about Miaoshan, then said, "On the surface she seemed a typical peasant girl. But again and again she has shown a deep capacity for deception and manipulation. With Tsai Bing there probably was love, but they'd known each other from birth and grown up together. Theirs was a familiar love. Knowing they were to be married, they'd had sex as comfortably and unemotionally as an old married couple."

(Now, that was a worldview that under different circumstances David would have pursued with the woman he planned to spend his life with, but now wasn't the time.)

"Tang Dan?" Hulan continued. "Who can tell? Maybe Miaoshan wanted the experience of an older man. Maybe she feared she'd never get out of the countryside and thought that at least she could marry the richest man in the county. That story is common the world over."

"What about rape?" Henry asked. He didn't know who this Miaoshan was, but he was intrigued.

"Could be," Hulan answered. "Rape is probably the most taboo subject in all of China. It's the worst shame. If she'd been raped, she would never have said a word." Hulan paused. "But I think not. Siang, Tang's daughter, said she saw them together. She was disgusted, but I don't think she would have mentioned it if there'd been a struggle. No, it wasn't rape."

"Guy Lin loved her," David said. "There's no question in my mind about that."

"Who's that?" Henry asked.

"He's the one you've seen on television with Pearl Jenner," David responded simply.

"Yes, he loved her," Hulan concluded. "But he lost his usefulness when she no longer needed him. Which brings us to Keith."

Hulan's mind felt clouded by the heat and humidity. She looked at the others. They all seemed to be waiting for her to continue. With great effort she gathered her thoughts and asked, "Did Ling Miaoshan—beautiful, manipulative, cruel in matters of the heart—actually love Keith Baxter—a man twice her age from a culture that was immensely foreign yet at the same time attractive to her?" Hulan let the question hang in the air, then resumed after a moment. "I've slept in her bed. I've smelled the White Shoulders on her sheets and in her pillow. I've seen the things he gave her folded in their tissue and wrapped in their ribbons. I've thought a lot about what she had to have done to be with him—repeatedly sneaking out of the dormitory, changing her clothes and her entire appearance to be more comely to him, and keeping the secrets of those papers when she was killed. Yes, I think she must have loved him. Was it a true-heart love or a simple infatuation that would have changed over time? I don't know. But I think she was in love. What about your friend? Could he have really loved her, or was it just sex?"

"He was ready to bring her home to meet his family," David said. "He was trying to get her out of the country. He may have been crazy, but I think he must have been in love too."

David turned and looked out the window. Hulan could see the impatience in his features. The traffic wasn't moving at all. She leaned forward and spoke a few words into Lo's ear, urging him to find another route. When she sat back, David said, "But to what lengths was he willing to go? When I was talking to Anne, I thought Keith had given his papers to the government. This would have violated his duty as an attorney, but I think they would have been enough to get Miaoshan out. If they are some kind of key, they would have opened a massive federal investigation into . . . Well, into your company, Henry, and Tartan. Seven hundred million is a lot of money. The Tartan and Knight stockholders would need to be answered to. There would have been the various corruption charges."

"I'm telling you, Sun is innocent," Henry repeated for what seemed the millionth time this morning.

"Sun wouldn't have been the target of a federal investigation, Henry, but you and to a different extent Tartan would have," David said. "But Keith didn't give the key to Rob. Keith loved Miaoshan, but he wasn't willing to sacrifice everything he'd worked for to have her."

"Then why was he so upset the night you had dinner with him?" Hulan asked. "If he'd made his decision, why worry?"

"Because Pearl already knew about Miaoshan's papers and probably told him so," he answered. "Because Keith knew that he'd lost the love of his life, that everything was going to come to light, and that there wasn't much he could do about it."

Henry cleared his throat. "I'm not used to this sort of thing, but if you don't mind my saying so, I think how Miaoshan got those papers is important."

David and Hulan looked over at the older man questioningly.

"If what you say is true—that none of this would be happening if that Pearl woman hadn't gotten these papers—then whoever gave them to Miaoshan in the first place had a strong motive to destroy . . ." He faltered, then finished up with, "To destroy me, I guess." David instantly thought of how Sun had used those exact same words last night. Henry went on uncertainly. "I mean, wouldn't you have to say that was the case? That this was some kind of plant by Tartan to get my company on the cheap?"

David and Hulan looked at each other, absorbing this new angle. Then Hulan leaned forward again and spoke in rapid Mandarin to Lo. He made a U-turn, swerved up a side street, and began beeping the horn.

"What's happening?" Henry asked.

"We've got to get over to the Holiday Inn," Hulan said. "What you say has truth. Part of that truth is that Pearl and Guy have accomplished what the killer wanted them to do. Since that's so, their lives are in danger. We must try to warn them."

"That snake of a woman?" Henry asked.

"Um," Hulan agreed, "but we must."

A few minutes later, they arrived at the downtown Holiday Inn or, rather, they got within a few yards of it. Police cars and ambulances blocked the parking area and porte-cochere. Bellboys in bright uniforms decorated with gold braid and passersby gawked as the managers of the hotel argued with the policemen to please move their vehicles. Amidst all this was a large contingent of plainclothes agents from the Ministry of Public Security.

"We're not going in there!" Henry half yelped when he saw David open the door. "You have to figure they're dead, right? We're too late."

Hulan grabbed his arm and gave the older man a not-so-gentle push. "We're absolutely going in there, Mr. Knight, and you're going to lead the way. You're the VIP-er. Do what you're supposed to do—bluster, bluster, bluster. We'll be right behind you."

And so, with Henry Knight out in front, they walked straight into the air-conditioned lobby of the hotel. When a young Beijing policeman tried to stop them, Henry said imperiously, "I don't understand." When the policeman, seeing that Hulan was Chinese, said they weren't permitted to pass, she looked at him uncomprehendingly, and David said, "We're in a hurry! Business meeting! Foreigners! Foreigners!" Henry boldly pushed past the policeman and walked to the bank of elevators with David and Hulan following close behind. As the elevator doors closed, they saw the policeman face front as though he'd never let anyone past.

"Which floor?" Henry whispered, then colored as he realized no one else was on this car.

"We'll go to the top and work our way down the stairs," Hulan said.

Of course, the stairs weren't air-conditioned, and by the time they'd gone down five flights they were all sweating. Hulan worried about Henry—a heart attack was the last thing they needed—but he seemed spry enough. On the other hand, the same lethargy that had gripped her in David's office now came back full force, and she wished she could step into one of the air-conditioned hallways, find a room, and lie down.

They continued down, opening the fire doors and checking for activity. On the ninth floor they found what they were looking for. Hulan wiped the sweat from her forehead with a tissue and said to her companions, "Follow me, but don't say anything."

She pulled out her MPS credential, stepped into the hallway, and walked purposefully down the hall. A policeman sat with his back against the wall, looking green, beside him a splash of vomit. A few of his buddies stood around in support, offering by turns cigarettes and bottled water. But the truth was, they looked none too well themselves. It must be bad, Hulan thought, very bad.

At the door to the room Hulan held up her credential, although the person guarding it was well known to her. Yang Yao had worked at the Ministry of Public Security for almost thirty years, but he'd never risen above the rank of investigator third grade. An announcement of his impending retirement had recently circulated around the office. It was about time. Still, Hulan had hoped he'd be here. Yang was slow and infinitely dumb, which was why he was always assigned to watch the door instead of investigate. He nodded to Hulan and made not one movement and said not one word to prevent the foreigners from going in after her.

The smell of death even in this highly air-conditioned environment assaulted them: the rustiness of blood, the sour odors of excrement, the nervous perspiration of the officers in the room. All death was gruesome—even for those who supposedly died peacefully in their sleep—but even Hulan, who'd seen more murder scenes than she cared to remember, had a hard time processing what had happened to Pearl Jenner and Guy Lin.

They were on the double bed together, both naked. They looked to be involved in some sort of sexual act, although Hulan couldn't fathom the wheres and hows of such an act. Pearl's wrists and ankles were bound together behind her by a length of rope. The rope had also been looped around her neck, stretching her whole body back—knees pulled open to accommodate the inhuman position—so that her private parts would have been totally exposed if not for the other victim positioned against her. From the knots that bound Pearl's ankles, the rope led to the other victim. Guy Lin was bound in much the same position, his loins pressed to Pearl's.

In her weakened state Hulan felt the blood drain from her head, and she thought she might faint. Then behind her she heard shallow panting. With great effort she pulled herself together and turned to escort David back out of the room. Only it wasn't David. He was fine—as fine as could be expected given the spectacle—but Henry had gone completely white and was trembling like the old man he was.

"Investigator Yang," Hulan commanded imperiously. "Take this man to the hall. Find him some tea and a chair." Yang did as he was told. As she turned back to the hideous tableau, she saw that David had edged closer to the bed where Pathologist Fong squatted, gloves on, bifocals perched on his nose. When Hulan approached, Fong looked up and beamed.

"They always send you out to see the pretty ones, hey, Inspector?" Fong said in heavily accented English for David's benefit. Fong didn't stand up. He never liked to be reminded how much shorter he was than Hulan. To cover this, Fong cocked his head back toward the bodies. "Foreigners," he grunted. "The propaganda tells us they are decadent, but you have to see something like this before you really believe it is true."

"How long have they been dead?" Hulan asked.

"That's my inspector!" Fong announced cheerfully to the room. "We have a case of autoerotic death, and she wants to know how long they've been dead!"

Some of the others in the room, who were dusting for fingerprints, looking through luggage, and picking through the trash receptacle, chortled. Hulan was not amused.

Fong rocked back on his haunches. "Two hours at most."

"How were they discovered?"

"The maid came in. Imagine what she thought!" Fong grinned again, then finally turned serious. "Last year I went to an international symposium on forensic medicine in Stockholm. They had a panel on autoerotic death. I went—curious. I had never seen a case myself, but I'd read about it in foreign literature."

He pointed at the bodies and assumed a scholarly tone. "You see how it works, don't you? With every one of his thrusts, her ropes are pulled tighter. Every time he pulls back, his ropes are pulled tighter. The lack of air is supposed to heighten sexual pleasure. People die like this all the time in the West," he said more in wonder than disapproval.

Neither Hulan nor David enlightened Fong about his misconception.

"But you see the problem, don't you, Inspector?"

Hulan stared at the bodies. The faces were purple. Pinpricks of broken blood vessels dotted the whites of their eyes, their faces and necks. Hulan shook her head.

Fong glanced over at David. "But you do."

"I think so," David said. "I understand the anatomy of what's happened here, but who tied the knots?"

"Precisely!"

Hulan, blaming her queasiness on her pregnancy, looked numbly at the two men, while David wondered where her mind was. She was usually so far ahead of him in these matters.

"Pretend you're going to have this kind of sex," David said. "You want to heighten your experience of orgasm. You cut off your partner's blood supply. Maybe she cuts off yours. Maybe you rig something that will help both of you. But look, Hulan, look at how they're bound. Once she's tied, she can't tie him and there's no way he could do that to himself. It's murder made to look like a sexual mistake."

"I agree," Fong said. "But when I get them back to the lab, I will test for semen just to make sure. I will send you the report . . ."

These words jolted Hulan. Fong didn't know about her problems. Either that or he knew but chose not to mention them, which was completely out of character. When things were bad, her colleagues enjoyed making furtive asides just loud enough so that she could hear them. But this morning no one had stopped her or even questioned her about the story that was on the television and in the newspaper. This could only mean that Zai or someone higher wanted her to see this.

"One last question, Pathologist Fong. Has the team found a satchel or any papers?"

"Passports and the like. It's a very clean room except for this."

With that, Hulan pulled on David's sleeve. Without good-byes they left the room, picked up a pale Henry Knight in the hall, rode the elevator down, and walked back into the brutal heat without one person stopping them or making a single comment.

"Did the same person kill all of these people?" David asked when they got back in the car.

"I think the better question is, are we supposed to think so?" Hulan replied. "Are we supposed to take that scene at face value—a mistake of sexual deviance? Or are we intended to recognize it as a cleverly staged murder?"

The car pulled onto the toll road. The traffic cleared immediately, and Lo was able to drive at a steady, though still restrained, pace.

"I assumed murder," David said, "because it was so obvious, so dramatic. He wanted to flaunt what he was able to do."

"Jesus Christ!" Henry exploded. "What's wrong with you people? What we saw in there . . . God, it was horrific!"

"Is it the same person?" David repeated, totally ignoring Henry's outburst.

"If you look at the modus operandi, it could be. Suffocation has been the key. Miaoshan—hung from a rope. Pearl and Guy—also hung by a rope."

"But Keith and Xiao Yang were different," David said.

"Yes, theirs were more physical deaths—hitting someone with a car, throwing someone from a roof. To me, those murders imply a person with a desire for a *physical* act, while the suffocation and ropes suggest a tighter mind, someone who wants to be *hands-on* during the project, someone who wants to feel and watch the breath stop. So to my mind, this could be one person who's acquired a taste for murder and is embellishing the methods by which he kills, or it could be two or more people. We just don't know yet."

The car slowed as it got off the toll road. The airport wasn't set up for private planes. There was no VIP lounge or even a private airfield. Instead, those few people who flew into China on private or government jets used a side entrance—the same one used by maintenance—to reach the tarmac. Up ahead they could see the guardhouse that protected that entrance and the two People's Liberation Army soldiers in their summer greens with machine guns draped over their shoulders flanking it. Lo asked, "What do you want me to say?"

Hulan looked over at Henry. "You know what to do," she said.

Henry shrank into his seat.

"You want to help Sun?" David asked. "The only way we're going to do that is if we get on your plane."

Henry nodded, resigned. It was one thing to talk bravely about saving an old friend, David thought sympathetically. It was another to risk arrest in China.

The car moved forward. When they reached the gate, Henry pushed a button and his window glided down. The guard approached, surly and stiff, but before he could speak, Henry snapped his fingers and said loudly, "Come over here, boy."

The guard glanced over the roof of the car at his companion. What impertinence was this? his look seemed to say.

"Don't dawdle!" Henry blasted. He hit the side of the car with his fist. "Come here!" The guard swaggered over. Henry pointed right at the guard's chest, an insult of the highest order. "You! See that plane over there?" Henry dragged his finger away from the guard to the direction of his plane. "That's my baby. Let me pass!"

The guard bent down to see who else was in the car. Henry pressed a button and the tinted window rolled up. The guard banged on the window and started yelling. Lo kept his eyes forward. David and Hulan pretended they didn't hear a thing. After a moment Henry cracked the window an inch or so.

"Get out of the car," the guard said in Mandarin. To emphasize his point, he tapped the muzzle of his machine gun on the glass.

"No speakee Chinese!" Henry yapped. David groaned. "Now look, buddy," Henry went on. Somewhere along the way he seemed to have added a broad Southern accent. "I'm a personal friend of President Jiang Zemin. Jiang Zemin! Get it?" Henry snapped his fingers in the guard's face, each time rapping out, "Hurry! Hurry! Hurry!"

The guard, flummoxed by this spectacle, motioned to the other guard. The gate rose, and Lo stepped on the gas.

Henry sank back into the leather seat. "You wanted bluster. I blustered."

"You did a good job," Hulan said.

"I acted like a total asshole and thoroughly insulted your countrymen."

"It worked," she replied.

The car stopped next to the plane. The pilot and copilot stood at the bottom of the stairs, sweating in the sun. "We're ready to go, sir," the pilot said.

"Just get us out of here as soon as you can," Henry said, and with that they boarded the plane.

# 22

A S THE PILOT STARTED THE ENGINES, HENRY QUICKLY checked to see if the fax had come through. It hadn't. They belted in, the plane taxied out to the runway, and after a short, though agonizing wait, they were given permission to take off. When the plane reached cruising altitude, Henry unbuckled his seat belt and said ironically, "I haven't had this much excitement since the war. And I want you to know right now, I'm not enjoying it any better."

David smiled. It took a special person to deal with this kind of danger with humor. He looked over to see if Hulan had had the same reaction, but she'd fallen asleep. He knew that sleep was a way to escape tough circumstances, but he'd been in life-threatening situations with Hulan before and he'd never seen her shut down like this. He reached over and touched her cheek. It was burning hot.

"Hulan? Honey? Are you okay?"

Her eyes blinked open. She straightened in the seat and smoothed her hair. "I must have dozed off."

"You're burning up," David said.

Hulan shook her head. "Of course. It's about forty degrees centigrade and ninety-nine percent humidity."

Outside, David thought. In the jet it was a comfortable seventy-two.

"If I could have a little water," she continued, "I'm sure I'll be fine. I'm probably just dehydrated."

Henry got up and pulled a bottle of Evian out of the refrigerator. Hulan unscrewed the top and drank straight from the bottle. She looked over at David and said in a voice that made it clear she wanted no argument, "Really, I'm fine."

What could he do but take her word for it? David glanced over at Henry, who only shrugged. His look seemed to say there wasn't much you could do if a woman wasn't going to be square with you.

"Mr. Knight," Hulan said, "you're going to a lot of trouble for Sun. Are you ready to tell us why?"

Henry stared pensively out the window, then, without looking at David or Hulan, he plunged in. "As you know, I was sent to China during World War II. I flew in over the Hump—the Himalayas. You always hoped you'd make it over, but you wore your parachute just in case. Then you'd get to Kunming in Yunnan Province. We had all kinds of names for that place—City of Rats, Black Market Town. First we stayed in these thatched huts. Rats lived up in the straw thatching, and when you woke up you'd see their beady little eyes staring down at you. There were so many rats that the army announced a rat-tail redemption campaign. In three months the locals turned in over a million tails, but that still didn't put a dent in the number of rats. The army did an investigation and found over a hundred rat farms that had been started just to cash in on the campaign. That's what Kunming was like."

Anne's fax still hadn't come through, but David was anxious for Henry to get to the point. "How did Sun get over to Kunming? I thought he was from Shanxi Province."

"I never said I met him in Kunming," Henry responded. For a moment it seemed he wouldn't continue. Then he sighed and said, "I told you before that I wanted to spend my life in China. What I didn't say was that I'd had that desire long before I ever got here. As a kid, I was fascinated with the place. I was particularly interested in old religious sites. I know it sounds crazy and maybe it was. You can imagine what my father thought! Things were different back then. I was only the third generation in my family to be in America and only the first to be born here. My father expected me to go into the family business and I did, but that didn't stop me from studying on my own or finding a Mandarin tutor. When the war broke out, everything changed, especially after the army found out about my interests. It's surprising what an armchair archeologist knows. I'd spent years studying the early Buddhist cave sculptures of Yungang, Luoyang, and Gansu. But I'd also researched the lesser-known cave sculptures of Tianlong Shan, which lay in the mountains to the south of Taiyuan. I wasn't the only person interested in those caves. A few years before, the Japanese had sent a team of art historians to Tianlong. They documented everything and published several books which were very popular in Japan."

"So in 1937, when the Japanese invaded, they knew exactly what to look for," Hulan concluded.

"The Japanese chopped off the heads of the Buddhas and carved out the relief sculptures from the walls. They were systematic and thorough. But as the war progressed, those caves offered something besides art."

"Protection," David said.

"That's right. They fortified themselves up there, and it seemed there was no way to rout them out. Even today the caves aren't that easy to reach, but back then the only way up was by foot across the mountains. It wasn't that the altitude was so bad—the 'mountains' are really just large hills on an already high plateau—but that the terrain was rocky, steep, and unstable. The Japanese looked to be up there for good. The Joint Intelligence Collection Agency thought I was the perfect person to go and take a look-see."

Japanese-Occupied China had covered a huge area. The Japanese were able to control strategic garrisons, but vast areas inhabited only by peasants and missionaries were left alone. It was through these areas that intelligence operatives traveled. "I flew into Xian, where we had other intelligence people," Henry continued. "Bishop Thomas Meeghan had an orphanage there for Chinese boys, who were trained to be totally reliable. A couple of those kids took me east. We rode on—I don't know what you call it—one of those things you pump up and down on a railroad track? We traveled at night, stopping for food and shelter at American, French, or Norwegian missions."

"How did you know where to go?"

"It was a network," Henry said. "The missionaries and the peasants didn't want the Japanese there. They were sympathetic to what we were doing. If a B–29 ran out of fuel flying back from a bombing raid on

Japanese-Occupied China and the crew had to bail out, all they had to do was show the Allied patch they wore inside their jackets and they were passed west through the network. We wore those same patches. They were like a passport. Anyway, we kept to the main railway line which divides the country between north and south and eventually runs through Taiyuan."

"Which is where you finally met Sun Gan," David said.

"Everything we told you before was true," Henry said. "Sun was just a scrawny kid when I first met him. At first I thought he was about eight years old, but he was thirteen. Half of his life had been during wartime. He hadn't had much food or nourishment other than what the local mission gave him. But the kid was smart. Street smart, of course. You had to be a good scavenger in those days to survive. But it was more than that. He seemed to understand what we wanted, and then he got it for us."

"So what did he do? Save your life?"

Henry smiled patiently. He was going to tell his story in his own way.

"Taiyuan—the whole province actually—has a bloody history because of its strategic position as the gateway to the fertile plains to the south. The Japanese understood this, which was why they were there. At that time we didn't know about the atom bomb. We thought, despite Chiang's desires, that we were going to have to fight the Japanese back inch by bloody inch. If we were ever going to take back China, Taiyuan would be—as it has always been—vitally important. I was some dopey know-nothing kid with a secret passion that suddenly had value. We had air reconnaissance, but the brass wanted me to sneak up the mountain and see just how fortified the Japanese were. Sun Gan tagged along with us—part scout, part mascot, part translator. But because he was from Shanxi Province, he understood the land in a way none of the rest of us did—not even the other Chinese."

They'd gotten halfway up the hill when they were spotted. "The Japanese were above us in the caves and below us too," Henry recalled. "It was like target practice for them. Any of us moved and *bam!*" Henry smacked his hand, the sound startling in the small confines of the Gulfstream. "One of those mission kids got his arm shot off. The other kid got a bullet in the gut. His intestines were hanging out, and he was trying to stuff them back in."

Henry shook his head as the memories came back.

"We were all going to die up there. Sun Gan stepped forward—well, it was hardly that. He crawled along the rock face, trying like the rest of us not to get his head blown off. When he disappeared I thought, that's it. He's run off and I'm dead. By the time Sun got back, the two mission kids were dead. I hadn't been able to do much for them. One kid bled to death; the other blew his brains out. He knew what would have happened if he'd been captured. So Sun, this little kid, comes crawling back, takes in the two dead guys, sizes me up, and tells me what we're going to do. 'You're here for a job,' he said. 'So am I.' And he slithers off into the darkness, leaving me alone."

Henry snorted. "I'm thinking, not on your fucking life am I following you! But here's the thing. I couldn't go up and I couldn't go down, because the enemy was in both places. And staying there wasn't much of an alternative either. The Japanese would have found me eventually. I was looking at a quick execution if I was lucky, or a prisoner of war camp if I wasn't. So I started crawling along behind Sun. This meant creeping along those damn cliffs at the same elevation, circumnavigating that fucking mountain. The whole exercise was dangerous, suicidal. But you know, you can sit still and die, or you can move forward and die."

Henry leaned over, resting his forearms on his knees, looking weary. "I'm eighteen fucking years old. I'm thinking, if I'm going to die, I'm going to do it on my own terms. And maybe, just maybe, I'll see those caves in the process." His mouth spread in a toothy grin. "Okay, I was young, dumb, and stupid. That's why they send boys to war. They don't know any better."

After a moment he continued. "Finally we come up over the back of the mountain. There was a moment when I think each of us thought, I could just crawl down this mountain, hole up somewhere, and wait it out. The impulse to live is strong."

David and Hulan knew what Henry meant. They'd been there themselves.

"Maybe because Sun was an orphan, maybe because it was his homeland, he stood firm. We crouched together and he mapped out a plan. He brought me into it, because I knew the caves better than he did. The sun would be up in a couple of hours. If we were going to make our move, it had to be now. Well, you can guess the rest. We made it. Sun saved my life."

"You're not getting off that easily," David said.

Henry looked over at Hulan. She too looked at him expectantly.

"Just as Sun planned, we dropped down over the top of the cliff with ropes and *swung* right into those caves like we were a couple of Tarzans. The Japanese were surprised, but ready enough. It was a classic hand-to-hand fight. We were outnumbered, but not as badly as I thought. There were only eight men up there. I don't know how many were down below on the mountain. We were out of there before they could reach us. But still, the men in the caves had gotten sleep. They'd had fires to keep them warm. They'd eaten. They'd been up there for months, while I'd been pumping my way across the interior, climbing that mountain, watching friends die. I think the only reason we lived was because we expected to die. We had nothing to lose, so we beat them back. We had to kill them. I mean, we couldn't take them captive. What were we going to do, seesaw them back across China to Xian and on to Kunming? And they had to kill us too as a point of honor. We left the bodies where they dropped and met again in the largest cave, where there are two huge Buddhas—each about fifty feet tall. These statues were still in good shape, because the heads were too big to get out of the cave. But all the smaller ones had been vandalized and shipped back to Tokyo. I was looking at what was left in wonder, when this soldier—not dead obviously—pulls out a gun and aims right at me. I was completely oblivious—standing in that cave was a dream come true—when Sun shot him. So see, I would have been dead a couple of times over if it hadn't been for him."

Henry fell silent. The only sound was the drone of the G–3's engine.

"Sun's hiding in those caves," David guessed.

"If not in the caves, then somewhere on that mountain," Henry agreed.

For a moment everything seemed settled, but Hulan wasn't satisfied.

"You're sure that Sun was mission-educated?" she asked.

Henry nodded.

It explained Sun's near-perfect English, but why hadn't this been in his *dangan*, which said that—far from being an orphan—his parents were from the reddest class, the peasant class? How could all this have been kept a secret? How had this not come up during the various purges that had so shaken China over the years?

"And you say you didn't have contact with him again until seven years ago?" Hulan continued. "So much has happened in China. How did you find him, and weren't you surprised at what he'd become?"

"I didn't see him again until 1990, but that doesn't mean I'd lost contact with him," Henry admitted. "After our escapade I stayed in China for another two years. I did everything I could for the boy. I brought him west to Xian and later to Kunming. I made sure he ate, and he began to grow and fill out normally. He picked up more English, but what can I say, he was around soldiers so his language was pretty much in the gutter. Still, I gave him books. In those days almost everyone in China was illiterate, so I made sure he learned to read and write in his own language too."

As Henry spoke, Hulan began to put the pieces together. Sun's *dangan* said that he'd been involved with the local Communist party from an early age. Was it possible he'd already been a Communist when he'd gone to the mission? Had he been sent there by the local cadres? It explained his attitude on the mountain. If he'd been a Nationalist, he'd never have fought the Japanese, because the threat of retribution was so great. And later, when Sun had gone west with Henry, he would have been able to report not only on the Nationalists but the Americans as well. It made sense, but again, none of it was in the *dangan*.

"Once my tour was up," Henry was saying, "my dad wanted me to come home, which I did. But I still wanted a life in China. My father continued to take a very dim view of that idea, but I was working on him. In the meantime I kept sending money back to help Sun. The Chinese called it 'tea money.' But after the war the Nationalists and the Communists went back to their own bloody fight. In 1949 Chiang Kai-shek was beaten back to the island of Taiwan, Mao marched into Beijing, and the Bamboo Curtain fell. Both of you weren't even born yet, but back then anti-Communist sentiment was strong, vicious. To have any contact with China became very dangerous. By 1950 an embargo was in effect, McCarthy was doing his mad dog thing, and little tea money at all crossed the Pacific."

"People here would have been scared too," Hulan said. "How do you explain to your new comrades that you're getting money from foreign imperialists?"

"Without question it was dangerous," Henry agreed, "but you can always find a crack, and if you're smart, and Sun Gan was, you learn how to hide your money, live frugally, and spend carefully. And you have to remember, I wasn't sending a fortune, just fifty or a hundred here and there. It was enough to buy him food, enough to get him to college, and later, as China became increasingly corrupt, enough to get himself out of various jams."

Again Hulan thought about Sun's *dangan*. Sun had taken Henry's money for years. If he was a true Communist, how could he have done this? Could he have turned the money in to the government? Not according to the *dangan*. So he must have squirreled it away, which had to explain how he'd been able to buy his way out of trouble during the Cultural Revolution. But how could it not have come to light? Could he have used his stash to buy his way into the file, hire someone to make the critical changes, and clean up his past?

"Not one word of what you've said reassures me," David said, verbalizing what Hulan was thinking, "because in a sense you've been paying Sun bribes for over fifty years."

"I was helping a friend!" Henry sputtered. "What I sent him was nothing compared to what he'd given me. He saved my life! Can't you see that?"

"I see a nice man who tried to do the right thing, who may have chosen to call an apple an orange—a bribe a gift—and in doing so became a pawn in Sun's game."

"You are blind and stupid," Henry retorted.

The two men scowled at each other. Henry was the first to break eye contact by standing and going to check the fax machine. Still, nothing had come through. He came back to his seat, strapped himself in, and looked out the window. David too looked out the window, putting aside all he had heard and plotting their next moves. Once the plane landed, they would need to proceed quickly and efficiently. He also thought about Hulan. No matter what she said, he could see that something was wrong with her. She looked hot even in this air-conditioned environment. She was falling asleep every chance she got, and her mind didn't seem all there. He needed to get all this over with so he could get her to a doctor.

As they had done many times before, Taiyuan airport authorities gave Mr. Knight's plane permission to land, which it did without incident. But from this point all activity associated with Mr. Knight's Gulfstream deviated from anything they had seen before. Fortunately, they showed no curiosity about this. They didn't even come out to investigate why no one except a solidly built Chinese man who looked suspiciously like a law enforcement officer stepped off the plane, trotted across the tarmac, exited the terminal, bargained fiercely and paid handsomely to "rent" a car from a driver (which really meant that Lo flashed his MPS credential and made a few bone-chilling threats), then drove back around through the airport's south gate, back across the tarmac, parked, then disappeared back into the private jet, where there appeared to be no further activity.

Inside the plane the minutes dragged on as everyone waited for Anne Baxter Hooper's fax to come through. One by one they checked to see if all of the fax lines were plugged into the right places. David became increasingly convinced that the call was being blocked in some way, but Hulan—who'd awakened from dreams filled with unsettling images of war and the Knight factory floor, of mutilated bodies and dirty money— doubted that could be so. Finally the machine hummed to life and the papers began to spew out. David picked up each sheet as it came through. As with the others, they made no sense by themselves or even when compared to the papers Sun had given him.

Over Henry's objections, they decided not to look for Sun. "If your friend is hiding on Tianlong Mountain, he'll be hard to find," Hulan offered reasonably after Henry had shouted at David that his judgment was clouded and that he was only concerned with saving his own hide. "For now he's probably better off where he is. Let's get this resolved once and for all. If Sun is innocent as you say, Mr. Knight, then we can bring him out safely. If he's guilty, then he'll be found, prosecuted, and shot no matter what we do."

"All I'm saying is that your boyfriend here keeps forgetting that Sun is his client—"

"I've told you twenty times, Henry, I haven't forgotten that—"

"Can we just go?" Hulan asked.

The copilot released the door and stairs. The heat and humidity hit the travelers, instantly drenching them in sweat and sticky, polluted moisture from the torpid air. Lo and Hulan got in the front seat, and Henry and David got in the back, of a Wuhan-manufactured Citroën. Lo drove them back through Taiyuan City, across the anemic Fen River, then south on the toll road. Lo pulled off at the exit for Da Shui Village, and they proceeded west until they reached the crossroads. From here Lo turned again and drove the short distance to Suchee's little farm.

Midday hung heavily on the little compound. The cicadas shrieked with heat, and the roasting air undulated off the fields. Hulan ducked into the house to make sure Suchee wasn't there, then came back outside and called out across the fields to her friend. Shortly they saw Suchee emerge through a distant cornfield, then trudge across another field of her home vegetables. When she reached them, Hulan introduced Henry. Realizing that this was the man who'd hired her daughter and who in her eyes had corrupted the village, Suchee stared at him with steady, unforgiving eyes, ignoring his passable attempts at polite conversation. Without shifting her gaze, Suchee asked Hulan, "Why have you brought him here?"

"We need to see Miaoshan's papers again."

Suchee stood as still as an ox under the beating sun, thinking, weighing. Then she turned and with heavy steps plodded slowly to the little outbuilding where she kept her tools. A few minutes later, she returned and led the way into her house. Lo remained outside to stand guard.

The heat inside was almost unbearable with the temperature hovering at about a hundred and fifteen degrees. Suchee began to unroll the plans, but David said, "Not those. The other papers." Suchee left the factory plans on the table, and as they waited, Henry smoothed them out, looking at them with sadness. David took this time to check on Hulan. She'd dropped onto one of the overturned crates. Her face was pale, and sweat dripped down her neck. She too stared at the factory plans, but David could see that her eyes were unfocused.

"Here," Suchee said sharply, putting the papers with the columns and numbers on the table.

Henry set the fax down on the table next to the other papers, then looked expectantly at David, who hesitated. Sun was his client. If he was guilty, David would be exposing him. But if he was innocent, this was the only way to prove it. Reluctantly he reached into his briefcase, pulled out Sun's papers, and set them on the table with the others. The four of them stared at the papers, trying to decipher them. After a painful moment Suchee turned away. But to the others a pattern began to emerge. Ann's fax really was the key, providing the various bank names, account numbers, and pathways between the SUN GAN accounts and the dummy corporations.

Each week monies had left the main Knight International account from the Bank of China branch in Taiyuan. From here varying amounts had traveled into other accounts in the same branch, where they never stayed for more than a day. These accounts were the ones that matched Suchee's list and used the Sam & His Friends characters to spell out SUN GAN. Then these monies were wired abroad to what looked to be Sun's actual accounts in the U.S. However, Sun's actual account numbers meant absolutely nothing in the scheme. They had been placed in the columns next to the names of the dummy corporations only to deceive, which they had done quite successfully. This was where Keith's key provided another list of accounts. These covered an unusual spectrum of primarily West Coast American- and Asian-owned institutions, the first letters of which also spelled out SUN GAN—Sumitomo, Union, National, Glendale Federal, American, and Nippon Kogyo Ginko. The monies had stayed in these accounts sometimes for a day, sometimes for as much as two months, but then they'd been moved again, traveling through another series of accounts in the United States, Switzerland, the Cayman Islands, and, finally, back to China to accounts at the Bank of China, the China Industrial Bank, and the China Agricultural Bank in Taiyuan. By the time the monies reached these institutions, they'd been perfectly laundered, appearing as pristine American dollars deposited directly into the Chinese accounts of Henry Knight. The proof was irrefutable.

At last, and with some embarrassment, Hulan and David turned to Henry. He stared at them with agonized eyes. He didn't try to deny what they'd found, nor did he try to defend himself, which made the moment all the more awkward. He'd lied to them and lied some more. He'd bluffed and they'd called him on it. But before any of them could speak, a scream rang out in the distance. Then another, and another. Each one came closer. Hulan looked around and saw Suchee with her hands over her ears, trying to block the sound as if it were coming from inside her own head. But it wasn't, and Hulan watched Suchee's face change as she realized that the horrible, primitive wail was coming from outside.

# 23

T HEY RAN OUT OF THE HOUSE. LO LOOKED AROUND, GUN drawn. Suchee took off in the direction of the sound, and the rest of them followed. David shoved Henry ahead of him, keeping him within grabbing distance. Running in this heat made Hulan's entire arm throb, but she pushed on, staying right behind Suchee as she led the way through the fields toward—Hulan suddenly realized—the home of the Tsai family. Without warning, a woman burst through the green wall of corn ahead of them. Her hair was disheveled, her eyes frenzied. "Tsai Bing! Tsai Bing!" She pointed behind her, turned, and retraced her steps to her own little farm.

This place was almost identical to Suchee's homestead. There was a house made of mud brick, an outbuilding or two, some chickens, a pig. Next to the well lay the sodden form of Tsai Bing, Miaoshan's betrothed, beloved of Tang Siang, and only child of the Tsai family. Tsai Bing's father was trying to resuscitate his son. Hulan knelt at his side and gently pushed him away. She felt for a pulse in the boy's neck, but his milky, unseeing eyes told her he'd been dead for some time. She put her fingers on his eyelids and closed them, triggering a new round of bone-chilling wails from the dead boy's mother.

"Investigator Lo," Hulan said, "please go to Da Shui. You will find Captain Woo at the station house in the center of the village. We need his presence here."

While they waited for Lo's return, Hulan inspected the body, checking his fingernails, his eyes, his mouth, gently running her hands over his limbs. Under the hot sun Tsai Bing's clothes dried quickly, making the body seem somehow less pathetic. At last Hulan let the boy's parents come close. They knelt on either side of their son, tears streaming down their cheeks. Tsai Bing's mother held his hand to her chest, imploring him to speak to her.

Hulan retired to the one spot of shade she could find, a foot-wide stretch alongside the mud-brick wall of the Tsais' home. She sat down on her haunches as any peasant might do, except that she cradled her burning arm between her chest and her raised knees. From this position she took in the scene around her. David was staying with—no, guarding—Henry, who had turned away from the body and was looking out across the fields. Suchee had moved to Tsai Bing's mother's side and had an arm around her. The two women—one pale in the shock of tragedy; the other ravaged by loss and bitter acceptance—were now united by the worst pain a mother could experience.

Tsai Bing's mother's cries had alerted other neighbors as well, and they stepped through the fields and onto the hard-packed earth, some armed with the tools they'd been working with, others empty-handed but all with a shared look of dread. Hulan recognized only one of them. Tang Dan had been one of the first to arrive, and he circulated among the others, keeping them at a respectful distance from the body and its parents. At one point he ventured toward the quartet near the well, put a reassuring hand on Suchee's shoulder, and held it there. His strength seemed to travel down through Suchee's body, and she in turn seemed to tighten her arm around Madame Tsai's shuddering form.

About twenty-five minutes later, two cars arrived in a swirl of dust. Lo led Captain Woo to the body, while three other officers in green short-sleeve shirts pushed the neighbors farther away. Woo barely glanced at Tsai Bing, then ordered the parents to step aside. Then he began writing in his notebook. Never did he stoop down to look at the body. Never did he attempt to question Tsai Bing's parents. He did, however, stroll to the well and look into it. He made a few more notes, snapped the notebook shut, and strode to his car while calling for his men to follow.

Hulan stood, felt a wave of dizziness come over her, reached out a hand to steady herself on the wall of the house, then stepped forward.

"You can't possibly be done," she said.

Captain Woo's eyes raked her from head to toe and back again.

"This is none of your business," he said. "Leave it to the police."

"What do you think happened here?" she asked.

He stared hard at her, unaccustomed to being questioned. "You ask for trouble, *taitai*."

But Hulan didn't move from her spot. The peasants who'd clustered here gawked openmouthed at her impudence.

Suchee, sensing the danger her friend was in, took a few tentative steps, and warned, "Hulan . . ."

"I remember you," the captain said to Hulan. "You came to my office before. We don't like troublemakers in our county. Now, I will tell you again, this is an official matter, but if you wish to interfere, I will have no recourse except to have my men take you down to our office. I can assure you that you will not find the experience very pleasant."

All of this had taken place in Mandarin so David didn't understand what was happening. The others did, however, and not wanting to be associated with any disturbance that might come back to haunt them, began to shuffle off into the surrounding fields.

"Wait!" Hulan commanded. "Please come back, all of you." As the neighbors hesitated, she reached into her purse and pulled out her Ministry of Public Security identification and held it up for all to see. The effect was immediate. The neighbors stopped in their tracks.

Captain Woo, however, was not so easily cowed. "You have no jurisdiction here."

Hulan felt another wave of dizziness, and she swayed as she waited for the blackness to fall away from her eyes. She didn't think she had the strength for this. Then Investigator Lo came forward. With one hand he held out his credential, while the other rested on the grip of his weapon. A couple of the neighbors gasped. This was not a good place to be.

"I think," Lo said in a menacing tone, "you will be wise to listen to what Inspector Liu has to say."

Out of the corner of her eye Hulan saw David edge toward her. He may not have understood the words, but he couldn't mistake the stand-off that was taking place before him. Henry grabbed his shirtsleeve to hold him back. Captain Woo perhaps had not seen the foreigners. Their appearance could only complicate things.

"With great respect, I would like to ask you again." Hulan spoke evenly, hoping to temper the situation. "What do you think happened here?"

"It is very clear," Woo responded at last. "The boy must have fallen into the well. Either that or he committed suicide." Woo now addressed the neighbors. "We all know that he was engaged to Ling Miaoshan. He must have been despondent at her death."

"You did not look at the body," Hulan said. "How can you know this?"

"The boy drowned. Of that I am certain."

"What he says is true," Suchee said. "You saw him. He was wet, and his body came out of the well."

"That's right," Woo said. "You knew the boy. You knew the situation. Tell your nosy friend how it is."

Hulan looked at Suchee sadly. Of course, Suchee—even knowing what she did about her daughter—still was hoping to paint a picture of true love between Miaoshan and Tsai Bing.

"Captain Woo, please, come with me," Hulan said. She walked to the body and knelt at its side. Reluctantly Woo came to stand next to her. Hulan called out to Lo, "Keep the others away, but don't let anyone leave." Then she lowered her voice so that only Woo could hear. "I know you aren't familiar with corpses. I'm sorry to put you through this, but please, take a look with me." The policeman squatted beside her. She smelled his frightened sweat. Looking up from under her lashes, she saw that the color had drained from his face and she hoped that he wouldn't vomit. Any further loss of face would make what had to come next even more difficult.

Keeping her voice low, she asked, already guessing the answer, "Did you examine the body of Ling Miaoshan?"

Woo almost imperceptibly shook his head. Hulan sighed. What might have been found on the dead girl's body if only this policeman had had the courage and/or the experience?

"I will not go into the physiology of drowning, because Tsai Bing did not drown. Instead I will ask you to look at some other markers. Please note that his eyes are pricked with red. His chest and face too have broken capillaries. This is consistent with suffocation. Hanging, strangulation, garroting."

"But wouldn't that also be consistent with drowning? Don't you suffocate that way too?"

Good, Hulan thought. He's beginning to focus.

"I have already explained. Tsai Bing didn't drown."

"Then what?"

"Look at his hands, at his fingernails in particular," Hulan ordered gently. It was important that this appear as though Woo had made the discovery. "What do you see?"

"His fingernails are broken and bloody. He must have struggled to get out of the well."

"He was dead when he went in the well. I guarantee that," Hulan said. "What else do you see?"

"The color under his nails is good. Pink."

"Too good, wouldn't you say?"

Captain Woo didn't know. This was only the second body he'd ever had to deal with and only the first that he'd really looked at.

"Tsai Bing is cyanotic," she said.

"Do you mean cyanide poisoning?"

"Do you smell almonds?" she asked gently.

Woo shook his head.

"Neither do I," Hulan said. "But there is another possibility. Carbon monoxide poisoning mimics these symptoms. If we were somewhere else, I would say that Tsai Bing might have committed suicide by locking himself in his car and rigging the exhaust pipe to come back inside. He would have died quickly and nearly painlessly."

"Tsai Bing didn't have a car—"

"And wherever he was, he struggled to get out," Hulan added.

They were silent for a minute. Other than the cicadas there was dead quiet. Even Madame Tsai had stopped crying. Hulan let the silence drag out, hoping Woo would figure it out for himself. At last he spoke.

"In Da Shui Village the cars are all government-owned. Our police department has two sedans. The doctor also has a car. We have one other that is shared by a consortium for driving people to other villages for a small fee. Other than this, we have buses and trucks used for transportation of people and merchandise. However, we do have one other category of vehicle that uses gasoline."

"Farm equipment," Hulan said.

For the first time Woo's eyes met hers. Suddenly what had been clear to her from the moment she saw the body registered on Woo. His eyes widened and she nodded. Yes, his conclusion was correct, she seemed to say.

Woo heaved himself to his feet and addressed the assembled neighbors. "We have a saying in our government that I would ask you all to hear again. Leniency to those who confess, severity to those who don't."

The neighbors—all from the poorest class—looked nervously at their feet. Tsai Bing's mother began to weep again with the realization that her son's death had not been a horrible accident.

"Our neighbor and friend, Tsai Bing, was murdered by one of our own," Woo said. "The murderer has one minute to reveal himself." Woo looked at his watch, then around at the peasants. "When this minute is over, any leniency that I or the courts or your neighbors would see fit to treat you with will evaporate forever."

No one spoke, but instead of staring at their feet, the people had begun to look around the courtyard, checking the familiar faces of those they had known for years. Woo, now emboldened, circulated among the peasants.

"There is only one person here whom we all hold above reproach," he said loudly so that all could hear. "He has done much for our community. As his wealth has grown, he has shared his mechanized farm equipment with his neighbors. He is the only man who has the capability of killing Tsai Bing, and I'm sure when we inspect the garage where he keeps his equipment, we will find Tsai Bing's blood on the door, for this poor boy tried to scratch his way out until he was too weak to fight anymore."

The peasants knew of whom Woo was speaking but couldn't believe what they were hearing.

"There is only one person here who fits this description, and we all know who he is." Captain Woo stopped before Tang Dan. "The only remaining question your neighbors have is, why?"

Madame Tsai screamed in anguish and collapsed into her husband's arms.

Tang Dan stared proudly at the policeman.

"Why!" Woo shouted.

Tang Dan blinked, then said, "I believe my minute is up, so it doesn't matter what I say." He held out his wrists to be handcuffed.

Woo glanced back at Hulan, unsure of what to do next. She nodded. He brought out his handcuffs, roughly clasped them on Tang Dan, then gave the murderer a shove toward the police car.

Suddenly Suchee rushed forward and slammed into Tang Dan's chest with both fists, sending him into the dirt. "Why? Why? Why?"

The other neighbors circled in closer, now gripping their hoes and other tools as weapons. Even those who were empty-handed crept closer, their bodies taut with anger and the desire for revenge. A boy, an only son, had been murdered by a man who had grown rich while they had remained poor.

"He comes from the landlord class," someone spat out.

"You can't change a tiger's stripes," said another, quoting an almost universal epithet.

"Pig ass!"

"Mother of a fart!"

Chinese villagers had five thousand years of precedence for dealing with such a crime. In the olden days a robber, kidnapper, or vandal was brought before the populace of a village and made to walk among them, where they might scream out his crimes and what they thought of him, where they might throw stones or beat the evildoer with sticks. The criminal might be made to wear a *cangue*, a huge wooden collar that made it nearly impossible to eat or even to shoo away flies. His wrists and ankles might be locked into a public stock so that everyone in the village might know that this was a bad person.

According to Confucian tradition, punishment was meted out no less swiftly or brutally for domestic crimes. If a son hit his father, then the father had the right to kill his son. If a father hit his son, there was no punishment. If a landlord stole from the people or raped a daughter, then nothing could be done except to kowtow to that landlord and hope it didn't happen again. If a peasant dared to do anything against a landlord, then punishment was brutal and final. For five thousand years retribution had been carried out thus; then the Communists had come into power. The forms of crime changed but the punishments very little. Now it was the government that acted swiftly. As the saying went—you sometimes had to kill a chicken to shock the monkeys. And yet the government understood that the masses still needed to have their moment of power, which was why the civil war and the Cultural Revolution had been so cruelly savage.

"Beast!"

"Murderer!"

"The devil rings his bell when he comes to get your life," someone else shouted. "Well, it's ringing now, Tang Dan!"

Hulan had seen crowds like this before, been a part of them. They demanded, insisted upon, blood for blood. Looking at Captain Woo and the other policemen from the local Public Security Bureau, she knew that they would do nothing to stop the crowd. It was so easy to look the other way. It made for less paperwork, and it satisfied the villagers. In fact, Woo and his comrades might even participate themselves. She was glad—if that was the word given the circumstances—that Siang was not here to witness this.

Hulan pushed through the crowd and stood between Tang Dan and Suchee.

"I have something to say," she announced. She searched for David, found his puzzled face in the crowd, and wished she could speak in English for his benefit. Then she saw Lo edge in next to David and begin to speak softly, explaining what was happening. Hulan looked around her, taking in the faces worn by hard work and hard times. These people had never been given a break. They had known only suffering. Always their joys had been simple—the birth of a child, a good harvest, a suspension of a political campaign. Now two of their neighbors had lost only children—those life-affirming gifts made all the more precious because of China's daunting childbirth policies.

"You are right when you say that this man is from the landlord class," she said, "for his problems stem from old ways that we all have tried hard to forget. Some of you here are old enough to remember what the landlords were like. Insidious, cruel, ruthless, but most of all they were greedy. Tang Dan is a greedy man, and although I have no firsthand knowledge of this, I think if you look back you will remember that he has always been greedy."

Again Hulan sought David's face in the crowd. She saw Lo translating her words, while already a few people in the crowd murmured their agreement. She observed David's look of confusion as he realized that her words, instead of calming the heated tempers, were only inflaming them. Aware that his eyes were fixed on her, she turned away.

"I am only a visitor to this county," Hulan said. "I was here once many, many years ago and then again now. Since coming back I have seen the changes that have happened in Da Shui and all around the countryside. We can all agree that conditions are better. You have electricity, television, some of you even have refrigerators. All this"—her arm took in the expanse around them—"is better, and at first it made me blind, as it has made you blind, to the changes that are so basic to our Chinese life."

She paused, circling slowly, looking at the faces before her. "Fire, water, air, wood, earth—these are the five elements basic to Chinese life and beliefs. We see the sun and know there's fire. We stand on the earth, we breathe the air, we use wood in our homes, but what of water? Twenty-seven years ago when I first came to Taiyuan, the Fen River was a huge, roiling beast. Remember when the government built the bridge to unite the two banks no matter what the river's conditions? Could you have imagined back then that today the Fen would be but a stream? That the riverbed would now be a place to picnic and fly kites? Or that the Three Everlasting Springs so famous in this area would be but one spring in danger of everlasting no more? I saw that and I didn't think, because all of China, despite our yearly floods, is losing water. Our rivers, our lakes, our springs, our wells are all going dry."

She spun around to find Tang Dan, who'd raised himself to his knees. Red soil smudged his clothes. Dust had also settled on his face, mixing with his sweat and running in red rivulets down his face.

"Since land reform many of you have abandoned farming," she continued. "You have gone into brick making or worked at a local factory. I say this not as a reprimand. It is merely fact. And when you or your children or your neighbors have left your farms, you've subleased your land or even given it back to the government to redistribute. Much of that land has gone to Tang Dan, and who among us today can say that he has not done a good job with it?"

She gazed at the neighbors, but none could contradict her.

"When Ling Suchee's daughter died, she asked me to come here and find out what happened. I knew that to find the killer I would have to know the victim. I came to know Miaoshan. I came to understand her value to her murderer. She had access to the one thing he was missing."

"Water," the people answered as one. Their eyes had turned to Tang Dan again. Their hate was palpable.

"Water," Hulan echoed. "You live in Da Shui, Big Water, and yet you were blind to its growing scarcity. But this man wasn't, and he began to look for land that had access to water." Here Hulan lowered her voice. "You all know whose wells could be counted on."

For the first time Hulan looked for and found her friend. "Ling Suchee has such a well. She is a widow and could never work her land as well as a family with a wife, husband, and son, so her farm has never prospered. But under that soil lies something so valuable that Tang Dan was willing to lie and cheat and eventually kill for it."

Hulan expected to see her friend overcome by grief, but Suchee was a mother who still needed to protect her daughter. She stared hard at Hulan, pleading with her eyes. Hulan answered her friend with a barely discernible nod. The neighbors didn't need to know the squalid details that would make Suchee and her daughter look like fools for years to come.

"I will say only this," Hulan went on. "When Tang Dan knew he couldn't get the water from your neighbor Ling Suchee, he killed her daughter." She addressed Tang Dan directly. "You hoped that as an end-of-the-liner Suchee would give up her farm and move into the village. When this didn't work, you unleashed your next plan, for the Tsais' well was also bountiful."

Hulan bent her head, and her shoulders trembled. David took a step forward, but Lo held him back. "I blame myself for what happened next. I didn't see what was right before me." She hesitated, then said, "I have gotten to know Tang Dan's daughter. You all know her. You all know that she was in love with this dead boy, even though he had been betrothed to Miaoshan. Once she was dead, however, the path looked clear for Tsai

Bing and Tang Siang. They were young and Siang has what we could all agree is a strong personality, but I think they would have been happy together."

The villagers looked from Tang Dan to Tsai Bing's lifeless form to his pitiable parents. Yes, all this had been right before their eyes, and yet they hadn't really seen until now.

"What horrifies me as I stand here today," Hulan said regretfully, "is that Tang Dan could have gotten his water just by letting his daughter marry Tsai Bing. But here is where his past once again exposed its ugly face. Tang Dan couldn't and wouldn't allow his daughter to marry a peasant when he had come from the landlord class and had become a millionaire in his own right. He had other plans for Siang, and they didn't involve Tsai Bing."

Hulan raised her voice. "The rest is as Captain Woo told you. Tang Dan enticed the boy to his farm, set his machinery to running, locked the boy inside, and let him die. To cover his tracks, he threw him in the well. Why?" She gestured to the Tsais. "Could this couple now drink from the well where their son died? Never! That, combined with being end-of-the-liners, would leave them no choice but to abandon this land. You all have seen Tang Dan with his sympathetic face. He would have come here. He would have made promises. And soon this land and its well would have gone to him."

Hulan stared at Tang Dan. His face showed no remorse, but he did look frightened, knowing he might be dead in a few minutes. Hulan, however, thought this outcome too good for him. He deserved to suffer longer as a small repayment for all the misery he'd caused.

"Captain Woo," she said, once again adopting her most official tone, "please take the prisoner to your jail."

Tang Dan began to shake as the reality of her words hit him.

"We will let the courts decide his punishment," she continued. "In the meantime, we all trust you to make sure he's treated like the low dog he is."

With a curt signal from Woo the other officers roughly hauled Tang Dan to his feet. On the way to the police car he wordlessly accepted a few blows to his head and a couple of kidney punches. Tang Dan would be dead in a week, but it would be a painful week.

*   *   *

Once the police cars had driven away, David rushed forward to Hulan, who hadn't moved from her spot in the middle of the courtyard. When he reached her, she sank into his arms. Holding her, he felt her heart fluttering against his chest. Then she pulled away from him, staggered to the side of the Tsais' house, bent over, and retched.

Not for the first time today David worried about her. She shouldn't be out in this ghastly heat. She shouldn't have the stress of flying back and forth to Beijing, of tracking down criminals, of crowd control. But as he stood there with his hand on the small of her back, he couldn't help but be impressed with what she'd just accomplished. He'd known her for a long time now. First as a young and shy associate at Phillips, MacKenzie, then as his quiet and pensive lover, now as a woman who even still kept her secrets. But God, he'd never seen her like this!

How beautiful she looked standing there under the bleaching rays of the sun as she spoke to the crowd! How powerful she looked with her right arm raised like a revolutionary heroine exhorting the peasants to revolt! Always he'd seen her authority as a professional attribute, something cultivated over many years in a career that demanded and constantly received respect. But her family had also been imperial performers. The actress, the avenger—both of these characteristics were in her blood. He realized that this was how she must have looked all those years ago when she was at the Red Soil Farm, proclaiming, inciting, denouncing, that she had always carried this authority in her, that sometimes it had worked to her advantage but more often to her detriment and that of others. This woman he loved was always willing to pay the physical and emotional price of her nature.

She slowly straightened and rested her head in the crook of her arm against the wall. He leaned in close and whispered, "Are you okay? Is there something I can get you?"

She shook her head. A moment later she asked, her voice weak, "Henry?"

David looked around. Investigator Lo wasn't taking any chances. He held Henry by the back of the neck.

"Lo's got him," David said.

Hulan didn't respond, just kept her head buried. David waited at her side and watched as the neighbors gradually dispersed. The Tsais resumed their positions next to their son. Suchee knelt beside them, speaking soothingly. Just as the thought that they'd have to get the boy out of the sun crossed David's mind, the threesome stood. Tsai Bing's father picked up his son's shoulders, while the two women each took a leg. As they started for the house, David turned away, uncomfortable at the sight. A year ago he had not seen a dead body. But since January he'd seen nine. What struck him—beyond the horrible and cruel images of what had been done to once living, breathing creatures—was the matter-of-fact way these peasants handled their dead. In America he'd seen policemen and FBI agents and coroners and forensics experts and paramedics and minimum-wage drivers from funeral homes. The physicality of death was something that was kept far away from the surviving loved ones. But here in the Chinese countryside the body was given over to the family to be washed, clothed, and cremated or buried. And David thought if this were Hulan or his own child, he might not have the strength to take that lifeless form into his arms and touch it so intimately, even as a last act of love.

He felt Hulan move. She turned and faced him. Her cheeks were drained of color.

"Let's go back to Beijing," she said.

She pushed away from the wall and, while David waited, went inside the Tsais' house to say good-bye to Suchee. She reemerged quickly, headed across the dirt expanse, and stepped into the cornfield. David, Lo, and Henry followed swiftly. When they reached Suchee's farm, Hulan took one last look around, then ducked into the front seat of the car Lo had commandeered. Once David and Henry settled in the back, Lo started the engine and they pulled out of the little compound.

Each person seemed lost in his or her thoughts as they bumped across the rutted dirt road leading back to the main highway. Hulan slumped in the front seat, her head resting against the window. She felt hot, sick, exhausted. Next to her, Lo drove with his usual quiet determination, yet his thoughts were very much on the report he would give to his superiors back in Beijing. How would he explain Hulan's actions at the Tsai farm? In the backseat, Henry stared morosely out the window. David contemplated Henry, thinking.

When they reached the crossroads, Lo asked Hulan where she wanted to go. "Back to Beijing," she muttered in Mandarin. When his eyes continued to question her, she expanded. "On the expressway. We can't take Knight's jet. The man is a criminal of the worst sort. Once we get in the air, we are with his people. We can't allow that to happen. Just drive, Investigator. We'll be back home soon enough." Lo turned right and began to speed along.

David sat forward and asked, "How'd you know about Tang Dan?"

Hulan sighed tiredly. "It always bothered me that the killer didn't take Miaoshan's papers. He took Guy's and those were only copies, which verified that Miaoshan hadn't been killed for them. She'd been killed for another reason altogether."

David leaned back. How had Miaoshan gotten the papers? Guy said an American gave them to her. She didn't get them from Keith; she gave them to him. Was Aaron Rodgers still a possibility? Or Sandy Newheart? They came to the turnoff to Knight International. The compound was hidden behind a low rise, but David glanced in that direction and saw Henry looking suddenly alert. His dreams and his failures lay just over that rise, and as soon as they passed it Henry drooped down once again, looking more dejected than before.

"Lo, turn around," David said.

"Attorney Stark?"

"Stop the car and turn around."

Lo slowed, and Hulan said, "No, keep going. Let's get home."

The car sped up again.

"No! We have to turn around!" David put a hand on Lo's shoulder. "Please!"

Lo pulled over. Hulan turned in her seat to look at David. Her face was ashen and covered with a thin sheen of sweat.

"We've done what we came to do," Hulan said, utterly exhausted. "I solved Miaoshan's murder. You found the person behind the bribes. I suspect that with further questioning at Beijing Municipal Jail Number Five, Mr. Knight will confess to killing or hiring someone to kill your friend."

"This isn't finished," David said, then turned to Henry. "Is it?"

"The inspector is right," Henry said. "We should get back to Beijing."

David smiled. Sadly, triumphantly, Hulan wasn't sure which.

"Let's go back to the factory," David repeated.

"There's no reason to do that, Inspector Liu," Henry said. She stared at him. He was a broken man, but she didn't feel sorry for him. As if reading her thoughts, he continued. "I've made some terrible mistakes in my life. One of the worst was underestimating you and Mr. Stark. As you say, we're all tired. Let's go back to Beijing. Once we're there I'll explain everything. You'll have your case, and I suspect you'll be a hero . . ." He tipped his head and amended, "A heroine."

Hulan passed her good hand over her eyes. They ached and she longed for ice to put on her lids, for a cold drink to refresh her parched throat, for cool sheets to appease her burning skin, and something, anything, to stop the throbbing in her arm.

David pressed his case. "We should secure the records in the computers. They may have already been erased, but I think we should see if they're still there."

Tired, Hulan ordered Lo to turn the car around.

"Please, no!" Henry blurted. "There's no reason to go back."

But whatever sympathy Hulan might have had had been used up in the last hour, and she wordlessly stared out the windshield.

The car turned onto the side road that led to the factory. As they passed the billboards with the gaily rendered Sam & His Friends, Henry increased his ranting, his confessions, his pleas to go on to Beijing.

"I was at fault for all of it. I allowed the employees to live and work in bad conditions. This is why I came to China! No one was looking and I thought—I knew—I could get away with it. And that woman? David, remember that woman who jumped off the roof? You were right all along. She was thrown off and I did it. And that reporter and that unionizer? They got what they deserved."

"How could you throw Xiao Yang off the roof when you were in a meeting with me? And why try to frame your old friend Sun?" David asked as Lo stopped at the compound's gate. When the guard came out to see who it was, Lo jerked his thumb toward the backseat. The guard peered in, saw his employer, and quickly retreated inside his kiosk to press the button for the gate. Lo pulled through, drove directly to the Administration Building, and parked between a Lexus and a Mercedes, the drivers of which were nowhere to be seen.

Lo and Hulan opened their doors and got out. Henry looked desperately about him, but there was no place for him to run. David could see some activity around the warehouse. A forklift loaded a pallet of what David presumed were Sam & His Friends onto the back of a flatbed truck. But otherwise the large, barren courtyard was deserted as usual, while behind the windowless walls hundreds of women labored on the assembly lines.

"I'm sorry, Henry," David said quietly.

Henry's eyes widened. Then a curtain of utter resignation closed down over his face. "Please," he begged.

David weighed the word. In that single syllable was all of Henry's life. It was an appeal for compassion, forgiveness, and an acceptance of the way things were. "I take full responsibility," Henry added. "Let me take the blame for everything that's happened."

David hardened himself against these words, then answered Henry by opening the door and getting out.

# 24

D AVID PUSHED OPEN THE BIG GLASS DOOR OF THE ADMIN-
istration Building, and the four of them entered. At the end of the
hall they came to the heart of the company, where almost a hundred
women dressed in nearly identical business suits sat in their cubicles,
staring at computer screens or speaking on phones. David pushed Henry
into one of the cubicles. The woman working there looked up startled,
then, seeing Henry, stood up in some attempt at attention.

"Open the files, Henry," David ordered.

"I don't know how."

"Then ask her to do it."

Henry started to speak, but only a croak came out. He cleared his
throat and said, "Please, Miss, can you look up my personal financial
records?"

The young clerk stared at him, perplexed. Then she looked over his
shoulder, past the other foreigner to Lo and Hulan. The woman looked
sick; the other man, with his thick build and sour expression, was surely
a government agent of some sort. The clerk's eyes came back to the
owner of the company. "I don't have access to those records, sir," she said
softly in English. "I only process our purchase orders from America."

Henry turned to David. "As I said before, this can't be of any help."

David signaled the woman to leave, and she edged out of the cubicle.
David motioned for Henry to sit. "Type," David said.

Henry glared at David. "I told you I don't know how to use the damn thing."

"You're telling me that you—an inventor, a businessman, and a financial criminal—don't know how to use a computer?" David asked dubiously. When he spoke next, his tone was much harsher. "Look up the files."

Henry turned to the screen and put his fingers on the keyboard. He exited the program the young woman had been working in, went to the main menu, typed in his password, then his name, and up came a list of files: bio, company history, phone logs, travel, correspondence, but nothing on financial transactions. "Try Sun Gan," David said. Henry obeyed. Of course nothing happened, but David wanted further confirmation of Sun's innocence after having doubted him for so long. For the next ten minutes David ordered Henry to type in a variety of key words— expenses, payments, financials, financial records, bank records, Bank of China, China Industrial Bank, and China Agricultural Bank. Some of these revealed legitimate transactions; others revealed nothing but a blinking cursor or the terse words NOT FOUND. There was nothing that came close to any of the damning financial records that David had in his possession. That didn't mean they still weren't in the computer. A forensic accountant would be able to retrieve erased, encrypted, or hidden data.

David put a hand on Henry's shoulder. "I'm sorry, Henry. I know it would have been easier this way." Even in the air conditioning, Henry's shirt had turned damp with nervous sweat. David leaned down and said gently, "Let's finish this."

Without turning, Henry said softly, "I can't."

"You can. You have to."

Henry looked up at David, his face tormented. "Why?" The way the word ripped the air, David knew Henry was asking a fundamentally deeper question than simply responding to David's request.

"That's what we're going to find out. Let's go."

Sensing that something was amiss, the women had stopped working, had stood, and now silently gaped at the group as they threaded their way to one of the other corridors that led from the heart. They passed Sandy Newheart's office, but he wasn't there. They passed the posters of Sam & His Friends, each character colorful, harmless, innocent. At last they came to the conference room. The door was closed, but they could hear raised voices inside. Henry glanced at David again, a final plea. But David reached out, turned the knob, and entered the room, where Douglas Knight and Miles Stout sat across from each other at the long rosewood table. The Knight-Tartan contracts lay in sloppy disarray between them. Amy Gao, Governor Sun's assistant, stood against the far wall, looking decorative in chartreuse.

Doug stood. "Dad, thank God. I've been hoping you'd show up. I've got good news. I've told Tartan I'm not selling. We're keeping the company. They can try their hostile takeover, but I've told Miles that I think we can fight them off."

Henry brought his hands to his face and held them there.

"Dad? Are you all right? Here, come sit down."

Doug took a step forward, but Henry's hand shot out. "No!"

Doug frowned, then shrugged as if to say, you simply couldn't predict the old man.

"It's over, Doug," Henry said at last.

"That's what I'm trying to tell you, Dad. It's over. I've shown Tartan the door."

"It's not as easy as he's making it sound," Miles said, his voice gritty. "Knight's gone too far to pull out now."

Doug's gaunt face turned crimson. "Don't listen to him, Dad. I've got things under control. I've made mistakes, and I hope you'll forgive me for them. But last night I saw what a fool I've been. Amy helped me. She made me realize this is *our* company. You and Grandpa built it. We can't let it go. I understand that now."

Henry, his wiry body looking so frail now, stared uncomprehendingly at his son, then suddenly walked past him and sat down at the table. The others, following his cue, also took seats. Henry shook his head, then said to David, "I can't do this."

"David, what's all this about?" Miles asked, slipping easily into his professional mode. "We had a deal on the table. It was accepted. We went forward. Then everything went to hell. Why? Fuck if I know. But I'm here because Randall's willing to put yesterday's rigmarole behind him. I'm guessing you're here because you've talked some sense into Mr. Knight. So, let's finish this up and go home."

"You forget," David said. "I don't work for you anymore."

"I was out of line," Miles admitted. "As you pointed out, I can't fire you without a vote of the full partnership."

"Semantics," David said. "I quit. Does that satisfy you?"

Miles's forehead creased as he processed this information. Then he said, "I apologize. Now, let's let bygones be bygones and get on with this." He reached out to the middle of the table and pushed the stack of contracts toward Henry.

The older man fingered the edges of the papers. "If I sign, this will all be over," he said. Again he turned toward David, waiting for an answer.

David weighed these words. Could he let what he knew had happened go by unpunished for the sake of this old man? A year ago it wouldn't have been a question. His duty would have been clear. Punishment to the full extent of the law. No mitigating circumstances. No mercy. But since he'd found Hulan again, he'd changed. Sometimes the greater good meant looking the other way. What did Hulan call it? The one-eye-open, one-eye-closed policy? Henry's statement had also implied a question, and as David surveyed the faces in the room, he saw the myriad crimes and secrets that wouldn't be solved by a series of signatures.

"No, Henry, it won't be over," David said.

"Dad," Doug interrupted impatiently. "I've already told you. We can keep the company. I want us to keep it. I know I can build it for my sons—"

"Shut up, Doug," Henry rapped out, then, "David?"

They were all staring at him now. David understood that at this moment he held in his hands the power to destroy lives as easily and perhaps more brutally than if he'd held a gun. But so many lives had been lost already. It had to stop now. He looked around. This place seemed so civilized with its pretty pictures on the walls, the air-conditioning, the expensive rosewood table, but violence had occurred here in many forms. He didn't have a weapon, but he knew Lo did and assumed Hulan did as well. If anything happened, they'd be ready. He thought of how he'd seen Hulan at the Tsais' farm. Her method was so Chinese, but she had laid out the facts as any prosecutor would. That's what he had to do now.

"Three weeks ago a girl was killed not far from here," David began. "It looked like a suicide. It turned out to be a murder. We know now that her death had nothing to do with Knight International, but for a while there seemed to be a link. Back then, after I found out about the girl's death, I had dinner with a friend, Keith Baxter. When he was murdered, I blamed myself for reasons that don't matter."

"Do we have to hear all this?" Miles asked, pushing his chair away from the table.

"Stay where you are, Miles," David ordered. Lo, on unspoken command, stood, crossed the room, took a position with his back against the door, and unbuttoned his jacket so everyone could see his weapon. "You see," David resumed in an even tone, "there are so many layers here, so many betrayals, I think you'll all want to hear me out. Especially you, Miles. This next part particularly concerns you."

Miles didn't move. The air in the room, despite the air conditioning, suddenly felt heavy.

"At Keith's funeral," David continued, "I listened, but I didn't understand the words. Miles, you're a smart man, and you played us all so well simply by speaking the truth. Remember what you said about the last time you'd seen Keith? It was something along the lines of 'Keith showed me some papers. He saw the problems. He saw the mistakes.' You flaunted that in front of Keith's family, his friends, and his partners. And not one person understood what they were hearing, isn't that right?"

Miles didn't answer, but the coldness in his blue eyes told everyone in the room that there was truth in David's words.

"Keith confronted you with the lies and omissions in the financials, and you didn't do anything about them. You knew the kind of shop these people ran, and you didn't do anything about that either. You were willing for this deal to go forward *at any cost*. This has meant," David said, now including the others in the room, "that he was willing to forgo any professional ethics he ever had by lying to the government, by lying to his client, by lying to his partners. In our profession we consider these to be the worst possible breaches, but these are nothing compared to taking a human life. Remember at your house when I said that Keith's sister blamed me for her brother's death? You said something like, 'How could she? She wasn't there.' But *you* were! You killed Keith Baxter and you hired me, guessing accurately that since I blamed myself, I wouldn't see the truth."

"I didn't kill Keith," Miles said. "I couldn't possibly—"

"It's not my job to prove it," David said. "But I'm sure the LAPD will be interested in looking at your car—if you still have it. The rest, it's true, is circumstantial. But remember years ago how you taught me to explain circumstantial evidence to a jury? You don't need to see the actual bunny to know it's been in the snow. All you need to see are the bunny's tracks. Well, you've left plenty of tracks, and I think there's enough of them to get a conviction, especially when you add in the motive."

Miles grimaced. "I have no motive."

"Yes, that was a problem," David agreed. "For the longest time I didn't see one, just as I hadn't seen the other things that were so obvious. But you see, that was the key. *The obvious.* What did I know about you? You were always a climber. Smooth, but a climber. The golf with Milken. The premieres with the studio execs. Mary Elizabeth's charity work. You wanted to be a player."

Miles knew the same lawyer's tricks David did. Watch the eyes. If he looks up, he's scrolling through memories. If he looks left, he's lying. Miles kept his eyes focused on David, but he couldn't control what happened involuntarily. Color had flooded his cheeks—in frustration, in shame, and finally in anger.

With athletic grace Miles leapt to his feet. "I didn't kill Keith!" He looked around the room, searching for someone to believe him. "The rest—"

"The rest could only happen if you became secret partners with—"

"Aw, hell." These words were spoken quietly by Doug Knight, but he'd been underestimated for so long, even by those in the room who knew the truth about him, that no one glanced in his direction. That is, except for Miles Stout, who thought he'd heard in that voice a modicum of sympathy. Miles looked at the man attached to the voice. Then his eyes widened, and his hands instinctively flew up in an attempt to protect himself, but mere bones and flesh could not stop the bullet that shot out of Doug's gun, entered Miles's skull just above his left eye, and took off the back of his head. Miles's body slammed against the boardroom wall and dropped to the ground.

In that split second before anyone moved, Doug stood, reached out, grabbed Hulan's hand, and yanked her out of her chair. She shrieked, high, loud, and very briefly. Then they watched as her eyes rolled up, her face tilted back, her body lost its structure, and she collapsed to the floor. Doug stared down at her, then at his own hand as if trying to ascertain how his grip could have caused such a result. David understood that Hulan had hoped to con Doug into that moment of confusion. After a quick glance at Lo, who was reaching for his weapon, David lunged toward Doug, but he was brought up cold by the sickening metallic sound of a revolver being cocked and the chamber moving into place. Then he felt the muzzle of a gun press just below his left ear and Amy Gao say in her melodious voice, "Step back slowly."

"You'd better obey her, Stark," Doug said to David, then turned to Lo. "And you'd better drop your weapon."

Both men did as they were told.

Hulan's attempt to divert their attention hadn't worked, but she still lay in a rag-doll heap on the floor.

"Get up, Inspector!" Amy Gao's voice reeked with contempt.

Hulan still didn't move.

"I think there's something wrong with her." Five pairs of eyes turned to Doug, who held out the hand he'd grabbed Hulan with. It was streaked with blood.

David took a step forward. Doug's gun swiveled in his direction. "Wait!" David held his position as Doug nudged Hulan with his foot. When she didn't move, he reached down, pulled out her gun, and tossed it across the room. Then Doug motioned to David.

David knelt by Hulan's side.

"Hulan," he said tenderly. When he got no response, he repeated her name louder. Still no response. He put his hand on her face. Her skin was hot and dry and dead white. Her breathing was shallow and ragged. He checked her body and saw nothing wrong except for her bandaged hand. He picked it up. It lay limp in his palm. The bandage was soaked through. He unwrapped the sodden gauze. Thick green pus and blood coated her hand. The wound itself was open and oozing. The swollen skin around it was a rupture of deep purple with dark streaks emanating from the center like some strange sea creature. Slowly, carefully David pushed her sleeve up from her wrist to her elbow. The horrid streaks made crimson rivers along the skin up her arm. He felt higher to her armpit. The glands were swollen and hard. Blood poisoning. He had to get her out of here.

Doug Knight and Amy Gao, with their weapons aimed at him, were not prepared either for the swiftness or ferocity with which David acted. He lunged into Doug's gut, sending the raw-boned man flying across the room. Lo followed up with a flying kick to Doug's back, while Henry threw his right elbow into Amy's face. David heard a report from a gun— whether Amy's or Doug's he wasn't sure—because he'd swept up Hulan in his arms and was running down the hall back through the heart, where a hundred women in business attire were trying to figure out what was happening.

He made it to the courtyard. Lo's rental car was at the bottom steps. Of course, the keys weren't there. David tried the Mercedes and Lexus; both were locked.

"David! Hurry! Come with me!" It was Henry, taking the Administration Building's steps three at a time.

David adjusted Hulan's inert form in his arms and took off after the older man. They raced across the courtyard, passing the cafeteria and the dormitory. More shots rang out, tufting up the dirt ahead of David and Henry.

They ducked into the Assembly Building. Jimmy, the Australian guard, wasn't at his post, so Henry was able to reach under the desk and hit the release button for the door.

"Grab it!" he ordered.

David struggled to get the door open; Hulan moaned and twisted in his arms. As soon as Henry saw the door ajar, he ripped the wires for the release mechanism out of the desk. Then he hurried to David, and together they entered the hallway. The door closed behind them and locked into place.

David leaned against the wall, gulping for air, sweat streaming down his face. Henry bent over, placed his hands on his knees, and tried to catch his breath. Looking down at the older man, David registered the oddest detail: he could see the blood pounding through the veins in Henry's neck.

"Lo?" David asking, gasping.

Henry shook his head. "Shot. I don't know."

"We can't stay here."

"There's a phone. Remember?" Henry straightened, still panting. "Aaron Rodgers has a phone in his office."

With the soundproofing in the building, the corridor seemed fearfully quiet. Although they couldn't hear any activity from the factory floor, they could feel the reverberations from the pounding of the heavy machinery. Then they heard noise on the other side of the door.

"Let's go," David said and propelled himself off the wall and down the corridor. He made the first turn and pulled up short. Henry peered around him and saw blood and brain matter splattered on the walls. Sandy Newheart lay dead, with at least one bullet to his head and several others to his body. They had no choice but to walk right through the crime scene, destroying evidence in the process. David's shoes slipped in the blood, and his shoulder crashed into the wall. That blood belonged to someone he knew—a young man who'd spoken just the day before yesterday about going home.

Once on the other side of the body, they picked up their pace, hurrying first down one corridor, then another. "Do you know where we're going?" David asked. Henry didn't answer. He didn't know the way through this maze any better than David. Behind them they heard more gunshots and the door splintering. Again and again Henry tried opening different doors, but they were locked. Behind them in the corridor they heard shoes tramping on the linoleum, getting closer.

Henry tried another door. As it opened, the sound of the running footsteps was completely lost in the din of the machinery in the main assembly room. Henry ducked inside, with David carrying Hulan right behind him. They darted across the floor, dipped behind one of the machines, and hunkered down. All this happened so fast that most of the women hadn't even noticed. David laid Hulan on the ground. She opened her eyes. He put his face down close to hers.

"David?" she whispered. "Where are we?"

"In the Assembly Building," he answered.

She closed her eyes against the terrible noise. Yes, she was in the assembly room. She opened her eyes again, rolled onto her side, and pushed herself into a sitting position. Her face turned the color of pale green marble.

"You're sick, Hulan," David said. "I think it's blood poisoning. We've got to get you to a hospital."

"Help me up," she said. When he hesitated, she ordered him gruffly. "Get me up! We don't have much time, do we?"

David did as she asked. Once in a standing position, she wavered, reached out for the corner of the flocking machine, and steadied herself. She reached for her weapon, but of course she didn't have it. The two men stood before her, staring at her worriedly. Lo wasn't with them, and she assumed the worst.

This was a police matter now. They needed to follow her lead, but she was in no condition to do much of anything. She stood perfectly still, pale and frail compared to the woman who'd been so righteous in the Tsais' courtyard only an hour ago. As far as she knew, there was only one way out of here—the corridor, and she concluded that that was the way they'd gotten in this building. The only reason David and Henry would have brought her here was if they'd had no other choice, which meant that people were after them.

"Excuse me, but you're not allowed in here," a woman's voice said loudly in Mandarin. They turned and saw Madame Leung, the party secretary. "This room is not for foreigners or visitors. And," she added, her tone severe, "no men allowed!"

"Madame Leung, it is I, Liu Hulan. And this is Henry Knight."

The party secretary seemed not to understand. This woman, obviously sick but dressed in her fine silk suit, was no one she knew. As far as the old man? Yes, it was him, but he never came in here during working hours.

"We're in trouble," Hulan continued rapidly. "You must help us."

"This is no place for visitors!"

A shot rang out. Even with the racket of the machines the sound was loud, sharp, and distinctive. Madame Leung turned and saw Doug with the weapon in his hand, Amy Gao at his side. He lifted his weapon again and aimed for the little cluster of people. Before he could pull the trigger, his targets scattered. He fired anyway. Women screamed. Some instinctively fell to the floor. Others made as if to run, but he and Amy blocked the door. There was no place to go.

Hulan peeked around the flocking machine and saw David and

Henry about ten feet from her, behind the engine for the main assembly line. Their heads were down by the exhaust, the fan blowing David's hair away from his forehead. Then Hulan took in as much of the room as she safely could. No one had been shot as far as she could see. There was no movement except for Party Secretary Leung, who slowly crept on all fours under some machinery against a nearby wall. Hulan turned back to Doug. He was saying something to Amy and motioning to the wall not far from Madame Leung. Amy strode forward purposely, unafraid. Why should she be afraid? She held a gun and she had backup. Madame Leung fell flat as Amy passed the machine she was under, but the woman with the gun didn't notice. Amy got to the wall, reached up, and pulled down several levers. One after another the machines ground to a halt. The room fell silent.

"Come out, Dad," Doug called across the cavernous room. "You're in no danger."

"What's happening?" a girl yelled in Mandarin.

Doug waved his gun toward the sound of the voice. Again, silence. Hulan edged around the machine. She saw Siang and Peanut huddled together.

Doug reached down, grabbed a girl of about twelve, and held the gun to her head. "Dad, I'm asking you to come out and talk to me or this girl dies."

Henry started to stand. David grabbed a handful of Henry's shirt to keep him down, but the older man jerked the fabric out of David's grasp and stepped out from behind the conveyor's engine. Doug tossed the girl aside. She fell, then quickly scrambled for cover.

"Did you always know, Dad? Is that why you wanted to sell?"

"No, son, I didn't know it was you until I saw all of your papers together. And during this last hour I've been trying to understand, but I can't."

"Then why sell?"

Henry closed his eyes as if in pain. When he opened them again, his eyes were hard. "Are you going to let these people go?"

"Why sell?" Doug demanded.

"I thought you'd get a better price while I was still alive, and together we could deal with the tax consequences."

This, of course, was what Pearl Jenner had written in her coverage of the sale, and it had been the accepted reason bandied about on Wall Street, but Doug didn't believe it. "You didn't want me to have the company," he stated matter-of-factly.

"If that's what you want to believe—"

"Admit it!" Doug aimed the pistol.

Henry raised his hands in supplication. "I'll admit it if you'll let these people go."

Hulan took this as her cue. Drawing on her last reserves, she edged back out of sight, then crawled along the floor. This meant putting weight on her hand. The pain was excruciating, and with every yard she gained she thought she would pass out again.

"Dad, you know I'm not going to do that. I can't. Things went too far."

These words chilled Hulan. Either that or she shook from pain and the cold sweat that had broken out over her body. She reached a little group of women, whispered instructions, and moved on. David too had begun to move, making his way slowly and quietly to a position behind Amy, who stood with her gun aimed at Henry's back.

"Tell me why, son. Isn't that what you're supposed to do now? Tell us why."

Doug didn't respond. Instead he looked around the room apparently searching for something.

"Doug!" Henry shouted. "I'm talking to you!"

Doug looked back at his father. "What is it, Dad?"

"I need to know why."

"But there's so many reasons, and"—he grinned—"so little time."

"Tell me we have time for this at least. Accord me that courtesy."

Across the room, Madame Leung kept moving, also stopping occasionally to whisper to girls and women. Did she have the same idea as Hulan? Or was the party secretary just trying to make her way to the door? If she was and Doug or Amy caught her, she'd be dead in a second.

Doug sighed. "Okay, but if you're stalling for time, it won't do any good. As everyone has said before, this place is in the middle of nowhere. What has to happen now can't be stopped."

Henry agreed with an abrupt nod.

"I was never interested in the company, Dad. You knew that. Everyone knew that. You thought I wasn't good enough. Everyone else thought I wasn't talented enough. I've heard it my whole life at those toy conventions—your dad's a hard act to follow, or you've got some pretty big shoes to fill. Then you got sick and you sent me here to get this place built. I met Governor Sun and, of course, his assistant, Amy. She was the one who first told me how profits could be made without any outlay of capital."

"Skimming off the salaries," Henry said.

"I know it doesn't seem like much," Doug said. "But look, three hundred thousand a year tax-free ain't bad."

"That's chump change."

"It's not when you start adding in other factories. Once I got here, I saw we could expand easily—just as Mattel and Boeing have."

"Those are legitimate businesses."

"It doesn't matter how you get there. What matters is the profit. Do the math, Dad. Four new factories, each with a three hundred thousand skim—"

"But it still wasn't enough."

Hulan reached her old workstation. She brought a finger to her lips to keep Siang and Peanut from making a sound, but their eyes widened in disbelief and surprise as they recognized her. Then she leaned in and whispered. It was her last act before she lost consciousness again. From his position across the room, David saw Hulan sink to the floor and the two Chinese girls try to wake her.

"Exactly!" Doug said. "The turning point came with Sam & His Friends. You're home, supposed to be resting, and you come up with this great idea. That's what makes you a genius. That's why you're in the Toy Hall of Fame. But you didn't see the potential."

"I saw it. That's why I wanted to sell now. We'd get the best price while I was still alive."

"*No*, you don't see what I see. The dolls are *nothing*. The money's in the technology. If you'd spent any time with Miles and Randall, you'd have seen that's what they wanted."

"Was Miles your partner?"

Doug humphed. "He's a lawyer, Dad. Give me some credit."

"But he knew what you were doing out here."

"Sure. But he had his eye on a bigger prize. Seal the deal, leave his firm, and go over to Tartan. They were talking stock options, the works. You would have known that if you'd paid any attention." Doug shook his head. "But you didn't pay attention, which is why we're here. All you had to do was spot trouble, i.e., our company was paying Sun Gan bribes, and you would have nixed the whole thing, because you'd do anything to protect that guy. Am I right?" When Henry didn't respond, Doug screamed, "Am I right?"

"Yes."

"But you didn't back out of the deal because nothing went as it was supposed to. I gave that little tramp the information, and what does she do? She fucks it all up. I wanted her to give the works to that measly little do-gooder who'd been nosing around. But instead she splits it up. Keith shows a variation of it to Miles, who buries it for his own personal gain. Keith died because he didn't have the guts to expose what he knew. She also sends some of the papers to Sun, and he does everything he can to cover his ass. But I still counted on Guy Lin. He at least did what he was supposed to do."

"But for what end? I still don't understand."

"Any piece of it—the bribery, the problems on the factory floor—should have been enough to alert you. I knew you'd start an internal investigation, and once you did you'd pull out of the Tartan deal, because the idea that Tartan would keep the place running like this would make you sick."

"What you've done here does make me sick. You could have avoided all this just by telling me what you wanted. Did you think I wouldn't pull out if you asked me to? And why promise to sell your shares to Tartan, then back out of that?"

"You still don't get it, Dad. Think Knight. Think chess. Think *next move*. Finally, rather later than I expected, you did *exactly* what I wanted. You heard about the hostile takeover and ordered your brokers to start buying stock. You were to increase our shares overall."

"Meaning more profits to you. But," Henry said, gesturing around him, "this can't be the checkmate you wanted."

A small smile played on Doug's lips. "It will do."

"Come on, Doug," Amy interrupted. "Let's get moving."

Doug nodded and motioned for Amy to get to work. The woman tucked her revolver in the waistband of her skirt and began pulling handfuls of fiber out of big burlap sacks and tossing it on the floor. The intention of this action was immediately felt by the hundreds of women in the room. These foreigners planned to light a fire.

"And what will this get you? You'll destroy your prize," Henry said.

"It covers this mess," Doug answered. "I figured we could deal with a lawyer, but the police? Once the inspector showed up we had to change strategies. But don't worry. We've made plans to pick up from the ashes."

David's eyes darted back to where Hulan had collapsed. She hadn't moved, but the two girls had. One was on her feet, darting from the safety of one machine to another, while the other crawled along more cautiously. Both were passing word of some sort. Their movements went unnoticed by Amy Gao, who now looked ghostly in a cloud of fluff, while the two men in the center of the room seemed completely unaware of the electric fear pulsating throughout the room.

"All you had to do was walk away from the deal," Doug said. "But *look* what it took! It makes me think you're not as smart as everyone says."

"And you're still telling me you did this for the technology?" Henry asked skeptically.

"Dad." The word was drawn out and as patronizing as any from a rebellious teenager. "It was the skim. It was the potential of this land. I mean, my God, look around! We could have had all of it for *nothing*. But yes, it was the damn technology. You hit it, Dad. You actually hit it. It's so much bigger than Sam & His Friends. The other toy companies want it. The studios have been banging at the door. Think what this could mean to Warner Brothers and the *Batman* films or to Paramount and the *Star Trek* franchise or to Lucas and the *Star Wars* empire. Everything that's old could be new again, and everything that's new could be . . . Well, others have talked about interactive toys, but you *did* it. Seven hundred million was peanuts. Even if we make one hundred million a year and the stock market values us at thirty times earnings—which is modest these days— we'll have a company worth three billion, with nowhere to go but up."

Henry's face was unreadable. Finally he said, his voice disappointed, "Our family has been in the *toy* business. Did you once stop to think what that meant?"

Doug turned his eyes away from his father and settled on some women cowering nearby. Seeing them seemed to remind him what had to happen next. When he looked back at his father, he seemed determined. "I'm sorry you see it that way, Dad." Then, "Amy, I think that's enough. Let's go." Amy walked to his side, her heels clicking staccato against the floor and wafting bits of fluff and lint behind her. Doug reached into his pocket and pulled out a lighter, weighing it in his left hand.

"There's just one thing I need to know," he said. "Did you ever think I could run the company? Did it ever just once cross your mind?"

David moved into a crouch, ready to pounce. He kept his eyes on Henry, primed for a signal, so he saw, just as Doug saw, the look that came over the older man's face.

"No, Doug, it didn't," Henry admitted sadly, and as he spoke these words it was abundantly clear that the realization that he'd so little faith in his son was even more painful than the fact that his son was a murderer.

Doug, the revolver steady in his right hand, flicked open the lighter. Just as he did so, hundreds of women rose en masse. Immediately they were joined by those who hadn't gotten the word that had circulated. Whatever opportunity David had to attack was blocked. In that same instant a shrill voice screamed something in Mandarin, something clicked and clicked again, and the machines revved to life.

Doug took a step backward and waved his revolver around. Amy reached for hers. In that second the women rushed forward. Amy was wrestled to the ground. Doug struggled, got off a couple of shots, pushed away from the grabbing hands, lost his balance, and flew back into one of the machines. Blood spurted from the center of the crowd of women. Doug's scream was cruel and very short.

A moment later the machines were shut down and an eerie quiet fell over the room. David picked his way through the pink-smocked women. Doug had been grabbed by the claws of the fiber-shredding machine. His body was a mangled and bloody mess. Henry stood at Doug's side, a hand touching his son's lifeless ankle.

David heard Madame Leung's voice over the loudspeaker, giving instructions of some sort. The women obeyed and began drifting in an orderly fashion toward the exit. David hurried to Hulan's crumpled form. Two girls—one about fourteen, the other also a teenager—kneeled at her side. He felt for a pulse and didn't feel one. He put his ear on her chest and heard nothing.

Then someone screamed. Then another scream, and another, and another as the preternatural calm of moments before was replaced by panic. One of the girls holding Hulan's hand looked at David in terror. She moved her lips. He didn't understand the word. She repeated it again and again. Finally he understood the word through her heavy accent. Fire.

He scooped Hulan up into his arms and stood. Now that he was upright, he saw the flames kicking up from the fiber fluff. Hundreds of women shoved and pushed to get out the door as the flames spread quickly through the piles. David, holding Hulan, with the two girls clinging close to his side, joined the others in a desperate attempt to escape. Acrid smoke filled the air, creating even more panic. A lot of people would die in here if someone didn't do something. David lowered Hulan's feet to the ground and motioned for the two girls to take her arms and get her out of the building. He took one last look at Hulan's ashen face, then turned and walked into the smoke.

## 25

BECAUSE OF THE SOUNDPROOFING IN THE BUILDING, MOST of the fatalities were in the final assembly room. By the time the fire had spread far enough to alert the women there, the fumes from the burning plastic and fiber had made any chance of survival impossible. Fortunately, almost all of the women had made it out of the primary assembly area where Hulan had worked. But here too many women lost their lives due to smoke inhalation or being crushed in the stampede. The remoteness of the factory had done little to help matters. Many women died on the way to Taiyuan. More died in the hospital, inundated as it was by so many injuries. The final death toll reached 176.

David had done his best to fight back the fire, swatting the flames with the empty burlap bags that had once held the stuffing for Sam & His Friends. Madame Leung, who stayed at David's side until the very end, helped his efforts. Miraculously, she'd found a couple of fire extinguishers. If not for these, they wouldn't have made it out of the building alive. For her efforts Madame Leung was given a medal by the central government.

And then there was Hulan. When David emerged from the burning building, choking, his eyes running, his lungs scorched, he found Hulan stretched out on the ground, the two girls who'd brought her out still at her side. The only way he knew she was alive was that her skin radiated an intense feverish heat. He knew that when the medical teams arrived, the doctors would dismiss Hulan as less urgent, for she looked peaceful and physically uninjured compared to the others who were in such agony from their burns. He half staggered, half ran back to the Administration Building, made his way back through the deserted hallways to the conference room, thinking that he'd have to take the car keys off Lo's body. Instead he found Lo shot but conscious. David helped Lo out to the car, drove to where Hulan was, put her in the backseat along with Siang, the girl who spoke a little English, then, under Lo's directions, pulled out of the compound and made it to the hospital in Taiyuan before the hundreds of others arrived.

It was a good thing David thought to bring Siang, because by the time they reached the hospital Lo had gone into shock. With eyes wide, Siang presented Lo's and Hulan's Ministry of Public Security credentials to the nurse, who quickly summoned help. Hulan and Lo were wheeled away, and David waited.

Siang didn't have the language skills to translate the doctors' words, but eventually someone was found who'd studied at Johns Hopkins. Still, the words—tachycardia, oliguria, anoxia, tachypnea—were as foreign and had as little meaning for David as the Mandarin. Even the terms he understood he couldn't allow himself to comprehend. The doctor seemed to be telling him that the sepsis had gone so far that Hulan's heart, brain, or liver could be overwhelmed at any moment. If the poisoning turned out to be viral, the doctor added regretfully, there was nothing anyone could do. They had twenty-four hours, if Hulan lived that long, to wait for the results of the blood culture. In the meantime Hulan was intravenously dosed with broad-spectrum antibiotics.

Those twenty-four hours were the worst of David's life. Now that he knew what Hulan had, all of her ailments of the last few days fell into place—the flu-like symptoms, the lethargy, the fever followed by chills, her rapid breathing, her racing, then feeble pulse. The guilt he felt over this was superseded only by the terror at the prospect of losing her.

Eventually the right cocktail of antibiotics was found, and Hulan's doctors announced that she would probably live. The survival of the baby, however, was still an issue. The baby's heart continued to beat, but more tests needed to be run.

By that time much had happened. Henry Knight, who survived the ordeal at the factory, led an expedition up Tianlong Mountain to ferret out Governor Sun, while Siang was informed about Tsai Bing's death and her father's hand in it. David, who never left Hulan's side, spent hours on a cell phone, talking to the partners at Phillips, MacKenzie & Stout, to Anne Baxter Hooper, to Nixon Chen (who was enlisted to help Henry), and to Rob Butler at the U.S. Attorney's Office. Rob and David had much to discuss, but in the meantime Rob negotiated for and won the right to send a team of forensic accountants from Los Angeles to the Knight compound to try and pull up the financial records that Doug had tried to eliminate from the computer. Through it all, David had the help and support of Vice Minister Zai, whose concern for Hulan's well-being seemed sometimes to surpass even David's.

One day Hulan's doctors crowded into her room and announced that the tests on the baby looked good. This news gave Hulan a surge of energy, and she began to regain her strength. Though Zai and the doctors preferred that Hulan be spared the details, she was adamant that she hear everything. She reviewed the media coverage, studied the photos of the burned-out building, read over the casualty list, and cried first at the number of names, then at the individual names of people she'd known. Once she was deemed well enough to return to Beijing, they flew to the capital on the Knight jet and settled back in the compound with round-the-clock nurses. Hulan's mother and her nurse came back from the seaside. Cooks and maids were brought in to help, and the compound bustled with activity. Finally there came a day when Hulan told David that he had unfinished business to attend to and that she'd be fine with all her extra caretakers. With deep misgivings, David did as he was told.

Many questions still needed to be answered, but those who might have answered them most truthfully—Miles, Doug, and Sandy—were dead. That left Aaron, Jimmy, and Amy. Aaron Rodgers, who had the great fortune to have been in Taiyuan on the day of the fire, admitted to a healthy libido befitting a twenty-five-year-old placed in the happy circumstance of being one of a handful of males amongst a thousand females. Ling Miaoshan had been the first of many conquests. His age, his isolation in the Assembly Building, and his stupidity (which became apparent to all concerned as the investigation unfolded) conspired to keep him blissfully in the dark to the financial shenanigans. As for conditions in the factory, Aaron used the predictable and well-worn excuse that he thought that's how things were supposed to be in China. As his mother and father, who flew out to Taiyuan, said, their son didn't know any better. No criminal charges were filed. He gave testimony against Jimmy and Amy in court; then his parents took him home. He would never again return to China.

David then turned his attention to Jimmy and Amy. David wasn't the only one who wanted answers, and so it was that Henry pulled himself away from the ruins of the Knight factory, where he'd worked practically without sleep since the fire, to accompany David to Taiyuan's provincial jail. On their arrival they were handed a file pertaining to one James W. Smith, which had been faxed from the Australian authorities. As Hulan guessed when she'd first seen Jimmy, he had an extensive criminal background, which included armed robbery and a couple of cases of battery. He'd been in and out of prison since the age of eighteen. Two years ago yet another warrant had been issued for his arrest, but he'd managed to flee, ending up, the record showed, in Hong Kong. It was presumed that he had met Doug in that city, been hired, and had moved into the Knight compound even before the factory opened.

Also, as suspected, the Knight records showing that women who'd suffered injuries of one sort or another and had chosen to "go back home" proved false. Using the doctored files, Chinese investigators had contacted local Public Security Bureaus across China and ascertained that those women had never returned home. No wonder Xiao Yang had screamed so when Aaron had carried her off the factory floor. No wonder she'd been found dead not long after.

But had this murder been too hasty, a matter of convenience on a day that was busy? Or had it been part of the plot to keep pushing Henry in one direction so he wouldn't look in another? Had Jimmy thrown Xiao Yang off the roof? Had he run down Keith? The record showed that he'd been in Los Angeles on the date in question. Was he the one who'd killed Pearl and Guy? The answers to these queries would help address a major underlying question: How much of a monster had Douglas Knight been? But Jimmy Smith wasn't talking. David pleaded. Henry begged.

Obviously the local police had tried persuasion of another sort, all to no avail. Whatever Jimmy knew would die with him.

David and Henry were dealing with a bureaucracy, and for their next meeting they were asked to move to another room. The pitiful room that passed for a visiting area was filthy and stiflingly hot. Amy Gao, who ten days ago had looked so snappy in her suit at the banquet at the Beijing Hotel, now wore a dirty prison uniform. She had not been allowed to bathe, wash her hair, or brush her teeth since her confinement.

Like Jimmy, she kept quiet at first. But as David peppered her with questions, he could see her mind begin to work. David, a prosecutor, had seen that look a hundred times before. If Amy gave them information, what could she get in return?

"What do you want?" David asked when Amy finally revealed her thoughts.

"What do you think they'd be willing to give?"

"In China, as it is in the U.S., a lot depends on what you tell us . . ."

It was the thinnest shred of hope, but the desperation with which Amy grabbed hold of it made him realize just how young and inexperienced she was. He almost felt sorry for her, almost, that is, until she opened her mouth. With no promises written or otherwise, she plunged into her story.

Jimmy had not driven the SUV that killed Keith. Doug had been at the wheel; Amy had fired the warning shots. That David had been with Keith that evening was just an unlucky coincidence. The other women who'd disappeared from the factory had fallen under Jimmy Smith's job description. What he did with them, Amy didn't know. Pearl and Guy? She smiled when their names came up. "That was your son's genius at work, Mr. Knight," she said. They didn't ask for more details. Had Sandy Newheart been a part of the conspiracy? No. "We were always working *around* him," Amy explained. "He had his paperwork. We had ours." Why had he been killed? Amy sighed. "That last day things got a little out of hand," she admitted. Sandy Newheart simply had the misfortune of being in the wrong place at the wrong time.

"Who pulled the trigger?" Henry Knight asked.

"Let's just say that someone didn't think that through," Amy said. Her remark, so boastful really, placed blame squarely on Doug.

"Did you get what you wanted?" David asked.

"Obviously not." She smiled wistfully. "But I think you're really asking me if the ends justified the means."

"If that's how you want to put it."

"You in America and the West want us to be like you," she said. "You believe that we should have democracy in your form. You believe we should be able to make money and spend it on consumer goods—*your* consumer goods. For centuries the West has wanted a piece of us. Sometimes you've gotten it. To me it comes down to exploitation. In the last century the British intoxicated us with opium, forced us to open our ports, and very nearly destroyed us. Now you want to come in here—into the very heart of China—and force your will upon us. You're allowed to do your very worst, and your people look the other way."

"I think you have it backwards," David cut in. "What *you* were doing was criminal—"

"No, it was purely American."

David looked at her aghast. This woman was either deluded or crazy.

"Can you show me one thing that we did that wasn't done somewhere along the line in America's rise to prominence?" she asked. "Look back at your history. Your growth was accomplished on the backs of slaves. You were able to finish your westward migration because of the work *my* countrymen did building the railroad. And you didn't limit yourselves to people of—how do you so euphemistically call it?—people of color. No, you sent women and children into factories and into mines."

"All that was a long time ago."

"But today, looking back from a position of world domination and tremendous prosperity, wouldn't you have to say that the ends justified the means?"

"And what were you going to get out of it?"

Amy sneered. "You still don't see it? With Henry and Sun out of the way, we could do anything. I helped Doug, he helped me. Doug wanted your company," she said, acknowledging Henry. "I wanted the governorship."

Amy's confession, for what it was worth, gained her little but some soap, toothpaste, the promise of bottled water, and a towel.

\*         \*         \*

One day when Hulan's mother and her nurse had gone to see Dr. Du and David was on a trip to Los Angeles, Hulan heard a ring at the front gate. She padded out through the courtyards and opened the door. Though it was the middle of the day, the alley had been cleared of all people except for a man who announced that her presence was required elsewhere and she should get in the car please. She obeyed, knowing that if she didn't come back, no one would ever know what had happened to her.

The driver took her through the narrow alleys of the *hutong*, then popped out on the opposite shore of Shisha Lake from Hulan's home. Here the driver's progress stopped while he waited for a flock of Secrets of the Hutongs Special Tourist Agency pedicabs, each loaded with one or two Westerners, to pass. This tour was a new fad in Hulan's neighborhood, and she wasn't quite sure how she felt about it. On the one hand, she didn't like to see so many foreigners in this little enclave; on the other, the success of the state-owned agency might help to keep the neighborhood from being razed. As the sweating pedicab drivers slowly pedaled out of the way, Hulan stared out across the lake. Old men with fishing poles dotted the shore. Just outside her window, three skinny boys took turns jumping into the water. Their hollers, hoots, and squeals came to her on a soft breeze.

The sedan began to move again, and a few minutes later the driver pulled up to a gated compound. Like any traditional compound, the exterior walls were unpainted and gave no indication of hidden wealth. A guard ticked their names off a list, and the driver pulled inside.

Hulan had come here many times as a child and expected the compound to look smaller and less impressive. In fact, she had just the opposite sensation. The grounds were more beautiful than she remembered from those long-ago days. Gingko, camphor, and willow trees created a shadowed oasis. A stream—and Hulan remembered this vividly from playing out there with the other children of high-ranking cadres—meandered along the inside perimeter of the compound. Sponge rocks jutted from the sides of the stream. Stands of bamboo sheltered pavilions and summer houses. Birds chirped and twittered and cooed in the walls of greenery, reminding Hulan that there'd once been a dovecote behind the main house. She wondered if it was still there.

She followed the driver up the steps and into the foyer, which smelled of mothballs and mildew. They passed several formal parlors where the furniture was draped in dingy sheets, then traveled up a back staircase and down a hall with high ceilings. The driver tapped on a heavy door, slowly opened it, and motioned for Hulan to enter. As soon as she did, the door closed behind her. Five men, not one younger than seventy, sat in overstuffed chairs in a semicircle facing her. Each face was as familiar to her as if it had been her father's. Behind these five men sat two others, Hulan realized as her eyes adjusted to the gloom. One was Vice Minister Zai; the other was Governor Sun.

"Please sit, Inspector Liu Hulan," the man in the middle said, gesturing gracefully to a straight-back chair. When she hesitated, he added, "Don't rely on tradition. We know you are still weak. Sit."

Hulan sat, folded her hands in her lap, and waited. A matronly woman appeared out of the shadows along the wall, poured tea, then backed away again.

"How is your health, Liu Hulan?"

"Very well, sir."

"And your mother?"

"She is happy to be home."

"Yes, we have heard this as well. It makes us all so . . ." The old politician groped for the appropriate word and failed.

Another man said, "So many traditions, eh, Xiao Hulan?" She started. She hadn't been called Little Hulan since before she'd gone to the Red Soil Farm. "They tell us how to be loyal, how to conduct conversations, how to negotiate, how to meet as husband and wife. They can be so tiresome, don't you think?"

Hulan didn't know how to respond.

"I say, we are old friends here," this second man went on. "We are not family, but I can remember when you called me uncle."

Hulan's eyes stung with tears at these words. This compound with its memories. These men—the most powerful in her country—old now, dredging up times that were perhaps better left forgotten.

As if reading her thoughts, the second man said, "We have never forgotten your family or you. There are some people in this room who wouldn't be here if not for the long-ago courage of your father and mother. And what we want to say is that your work for our nation has not gone unnoticed and we are grateful."

"We also know," the first man resumed, "that your job has come at a high price."

Her father's death. Being belittled in the press. Becoming an object of scorn in her own country. Almost losing her life and that of her child. Yes, she had paid a very high price.

"We are sorry," he said.

*Up to a point,* Hulan thought.

"The people of our country think one thing about you," the man continued, "but you may keep your mind easy. We know the truth."

"Yes, but I live among the people. I work among the masses."

The men looked at her in surprise. She wasn't supposed to speak at all, let alone make even the slightest criticism. Over their shoulders Hulan saw Vice Minister Zai put a weary hand over his eyes.

"We need you, Liu Hulan," the man in the middle said. "You have an understanding of the truth. You are fair. You have always been unflinching."

*I've followed the wind. I've been swayed by government propaganda and thereby lost people I've loved,* she thought.

"We need you more than ever, Liu Hulan," he continued. "You understand better than most about corruptibility. Sad to say, this is your family legacy, but you have used it to advantage. You also understand these foreigners who are coming into our country like ants looking for sugar." The man paused. All this time his face had been the mask of a beloved uncle. Now he added a look of concern. "We know you don't want to leave your homeland. We are proud of you for wanting to have your baby here when it would be so easy for you to travel to the homeland of its father."

"David will be back."

He nodded. "We know that, of course."

A silence settled. Dust motes drifted in a stream of light coming through the window. Finally Hulan broke with ceremony. "What do you want?"

The face of the man in the middle stretched into a thin, triumphant smile.

"On the exterior you are so Chinese, Liu Hulan," he said. "You know how to say the proper words of a filial daughter, you know all the etiquette of centuries-old tradition, but inside you are like a foreigner." On the surface these words conveyed a supreme insult, but his voice resonated with admiration. "We have an open door policy and we will not back away from it," he went on. "But with that open door we have to deal with these outsiders. We want you to help us with that." He held up a hand. "I am not asking you to leave the Ministry of Public Security. No, we want you to stay exactly where you are. You have your credentials. You have your own money. These two things give you power on the street."

"So I continue my life as it is."

The man nodded.

"With no other strings?"

"To the contrary. We are prepared to look the other way. David Stark will be allowed to return to China. You will be allowed to have your baby."

Hulan glanced over the man's shoulder to Zai. Her mentor's face was white with worry. She could almost hear him shouting at her, Take it, accept it.

Hulan cleared her throat. "One does not like to bargain with family."

Zai once again covered his eyes. Even Sun looked appalled.

"This is not a negotiation," the man on the right said sternly.

"Nevertheless," Hulan said.

"What can we do for you, Xiao Hulan?"

"Three things."

"Three?" The old men exchanged glances. This kind of request was unheard of. The man in the middle waved his hand, signaling an agreement. The man to his left said, "Tell us what they are, then we will see."

"Why were we able to leave Beijing after the murders of Pearl Jenner and Guy Lin?"

"This is your request? This is hardly worth asking!"

"But I still want to know," Hulan said.

"Vice Minister Zai advised us to give you free rein. He proved to be right about you, as always."

Yes, of course this was how it had been. She'd intuited it during her encounter with Pathologist Fong.

"This second comes from my own curiosity," she went on. "I will never repeat it. I know what will happen if I do."

"Yes?"

"I had occasion to see Sun Gan's *dangan*." As she spoke these words she didn't look in Sun's direction. "There are some discrepancies to what I know to be the facts. This makes me think that he had men like you behind him. I wonder how this happened."

A heavy silence hung in the room. At last the man in the middle said, "No, not men. One man. The late but revered Premier Zhou Enlai."

As he continued speaking, the pieces clicked into place. Local cadres had sent the young Sun Gan to a mission school. His heroism at Tianlong Shan with Henry Knight had been noted and he'd been sent west, this time to spy on the Americans. However, the story in the *dangan* relating Sun's valor at the battle of Huai Hua was a complete falsehood. He'd been elsewhere. The place and the circumstances would remain a state secret, but he'd saved Zhou's life just as he'd saved Henry Knight's. Zhou, like Knight, had been grateful and had smoothed the way to position and promotion for his protégé. These simple acts, combined with Henry Knight's "tea money," had assured Sun safety during various political campaigns, not the least of which was the Cultural Revolution.

"Sun Gan was in great trouble during what we may call the Chaos," the man in the middle said. "But instead of trying to save himself, he petitioned Premier Zhou to protect one of our country's treasures. This is why, if you were to visit the Jinci Temple famous in Shanxi Province for its Three Everlasting Springs, you would know that Premier Zhou sent— at Sun Gan's request—an armed guard to protect . . ."

Another piece fell into place, this one from Hulan's own past. She remembered leaving the Red Soil Farm on an excursion to Jinci. The monks had been ridiculed and struggled against. In the newer buildings Hulan and her compatriots had destroyed paintings and sculptures, but they'd not been allowed to touch the oldest and most beautiful building at Jinci, the renowned Mother Temple, defended as it was by Premier Zhou's personal guards. It was as Henry Knight said that day flying back to Taiyuan: Sun Gan, even in the most difficult circumstances, "stood firm." Unlike others in this room, herself included, he'd never wavered in his beliefs or his duties.

Hulan became aware of the others' eyes upon her, judging her, testing her loyalty and her memory.

"You have a final request, Liu Hulan," a voice said from the back row. It was Sun Gan. "Perhaps this one will be more beneficial to you personally."

She answered, "There is a man. Bi Peng. He works for the *People's Daily*."

"Yes, we know him."

"I'm sure you do. He's written many things about me and my family at your direction."

Four of the men shifted uncomfortably in their chairs until the man in the middle laughed. "You want him sent to labor camp?"

"Perhaps he can simply be reassigned to something less malignant," Hulan said.

"It won't make you free," someone said.

"I just don't want lies being used to control me," Hulan said, her eyes searching the faces to see who'd spoken.

"What do you suggest, then?"

"I agree to your conditions. You agree to mine. I have far more to lose than you. I think you are ahead in the game. May we leave it at that?"

A few minutes later, Hulan was once again ensconced behind the tinted windows of the Mercedes. This time no attempt was made to clear the alley before her house. She left the car, ignored the worried looks of her neighbors, and ducked into the quiet of her compound. Her mother and the nurse were still out. David was still across the Pacific. She hoped they would never know of her visit to the other side of the lake.


In Los Angeles, David bunked at his house under the Hollywood sign with Special Agent Eddie Wiley. It had been a little over a month since David left Los Angeles, but already the city, his house, his own bed seemed foreign to him. He longed to be home with Hulan. Still, he went about his business. He stopped in every day at Phillips & MacKenzie, the "& Stout" having been dropped. The publicity had been bad, but as Phil Collingsworth and the other partners assured David, they'd known nothing of Miles's shenanigans. They were at pains to verify that their invitation to come back to the firm had not only been sincere but had been in the pipeline for many months before making the offer. (In retrospect, Phil recalled that Miles—while finally joining the unanimous vote—had been the only partner to voice last-minute opposition to David's return. Once he was in, Miles had manipulated the situation as only a fine—though ultimately corrupt—mind could.) Miles had been the firm rainmaker, but the firm was bigger than one man. In fact, billable hours were up thanks to Randall Craig and the various federal investigations nipping at Tartan's heels. The only real cost to the firm was in redesigning the logo on the door and reprinting the firm's stationery.

Phil and the others encouraged David to stay with the firm and keep the Beijing office open. David, whose belief in the law had been so tested during this past year, found himself drawn in by his partners' sentiments. If anything, his love of the law had been reaffirmed. Justice didn't always follow the rulebook. The outcome could often be unsatisfactory and unsatisfying, but this time around David felt that, despite the twists and turns, justice might be served.

His duty to seeing that happen was not yet done. All of the principals were either dead or awaiting execution in China. However, the story had indeed sparked the interest of the U.S. Attorney's Office, which had initiated a thorough investigation into Tartan's overseas operations. As a result David spent several days testifying before the grand jury, but most of his responses consisted of "I can't answer that due to attorney-client privilege." Since he no longer had an office in the criminal courts building, he holed up in Rob Butler's. There weren't many witnesses who were accorded such VIP treatment, but David and Rob were friends. That friendship made it all the harder for David to ask Rob why he hadn't told him about Keith.

"Told you?" Rob said. "What could I have told you? He came in here wanting to get political asylum for that girl, but he had no proof that she was in any political danger or that she was an important dissident. Then he asked me if the reason I wouldn't help was because we were investigating him. I told him we'd checked out what that reporter had written months before and had found nothing. But Keith didn't believe me."

David thought back to Keith's mood on that last night—his desperation, his anxiety, even his anger. So much misery could have been prevented if Keith had only told the truth. Rob and David too, for that matter.

"Before I went to China I asked you straight out—"

"If there was a Keith Baxter investigation and if there was any chance that Keith could have been the target and not you on that night," Rob finished for him. "First, I want you to know that I never would have let you go to China if I thought Keith had been the intended victim. But how could I have thought that anyway? Keith came to me about a girl—"

"What about the investigation?"

"That day Madeleine said there wasn't one, and there wasn't. But I also said that maybe his name had come up in another matter."

"And what was I supposed to take from that?"

"What I would have taken if the tables had been reversed. Nothing. Look, I couldn't tell you why he was here, just like you couldn't tell all of us what was happening in China. We have that pesky thing called confidentiality. And remember, Keith was my friend too. He was dead. Was it any of your business that he'd come in here with some crack-brained scheme—lying to me the whole while, by the way—to get his girlfriend over here? I decided the least I could do to protect his memory was keep my mouth shut. You can't tell me you wouldn't have done the same."

This caused David to look even closer at his own actions. What if he'd confronted Miles at the funeral, pushing past the platitudes and facile excuses? But like Rob, David had made protecting his friend's memory a priority. Then, when the job offer came up, it had been so easy to bury his concerns as he became consumed with the idea of getting back to Hulan. He'd have to live with the knowledge of that moment of selfishness for the rest of his life.

Two days later, after completing his testimony, David found himself drawn to the Stout estate, having heard that Mary Elizabeth was going back to Michigan. The driveway was chockablock with trucks from moving companies, auction houses, and charitable organizations. David wandered inside and found Mary Elizabeth, in jeans and a T-shirt, orchestrating the packing and giving away of her family's worldly possessions. A sorrowful look came over her face when she saw him, and wordlessly she motioned for him to follow her. They stood out on the terrace. It was a beautiful late summer day, and the scent of roses filled the air.

"I never wanted all this." Mary Elizabeth's gesture took in the gardens, the mansion, the view, the life she and Miles had built. "But he wanted it. He wanted it badly."

"How much did you know?"

"I only knew his dreams," she answered. "And even those were always . . . I knew he was unhappy. Remember back when Michael Ovitz left CAA and moved to Disney? He was arguably the most powerful man in Hollywood, but he still had to fetch Julia Roberts a glass of mineral water if she asked for it. Well, that's how Miles felt. He made tons of money, but he had to be available whenever a client wanted him."

David remembered what Doug had said about Miles. "Is it true that Tartan had offered him a job?"

"Yes, as general counsel. He would have been the client, don't you see?"

There seemed nothing more to say, and they turned back toward the house. Mary Elizabeth reached out and put a trembling hand on his arm. "Did he . . ." She began in a quavering voice, but she couldn't finish.

"No, he didn't suffer. He didn't even know what happened."

In early September, Hulan was resting on a chaise longue in the central courtyard of her family compound when Neighborhood Committee Director Zhang paid her customary call. The old woman, wearing a black jacket and black trousers, hung onto David's arm and wrinkled her face up at him in delight as he escorted her outside. She sat down opposite Hulan on a porcelain garden stool. As soon as David went inside to make tea, Madame Zhang said, "He is funny, that one. I see he is practicing his Mandarin, but aiya, to my ears it is frightful and hilarious at the same time."

Hulan had been trying to teach David basic sentences: Welcome. How are you? Okay. How much? That's too expensive. How is your son? Can you tell me . . . But he was as competent as a toddler in split pants. Lately she'd begun to think it would be better for him to forget the project entirely because his tones were abysmal, and, as Madame Zhang noted, they resulted in some amusing mistakes.

"What did he say today?"

"*Qing wen . . .*" Madame Zhang said, purposely missing the fourth tone of *wen* and replacing it with a third, thereby changing the meaning from "Please, may I ask" to "Please kiss."

Hulan smiled as the Neighborhood Committee director cackled in pleasure.

"He could kiss me if he wants," the old woman added. "He is not so ugly as I once thought."

David returned with the tea, set it on the table, and retired to the other side of the courtyard, where Hulan's mother, her nurse, and Vice Minister Zai sat under the twisting branches of the jujube. Jinli didn't understand who David was, although she accepted his presence without question; nor did she understand that she would soon be a grand-mother. But she seemed to find comfort in her childhood home and, while still not appreciating the raucous cymbals, gongs, and drums of the *yang ge* troupe, had grown more accustomed to the cacophonous morning ritual. David had found another way to deal with it. He'd joined the troupe.

"He is a foreigner," Madame Zhang continued. "This we can never forget. But he isn't so bad." This compliment was of the highest order, and the old woman moved quickly to ward off any evil that might result by cautiously explaining herself. "He minds his own business. He knows enough to sweep the snow in front of his own doorstep and not bother about the frost on top of his neighbor's roof. And yet he has shown high regard for our neighborhood and our neighbors. He is polite and respect-ful. And you should know"—she leaned forward and put a gnarled hand on Hulan's knee—"the neighbors are appreciative of the way he cares for you."

"I'm pleased that they're happy," Hulan said diplomatically.

A gauzy look came over Madame Zhang's wrinkled face as she gazed over in David's direction. Despite all of her attempts to remain critical, she was as smitten with David as if she were a schoolgirl.

"For so many years," the Committee director continued dreamily, "the government has talked about what is good for the masses. But these days I wonder. What if individual happiness can serve the people more than anything else?"

"I would never argue with our government," Hulan said.

The old woman frowned at her neighbor's stupidity: always this girl was mindful, so careful of every word. Madame Zhang had come here not completely in her official position—although she never forgot her duty—but as an old woman who had seen her neighbor happy and at peace for the first time since she was a small child. This house deserved to have joy and tranquility again, and she would do what she could to make that happen. So, instead of debating with her obtuse neighbor, she went on as though Hulan had not spoken at all.

"In this spirit," Madame Zhang said, "I've been thinking about a marriage certificate. Your David is a foreigner, yes, but I think I can make a recommendation that even the old-liners will accept."

Did the Committee director expect Hulan to believe that these were her own original thoughts? It had probably been the old men from the compound across the lake who had sent her here today. But what use was there in pointing this out? Instead Hulan folded her hands over her swelling stomach and looked across the courtyard at David. He chanced to look up and cocked his head as if waiting for her to ask him a question. With their eyes locked, Hulan said softly, "We'll see, auntie, we'll see."

Her duty done, the old woman paid her respects to Jinli and left. David came to sit at Hulan's side and, as they had repeatedly over these last few weeks, went back over the events leading to the conflagration at Knight. His orderly mind had boiled everything down to greed. The old men in the Silk Thread Café had been greedy, getting their kickbacks from Doug via Amy Gao. Tang Dan and Miles Stout had clearly been motivated by greed. And it had all started because Henry Knight was greedy in his own way.

Unwilling to share his company with his less talented son, Henry had unwittingly set the whole catastrophe in motion. And as much as David liked the man, he couldn't help but acknowledge that greed was what was keeping Henry going now. A makeshift assembly area—based on Doug's plans—had been set up in the Knight warehouse, and even now women were working overtime to get boxes of Sam & His Friends in the stores by Christmas. With all the additional publicity, the supply really couldn't meet the demand. More than that, the articles in the papers—and there'd been countless—had portrayed the Sam & His Friends technology as so revolutionary that it had caused . . . Well, the whole thing sounded positively Shakespearean.

In the meantime, Knight International's stock had gone through the roof, and Henry had, to considerable acclaim, unveiled a plan to link executive pay to fair labor practices, especially regarding child labor, since, as he kept repeating, "We're in the toy business. We create toys for children, not jobs!" Community groups, a reorganized board of directors, as well as a consortium of international watchdog organizations would carry out inspections. (This one action, if it was to be believed, wiped out half of Knight's workforce. Peanut and so many others had been sent "home," meaning that they'd simply moved on to other factories with less discriminating owners.) Henry's actions were not as noble as it seemed at first glance. When he wasn't giving interviews or testifying before Congress, he was talking to studios and conglomerates all over the world for what the international media was calling "the largest global out-licensing campaign of all time." It seemed that Doug's predictions had been frighteningly accurate.

Of course, all the attention had spurred the media to cover a different aspect of the story. Chinese woman migrant workers were changing the face of the countryside. Unlike their male counterparts, these women either sent their earnings home to their peasant families, increasing the household income by forty percent, or were saving their salaries so they might return to their villages to open little businesses. It was estimated that women who'd returned from foreign factories owned nearly half of all shops and cafés in rural villages. Suddenly Chinese peasant girls were seen by their families as leaders of social and economic change; as a result, in the last calendar year female infanticide had dropped for the first time in recorded history. As a Ford Foundation scholar noted, female migrant workers were the single most important element transforming Chinese society. "This is happening on a scope unprecedented worldwide, and it means radical, revolutionary changes for women." If anything, these stories soothed the consciences of parents around the world who needed to have Sam and Cactus and Notorious and the rest of the Friends in time for the holidays. Or, as Amy Gao might have put it, if there was one thing Americans admired, trusted, and believed in more than democracy, it was capitalism.

Hulan had heard all this before and once again repeated her view. "This wasn't caused by greed. It was love."

When she'd first said this back in the hospital, David hadn't believed her, for she was not a woman given over to mushy sentiments. But she had stuck to her theory now for weeks without much other explanation. In fact, since his return from Los Angeles, he'd noticed a certain bitterness in her thoughts, but perhaps after what she'd been through this was to be expected. That day in the factory she'd drawn on her last bit of strength to save not only David and Henry but all those other women. She'd been left so physically weak and emotionally frail that her usual defenses were in tatters.

"I've never experienced unconditional love like Suchee's for Miaoshan or even Keith's for Miaoshan," she said, finally expanding on her idea. "She had a lot of faults, but she must have been a remarkable woman to elicit that kind of devotion."

"Maybe they weren't so blind," David interrupted. "Yes, she was manipulative, but somewhere along the line she shifted. She had nothing personal to gain from trying to organize the women in the factory, and the way she divided up the materials tells me that she really wanted to make sure that information got out. She had energy, brains, and in other circumstances things might have turned out differently for her." He paused, then asked, "What about Doug? You can't believe he acted out of love."

"Him most of all. Think of what he did to prove himself to his father. Then think of how on that last day, Henry was willing to take the blame for everything—the corruption, the murders—to protect his son. He begged us to bring him back to Beijing to face the consequences. And in our own ways we deceived ourselves and each other despite love, for love. . . ." She closed her eyes. When she opened them, he saw nothing but sorrow. "I look back at my parents and the way I was brought up, and I wonder at all of it. I think of my work and how I see the very worst in people. But for me it's easier than the alternative."

"The alternative?"

"To give myself over fully to love," she said, at last admitting her deepest fear. She looked away again and stared over at Zai, her mother, and her nurse. "Suchee says I've run away my entire life. Maybe I have,

because staying opens up the possibility of losing love and being hurt."
When she turned back to him, her eyes glittered with tears. "I don't
think I could stand losing you or the baby."

"You're not going to lose us," he said. "I'm here and the baby's coming." He tried to be light. "You're always so good with your proverbs.
Well, I have a few of my own. You can run, but you can't hide. It's better
to have loved and lost than never to have loved at all. You don't know if
you don't like spinach unless you've tried it."

"Those aren't proverbs! They're clichés."

"Well, hear this, then." He took her hand and kissed it. "I'll never
leave you, Hulan. That's just the way it is."

# Epilogue

T HE DEAD HEAT OF SUMMER FINALLY PASSED, AND A KIND of languid somnambulance fell over the countryside as the crops ripened and the people readied for harvest. The heads of the sunflowers, drooping from the weight of their seeds, could no longer look up to the sun. The fields of millet and sorghum had already been harvested, the land cleared, and some farmers had begun preparations for their winter crops, for every day the sun rose less high in the sky and daylight waned minute by minute. The cicadas had grown quieter in recent days as the humidity, stickiness, and thick air disappeared as it always did at this time of year. Ling Suchee imagined—for by any measure temperatures were still warm, hot even—a coolness drifting on the air.

Suchee tore an ear of corn from the stalk, peeled back the outer leaves, and examined the kernels. They were plump and a pleasing shade of yellow. There were no bugs and no diseases. She took a bite and the raw corn felt fresh and sun-warm in her mouth. Yes, in another day or two this field would be ready for harvest and she would hire a couple of boys to help her. She walked on, passing through the rows, feeling the rustle of the stalks against her arms and the warmth of the soil beneath her bare feet.

But inside, where her heart kept its steady, relentless beating, she ached. Not a day, not a minute went by that she didn't wish for a hardness to form over that delicate but persistent organ. She knew, of course, that the physical heart—the chambers and valves and aortas that she'd seen in a book—did not really suffer from loss, but then how else could you explain the pain, the sickness that lay heavy in her chest every morning when she woke up and that she carried with her as she went about her chores?

The barefoot doctor had recommended that she leave this place and move into the village. Instead she'd come away with a packet of herbs and instructions to boil them, strain them, boil them again, then drink one cup three times a day for ten days. She'd done as the doctor ordered, but that bitter liquid could not cure her.

Nor would her neighbors' suggestion to join them in the village. Tang Dan had been right in his assessment of the Tsais. Everywhere they looked they saw reminders of their son—the *kang* where he'd slept, the well where his body had been found, the land where he'd been with them literally every day since his birth. So within days of Tsai Bing's death, his parents, without completing the harvest, had handed their land back to the government and had moved to the village house for end-of-the-liners.

"It is not so bad," Madame Tsai said. "We have our own room. They tell us it is dry in winter and that the local government will provide all the coal we need to keep our old bones warm when it gets cold. We get rice three times a day. Every day is a banquet. Breakfast, lunch, dinner— always we are with other people. There is a communal television set. At night we have more companionship than we ever had on our land." Suchee understood what her friend was saying. That television, the yakking of the other end-of-the-liners, could not actually fill the void, but they did make a noisy cover for it.

But how could Suchee leave this land? As she looked at the uncompromising red earth all around her, she thought of the decomposition of vegetable and animal matter that gave the land its fertility. She thought of the lies and deceptions that insinuated themselves into the soil as surely as water and sunlight. She thought of how so many of those lies and deceptions had come through her, had radiated right through her from the sky, into the human and down through the soles of her feet into the earth.

Suchee had always believed in her government's policies. Her life, like so many in the countryside, had improved from the days when her parents and grandparents had worked the fields in this region for land-lords who'd sucked the very life out of them. Now she looked around her and saw that whatever advances had been made were eroding as easily and ruthlessly as the way a dust storm swept away the earth. They said she now could have electricity and television, but they only gave her a window into the outer world where she could see exactly what she didn't have and would never, ever have.

They say there are nine hundred million peasants working the land in China, one-sixth of the world's population, Suchee thought, and somehow—amazingly, ridiculously—her government believed she should accept her lot as her ancestors had accepted it before her. Miaoshan had seen this. She understood it in a way that only the young can. She understood what the leaders of China didn't when they said to the coun-try's peasants, "You are the life blood of China. Don't come to the cities. Stay where you are." She understood that the foreign outsiders were engaged in their own lies and deceptions. It was too late for Suchee, but there were hundreds of millions of others like Miaoshan who would not sit back any longer and let the world do to them. They would eventually rise up, as Chinese peasants had in the past, and make the world come to them by giving their blood, by sacrificing their respect for the past, by looking out to the horizon, by demanding what was theirs by human and political right.

But all that was almost too large for Suchee to contemplate, because her world had always been and always would be confined to what she knew was a very small and insignificant life. And in that life she had told herself numerous lies.

She had believed in the ideals of friendship, but Liu Hulan and Tang Dan had not been true friends. Yes, they were in the same place in her damaged heart, for they had both acted coldly with no respect for the consequences. Tang Dan's deceit had stemmed from avarice, and the con-sequences had been tangibly recognizable and condemned by the larger society. But Hulan's crimes had been done without thought to the conse-quences and would never be punished. If Hulan had never come to the Red Soil Farm, had never turned in Suchee and Shaoyi, had never intro-duced Suchee to the larger-world concepts of privilege and deprivation, Suchee's life would have been very different.

Suchee had believed in love, but her love for Ling Shaoyi had only been a matter of bad circumstance. The lies Suchee had told herself about Miaoshan were the most cruel and devastating of all. Her daughter, for all of her supposed idealism, was a liar, a cheat, a loose woman of no morals, and greedy almost beyond words. Suchee had deliberately chosen not to see it, and that had caused more bloodshed and more suffering than she ever could have imagined.

All this torture and the resulting suffering were in the air and soil around her. This place would be a daily reminder of that.

Suchee walked to a little clearing where she had left a thermos of tea, a bun for lunch, and a few tools. She picked up her hoe, waded back into the field, drove the blade hard into the red earth, then with a swift, strong movement lifted the aromatic soil to let the air down into it.

# Acknowledgments

In 1996, while in search of bear farms for *Flower Net*, I found myself in a small and extremely remote village in Sichuan Province. The village had no telephone service and had running water for only two hours a day, but in the café where I took my meals was a television tuned to CNN. That slice of Chinese life—so far removed not only from what most people think of as contemporary China, but also from what most tourists visiting the Forbidden City or the terra-cotta warriors ever see—has stayed with me. So too did a 1996 article written by Kathy Chen in the *Wall Street Journal* about the misadventures of a young Chinese migrant worker laboring in a factory in Shenzhen. Sometime in that same year we had a barbecue at our house for Pamela Rymer (a judge on the Ninth Circuit Court of Appeals), Brad Brian (a former assistant U.S. attorney), and Claire Spiegel (a writer with the *Los Angeles Times*). As a writer, you will get no better advice than from people who defend, prosecute, adjudicate, or report on criminals. Our charming dinner quartet certainly set my mind to racing with the ways in which Americans could commit crimes abroad and how they might get away with them. With my imagination captivated, my own adventures began.

I was blessed with innumerable kindnesses from relative strangers, as well as by the generous acts of friends. In China, my guides, translators, and drivers were indefatigable and amazingly open. On this side of the Pacific, Paul Moore of Crown Travel got me to ever more isolated villages, David Li contributed to my aphorism collection, and Xuesheng Li patiently drilled me in Mandarin and assisted with other matters of translation, as did Sophia Lo and Suellen Cheng (and her siblings in Taiwan). William Krisel shared some extraordinary tales about China during the war, imparted some great recommendations and warnings about places to see, and lent me his complete collection of the *Ex-CBI Round-up*. Rick Drooyan, former chief of the criminal division at the U.S. Attorney's Office, offered his insights on the Foreign Corrupt Practices Act and other matters. Dede Lebovits, a wonderful friend who knows the world about private jets, managed to get me on a short hop and answered questions about fuel, runways, landing rights, and the like that ultimately did not end up in these pages. I also interviewed several people who do business or manufacture in China. For obvious reasons, they prefer to remain nameless. However, I must single out Poppy—a childhood nickname—for his great details, particularly in regards to the fiber-shredding machine.

I hate to see death or illness either romanticized or glorified. To keep that from happening in my own work, I have relied on expert advice from Dr. Xiuling Ma, Dr. Pamela Malony, and Dr. Toni Long. I am beholden as well to the librarians at the Louise M. Darling Biomedical Library at UCLA for their assistance.

I am continually inspired by those writers who've written memoirs or chronicled China's turmoil of the last century. For readers who'd like to pursue the subject, I highly recommend He Liyi's *Mr. China's Son*, Peter J. Seybolt's *Throwing the Emperor from the Horse: Portrait of a Village Leader in China, 1923–1995*, Huang Shu-min's *The Spiral Road*, and Chihua Wen's *The Red Mirror: Children of China's Cultural Revolution*. An afternoon spent in a Hong Kong bookstore uncovered *Ungrounded Empires*, which featured an eye-opening essay by Ching Kawn Lee, a sociologist who, I believe, is one of the few outsiders to work in and report on factories in Hong Kong and Shenzhen. Jim Mann's *Beijing Jeep*, G. Wayne Miller's *Toy Wars*, and Du Xichuan and Zhang Lingyuan's *China's Legal System* also informed my work.

The nasty Pearl Jenner aside, Chinese culture, U.S.-Sino relations, and the sometimes arcane world of toy manufacturing and marketing would remain mostly inaccessible and incomprehensible if not for the professionalism of many honest, forthright, and dedicated journalists. These include: Rone Tempest, Maggie Farley, Seth Faison, William Holstein, George White, Stephen Gregory, Sara Fritz, Henry Chu, Jonathan Peterson, Scott Craven, Ian Buruma, Fareed Zakaria, Craig Smith, James Flanigan, George Wehrfritz, and the aforementioned Kathy Chen.

A book like this can't be written without help and guidance. My agent, Sandra Dijkstra, and her wonderful staff have given me encouragement, astute criticism, and, most important, great peace of mind. I'm thankful as well to the wonderful work of Carolyn Marino, my American editor at HarperCollins, and Kate Parkin, my English editor at Century. Although Eamon Dolan has moved to another house, I continue to be grateful for his imprint on this story. I have been fortunate to receive further assistance from Arlene Gharabeigie, Alicia Diaz, Jessica Saltsman, and Sasha Stone, all of whom have been unstinting with their energy, hard work, and good humor.

Last but not least, I want to thank my family: Ariana, Baby Dash, John, Leslee, Anne, and my parents, Richard and Carolyn See. During the writing of the proposal my sister, Clara Sturak, helped me focus on the real purpose of *The Interior*; my brother-in-law, Chris Chandler, rescued me more times than I'd like to admit from computer hell. My husband, Richard Kendall, has shared in every aspect of this endeavor, while my children, Alexander and Christopher, are my bright lights. None of this would be fun or would matter without them.

LISA SEE is the author of the critically acclaimed *New York Times* bestselling novel, *Snow Flower and the Secret Fan*, as well as *Peony in Love*, *Flower Net* (an Edgar Award nominee), *Dragon Bones*, and the widely acclaimed memoir, *On Gold Mountain*. The Organization of Chinese American Women named her the 2001 National Woman of the Year. She lives in Los Angeles.

# ALSO FROM LISA SEE

Don't miss the spellbinding
Red Princess mysteries featuring Liu Hulan.

### FLOWER NET

From the teeming streets of Beijing to Los
Angeles and back, detective Liu Hulan and
American attorney David Stark are caught in
a perilous net of politics, organized crime,
family loyalties, and their own passion for
each other.

**"Murder and intrigue splashes across the
canvas of modern Chinese life . . . A vivid
portrait of a vast Communist nation in the
painful throes of a sea change." —People**

### THE INTERIOR

An old friend from deep in China's interior
asks detective Hulan to uncover the truth
about her daughter's suspicious suicide—a case
that will take her into her own buried past
and into the heart of a dangerous mystery.

**"See's China is as vivid as Upton Sinclair's
Chicago." —The New York Times**

### DRAGON BONES

Liu and David are swept into a maze of
murder and a deadly political power
struggle when the corpse of an American
archeologist is found at the mouth of the
Yangtze River.

**"An atmospheric, tightly plotted suspense
story . . . a treat." —The Washington Post**